THE PERSIAN

DAVID ALEXANIAN

Ink & Quill Publishers
2022
Henderson, NV 89002

The Persian
(Book 1 of *Empire of Ashes* Series)
David Alexanian

Line/Content Editor: Janelle Evans
Interior Design: Jo A. Wilkins
Cover: David Alexanian & Janelle Evans
E-Book Design: Richard R. Draude

p. cm.—David Alexanian (Thriller/Political
Copyright © 2022 /David Alexanian
All Rights Reserved
ISBN: 978-1-948266-52-9/Paperback
ISBN: 978-1-948266-76-5/E-Pub

1. Fiction/Thrillers/Political
2. Fiction/Thrillers/Military
3. Fiction/Thrillers/Espionage

www.iqpublishers.com

Henderson, NV 89002
Printed in the United States of America

1 2 3 4 5 6 7 8 9 10

For my father,
the Persian

Acknowledgments

When my father left Iran, the Shah was seated on the Peacock Throne, and Iran was a progressive and industrious country. It would be several more years before the fall of a monarchy that had existed for thousands of years in one form or another. Yet fresh out of the army, he sought a new life and new fortunes overseas. While attending University, his first occupation in Canada was that of a tailor. This story was inspired by him, and I wish to thank him for his many wonderful stories.

Disclaimer

This is a work of fiction. Although it is centered around the very real events surrounding the 1979 Islamic Revolution in Iran, the world woven into that fabric is an imaginary one. Space and time, when needed, have been rearranged to suit the convenience of the story, and with the exception of public figures, any resemblance to persons living or dead is coincidental. Depictions of the royal family and any historical figures were intended with all due sensitivity and respect. The opinions expressed belong to the characters and do not necessarily reflect those of the author or publisher.

رد تسود تسد دریگ هک دشاب نآ تسود“
“ یگدنامرد و یلاح ناشیرپ

“A friend is found in adversity like gold is found in fire.”

-Persian Proverb

PART 1

CHAPTER ONE

Tehran, Iran
January 16, 1979

"Who would have thought the world would end on a cold Tuesday?" Masoud said in Vartan's general direction. His voice sounded muted in the small, sterile-gray office. The heat from the two large radiators and the smoke made the air in the room stifling.

"What day of the week is better for it? I had nothing on my schedule," Abbas said, shrugging.

Listening to his companions, Vartan took a long drag on his cigarette before snuffing it out on the accumulated pile of butts. Ashes spilled from the ashtray onto the papers scattered across the steel desk. No one cared. He lit a new one. He loved American cigarettes.

Vartan and two other men, none of them older than twenty, sat in the unventilated office under a cloud of smoke and stress. A crackle of gunfire popped in the distance. Masoud stood and looked out the window, having to stand on his toes to see outside. Abbas did not seem to notice and just stared at his patent leather shoes. Vartan slid his pistol a little closer to himself on the desk.

A knock came at the door and it opened without waiting for an answer. The face of Hossain appeared in the gap.

"They are ready," he said in his grating voice.

"Okay," said Vartan. He disliked Hossain, but now was not the time to cultivate enemies. He closed the file he had opened on his desk. An Israeli spy had been caught and was being held at Evin Prison. His majesty had suggested she could be of some use and had ordered her unharmed. Taking the entire file, he pushed it through the paper shredder next to him where they had been mincing documents all night, destroying it in seconds.

Nodding to Masoud, Vartan crushed out his smoke and picked up his gun, holstering it away under his blazer but leaving the safety off. They followed Hossain out the door and into a long hallway.

In stark contrast to his steely office, the palace corridor was furnished in luxury and well lit. He stopped for a moment to take it all in for what, he was certain, would be the last time.

The space seemed to go on and on in both directions, lined with priceless works of art from not only the empire but from around the world. Busts of long-dead poets and philosophers kept silent watch at intervals of two meters. Vartan knew each one by name. The long train of hand-woven silk carpeting shimmered as it ran along the entire length in one magnificent piece. Its brilliant red and gold threads stood out against the white of the marble floor and walls.

He appreciated the art and the history, but most of all, Vartan would miss the royal library—to which he had been granted unfettered access. All that invaluable knowledge would slip from his fingers.

"It will all be turned to dust when they get in here," said Abbas, as if reading Vartan's thoughts.

"I know," he said. "People become like animals when they're in large groups."

The men continued on their way, brushing past frantic servants and armed soldiers. The Shah's own personal guard ran everywhere in the chaos. They were said to be loyal beyond doubt, yet Vartan eyed them with suspicion. He no longer knew who to trust, so he trusted no one.

He pushed open a panel in the wall where the marble gave way to glittering embossed silver slabs, revealing an opening just wide enough for one man to crouch through at a time. Short and stocky in stature, Vartan could walk in. However, his three tall and slender companions had to bend.

The passage to the empress's apartments had been a well-guarded secret up to that moment, but Vartan did not even glance around to see who might be watching. It no longer mattered.

They rushed through the dimly lit hallway just short of a run, emerging back into the light and to even more chaos.

Vartan scanned the hall. So many people. He could not account for everyone in the panic. No doubt valuables were being looted, but that would happen regardless.

"This is crazy," said Hossain. "Everyone has gone mad."

"They have reason to be afraid," Masoud said.

At the end of the hall, her majesty stood at the door of her sitting room. A vision of regal elegance, she spoke to her ladies in waiting. Vartan could tell from her tender gestures that she uttered words of comfort to those loyal women who could not leave with her. She placed something in the hands of each of them as they cried. It was American cash. Vartan's heart ached at the scene, but he felt pride also. She was a true queen.

"We have to get the empress out of here," he said. "There are too many people. She is too exposed."

"The cars are ready to take them to the airport. The plane is waiting." Hossain spoke over the increasing din.

Vartan walked toward the empress, but a sparkle of sunlight from under Hossain's uniform cuff caught his eye. He recognized it as a gold Rolex. He reached into his blazer pocket to thumb the leather clasp on his holster. Either he was compromised and paid off, or he was a looter. Regardless, Vartan would kill him before he got on the plane.

"Your majesty, the car is ready for you," Vartan called out with a bow. She handed a large fold of bills to a young, teary-eyed valet and touched his cheek in a motherly gesture, then looked up.

"I'm ready, Vartan-jan," she said, her voice calm. She looked around, sighed, and placed her fur hat upon her head as if wearing her crown. He could tell from her face that she knew she would never wear one again.

Careful not to make physical contact, Vartan extended his arm to direct her through the door.

"This way, your majesty."

His trained eye saw a subtle movement, a deviation from the norm. It was not Hossain as he might have expected. The move came from Masoud. His longtime partner raised his service revolver in what looked like slow motion to him. Drawn from behind, it moved in a low sideways arch toward the empress of Iran.

A loud bang echoed throughout the large rooms of the royal quarters. Blood spattered across the gilded paneling. Screams of horror followed after a brief pause of synchronized disbelief. Masoud lay dead on the Persian-rug-covered hardwood. Smoke floated up from the nozzle of Vartan's pistol.

A look of horror crawled across Hossain's pock-marked face. Little chunks of Masoud's traitorous brain clung to his blood-spattered brown uniform.

Abbas had his gun out too, scanning the room to see if anyone else wanted to try something. He stepped behind to cover the empress from the back.

Vartan looked up at his queen. If she was shocked, she kept it well hidden behind her customary graceful poise. Only a hint of distaste betrayed her flawless visage.

"Was that really necessary, Vartan?"

"I'm afraid so, your majesty," he said with a bow. "Please. This way. We had best leave through the tunnels so that—"

"Absolutely not," she said, calm but firm. "If they are going to force me from my home, I will leave from the front door."

For a fleeting moment he considered insisting, but he knew her well enough to know when she had made up her mind.

"As your majesty wishes," he said, bowing again.

Vartan kept his revolver out and to his side, following the shaking Hossain through the grand hallway toward the large, gold-plated doors where the convoy awaited them with a full contingent of the Shah's guards. His majesty stood by the open door of his armored Mercedes, waiting. A look of concern turned to relief when he saw his wife.

The Shah was a tall man, barrel-chested, with hair that had grayed much in the last little while. He held the look of a man greatly diminished, yet his pride and strength were still evident. The sight of him filled Vartan with a mix of sadness and admiration.

The royal couple entered the vehicle. Abbas got into the lead car, his firearm still in his burly hand. Vartan called Hossain over to him. He pulled him close and whispered a few words in his ear before getting into the front seat.

As the convoy pulled away from the White Palace for the last time, Vartan tilted his head to look into the side mirror. Hossain only stood for a few more seconds before crumbling to the ground. He wiped the bloody blade of his dagger on a white handkerchief and put it away. He then examined the gold Rolex in his hand. The driver looked over, but said nothing.

Vartan turned back to look at the royal passengers. The Shah sat with the empress leaning against him, her head on his shoulder. He looked at Vartan.

"I gather that Hossain won't be our pilot," he said. His keen eyes missed nothing.

"I'm afraid not, your majesty. I will find you another—"

"That's fine," the Shah said, "I'd rather fly myself anyway."

"Your majesty." Vartan reached back, bowing his head. "I believe this is yours." He handed the gold Rolex to the king.

"I was looking for this earlier. It was my father's. So many things have already gone missing. It's as if the vultures aren't even bothering to wait for me to stop breathing." He took the watch and placed it on his wrist.

The rest of the drive was silent. The highways were empty, having been cordoned off by the remaining loyalist guards.

A small group of high-ranking officials, ministers, and officers had gathered in front of the otherwise abandoned airport, waiting for them to arrive. Vartan searched the crowd, looking for any signs of danger.

The group disembarked and the bodyguards whisked the royal children to the plane while the Shah and Shahbanu took a last leisure stroll through the airport.

Vartan watched the king, hat in his hand, say his goodbyes as he walked across the tarmac on the red carpet. Some of his generals kissed his hand, others fell at his feet in lamentation, vowing to fight for him until the end.

He noticed that the newly appointed Prime Minister, Shapur Bakhtiar, was there as well, watching on in silence. His disdain for the Shah glowed off his thin face like a beacon.

Vartan kept his pistol drawn but under his jacket while he scanned in a continuous back-and-forth pattern.

At the stairs of the plane, the crowd backed off at last. The Shah began his ascent up the steps, followed by the empress. Vartan stopped. She turned to look in his direction, then stepped back down to him.

"You are not coming?"

"No, your majesty. I have some unfinished business to take care of."

The empress sighed again, then reached into her coat pocket and produced a small shiny item. It was a diamond bracelet.

"Take this. It was my mother's. You may find yourself in need. Come back to us when you are able."

"Your majesty, I can't—"

"Don't disobey your queen," she said, placing the bracelet in his hand.

He bowed low as she walked up the stairs. He turned to Abbas, who already had a hand extended. The two exchanged a long handshake.

"Take good care of them," Vartan told his last living partner.

"Take care of yourself. It's going to get a little unpleasant here."

Vartan, the young SAVAK agent, nodded and stepped back. Abbas climbed the steps and closed the aircraft door behind him.

He did not stay to watch the plane leave, carrying away the hope of his country's future. He slipped away from the crowd unnoticed and came out onto the street, hailing a cab and jumping into the back seat.

"Take me to Evin Prison," he said to the driver.

CHAPTER TWO

"If only that plane would just blow itself out of the sky and be done with it, Ahmad," said the Prime Minister of Iran, watching the blue and white Boeing 707 fly off toward the horizon. It was trailed by a cargo plane packed with crates full of imperial belongings. "I'd be a happy man." He turned to Ahamad, his aide-de-camp, daring him with a glare to contradict him.

"I know, sir, but it would be…unwise to let anyone hear that right now. Many here are extreme loyalists and would be glad to string us up just for looking up at it," said Ahmad, his voice lowered to a whisper.

Prime minister Bakhtiar sighed and grumbled under his breath. "I suppose you're right. Still, it would save us a lot of headaches. I was under so much pressure to keep him from leaving, but there was no other way."

"You did the right thing, sir. Public opinion is a fickle thing and doing so would only work against you in the long run," Ahmad said.

"Doesn't feel like the right thing. None of this does," said Bakhtiar, more to himself.

"He didn't register a flight plan. Where do you think he will go, sir?"

"Egypt, probably. No one else will take him. I hear that

it's impossible to get to Sadaat. The Mullahs sent an envoy to Egypt which mysteriously disappeared shortly after they tried to convince the president not to harbor him if he showed up there."

"They have a history between them. No surprise there. Sadaat is sentimental."

"Bloody fool," said Bakhtiar. "They will try to eliminate him there. He is in great danger now."

"I have no doubt that they have already made arrangements in any place he might try to find sanctuary, but it will be difficult. He'll be well protected. Also, they have a few of their top security agents with them."

"I won't lose any sleep over it if they succeed, Ahmad. Not one bit."

"Yes, sir. I know."

A soldier snapped to attention and opened the door as the Prime Minister and his security adviser strode up. Inside, the driver looked up at them through the rearview mirror, awaiting instructions.

"Damnit, it's cold today," he said with a shiver. "What's next, Ahmad?"

"We have to meet with Jack Smith, sir."

"God save me. Do I have to?"

"It's probably wise, sir."

Bakhtiar grunted. "Where is he?"

"Royal Garden Hotel," said Ahmad

"Royal Garden Hotel," he repeated to the peering eyes of the driver, who started off at once.

Taking the smaller streets helped them avoid the growing surge of protesters. They arrived at the hotel in good time. Pulling up to the front entrance, they jumped out before the driver could get out to open the doors for them.

Bakhtiar walked straight into the lobby, ignoring greetings

from the hotel staff. His security detail, having followed in subsequent vehicles, poured into the building, trying to keep up with the frantic pace.

An overweight man in a large white cowboy hat and wearing all denim sat drinking at the bar. His jean-clad thighs spilled over the stool like a cascading waterfall. Meaty arms rested on the brown marble bartop, holding a beer with sausage-like fingers.

"Mr. Smith, thank you for waiting."

"Mr. Bakhtiar. Thank you for meeting me." His English carried a strong southern drawl. "Is it done?"

"Yes. The Shah is gone."

Smith nodded and looked off into space as if turning the words over in his mind. "So, the Peacock Throne is no more."

"I suppose…" Bakhtiar loosened his tie and undid the top button.

"Good. Then we are willing to support your government, so long as American interests are looked upon more…favorably than your former boss was willing to allow. That is, as long as the incoming clergy play ball."

Bakhtiar swallowed the bitter taste that formed in his mouth before responding. "Of course. I have it on good authority that the incoming Mullah's will be dealing with our lax morality issues, implementing religious law, but will leave my government intact to run the country otherwise," Bakhtiar assured him and perhaps assured himself as well.

Smith relit the half-smoked cigar squeezed between his thick lips, not bothering to turn away when blowing the smoke. The Prime Minister did not react.

"Be careful there. That guy is not as benign as you might think."

"Don't worry," said Bakhtiar. "Let me handle him. What about the Shah?"

“What about him?” The cowboy cocked his head.

“Well, we don’t want him showing up at the front door of Niavaran Palace with his suitcase, wanting his chair back.”

“So what do you recommend?”

“What do you people usually do to someone you don’t want showing up?”

“Wow, Mr. Prime Minister, how very unparliamentary of you.”

“Laugh all you want, but the threat is real,” said the Prime Minister, stroking his mustache.

“I hear he’s not well,” said the American.

“Where did you hear that?” It was Bakhtiar’s turn to cock his head. Smith gave him a sly look in return.

“We hear things in the intelligence business, believe it or not.” Smith allowed himself a smile, but Bakhtiar was not amused.

“I don’t know what you might have heard, Mr. Smith. In any event, it doesn’t seem to be that serious, and I wouldn’t count on nature’s course as an insurance policy.”

“We never do, sir,” said Smith. “We never do. Anyway, he won’t be welcome in the states. So if push comes to shove… let’s just wait and see where the coin lands before making heads or tails of it.”

“Well don’t wait too long. Opinions change like ripples in the desert sands around here. If he gains any kind of momentum, everything we’ve worked for will go to hell.”

“What about the other one? Are you going to let him back into the country?” Smith said.

“What choice do I have? His supporters are tearing the place apart. His face is already plastered everywhere in the country. You people did your job well. Now I have to do something in order to appease the masses. They want their opiate. In any case, as I said, he has given me his personal assurance that he intends to let the status quo stand."

"Has he stated that publicly?"

Bakhtiar shook his head. "Back channels only, so far. But we expect a public statement soon."

"Careful, Mr. Prime Minister. You need to be really careful."

"Yes, so you keep telling me."

CHAPTER THREE

"Atah gibor l'olam adonay, m'chayeih hakol atah, rav l'hoshi-a. M'chalkeil chayim b'chesed, m'chayeih meitim b'rachamim rabim, someich nof'lim, v'rofei cholim, umatir asurim, um'kayeim emunato lisheinei afar, mi chamocha ba-al g'vurot umi domeh lach, melech meimit um'chayeh umatzmi-ach y'shuah"

Jaleh was not quite sure if she uttered the correct prayer. Not very religious, she had memorized many words but never paid much attention to any of it beyond that. Still, in the absolute vacuum from human contact, a conversation with an invisible being brought a small relief from this filthy green hole.

Evin Prison was a cold hell. For most prisoners the only escape was death, and they would not even let that come easy. They took great precautions to prevent her from killing herself. No bed sheet, no sharp instrument, no shard of glass, no fan. They had removed her belt, laces, undergarments, and did not allow her the luxury of long sleeves, even in winter.

The small window near the ceiling granted no view, but at least she knew if it was day or night. That was all she knew. And even then, the division between days had begun to blur into each other.

Her spartan surroundings consisted of a small, cold, metal

bed that offered no comfort, a tiny metal closet, a personal metal table with a bolted down stool and a small metal toilet with no seat, connected to a small metal sink situated near the doorway. The stench of waste and rotten meat was ever-present, and permeated the entire experience.

When Jaleh first arrived, she was placed in the woman's public cell-block, number 286. She was kept with twenty-nine other prisoners in a twenty square-meter cell, eighteen Africans, ten Iranians, and a Palestinian. This meant they could not lie down during the day, and at night there were only six triple-bunk beds available. The rest, including her, had to sleep wherever they could find space. She would find a piece of floor in one of the hallways or sometimes in the hossainiya, a religious congregation hall. Prisoners slept anywhere and everywhere, even close to the washrooms, packed like sardines in a can. The entire prison was a torture chamber.

Torture, for her, began right away. They took her from the dorm to a small windowless room and tied her to a bare wooden bed. She laid on her stomach while they lashed the soles of her feet with a length of cable that looked like a garden hose, but was not hollow.

They never asked any questions. They only told her they knew she was a Mossad agent and, if she was lucky, they would trade what was left of her for captured Iranian agents.

After a few months, the physical torture stopped. She was not told why. They took her from the communal dorm and deposited her in the solitary cell where she had languished ever since. A much harsher form of torture.

The food was a little better, at least, and that helped in her struggle to maintain her mental faculties. But it was a slow battle, and she was losing.

Still, in all her isolated despair, her chest seized with fear at the sound of her cell door opening. The silhouette that emerged in the brilliant backlight was the worst nightmare scenario—Behruz the brute, a prison guard well known for his excessive abuse and brutal raping of female prisoners. He had been eying Jaleh with the salivating lust of a slobbering hyena since she first encountered his disgusting face. She was only surprised he had taken this long to act on the instincts of his primitive brain.

"I have something special for you today, Jew," he said in his growling voice, as if he were Santa bearing a bag of toys. "Usually I would hose you down to clean you off first, but I don't have too much time, so this will have to do."

"Let me guess, you found a pair of balls and you came to show them to me," she said, searching for something to use as a weapon. There was nothing.

"Oh, I'm going to show them to you, you mouthy bitch."

"And me, without my microscope." Jaleh's stomach sank, despite her bravado.

He pulled down his uniform trousers, exposing his unmentionables in all their glory. She laughed at his gesture.

Her loud outburst was not the reaction he seemed to have expected. He made a clumsy lunge forward to grab her. But off balance, he waddled like a penguin with his downed britches.

Jaleh found her movements slower than she anticipated. Though she had kept herself as mentally sharp as possible, the effects of her incarceration had taken a physical toll. She dodged his blow by only a hair's breadth, rolling off her metal bed as he fell onto it. She was not so lucky with the second glancing blow. Struck in the lower jaw, she tumbled to the dirty concrete floor, hitting her head on the metal toilet.

A rough hand grabbed her hair, forcing her head down onto the cold, hard surface. Another tore at her clothes. She screamed. She would die before she gave in to this animal. Her arms and feet swung in mad thrusts, but could not find an effective target. Behruz placed a knee on her back to compensate for her thrashing.

Jaleh pushed off as hard as she could with her knees, throwing her hips upward and bucking like a horse. This forced him off balance enough that he had to let go of her to catch himself. The opportunity was not wasted. She twisted and struck him hard in the ribs with an elbow. The air gushed out of him. She jerked herself out from under his bulk and followed up with a clean jab to the throat before standing. He fell back, choking, his left leg free of his trousers.

A full force kick to the center of his gravity ended the struggle with a whimper and a crunch. He was done. She was not. By the time she dropped in exhaustion, her laceless shoe was covered in warm, sticky, blood. Behruz moved no more.

The cell door stood ajar, left so in his overconfident haste. She scrambled to find his keys from the pocket of his crumpled pants, grabbing a small wad of cash in the process. He had not brought his sidearm in with him, which was unfortunate. Jaleh stepped over the lifeless body, exited the cell, and closed the heavy steel door behind her.

She expected to be spotted right away but the whole segregation level looked abandoned. Where large numbers of guards once stood watch, there was no one, even the control area behind the Plexiglas was devoid of life.

No wonder that pig had decided to come try his luck. There is no one to stop him. Not that anyone was likely to have stopped him anyway. What is happening? Is the prison shut down? Her mind scrambled for possibilities.

Jaleh came to the huge door that led to the guard corridor. It was the only feasible way out. Would she run into anyone or were they really all gone? Perhaps, if she could reach the armory, she could shoot her way out.

She fumbled for the keys to the lock, but there were so

many. She cursed, then froze. The lock mechanism opened from the other side and the door flew open, just missing her.

Her fist flew into the nose of the first of two guards, sending him back in a spray of blood. By the time she moved into position to hit the second, he had his pistol drawn and pointed at her head. She was trapped. The first guard stood, holding his bloodied nose.

"Goddamn crazy bitch." He punched her in the face.

CHAPTER FOUR

The road the beige cab took through the streets of Tehran was not cordoned off. Filled with anti-Shah protesters, he saw overturned vehicles and burning American flags. People held signs plastered with the face of the exiled Ayatollah. Shouts of "death to the Shah" were heard over and over. Vartan shook his head.

"What have we done?" He muttered the question.

"It's a great day! We're taking our country back," the cab driver said, smiling at him through the rearview mirror.

"You won't be as happy about that by this time next year," Vartan said, annoyed.

"I'll be happy when they hang the Shah from a tree."

Vartan's blood boiled over with rage. Without a second thought, he struck the driver, bashing him on the side of the head just behind the ear. The hard hit caused the car to veer with a violent jerk to the left, the cabbie's head hitting his window.

Vartan braced himself for impact. The taxi slammed into a parked car and came to a hard stop. Steam from beneath the crumpled hood sprang forth like a geyser. He got out of the vehicle and dusted himself off, just a little dizzy. *Damn.*

At least he was only a few blocks away from the prison. He lit a cigarette and continued on foot, walking away from the crash-site where passersby and protesters were congregating around the scene.

He reached the prison gates before he had finished two smokes, taking alleyways to avoid the mobs chanting in the street.

You ungrateful bastards. They took you from a mud-hole village to a modern country and this is how you thank them.

He was seething by the time he reached the entrance gates to the large white building. The rugged greenery of the Alborz Mountains loomed large in the background.

Too beautiful of a spot for something so ugly.

He half acknowledged the solitary guard standing at the main gate, walking right by him without flashing his ID. The place looked almost unguarded compared to its usual state of high security. It did not bode well for what he wanted to accomplish. He walked in unchecked by anyone and sauntered up to the administrative desk.

"Where is everybody?" Vartan said to the white-haired man at the desk known as Yousef, one of the few remaining prison supervisors from the previous Shah's days.

"The prison has been pretty much emptied out. All political prisoners released. Only a few high-value inmates are left inside," Yousef said.

"Emptied? On whose orders?"

"Bakhtiar. Who else? But don't worry, it will be full again soon." He seemed pleased with that prediction.

"I need to see the Mossad agent immediately," he said with his usual authority, despite his youth.

"Who?" The old man looked confused.

"The Mossad agent. The woman. There can't be that many."

"You mean Prisoner 21826?"

"Yeah, okay. Prisoner 21826. Bring her into interrogation

on the lower level."

"I can't do that."

"I'm not asking."

"Seriously. I've been ordered not to move any prisoners. Rules are rules. Besides, what's the point anyway? Bakhtiar has already shut down everything. Investigations, interrogations… everything." Youseph looked up at him with deep sunken eyes and a cigarette hanging precariously off his lower lip.

"I want to press her for more operational details before they come and take her away too."

"Can't do it. Besides, it's a big waste of time, if you ask me," Yousef said.

"I didn't, because I don't care what you think."

"You realize that, technically, SAVAK is now defunct, therefore you have no authority. You secret police guys were disbanded and ordered out…so—"

"You realize that, technically, I can still cut your head off and place it on the desk in front of you so that you can take a good look at yourself…so—"

"Do you prefer room one or room two?" With Yousef's thick frosted mustache quivering above his lip, he picked up the phone, hands trembling.

Vartan headed past him, going through the door that led down to the belly of the prison. At the lowest level, he walked down the long concrete hallway of the interrogation unit. The once familiar screams that bounced off the crumbling green walls were silent. There were no guards except one. He stood at the door at the end of the hall, a young soldier fresh out of basic training. He stood as straight as a board, scanning left to right like a lighthouse beam, nerves obviously on edge.

"I'll need your sidearm, sir," he said in an unsure voice at Vartan's approach.

He couldn't be much younger than Vartan's own ripe age

of twenty, but he lacked the SAVAK training he had received and the resolve that came with it. So when he stared the soldier down, the young man gulped and stepped aside.

"Thank you," said Vartan.

"Be careful, sir. She is extremely dangerous. And she's unusually strong for a—"

"I'm sure I'll be fine."

"But—"

"Thank you," he said again, stepping into the room.

Inside the windowless chamber sat a young woman. Her left eye was purple and swollen, and her lower lip had a split in the middle. Though torn and dirty, she still wore the civilian clothing she had been arrested in—charcoal gray slacks and a sleeveless blue shirt. Her hair, as black as the night sky, was matted and tangled. He detected fresh blood on her. She looked tired and in pain, but far from defeated.

"Jaleh Farzani," he said as he closed the door behind him and locked it.

She looked up but said nothing.

Retrieving a small key from his pocket, Vartan walked over to her. He unlocked the shackles holding her to a bolt on the long steel table. He bent and did the same to her feet, noting blood on her right shoe. She stared in silence, but with a look of dread and distrust.

"Listen. We don't have much time. Some men are going to come here. They are going to want the information you have locked away in your head. They will break you faster than even we could."

"Whoever is coming can't be worse than the last guy who came into my cell," she said.

"You look like you've had a rough time here. That's unfortunate."

"I've been on worse holidays."

"Good to know. Anyway, I apologize for how you've been treated. That was not supposed to happen." Vartan lit a cigarette and offered it to her, but she refused.

"Listen, I told your people everything I know," she said, her tone now sounding weaker. "I'm not what you think I am. I'm just a seamstress."

"No. You're not. I've read your file. You are Mossad, and you are part of a network that has infiltrated the country. But that doesn't matter now. If they break you, your network will be finished, and I—we…might need that network later."

"Why would this so-called network want to help you?"

"Because now we have a common enemy—the new regime of clerics. If they get in, they will be no friend to the Jews, believe me. But you already know that."

"What new regime? What happened to the Shah?"

"The royal family has left the country and people are rioting in the streets."

"Oh, God."

He pulled out a small black pistol—an extra he kept tucked in the back waistband of his pants. He racked the slide to lodge a bullet in the chamber and handed it to her, butt first. Eyes wide, she hesitated.

"Hurry, we have to get you out of here. I need to get myself out too, for that matter."

"This is a trick—"

"No tricks. No games. We are leaving. You will disappear. If ever I need your resources, the dead drop is the statue in Ferdowsi Square. An X in chalk will mean a noon meeting the next day at the same spot."

She gave him a blank stare.

"Nod if you understand," he said.

She nodded and took the weapon. The way she pulled the slide back to confirm that it was loaded reaffirmed what he already knew about her. She knew her way around guns. Vartan half expected her to use it on him, but, at this point, he had little to lose. He would need all the help he could get to fight the new incoming government, and Mossad had the best resources in position to help with that—if they were willing. It was an intelligent gamble.

He turned his back to her, walked to the door, and unlocked it. He knocked hard on the thick green steel. The young soldier opened it, only to be greeted by the nozzle of Vartan's gun. Jaleh raised hers too. Vartan motioned to the table, and the confused and frightened young man complied.

"Shackle him," he told her.

With the hapless soldier secured, Vartan peered out of the room. The corridor was still empty. The only sound, a soft buzzing from the failing fluorescent bulbs flickering on and off. He motioned Jaleh forward and they left the room. They walked in the opposite direction from where he had come earlier. He was betting on the chance that no one was manning the security cameras.

He opened the door at the end of the hall. He walked into the storage closet and slid the metal shelf out of the way, revealing a wall of brick behind that. One of the fake bricks gave way to a row of numbered buttons. He entered a four-digit combination code, not bothering to hide it, and gave a push to the back wall. Another door popped open. He looked back. Jaleh stepped forward and poked her head in with reluctance.

"Where are you taking me?"

"Any place is better than here. Unless you want to stay," he said with a smile. He extended his arm invitingly into the darkness.

"After you," she said.

The door led to another long tunnel, dark but for a dim

light at the far end. He closed the door as she came through and they walked side by side.

"Were you born here, or did they send you?"

"I was born in Isfahan," she said. "My father is a university professor." He did not believe her but said nothing.

"How did they recruit you?"

"How did they recruit you?" she said with sarcasm.

"Okay, fine."

"How do you know I'll help you? How do you know I won't just disappear when you let me go?"

"Because if you think life is hard for Jews now, you are really in for a surprise when the Mullahs take power. Your government is going to need Mossad on the ground, and Mossad is going to need us. And, also, because you didn't shoot me."

"I didn't shoot you because I thought I might need the bullets once we got out of here."

"Good thinking," he said, amused.

"And when you say *us*, who do you mean?"

"Those loyal to the Shah, of course. You didn't think we'd give up without a fight, did you?" Vartan offered a wry smile in the dark.

"I've been out of the loop for a while, but if the Shah has left the country and a new government is coming, obviously it's what the country wants."

"It's what they think they want. What the western propaganda has led them to believe they want. They are in for a rude awakening," he said, shaking his head.

They arrived at the end of the tunnel, to a metal rung ladder that led to a heavy-looking trap door above.

"Where does this lead?" she said, looking up.

"To a rocky area just at the foot of the mountain." He handed her a small roll of bills. "You're on your own from here. I'm going back to make sure you have time to get away."

"Why would you risk yourself like this?"

"Dangerous times require dangerous risks."

"If you say so. Well, thank you." She started climbing her way to freedom.

"Don't thank me yet," Vartan said with a short laugh. "I may be sending you to a worse fate by letting you go after all. Who knows?"

"Try being a prisoner in this place for a while and see if you still think that's possible." She turned and disappeared up the ladder.

CHAPTER FIVE

Vartan could have left with Jaleh through the hidden tunnel, but the ruse would have been discovered much sooner, and she would not have the vital time needed to get to safety. Instead, he had returned to the interrogation room and shared a few cigarettes with the shackled soldier.

After he deemed enough time had passed, he departed, leaving the pack of Marlboros behind for the poor kid still chained to the table. He made his way back up to the main level and walked out, past Yousef, the administrator, to the courtyard. He made it only as far as the gate before six vehicles came to a screeching halt in front of him. Someone had figured it out.

Vartan drew his pistol and fired a shot in the air. The men starting to converge on him were sent scrambling, drawing their weapons.

The stone pillar of the guard house exploded into shards behind him, spraying him on the back of his neck. Out of sheer reflex, he ran toward the gunmen, zigzagging and hoping the abrupt movements would make him a harder target.

He jumped and slid across the hood of a maroon Impala and slammed both feet into the chest of a shooter, knocking him into another. He hit the pavement with a grunt and rolled under another vehicle. Once out the other side, he sprang to his feet and broke into a full sprint.

Zigging when he should have zagged, he caught a bullet graze in the shoulder. He saw no shelter—nowhere to hide—only a busy motorway. He ran for that. *How am I not dead yet?* He did not look back, but the gunfire ceased as he stepped onto the road.

The heavy traffic moved like molasses on cold pavement. He spun and fired several more shots at his pursuers, seeing them duck for cover. The movement sent stabbing pains through his body from the wound. He clutched his shoulder with his gun hand. The warm oozing blood made his fingers stick to the trigger.

He feigned left, then twisted right and took off against the flow of traffic.

Vartan was a runner. He ran every day and played soccer for hours on end growing up. He could have kept up this pace forever, if not for the pain from the bouncing wound. He jerked left again, sliding between two cars. After a screech of tires, the car narrowly missed him. He kept going, unfazed, turning to fire again. One of his bullets found its mark in the forehead of his nearest pursuer.

The others ducked down, causing several more tires to screech and horns to blare. Vartan counted six or seven more well-bearded men, all in civilian clothing. No doubt the clerics' supporters. Yousef must have called from the prison.

He looked around for a way out and found his chance. His only chance. Up ahead, the motorway became an overpass for the railway. A train was coming. He tucked his gun back in his shoulder holster, took a deep breath of the cold stinging air and upped his speed, keeping his knees high and his head low though his muscles screamed.

His pursuers seemed reluctant to fire into the traffic, but the moment he got to the edge of the overpass he had no doubt they would renew their barrage with fresh vigor. He would have to make a blind jump. Only a fool would do it, but only a bigger fool would follow.

Reaching the concrete barrier, the expected hail of bullets arrived, one skinning across his thigh like a hot poker. He did not pause for a second, stepping up onto the metal handrail and pushing off. Arms flailing in the air, he sailed down, catching the edge of an oil car with his ribs. The wind squeezed out of him, but he just managed to grab hold of the metal rungs and avoid the fast-moving gravel below.

Vartan looked up while his car rolled under the overpass. The men had run to the opposite railing to watch their prey get away. They fired several shots, one hitting close to where he dangled, but none of them found their target. Then one stood on the rail. *They can't be that stupid.* The man jumped, bounced off another oil car and dropped out of sight. *They are that stupid! Bloody zealots!* Another followed, then another. They all jumped in turn. One made it, landing on the flat roof of a boxcar. The last man jumped as well, but he was not even close.

The one that did make it was a giant of a man, tall to Vartan's eyes even from the distance between them. The giant steadied himself and got to his feet. He started to run, making short work of the gap between cars.

Goddamnit! Vartan pulled himself up with a grunt, climbing to the top of the cylindrical car. His bleeding shoulder and leg smeared the light-green paint, making it slippery. He held onto the metal wheel clamp at the top with his bad arm and pulled his revolver back out. He fired and missed—and then again. He pulled the trigger once more. The small clicking sound told him he was out of bullets.

The beast drew closer, leaping like a track star with surprising agility for a man of his musculature. Five cars to go. Four… He was almost upon him. Three… Vartan raised his arm. Two… The man leapt in the air to cover the final gap but was greeted in mid-flight by Vartan's well-thrown gun to his face. An audible crack emanated from the bridge of his nose and the giant dropped in between the cars and vanished.

Exhausted, Vartan flopped back. He slid higher on the car to stabilize himself and laid his head down, holding on tight.

The train tugged along the straight track, the cold making it difficult for his sticky red-brown fingers to cling to the metal. A reduction in speed made him look up. The train was nearing a junction. He glanced down at the ground, blurring past. The train jerked.

Vartan lowered himself one rung at a time with great effort until his feet stood inches away from the ground. The train lurched even harder, almost tossing him off. He held fast with a groan that got lost in the loud wind gusts.

With the junction upon him, the train would not be going any slower. *It won't get any easier than this. This is going to hurt.* With a cringe, he let go of the bar and dropped, rolling into a ball as he hit the ground. Small gravel stones cut into his arms, body, and face. He tumbled to a bone-grinding stop.

Vartan lay on the ground in a ball for a long time, heaving and withering in pain. It took a long time before he managed to prop himself up on his hands and knees. Blood dribbled down the sleeve of his overcoat and onto the small rocks. His ribs ached and his breathing was labored. His spinning head did not notice the arm go around his neck until it was too late. As his eyes faded out of focus, he could only think the giant had survived.

The next time his eyes opened, Vartan found himself chained to the very same table that had held Jaleh just a short while earlier. A man in a gray uniform, without any insignia, sat in the seat across from him smoking and drinking tea from a small copper cup. A matching plate of rock sugar rested next to the vessel. He popped a piece into his mouth and then took a sip of the steaming tea. His slicked back hair matched his oily beard, shimmer for shimmer. Behind him sat the giant, smoking in a chair in the corner. Dark circles ringed his eyes and gauze poorly covered the gash across his nose.

The intense pain in various areas of Vartan's body helped to quicken his reconnection to reality. He noted the angry look on his captor's face as his eyes focused.

"The Shah's lapdog is awake," the tea drinker said. "It's about time."

Vartan shook his head to clear the cobwebs. "Oh, great—a bunch of Turk donkeys."

"What did you do with the Mossad agent? How did she get out?" The giant yelled from the corner.

"Straight to the point, eh? Hey, did you know, if a donkey's eyes glowed in the dark like cats, your mom's hometown would look like Las Vegas at night?" Vartan smiled.

The giant roared and lunged. Tea-man intercepted but not before he landed a blow across Vartan's head, the chains impeding his efforts to dodge the strike.

"Easy, Hushang. We can all be civil here. We are not animals after all."

"Since when is a donkey not an animal?" Vartan offered his most charming grin through the pain.

Tea-man raised his hand in a preemptive motion to stay the giant. "You might want to reconsider antagonizing my friend here. I don't know how long I can keep him from tearing you apart."

"Don't do me any favors, donkey."

"Listen. The Shah is gone. His suitcase was never unpacked from the last incident. Your loyalty is admirable but there is nothing left to be loyal to. He's not coming back this time." He tossed a beige file folder, taken from a briefcase, onto the table toward Vartan.

"What is it?" Vartan said without bothering to open it. "Your resume? I'm not looking for a butler at the moment."

"Funny. No. It's your resume actually. Or, more accurately, your dossier. You are a good agent. Highly trained for your age and specialized in interrogation as well as being an expert marksman. It says you are exceptional at hand-to-hand combat. Judging by how many men I lost to bring you in, I'd say it is all true. Also, there is a big gap in your record, which tells me that you have skills beyond the scope of the average SAVAK agent. Trained by the CIA, no doubt."

"Is that a question or are you just making things up as you go?"

"It's not a question. A young man of your skill set can be quite useful to the new regime." Tea-man closed the dossier.

"Last time I checked, the constitution hadn't changed," Vartan said with a shrug. "There is no new regime."

"A mere technicality—paperwork to a foregone conclusion. Tell us where the Mossad agent is and you can go home, take a few days off and come back to a new, cushy job."

"And if I don't want a job?"

"Then you will get a crash course in the new and improved interrogation protocol, followed by early retirement and a room in this luxury hotel. Now, where is she?"

"Last time I saw her, she was riding off into the sunset on the back of a donkey," Vartan said, grinning through bloodied teeth. He pointed to the giant. "A relative of yours? Perhaps your sister."

Tea-man stood, shaking his head. He nodded at the giant and walked to the door.

"You brought this on yourself. You won't enjoy it, believe

me."

The door closed behind him. Vartan caught a glimpse of the young soldier he had shackled earlier just before it clicked shut.

The giant came at him fast, releasing a flurry of angry punches. Vartan's instinct wanted to block the assault but the chains stopped his hands short, and the hits connected. Lightning ripped through his already battered frame. He slumped back in his chair, mouth filling with more blood.

"How do you feel about me now, funny boy?"

"Your mom slapped me harder than that last night," Vartan said between globs of red spit.

The giant renewed his attack with vitriol, smashing his victim like a boxer's speed bag. Vartan slumped again, coughing and gagging out more blood—and a molar or two. The giant raised his hand.

"Wait." He groaned. "Wait. Yes."

"Yes, what?"

"Yes, that's how hard your mother hit me last night."

The giant lunged in a rage to grab Vartan by the throat, but a well-timed lunge of his own, limited by the floor shackles, landed his forehead square on the giant's broken nose. The large man howled, blood spattering over his white shirt. He picked up the metal chair in front of him and seemed determined to end the interview. Vartan braced for it, but the hit never came.

The door burst open with force. Tea-man was shoved hard to the ground, and a man with a gun fired into the surprised giant. With the chair raised above his head, he crumbled in a heap on the concrete. Tea-man went next with two loud pops to the back of his head. The young soldier sat cowering outside the door, having been spared.

Several masked men walked into the room. They placed a

dark hood over Vartan's head before unchaining him from the table. Keeping his cuffs on, they hauled him to his feet.

"Move it," said a gruff voice behind him.

"Listen, if it's about that library book, I can explain," Vartan said in a muffled voice.

His captors shoved him out the door and led him in darkness to an unknown fate.

CHAPTER SIX

Tossed without ceremony into a van, he had been driven around for so long he lost track of time. He fell in and out of consciousness from the pain tearing through his body. By the time they stopped, took him out, and propped him up in a chair, Vartan was in bad shape.

The hood came off with an abrupt yank, the bright fluorescent lights above him causing a moment of disorienting blindness. He clenched his eyes shut from the discomfort.

"Did that big Turk's mom send you? Because I swear, I didn't do anything she didn't get paid for," he said, unwilling to give them the satisfaction of seeing him unnerved.

"Do you ever stop?" A female voice said from what sounded like somewhere behind him. "Take the restraints off him."

Jaleh stepped into view while his cuffs were removed. He squinted up at her.

"Ah, you again." Rubbing his aching eyes, he hid his relief at seeing her. Without knowing their intentions, it was a bit early to relax. "Didn't we just part ways a few hours ago?"

"It appeared you weren't doing too well, so I decided to bail you out," she said, a smug grin on her face.

"I was just about to make my move when you guys busted in. You ruined my plan."

"Yes, it looked like you had it all under control. What was

the plan? Let them torture you until they told you everything?"

"Pretty brilliant, no?" He grinned back at her.

"Definitely thinking outside the box. Anyway, I had to give this back to you." She handed him the gun he gave her earlier.

Vartan didn't hesitate, checking to see if the weapon was loaded. "Thanks. How did you even know I didn't make it out of the prison?" He tucked it into his empty holster, replacing the one he had thrown at the giant's face.

"I saw you come out, then I saw them bring you back in," she said with a shrug.

"Makes sense. You stuck around. Why?"

"You were right. We are going to need each other if we want to prevent the Mullahs from consolidating their power. With our network and your military loyalists, we might just be able to stop them."

"You had me at 'you were right.' But how do you know I can provide all that?"

"You are SAVAK, aren't you? Only they would know of a secret tunnel out of Evin Prison."

"Touché," said Vartan.

"So, since you came to me, how do you want to proceed?" Jaleh stood with her arms folded across her chest.

"Well, for starters, I'm going to have to be able to get around if we are going to do this. I'm wanted now, so I need some ID. And weapons. I could go to my people, but I have no idea who is compromised yet."

"Done. We can get a full set of papers within hours."

"I'll need some intel on what's happening on the ground—who is still fighting and who has turned," he said.

"Already coming in. I've been getting briefed while on the way here."

"And I'll need to get to Ahvaz to see General Gholam."

Jaleh's eyes went wide. "That will be a little harder." She

looked at her agents.

"Intel, weapons, and an ID was the easy part?" Vartan smiled.

"Getting you in to see the general is next to impossible. The revolutionaries will be keeping everyone from getting in by locking down the roads, and the loyalists will be keeping everyone out by shooting at them."

"So what's the plan?"

Jaleh looked at one of her fellow operatives. He shrugged and took over.

"The trucker strikes are preventing any transports from moving around, so we can't go like that," the cropped-haired, middle-aged man said. "Nothing commercial. Roadblocks on all main roads in and out of Tehran, with random checkpoints along the way."

"How about an ambulance? We could get our hands on one of those," said the other agent.

"The minute it is reported stolen, we will be a flashing, moving target."

"Not if it's an air ambulance," Jaleh said.

Everyone looked at each other as the idea took hold. Even Vartan thought it was a good one. *Impressive.*

"Rajaie Hospital has two, though they must be constantly on the go with the chaos on the streets," said one of the agents.

"We'll have to catch one when they drop off a patient," said the other.

"Steal it right off the heli-pad. It's crazy. I like it," said Vartan. "I'm flying."

"I don't think so. I've flown plenty of times. I'll fly," Jaleh said, crossing her arms again.

"Don't you have a cake to bake or something?" Vartan regretted it as soon as he said it.

Her back straightened and her face flushed. "I'll bake a

cake with flour made from your bones." Her hand hovered over her sidearm. Vartan did not doubt she would shoot him in a heartbeat if provoked.

"Okay, okay, I'm kidding. I wouldn't eat anything you cooked." Vartan laughed, but the other male agents did not dare. "You fly."

Jaleh appeared to relax but did not show any humor. She must not be used to being teased, which meant she was well respected by her fellow agents—feared perhaps. Making a mental note to fear her too, he joined them in laying out the plans for a helicopter heist.

The Mossad agents were very professional, planning everything down to the last detail—especially Jaleh. She had a take-charge attitude and left nothing to chance. Vartan was not opposed to a good plan, as a guideline, but he preferred the seat-of-your-pants approach most of the time. The attitude had often gotten him in trouble throughout his short life, but it also had worked well enough to keep him alive so far.

They poured into the back of a cargo van with one of the male agents, Issac, at the wheel and headed to the hospital. They spent the short ride checking their weapons. Vartan had to admit they had access to some pretty good hardware. No wonder his own agency had spent so much of their resources trying to flush them out. Between spies and communist sympathizers, they took up half the resources of the now-defunct SAVAK. How strange that he was here now, getting help from his enemies to save his country.

Looking at Jaleh, he could not see her as an enemy. There was something about her. A feeling he could not shake, even though he tried. She must have sensed his thoughts because she looked up.

"So why did you decide to save me?" she said.

"I told you already."

"Yeah, but why me? You guys had another alleged Mossad agent in custody at Evin. You could have rescued him. Why me?"

"Pretty simple. You were able to walk out of the prison. He wasn't. Your file came across the Shah's desk and was given to me afterward. When things went south, I figured you might be more valuable on the outside than in prison, where they would get information on your entire cell."

"You think I would have broken so easily?" said Jaleh, eyebrows raised.

"No. Not at all. But I think they would have taken great pains to try and make that happen."

"Your guys held back quite a bit. No water board, no electricity. Just a foot massage, a few slaps, a black eye, and some bad food. Why?"

"Shah's orders. He was thinking the same thing I was." Vartan's thoughts wandered to how the royal family was faring.

She nodded her head.

"We're here," Issac called out.

The hospital's sterile-looking white brick building was surrounded by juniper trees. They abandoned the van a few blocks away and set off on foot, keeping their guns out of sight.

Vartan grabbed a wheelchair that fortune had left abandoned outside of the emergency room entrance.

"Get on," he told Jaleh. She grunted but complied.

The four of them strode into the hospital's chaos. From the protests and demonstrations, many injured people filled the space. They rolled Jaleh right past the triage desk with only a slight glance in their direction and went straight toward the elevator.

Once inside, they headed toward the top floor. Jaleh got

out of the chair and pulled out her gun, hiding it behind her back. The others followed suit.

"We are going to have to get off on the top floor and take the stairs up to the roof from there," she said.

The door opened and Vartan stepped out, followed by the others.

The top floor looked to be just as hectic as the ground floor. Nurses, carrying multiple pints of blood in their hands, ran past them, one after another. People on stretchers were being rushed into operating rooms. Bloodied patients lay on beds in the hall because of overcrowding. Through the bedlam, Issac pointed to a door at the end of the corridor.

They ran, getting there just as it opened. A man in a white coat, carrying an organ transplant box, pushed past them without giving them more than a cursory glance.

Jaleh caught the door before it closed and entered a stairwell. They only had one flight to the roof from there. Overhead the helicopter's rotors whirled.

"Let's go before it takes off again," Vartan yelled over the din, the wind tearing at his clothes and hair.

They sprinted to the landing pad, startling the pilot and copilot as they prepared to take off. Jaleh fired a warning shot past the cockpit and the two men raised their hands.

"Get out," she said, her smoking barrel still pointed at them.

"You can't take this helicopter. It's an air ambulance. We are trying to save people's lives here."

"And we are trying to save a whole country," yelled Vartan. "Now, do as she says or you'll be a patient here."

The pilots removed their headsets and jumped out, arms still raised in the air. The four newly minted skyjackers took their seats, Jaleh at the helm.

With everyone in, she opened the throttle and raised the

collective to her left. She stepped on the pedal and adjusted the throttle to increase engine speed. The helicopter moved in a slow, steady lift off the pad.

"Make sure your RPM is always in line with the collective setting," he told her over the headset.

"Really? Oh, what would I do without you?" She glared at him and pushed the cyclic forward. They were off.

It was a gamble, but it seemed to have worked out. Fuel was optimum and skies were clear, but immediate chatter came over the radio.

"Air Ambulance B-16, this is control. Please return to landing."

"B-16 to control, roger that, we are returning at once," Vartan said, smiling ear to ear at his pilot.

"You're a big kid, you know that?" She shook her head at him

"I've been called worse."

"I don't doubt it. But the night is young," she said.

"B-16... Hey...whoever has stolen this helicopter, you're in big trouble."

Vartan switched the channel to a quieter one. He looked back and saw Isaac scowling at him. The other one, Shahram, had the same look.

"Your friends don't like me much, do they?" he said.

"Can you blame them? SAVAK tortured a lot of their friends and family."

"Wasn't my department." He shrugged. "I was mostly on security detail for the royal family. Besides, I'm quite sure being captured by your people isn't a day at the spa. Just being rescued by you nearly broke me."

"Point taken."

"I'm a great guy, once you get to know me." He smiled again.

"I'll take your word for it," she said.

She was stoic, but he detected a faint lift of her lips this time, hidden in the play of lights and shadows on her face. He really enjoyed putting it there.

"So what makes you think the general is going to help you?" she said.

"Well, he owes me."

"Let me guess. You once saved his life in battle."

"No. But close. I saved his daughter from flunking math. I tutored her. They were my next-door neighbors in Tehran Pars."

"Well, as long as we have a solid foundation for your plan."

"Hey, what could possibly go wrong?"

"RPG," Jaleh said.

"Well, yeah that certainly would—"

"No. RPG!"

He saw the flash and the smoke trail of the rocket-propelled grenade streaming toward them. She jerked hard left and Vartan nearly landed on her, but for the restraints. The projectile skimmed by them, and the heat of the explosion lit their windows like a giant spotlight for a brief second.

As they tumbled out of the sky, Vartan yelled, "Pull up."

The entire vessel shook so hard the bolts creaked.

"I'm trying," she yelled back. She yanked at the collective and stomped on the pedals with all her strength, remaining calm all the while. The helicopter straightened out but still shook. "Rudder's gone. It was a near miss."

"More like a far hit. Can we stay airborne?" Vartan said.

"For now. But we can't maneuver much, and landing won't be fun."

"Told you to let me fly."

She glared at him.

The shaking got worse and the passengers in the back were

jostled about like dice in a backgammon shaker. A beeping started, the lights flashing randomly on the control panel and the engine noise changed. It seemed things were about to get worse.

"The airbase is up ahead. If we try to land too close, they will shoot at us too, but it's all trees everywhere else." Jaleh said.

The helicopter gave a violent kick forty-five degrees to the right. Vartan's stomach lurched upward as if on a roller coaster ride.

Under screeching rotors, Jaleh tried to keep the small aircraft in the air. But with each passing moment, the pitch blackness of the forest below inched closer and closer.

Struggling with the controls, she hung onto her rigging so she would not crash into the panel. He saw the base getting nearer and spotlights coming on, but they were all a blur.

Crashing through the trees, they began to roll. Vartan took a last look at Jaleh. It was a good last image before everything went black.

CHAPTER SEVEN

The starry black canvas hung like a brilliant Van Gogh, everything bigger and brighter, blurred in the most fantastic way. Vartan gazed upward, the midnight blue ceiling above all but erasing the usual carousel of worries from his mind.

Whisked away to his childhood home, he laid in the backyard beneath his father's date tree, dreaming of what the future would bring. The sound of cicadas pierced the silence of the night. Yet they soon grew so loud they made his ears hurt. Forgotten pains throughout his body came to life and the cicadas gave way to a high pitch sound, like what one would hear after a loud explosion.

Broken glass fragments, like grains of sand, dug into his eyes and face. The smells of wet earth and burning petrol fought for dominance in his nostrils. Muffled voices came from every direction and bright lights shone over him, making his closed eyelids red. His backyard had vanished like a cruel mirage. Everything came back to him at once. The RPG, the crash, Jaleh…

The screeching sound of a saw cutting metal was followed by the sensation of being dragged across the ground, pulled by his ankles. Pain shot through his legs, but he was happy he could at least feel them. He had survived, if barely. What about Jaleh and the others? He lifted his head to try and see them but could not quite open his eyes. His throat ached and the burn from the smoke made him cough. The jarring action brought more pain throughout his body.

He called out for water and was handed a canteen. After taking a large, slow sip, he poured the rest of it over his face, coaxing little bits of glass away from his eyeballs. With his vision cleared enough, Vartan could see the helicopter burning in the distance. Jaleh sat by a military ambulance having her arm wrapped up. He experienced a surprising flood of relief in seeing that she was not dead. He could not quite understand why.

Looking to the left, he saw that someone else had not been so fortunate. A white sheet covered a man-sized mass on the ground. Shahram had survived the ordeal with only a head wound. Issac was missing. What a terrible shame.

He nodded at Jaleh, and she looked a little relieved to see him. It was not a miracle, but her flying that had saved them. She had managed against ridiculous odds to save three of them. Though sorry for Isaac, he was still impressed.

His focus shifted to their rescuers. They were armed soldiers. The Shah's soldiers. They had guns trained on them even as they were being treated.

"Who's the commanding officer here?" Vartan asked the medic looking after him.

The man nodded in the direction of a staff sergeant who approached.

"Who are you, and why are you flying an air ambulance?" said the man in a gruff voice, his hand on his side arm indicating he had no qualms about annulling his survival.

"I need to see the general." Vartan pulled out his security ID with a slow hand. "I'm an old friend of his."

The sergeant took the ID and stepped out of earshot to make a call on his radio. The inaudible crackle in response seemed to snap the man to attention. Commands were shouted and vehicles approached. They were loaded onto an old army truck and driven at breakneck speed toward the base. Inside, they were taken right away to the general's office in the center of the compound. A vast, empty room but for an old oak desk and several chairs.

"Vartan-*jan*, my young friend." The general's voice, loud and boisterous, came booming across the room. "I couldn't believe it when they called me and told me it was you."

"Good to see you, sir. I'm happy to find you well. How is the family?"

"They are fine for now, but God knows for how long. I'm going to get them out of the country when I can, but we've been over-run by Kurdish mercenaries fighting for the rebels."

"We noticed them when they fired on us," said Vartan.

"Yes, they do that. I'm sorry about your friend."

"Me too." Vartan looked over at Jaleh, who showed no emotion.

"Why didn't you leave with the Shah?" The general sat against his desk looking fatigued.

"I wanted to stay behind and help stop this thing before they took over completely," Vartan said.

"They are practically there already. It's going to be a long fight. Even now, half the military is turning on us. We are all being pushed to the outskirts."

"Maybe we can help. I've made some inroads with Mossad."

"Mossad? Why would they help us?" He looked at Jaleh and Shahram, suspicion written on his face.

"The clerics are no friends of theirs. The Shah was much more friendly to the Jews than anyone in the region. We have a mutual interest in not losing the country."

"But Mossad…" The general still looked skeptical.

"This idea came straight from his majesty's lips to my ear."

The general looked at Vartan for a moment, as though sizing him up. "We have firepower and men. We can put up a good resistance."

"That won't be enough. We need contacts to move underground, to get people in and out of the country, to make surgical strikes on select targets."

"Cut the snake's head off," the general said, understanding at last.

"Exactly." Vartan put his hand on the weary old general's shoulder.

"We can get your family out with new passports and IDs," Jaleh said.

"How do I know we can trust you?"

"We are all drinking from the same well, general. It wouldn't make sense for any of us to poison it."

"Shakespeare said, 'misery acquaints a man with strange bedfellows.' I guess I shouldn't be so surprised." He scratched his thick, black hair.

At last, the general shook hands with his guests, giving a hug to Vartan—the union sealed.

"Thank you, general," Vartan said, relief slipping through the cracks in his facade for a moment.

"I knew you would turn out okay. You were always a good kid." The general gave Vartan a slap on the back. "Now, let's eat first, then kill some dirty rebels."

PART 2

CHAPTER EIGHT

Paris, France
March 3, 1980

"Are you sure he is the best person for the task?" CIA Station Chief Jack Smith raised his eyebrows at Bakhtiar who sat in the front of the Lincoln Town Car.

"He is the only person for it," Bakhtiar said, leaning forward out of the plush seats. "He is the only one who can still command the loyalty of what's left of our armed forces. The only one who is still respected by all sides. Plus, he is the only one with any real combat experience. That's a pretty essential quality, don't you think?"

"That's all great, but can he be trusted? We obviously made a huge mistake trusting the cleric. We can't afford to make another."

"Trusting him is not the problem. The question here is, will he trust me?"

"Why wouldn't he?" Smith asked.

"I can think of a thousand reasons, not the least of which is that I'm sitting here with you bastards."

"How would he even know that?"

"You CIA really believe that you are the only ones with a vast intelligence network, don't you? Underestimate him at your peril, but I'm willing to bet he knows what side of your coffee cup you drank from this morning."

"Well then, maybe he is the right man for the job. Maybe we'll even recruit him ourselves when this is done." Smith's southern drawl seemed thicker than usual.

"Good luck with that, Mr. Station Chief."

The black vehicle they rode in pulled to a hard stop by the curb.

"It's just down that path over there. Don't worry. We'll move in if anything happens," Smith said.

"Yeah, great. If this fails, I'm dead anyway."

"I did tell you to be careful."

"Yes, I remember it well. But you were also the one pushing for this change—'in the best interest of our two great countries' I believe was the phrase." A bitter taste formed in the back of his throat at Smith's words.

"I'm sure we will have plenty of time to point fingers later. For now, we need to deal with this unexpected problem—in the interest of our two great countries. Have some faith, Mr. Bakhtiar."

"Right…" Bakhtiar got out of the car and walked away without looking back. He headed for the cobblestone pathway off the main walk as indicated.

He considered this quite a desperate move on his part, fraught with danger and uncertainty. He stopped outside a stone courtyard, enclosed on three sides by quaint bars and small cafes—the typical scene of a European town square. A small, intricately carved fountain, shut off for the season, crowned the center of the scene.

Despite being late March, the snow still swirled about in a vibrant dance. He shivered from the cold, but perhaps it was more than the cold that caused Bakhtiar to shiver. The stakes in this game were so high, and this was more than likely the last good hand he would be dealt.

He took a hard look at the people walking by, eying them with suspicion. His French security detail had done an excellent job of blending in. Even he could not spot them with any certainty. He only guessed that a merchant selling roasted almonds was one, or the taxi driver sitting in his cab and reading a paper might be another.

He shivered again and took a tentative step toward one of the brightly lit windows. He looked around with caution and probably too much conspicuousness. One more step and he breached the threshold of the Cafe de la Paix. He made his way down the few wooden steps, removing his hat from his head.

The cafe turned out to be more of a bakery than anything else. Beyond the initially strong scent of fresh-ground beans, the blissful aroma of newly baked croissants and buttered scones bathed one's lungs in their delight.

He took a seat at a small table with thin legs. A waiter dropped off a laminated, folded menu. Bakhtiar took a long moment to peruse the many offerings while he blew into his free hand to warm himself. Summoning the waiter with a wave, he ordered a simple tea. He missed his beloved Persian style tea, the loose-leaf black tea with rosewater and cardamom, but he had been unable to find a place nearby that could prepare it.

His order soon arrived. He took a long sip of the scalding liquid, enjoying the burn down his throat. A little more relaxed, he sat back in his creaky wooden chair and took in the surroundings.

Walking in, he had noticed the mustard yellow paint on the walls, but from his vantage point at the back table he could fully appreciate the detail of the decor.

The painted flower murals. The posters of what he assumed were Parisian celebrities—none of which he recognized. The mosaic tiles that adorned the floor beneath his feet, depicted scenes from Rome long ago as if he was in an ancient bathhouse. He appreciated the ambiance, and yet he still thought that back home was so much...better.

A man playing a sad guitar riff sat in the far corner, his serenade lost within the chatter of conversation. Students sat in groups of four or five, laughing more than studying. An old woman dressed in clothes that, obvious to him, were once fine but had seen better days, sat and chatted with a young girl that might be her granddaughter. The girl paid little attention but delighted in her confections.

He turned his attention to the room's last occupant, startled to find him staring back. He had strong, rugged, clean-shaven features, with immaculate black hair and equally dark, piercing eyes. His thick hands gripped his coffee cup as if it was the neck of an enemy. Bakhtiar picked up his half-full teacup and approached the stout man. "General," he said, his hand on his heart and a slight bow of respect.

"Prime Minister," he said, gesturing to the empty chair.

"Former Prime Minister," he corrected.

"Yes. Are you alone?"

"I doubt it, but they are giving us space."

"They being CIA?" The general raised an untrusting eyebrow.

"No, the French. DST."

"Of course," the general said, though his face more than hinted at skepticism. "Shall we get right to it then?"

"Absolutely. What I need—"

"I know what you need. I just don't know if I can trust you." The man was always straight and to the point.

"We both want the same thing, general."

"I doubt that. You want power. I want my country taken back from these...mullahs."

"Our goals, I'm afraid, are mutually inclusive." Bakhtiar sipped his tea and found it already too cold.

"So what is the end game here? You disbanded the SAVAK, walked the Shah out the door, and let that bearded menace from Qom back in, hoping that if you licked hard enough at his feet he would keep you in charge, but that didn't work as planned. Now you want to get back in...and what?"

"Get back in and put the Shah back on his throne."

"You could have saved us all the trouble." The general scowled at him.

"Hindsight is always twenty-twenty. Look, general, we have always had the common goal of doing what is best for our country. We only differed in our opinions of what was actually best. We've come full circle and now believe that what is best is having the Shah back on the throne of a constitutional Monarchy, with reforms in mind."

"I hear he is sick."

"That's just a rumor. It's nothing serious." He kept his face stoic, impressed at the general's intelligence-gathering abilities.

"What if he dies?" the general said.

"There is the prince." Bakhtiar shrugged his shoulders.

"And you, behind him, whispering into his ear."

"The prince has a mind of his own, let me tell you. But I see it will be hard for you to trust me." Bakhtiar waved for another tea.

"Can you think of any reason I should?" The general leaned back in his chair and crossed his arms—not a good sign.

"They want me dead as much as they want the Shah dead."

"That just tells me you screwed them over too."

Bakhtiar sighed, put his new tea down, and picked up his hat. "If you don't want to help, I will find someone else."

"No, you won't, I'm afraid. Not someone who will be able to do what you need to get this done. Can you raise the funds?"

"I already have it."

The general raised both eyebrows this time. "Where did you get it?"

"Does it matter?"

"Yes. I don't want CIA money. We don't need the US running the country the minute we get it back."

"My personal funds. No Americans."

The general sat in silent thought for a minute. "I will get everything you need. Tanks, fighter jets, people. Loyal people. I have the best agents still on the ground for the messy bits. You do your part. Trust no one and tell no one. If this gets out, many people will die."

"I understand."

"If you screw me, Mr. Former Prime Minister, there won't be a country on this earth that can hide you."

Bakhtiar pulled some franc bills from his pocket. "Let me get this."

"Save your money." The general stayed the Prime Minister's hand with his own. "You have a war to finance."

He nodded and stood, offering a handshake. The general glared for a moment then stood as well, sealing the deal and the fate of millions of people.

CHAPTER NINE

Tehran, Iran
July 9, 1980

"Twenty-some-odd tanks, out of the one hundred and sixty in Khuzestan they promised us. That's all we could get? How is that even possible?" Vartan said, incredulous. He wiped the sweat from his brow, a preemptive move to prevent the salty solution from stinging his eyes. Yet his forehead, like the rest of his body, remained slick and glistening from the relentless heat of the summer sun. His clothes clung to his body in the most uncomfortable configurations.

"Give or take," said Omid's raspy voice, emanating from his skinny frame, also sweat soaked.

"How is that even possible?" Vartan shook his head.

"What do you want me to tell you?" Omid shrugged. "It's what they were able to get that was still functional."

"That's not nearly enough."

"It's more than enough. We have fighter jets too."

Omid was an old soldier who had seen combat, but had also seen better days, in Vartan's opinion. Still, he had absolute loyalty to the Shah, and therefore the country—the only thing that mattered.

"This whole thing feels wrong," Vartan said.

"You worry too much. It's going to work." Omid spat onto the roof near where they sat—a disgusting habit. He picked up his binoculars and scanned the area.

"How it got this far I'll never understand. We could have wiped out the leadership before they left Paris, and this would have been a simple cleanup operation. Now it's a Goddamned coup." Vartan wanted to light a smoke but did not want to give away their position.

"It's going to work." Omid scanned the buildings of the compound.

"So you keep saying. What do you see?"

"Nothing unusual yet. The president's guards are patrolling but their patterns are irregular. Bloody amateurs. The sniper on the clock tower finished setting up and is taking a break."

Vartan peered into the scope of his rifle. On a rooftop not far from the Presidential Palace that until only recently was the Shah's home, a revolutionary guard sniper sat watching. Beside him lay his rifle, and over his shoulders was slung a pair of field glasses. His thin, ascetic face looked young, despite the dark, heavy beard that had become the standard for the Ayatollah's lackeys. But his eyes had the cold gleam of the fanatic. The expression of a man who had too soon become used to looking at death.

He ate rice from a plastic container—*zereshk polow*. Through his scope he could even make out the barberries mixed with the long grains. Vartan's stomach growled. He had eaten nothing since the day before. It had been too hectic to eat. The bearded youth finished his simple meal and took a flask from his inner coat pocket. Taking a short drought, he returned the flask to its hiding place.

"Not so pious after all. These bastards, eh?" Vartan's words were more of a statement than a question, but Omid, who watched along through his field glasses, took it up as such.

"It's the one aspect of Islam that Persians never took to very well. You Armenians are lucky that way. Jesus liked wine."

Vartan couldn't help but laugh at that, even as he watched the sniper pause for a moment, cigarette in hand, appearing to consider whether he should risk a puff—a dangerous idea. The flash and smoke might give his position away, and someone could be watching. Vartan smiled at the irony as the man decided to take the chance, though he himself craved a cigarette more than he craved food. Placing the cigarette between his lips, the soldier struck a match, inhaled the smoke and put out the flame as fast as he could.

"As soon as we fire a shot, this guy will fire at us so be ready. A high velocity piece like this will leave a vapor trail leading right to our position," said Vartan.

"This isn't my first dance here, kid. You just worry about yourself."

"Good to know," Vartan wiped sweat off the lens of his scope.

"If we weren't so far away, you wouldn't need that type of firepower. You know this shot is next to impossible. Those buildings there don't give you much room for error. And ambient temperature is not optimal, so you'll need to shoot higher to account for bullet drop, which will be at least two inches at this range."

"See, that's why you're here. We have to be this far, or we won't get out of here alive."

"Yeah, I get it. But the odds are not—heads up. Something is happening," Omid said. "The president is coming out."

A slew of bodyguards emerged first, hands on the triggers of the machine guns hanging from their shoulders. They were serious looking men, scouring the area for any sign of danger.

A few seconds later, a man with thick curly hair and even

thicker eyeglasses came out onto the large terrace. His thin black mustache added to the features that marked him as President Abolhassan Banisdar, the first president of a country that had only known thousands of years of kings.

They had him. Vartan smiled and lifted his rifle above the edge of the parapet. The distance was more than eighty meters. A difficult shot in the best of circumstances, and his left shoulder still caused him much agony, like shards of broken glass grinding between the joints.

"Shooter ready. We have a positive ID," said Vartan.

"Target Alpha, eleven o'clock, eighty-six meters off."

"On target." He took steady aim, ignoring the slight tremble in his hand—perhaps from the pain or maybe the eagerness.

"Range is nine, five, two." Omid's pitch went up with his adrenaline level.

"Nine, five, two."

"Fire when ready."

Pressing his lips together, he took a deep breath through his nostrils and fired, deafened by the report. His arm shook with the recoil, the impact causing his unhealed ribs to shift. He peered across the clearing smoke.

"Target down." Omid uttered a muted cry of joy.

The shot had been perfect. The president fell against the parapet in the agony of death, grasping at the hole in his chest. He fell forward in slow motion as if part of a dream. A sheaf of papers fell from his grasp, scattered by the wind like so many white doves flying to freedom. The dying man bellowed and crumpled, falling forward over the handrail. The body turned over and over in space and hit the ground with a dull thud. He lay still on the concrete below in a pool of blood.

Vartan's stomach dropped. The brown turban he had been wearing came off, revealing a bald head. It wasn't the president, but a decoy.

They know.

From the sniper's roost, a shot rang out. Vartan dropped his rifle with a curse. The weapon clattered to the ground. He stooped to pick it up but could not lift it, his forearm hanging dead against his body.

"I'm hit," he said, but Omid did not respond—the shot had gone through them both.

Dropping flat to the roof, he crawled back to the parapet. With his left hand he felt the injured right forearm. Blood oozed through the sleeve of his coat but there was no pain—just a deadened sensation, as if the arm had been cut off.

With haste, he drew his knife from his pocket and cut off the sleeve. He found a small hole where the bullet had entered, having emerged on the other side creating a bigger hole. The bullet had torn through the bone, leaving it fractured. He ground his jaw to overcome the pain and closed his eyes. He had to get moving. The other choice would be death by torture, and he had already made other plans.

The streets below swarmed with armored cars. The expected low-altitude air strikes never arrived. The coupe had failed. They had been betrayed.

Vartan crawled through the door to the stairs to avoid being shot again, then took the steps as fast as he could. The jostling motion shot pain through his entire body but he reached the bottom. He tried to exit the building from the front, but the streets were filling up with soldiers. He ran to the other side, kicked the back door and ran into the alley. If he could make it to his car, or any car, he could make a run for it before they barricaded everything.

He found the alley empty and headed straight for the end where several cars were parked. A silhouette appeared in his path—a soldier. The man spotted Vartan and ran toward him.

Vartan thought to turn and run but the soldier drew his side arm and pointed it in his direction. At that range, his chances were not good.

"Hands in the air," said the soldier, looking serious.

Vartan complied as best he could with his injury.

From behind the man came a screeching of tires. A large blue Pontiac took the corner without slowing down. The soldier only had enough time to turn around before the fast-moving chunk of American steel struck him. He flew through the air, his face careening into the windshield and cracking it right in the center. The car came to a grinding halt next to Vartan.

"Well, are you coming, or did you want to stick around?" Jaleh said with her usual judgmental grin.

"I thought you'd never ask." Vartan hobbled into the car with great effort.

"I take it that it didn't go very well."

"It was a set up. I hit the wrong man. They knew we were coming." Taking out his field dressing, he ripped open the packet with his teeth.

As they sped down the alley, he broke the neck of the iodine bottle and let the bitter fluid drip into the wound. A spasm of pain swept through him. He placed the cotton wadding over the hole and wrapped the dressing over it. To tie the ends, again, he used his teeth.

For the first time since he met her, she looked fazed. They both knew what this all meant.

"Hang in there. I'll take you to someone to look after that." She nodded toward his arm and hit the gas hard.

"It's nothing. A flesh wound."

She shook her head as she drove on.

CHAPTER TEN

He could see no shadows about the streets. The July noon sun overhead sapped the energy out of every living thing in its oppressive presence. The man called Rostem looked down at the body. Half the head had caved in from the fall. The shot had struck their decoy's chest dead center—a fantastic, near-impossible shot, he had to admit. At such a distance and through the narrow gap between two buildings, the odds of success were astronomically low.

Impressive.

They had taken weeks to find someone who looked enough like the president to play the decoy, but he had not expected that they would have been able to kill him from so far away, thwarting the net they had cast. Loyal like a dog and twice as dangerous, Vartan Gharabian—if he was correct about the identity of the shooter—was going to be a problem. *An interesting problem.*

Iran's new top spy, Dariush Safahi, walked up to the scene now that it was safe. "He was insignificant. Don't give him a second thought. His family will be well compensated," he said.

"I'm just admiring the handy work as a professional," Rostem said without looking up.

"Yes, that was quite surprising. I'm told that the shooter may have been hit."

"They found a blood trail on the rooftop. His spotter was killed." Though Rostem was certain he knew who it was, he was not about to reveal it and play his whole hand. There was nothing in it for him.

"We need to stop him before he leaves the country. We don't need someone like that helping the resistance movement."

Rostem smiled. "There won't be much of a movement left after today. We have arrested hundreds of officers and servicemen at Nojeh Air Base near Hamedan."

"Good," Safahi said. "What about the former Prime Minister?"

"He is heavily guarded, but I will get him."

"That's what I like to hear. Now, tell me. Can you get to the Shah?"

"That is a more difficult matter," Rostem said, again keeping the entire story to himself. It was a dangerous game, but he was good at it.

"Surely in your position—and for what we pay you—it can be done."

"You don't know the kind of security measures they take to protect him and his family. Nothing short of an air strike could get to him." The man's insistence annoyed Rostem but he kept it to himself.

"Tell me that you are working on it."

"Of course. If there is a way, I will find it."

"Good. And about this hit man, what is being done to catch him?"

"We have all the possible routes out of the city locked down with checkpoints and the buses and trains are being watched, as is the airport. But he is well trained, he won't be easily caught."

"Report to me immediately when he is," said Safahi.

"Yes, sir."

Rostem watched the newly promoted head of Iranian intelligence walk away. He was a severe man, not quite as intelligent as his predecessor, but much more ruthless and fanatically dedicated to the new regime. He did not like him. More important than that, he did not trust him. Yet he was useful.

Several men came to collect the decoy's body. Rostem walked over to where the corpse of the rooftop spotter now rested at the gates of the compound, waiting to be taken to the morgue. He knelt and did a thorough search of the man's pockets. It turned up nothing more than a pack of cigarettes and some matches.

He tore open the man's shirt. A chain with the Star of David was tangled in a nest of blood-soaked, matted hair. Rostem tore it off his neck and examined it in the palm of his hand.

Could it be that the former SAVAK agents were now working under Mossad? He thought this to be an interesting development. It would certainly make them more dangerous. He decided to keep this new information to himself also—for the time being, pocketing the religious trinket. He needed to think how he could turn it all to his advantage. Revolutions were so lucrative.

For now, the time had come for him to return to Paris. He had a Prime Minister to kill.

CHAPTER ELEVEN

Jaleh had already seen too many bullet wounds in her short life, and this one did not come close to being the worst. Yet, for some reason, it sent shivers down her spine to see it and the urge to look away tugged at her head. Blood soaked the gauze wrapped around Vartan's arm, radiating outward.

Doctor Kashefi snipped the rest of his sleeve out of the way with a pair of scissors. He peeled back the wrap to show the dark hole in his never-seen-the-sun white skin. The doctor wedged a piece of thick fabric into Vartan's mouth and went to work with long tweezers, producing a tiny lead fragment.

"Shattered against the bone," the doctor said, depositing the piece into a metal tray. "It won't heal perfectly, but he will probably keep the use of the arm."

"Thank you, doctor. I know you are taking a big risk letting us come here right now."

"You know I am always happy to help, but I'm leaving for Canada myself. It's not safe for any of us anymore." Kashefi rummaged through his medical bag and produced a suture kit. He tore it open with his gloved hands and threaded it with care.

Jaleh locked her gaze on Vartan's dark eyes. He seemed transported to another place and did not even wince as the needle pierced his flesh. Jaleh winced for him, wondering why his pain affected her so.

Puncture after puncture, the doctor's expert hand brought the torn skin together, first at the entry point and then again with the exit wound. There would be a decent scar for sure, but Vartan did not display any of the pain she knew he must have been experiencing. She had been through the process herself once, to a smaller degree, and she had seen more than one man much larger than him pass out after the third or fourth stitch.

Impressive.

"You're a tough one, aren't you?" the doctor said, tying off his last stitch.

"You prefer to see me cry?"

"At least I'd know you were human." The doctor placed a sling around his patient's neck and nestled the now rewrapped arm into the hammock with a slow, gentle movement.

"Humans are overrated."

"I can't argue with that." Kashefi rose from his stool, taking his bag in hand. "Stay as long as you need. Stay off your feet. And try not to move that around."

"Thank you, doctor," said Vartan, admiring the handy work.

"Jaleh-*jan*, come upstairs with me," the doctor said. "I have the papers you requested."

"Are you going to be okay?" She winced at how nurturing the question sounded coming out of her mouth.

Vartan smiled. "I'll be here doing push-ups until you get back."

Jaleh shook her head and sighed, following the good doctor up the rickety steps, out of the basement and into his kitchen. His wife and daughter were finishing dinner preparations and did not look up as she came in. Kashefi took a thick envelope out of a bottom drawer and handed it to her.

"You will find everything you asked for. But it will be a

dangerous trip, and your friend is not in the best condition."

"He's stronger than he looks."

"He's stronger than anybody looks. Are you sure you don't want to stay here until things settle down? There's a safe-house in Arak—"

"No, doctor. We need to leave soon. If we are caught here, it's death…or worse…for all of you. We can do no more from Iran. The country has fallen."

"I understand. We will make arrangements."

"Thank you."

"No need to thank me. Your father did as much for me and more, back in the old days."

Jaleh smiled at the memory of her father. Kashefi handed her a bottle of pills.

"Tell Vartan to take one every day."

"What are they?"

"Pain killers. I know he won't take them, but it doesn't hurt to have them. And please, take some food to my patient. He's going to need all the strength he can muster." On cue, the doctor's daughter placed a tray with two steaming plates of *ghormeh sabzi* on white rice along with warm bread and a plate of pickled vegetables called *torshi*.

"I'll see that he eats it all," she said, taking up the tray.

"Navid will bring you some tea and a nice drink for our Armenian friend. Not to be mixed with the pain killers, of course."

Jaleh took the food back down the stairs, with the envelope tucked under her arm.

Standing on unsteady feet, Vartan lowered his good hand away from his firearm. "Sneaking up on a wounded soldier can be hazardous to your health."

"Coming down the stairs with your dinner is what you call sneaking?"

"Yes, with the way you do it—silent as a lioness on the hunt."

"I can't help that my training is better than yours,"she said. "Now, sit before you get dizzy."

Vartan grunted and sat while Jaleh put the tray down on the cot. She passed him the pills.

"What's this?" He turned the bottle over in his hand.

"Pain killers."

"I don't need those." He flashed her a smile.

"I know. Just in case." She took the pills back and put them in her pocket. "You need me to feed you?"

"I should say yes just to see you do it." Vartan took a piece of bread and scooped up some of the dark green parsley and red kidney beans, shoving it in his mouth.

Jaleh opened the envelope and poured the contents onto the cot beside him. Passports, American dollars, and an assortment of other documents spilled out.

"Wow, your people are fast." Vartan's eyes went wide and he picked up a passport.

"Well, we do our best."

"Vartan Vartanian? What the hell kind of last name is that?"

"I was in a hurry and I couldn't think of an Armenian last name."

"So you repurposed my first?"

"Hey, beggars can't be choosers." She stifled a giggle. "Besides, you can change it to whatever you want once we are out of here."

"And you're…my wife? Well isn't that a nice upgrade for you."

"More like a demotion." Jaleh wanted to smack off the smug look creeping across his face, but her words came out sounding more serious than she had meant them.

Vartan shook his head and sighed, grabbing another piece of bread dipped in parsley. Licking his fingers, he rose and headed over to a collection of copper piping of various sizes against the far wall. He plucked a smaller piece from the top of the pile and examined it.

"What are you going to do with that?"

"I have an idea. Here, help with this." He came back over and handed her the pipe. With painstaking care, he removed his injured arm from the sling and held it out. "Slip it over my arm."

"What? What for?"

"A little added protection." He grunted as she slid the pipe in but did not pull away. "There we go. As good as new. Like the six-million-dollar man."

"The Persian version of the six-dollar man."

Vartan gave a loud laugh. "We are on a budget."

"You are crazy. You know that, don't you?"

"My shrink seems to think so anyway." He slipped his armored appendage back into the sling with a satisfied look on his face.

"Crazy," she said again.

CHAPTER TWELVE

Tehran, Iran
July 12, 1980

"Someone betrayed us. Why else would the president have a decoy take his place?" Vartan said, standing next to Jaleh on the train station platform. His arm still rested in a sling but felt much better. He needed a cigarette, but it bothered Jaleh so he resisted the urge. Why he cared what she thought of it still baffled him.

"It had to be someone close. Very few people knew the plans. And more than three-quarters of our forces were arrested before we even started. Executions have already begun." Jaleh's eyes kept scanning the platform, ever cautious.

Vartan grunted. "Are we leaving through Turkey?"

"It will be safer for us to get out of the country through Pakistan—especially for you, Armenian boy."

Jaleh had acquired luggage containing a few changes of clothes and some dry food for them to make their voyage look more legitimate. Hand-guns and extra ammunition were also essential travel accessories. She covered her head with a hijab for good measure. The barehead ban was now in full effect for women.

"I hate that on you," Vartan said, irked by the sight of it.

"Are you my fashion consultant now?" A smile escaped her tightened lips.

"I'll send you my bill."

She shook her head. "If our paper-work holds up and/or if we're able to travel undisturbed, we'll be able to cross the border at night by jeep and get deep into Pakistan through old goat paths in the mountains, with the help of some well-paid Coyotes."

"Sounds like fun," said Vartan.

The train roared to a stop in front of them, tussling their clothes and causing a strand of hair to come loose under Jaleh's headscarf. He found that piece of hair hanging across her cheek quite pleasing, and his face must have said so.

"What?" she said.

"What?"

"You're staring."

"I...what? No." He cursed his inability to mask his thoughts.

"Eyes ahead, soldier." Her face looked stern, but the voice came out light.

Vartan laughed and shrugged, picking up the luggage with his good arm.

The train was busier than usual for the time of year, and getting in took some time. Once on board, they shared some *barbari* bread and feta cheese that Jaleh had packed.

"I forgot how hungry I was," he said to her. "I don't think I've eaten regularly in a very long time."

"That's not good. You need to take care of yourself." Her face told him she regretted the words the moment they left her lips.

"Is that genuine concern or are you practicing for the wife role?"

"Don't flatter yourself. You're no good to anyone dead. I may have need of you yet."

"I?"

"We. Mossad."

"Uh huh. I see."

"Just eat your bread." She scowled.

They took turns sleeping throughout the trip—shifts of one hour. During his turn to keep watch, he scanned the vast landscape and the mountains in the distance, the herds of sheep, old villages, and ancient ruins. Most of the time though, he found himself observing her. She slept with extreme lightness—trigger ready at all times. Her eyes would move in rapid flicks under her lids as she dozed, but only for a few seconds. Then they slowed down as if she would not allow herself to stay under too deep or too long. They had much in common.

She must have undergone some very intense training. He wondered where they taught their agents. Despite being gaunt from her stay in Evin Prison, she had the physique of a fighter. Her gait, though feminine, would sometimes render an unconscious betrayal of her readiness for physical altercations. A trained eye like Vartan's caught it, but he was certain that no one else would.

She remained cool under intense stress as well. He liked that. To his dismay, she was beginning to fascinate him and occupy too much of his attention. *My mother told me not to get involved with highly trained assassins—especially from Mossad.* Vartan was unaccustomed to such distractions.

His ever vigilant extra sense spotted trouble making its way toward them. He reached over to tap Jaleh's shoulder but her eyes sprung open before his hand got there.

"We have a problem," he whispered.

"What is it?"

"Revolutionary guard checking papers. He is down at the far end but heading this way."

"It's okay. I have travel documents."

"For the train?"

"Yes."

"When did you do that? We only decided to go by train an hour before boarding."

"No, the decision was made well before that. It just took you that long to reach the same conclusion."

He was certain he saw a faint smile. He cocked his head with skepticism. "Right. So if I search your bag, I won't find papers for the plane and boat as well?"

This time she smiled outright. "No, you won't find them."

She handed him his paper and closed her eyes again, relaxed as if she had not a care in the world. Vartan followed suit, closing his eyes but peeking through the slits of his eyelids every once in a while. Perhaps the guard would see the sleeping couple and judge them harmless, and let them be. A touch of a hand on his shoulder followed by a shake vanquished that hope. He resisted the intense urge to break the man's arm.

"Papers," said the guard.

Vartan made a great show of being disoriented for a moment, waking up with a start. He rubbed the pretend sleep from his eyes and searched several pockets before nudging his sleeping wife.

"Dear, this gentleman is asking for our papers."

"Oh yes, I have them here somewhere," Jaleh said, putting on an equally convincing show. She fumbled around until she pulled the folded papers from her purse.

The guard examined them with care, looking from the attached pictures to the passengers in question. Nothing was out of the ordinary until Vartan saw a nearly imperceptible flash of doubt cross the man's dark eyes. It vanished as soon as it came but it was unmistakable. He had found a problem.

They were made.

The dark-bearded guard handed the papers back to each of them like nothing was wrong and continued on to the next set of seats, repeating the process.

When he was out of earshot, Jaleh turned to him. "Did you see it?"

"Yeah. We are burned. As soon as he is out of sight, he will gather his buddies."

"Wait here, I'll fix it," she said, standing.

"Hang on, I'll go."

"Again. Do I look like I need saving, Mr. One-arm?" Her eyes flared.

"I saved you once already."

"And I saved you twice in return. Let's call it three now."

He wanted to argue his point more, but the look on her face told him it was a bad idea. Sinking back in his seat, he picked up the book he had been pretending to read. Tarzan, by Edgar Rice Burroughs. There would be no chest beating from him today.

Jaleh left the car, passing the guard as she did, heading for the restrooms. The man turned to watch her leave. He shot a quick glance in the direction of Vartan, who pretended not to notice, then disappeared after her.

Vartan turned to his book and read a few lines:

> *In his savage, untutored breast new emotions were stirring. He could not fathom them. He wondered why he felt so great an interest in these people—why he had gone to such pains to save the three men. But he did not wonder why he had torn Sabor from the tender flesh of the strange girl.*
>
> *Surely the men were stupid and ridiculous and cowardly. Even Manu, the monkey, was more intel-*

> *ligent than they. If these were creatures of his own kind he was doubtful if his past pride in blood was warranted.*
>
> *But the girl, ah—that was a different matter. He did not reason here. He knew that she was created to be protected and that he was created to protect her.*

Vartan closed the book with a snap and got up to set out after Jaleh. Walking as fast as he could without crashing through the throngs of passengers moving to and from the dining car ahead, he scanned back and forth for any sign of her or her bearded foe.

The men's lavatory car was empty, and she was nowhere to be found. He approached the ladies'. Pushing on the door with the palm of his good arm, he found it locked. He put his ear to the door and heard nothing out of the ordinary. Just running water.

He looked around. No one in sight. He reached under his shirt tail and pulled out his pistol. With a kick, the door gave way before him and he charged in.

"Shhhh, you're making so much noise. Hurry, grab his feet," Jaleh said, standing above the unconscious guard who lay prone on the ceramic floor. From where he stood, Vartan could see he was missing a few teeth and at least a pint of blood. He looked quite dead.

"I was just coming to use the restroom," he said, more than a little embarrassed. Putting his gun back in his waistband, he grabbed a limp leg with his good arm while she grabbed hold of the wrists.

"This is the ladies room."

"The men's was full, and I had to go."

"You weren't here trying to rescue me, were you, hero?"

"I...no, of course not. I—"

The door opening behind him cut off the rest of his denial.

"Don't move!" a voice commanded.

They both froze, still holding the man they were dragging toward the empty stall. Vartan did not have to turn to know there was a gun pointed at them.

Jaleh's expression did not look like she was ready to comply. "This isn't what it looks like," she assured the guard.

"Shut up and put your hands up slowly."

Jaleh's hands went up, letting go of the deceased guard. His head dropped onto the tiles at her feet with a thud. Vartan raised his free arm, dropping the legs.

"Both hands," said the gunman, stepping up to Vartan and pressing the nozzle of the gun right against his head.

"As you can see, I have one arm in a sling," Vartan said.

The man peered over to take a look. Vartan lashed out with his bad arm, twisting his head out of the line of fire and snapping the strap that held the sling in place. The copper pipe that encased his injured arm made a sweet ringing sound as it landed square on the second bearded man's temple. Another guard now lay crumpled on the floor. Vartan stifled a cry from the jarring pain.

"That had to hurt. You may be of some use after all," Jaleh said, feeling for a pulse. "He's dead too. Let's get these two bearded monkeys into the stall before any more come in, Mr. Vartanian."

"Yes, Mrs. Vartanian."

They made it back to their seats without any incident and resumed an uneasy rest, ever vigilant and ready to shoot their way off the train if they had to. Having placed an *out of order* sign on the restroom door after jamming the lock, they were not bothered for the rest of the trip. At least until just before the next station.

A flare up of activity told Vartan that the bodies had been

discovered. The sign had, by some miracle, done the trick for a whole twenty-four hours but their luck had run its course. The police would soon be scouring the train to solve this newest mystery, so at the first opportunity they disembarked and borrowed a vehicle from a nearby used car sales lot. It was the weekend, and the place was closed, perhaps giving them a day or two before it would be reported missing. They would be far away by then.

They took turns driving day and night, stopping only for gas and the occasional meal, arriving at Sistan-o Baluchestan without incident. Despite the stress associated with the journey, given its objective, this was the closest thing to a good time Vartan could remember having in a long time. The hours-long conversations ranged from the intense and philosophical to careless banter. He found her to be, at the very least, his equal in most subjects and, though he would not dare admit it out loud, his better in more than a few.

Despite himself, he had become quite addicted to her presence. But the time had come to put those thoughts aside and concentrate on the business at hand.

Jaleh had made contact with someone by pay-phone after abandoning their vehicle. A car arrived for them within a half hour. Whisked away to a staging point at a border town, they were transferred to a dark, windowless van and taken east. In the settling dusk over the craggy landscape only a hint of light still clung to the snow-capped mountains as they departed. They met up with other border crossers in a small camp beneath a rocky outcrop. For the most part, they were Iranian Jews that no longer felt safe under the new government.

The smugglers left them there for the night with three armed men to watch over them. One in particular kept a hashish-reddened eye on Jaleh.

"Aren't you going to get some sleep?" she asked Vartan,

laying down on her side with a towel for a pillow.

"I'll sleep sitting up. The ugly one seems to have some unsavory ideas."

"Which one do you consider the ugly one? The one with no teeth or the one who still has three?" She shifted and turned, trying to find a comfortable position

"Three teeth."

"Yeah, I see what you mean. Don't worry. If he tries to touch you, I'll shoot his kneecaps." She definitely enjoyed taunting him, and that elusive smile of hers almost appeared again.

"Thanks. I feel better already."

Very late in the morning, a convoy of three jeeps arrived to pick them up. They set out across the rocky desert to avoid the police checkpoints on the main roads. Vartan sat in the front passenger's seat. Jaleh had squeezed into the back next to two Jewish children. The long and bumpy ride and the machine gun crammed into the seat next to the driver caused Vartan a slight uneasiness.

Before nightfall, they stopped and were told to get out. From there they went on foot. In the growing darkness they held hands, making one long chain so as not to lose anyone. Jaleh's hand was softer than he had expected. At the whispered insistence of Three-teeth, they made a quick drop to the ground several times.

Near a small, abandoned outpost in the desert, a streak of light whistled past their heads. The group dropped once more and dozens of the same lights streaked by. The smugglers exchanged fire for a few minutes before the guns fell silent. They rose from the ground—everyone except No-teeth. There was no time to mourn, and it did not look to Vartan like anyone would anyway, though Three-teeth did take his Seiko wristwatch and whatever items he found in his dead friend's pockets.

They passed the bodies of the two Kurdish soldiers who had fired on them. Some of the smugglers conducted a quick search of the corpses for valuables and relieved them of their weapons and ammunition.

Taken to a house with two rooms and poor lighting, they were fed some bread, cheese, and some dried meat of an undisclosed variety. They slept on the floor for the night, being told they would cross into Pakistan in the morning. Outside, several more armed smugglers joined the group, engaging themselves in heavy drinking. Once again, Vartan stood watch.

Another truck arrived after a few hours, and they were loaded into the vehicle like so many boxes stacked together. They traveled through the wilderness and across dry riverbeds to avoid detection. Their van stopped every so often, allowing the group a few moments to stretch and get their blood circulating in their legs until they crossed a deserted portion of the border into Pakistan at last. Vartan's heart sank as he stepped out of the country he loved. He wondered if he would ever see it again and whether there would be anything left of it when he did.

The smugglers left them and the rest of the passengers there, promising that their main guide would pick them up later in the day. With only some fruit, bread, and a little water against ever increasing temperatures and no shade to be found, a collective feeling of terror traveled through the group. Jaleh did her best to reassure everyone.

It seemed like an eternity to Vartan, but their original guide did eventually pick them up. They were taken to a series of safe houses in the small, lawless villages along the Pakistani border, populated by smugglers and criminals. Transferred from one house to another, they stayed with different families.

A sense of danger hung in the air, more so for the women and young girls in the group. Vartan's presence and refusal to sleep, coupled with the fact that he and Jaleh cleaned their guns often, seemed to be enough to keep problems at bay. The smugglers were also distracted, telling Vartan that they were having difficulties transporting the group because of fighting that broke out between the various tribes in the city of Querta.

The waiting game continued until things were deemed safe enough. Then, under the cover of darkness, he and Jaleh and the rest of the group were brought to a safe-house in Querta—a large warehouse that stored freight containers.

They parted ways with Three-teeth and his men, boarding a train to Karachi. There they were met by a representative of the Hebrew Immigrant Aid Society.

Vartan, at last, breathed a sigh. They were safe.

CHAPTER THIRTEEN

Paris
July 18, 1980

"What are we waiting for? We've been here since 6:00am and could be eating breakfast by now." Anis Naccache growled, his anxious fidgeting becoming more annoying by the second. The former member of the Palestinian resistance group, Fatah, stood large and wide, with dark skin and a shaved head. He looked to Rostem like a man who enjoyed killing.

"Patience, my enthusiastic friend. There are far too many police around. The security detail will thin out during the day when the night shift goes home." Rostem looked back across the street from their vantage point in an apartment lobby, watching the group of uniformed police officers chat over morning coffee.

"Agh, let's just kill them all," Anis said, adding a few unintelligible words to his friend in Lebanese.

The other two, an Iranian and a Palestinian, just sat silent, looking more than a little uneasy.

What idiots they sent me. I could have done this all by myself. I should have just killed these men at the hotel.

The Prime Minister lived quite well, Rostem thought the first time he staked out the apartments in the Parisian suburb of Neuilly-sur-Seine. Still, it would be considered a significant step down from the opulence he had been afforded in his position back home.

Bakhtiar had grown fearful—of that there could be no doubt. His low-budget coup had failed, and he had to know that he had become the main object of retaliation—not only from the Islamic Republic but perhaps even from his own people. They would be wondering who betrayed them—who gave up their daring plans to the enemy. They did not know, but Rostem knew. He had been paid a tidy sum for the information. Playing both sides proved to be a prosperous endeavor, one he had every intention of keeping in play as long as possible. The only thing better than doing what you love was getting rich from it.

What Rostem did not like, what he could not stand, was being saddled with foreign help. Three days ago, the head of intelligence of the newly-formed VEVAK had called to let him know that a four-man team would be arriving in Paris to assist in his mission. The command had been non-negotiable—there was no room for error. But looking at them now—two hot-headed Lebanese, a young, green Iranian Turk, and a half-blind, thick glasses-wearing Palestinian—he could not imagine how this would succeed. Seeing these people with guns was as unsettling as watching kids skip with razor wire.

He looked at his watch. 8:43am. The conversations between police officers were winding down. Things would soon go back to the quiet norm. The street had already been empty for an hour, with the occasional Beetle or Alfa Romeo cruising by.

Rostem ran his hand along the gun in his shoulder holster. He did not like these frontal attacks, but anything else was too complicated to attempt with the likes of his unwanted hit team.

"Forget this." Anis threw his cigarette on the ground. "I'm going in."

"No. Wait," Rostem said, but the two Lebanese were already

crossing the street, guns drawn. "Damn. Okay, go," he ordered the remaining two. They got up and ran after the others. Rostem stayed back for a few seconds before following.

This is going to fail.

Anis had his gun blazing before he reached the door of the apartment. The semi-automatic weapon's fire hit two policemen—one right in the head. His companions fired at will, forcing the rest of them to scatter and take cover behind their vehicles. Coming up from the rear, Rostem shot over their heads at the panicking security, allowing his men to get into the building.

Soon they were under heavy fire from officers inside who had taken what little cover they could within the numerous doorways. The second Lebanese took a bullet to the chest. The rest of them burst through the door to the stairwell.

"Stay here and shoot anyone who comes out," ordered Anis.

Rostem delegated the task to the Iranian, who nodded wide-eyed in response. The remaining three made the climb toward the fourth floor, to Bakhtiar's apartment.

Before they reached the third floor, they came under fire again. A stray bullet hit the top of the Palestinian's foot. Screaming, he collapsed and grasped the bleeding appendage only to drop his gun over the banister.

"Great plan you have going here," Rostem said, shaking his head. *This is not going to work. Time to get out.*

"Shut up. Let's go," said Anis.

"I'm afraid this is where we part ways. I have no interest in being dead, or worse, getting caught by French Police.

"It wasn't a request." Anis pointed his gun at Rostem's head.

"Are you certain you want to go down this road?" Without waiting for an answer, Rostem disarmed the Lebanese hitman with blinding speed, turning his own gun on him.

"Hey, friend," Anis said with his arms raising in surrender, "we are all on the same team. I was just—"

"There is no "I" in team but there are two in idiot, and I won't be one of them. Good luck, friend." Rostem lashed out with the butt of the man's pistol, bashing him on the side of the head with destructive force. He fired a shot upward at the officers above him and stepped over the limp body, taking the door to the third floor.

He found the hallway empty and unsecured—a bit of good fortune. He sprinted the length of it, thinking to get to the stairwell on the far side but heard the sound of quick stomping boots approaching.

A solution dawned on him. While unsavory, it provided the only chance for him to live to kill another day. The locked door to the garbage shoot gave way under his strong shoulder. He eyed the size of the shoot. It would be tight but passable. He took the plunge feet first, gun in hand, and arms crossed over his chest.

Besides the nauseous smell, the sticky shoot slowed his slide down to a torturous crawl. After what seemed like an eternity, he emerged from the trap door into a large metal bin full of garbage, just when he thought the smell could not get any worse.

With the sirens and bustle focused on the front of the building, Rostem took the opportunity to leave from the back. He crawled out of the bin and jumped a fence into a neighboring lot.

His anger seethed, made worse by the filth covering him. Failure was not something he experienced all that often. He needed to kill someone but it would not be the Prime Minister for the time being.

CHAPTER FOURTEEN

Karachi, Pakistan
July 19, 1980

Karachi was the sun-kissed city by the mighty Arabian Sea. Jaleh did not think it was quite the sparkling jewel of her imagination, but still impressive.

"This city is something else, don't you think?" Jaleh said.

"Yes, it's amazing what you can build out of mud." Vartan laughed at his own humor. He did that a lot.

"Oh, stop. Not every place can be Tehran Pars."

"Not if you isolate yourself from your neighbors, no. You know the thing that strikes me about these big cities in this part of the world is the short memory span."

She resigned herself to the inevitable history lesson to come. "Okay, tell me."

"Karachi was a small, mud hut village in the middle of nowhere until the British came and turned it into an important, flourishing seaport. What do they do? They kick the British out. Tehran was also a mud hut village until Reza Shah rebuilt his capital. What do they do in return? Kick them out."

"There was a little more to it than that."

"Yeah maybe." He shrugged. "Still, this place seems to have

reverted back to mud huts," he said, referring to the rows of derelict buildings with corrugated tin roofs and rotting wood frames.

"It has its charms though." She pointed to the lavish temple in the midst of it all.

"Yes, the clergy are never poor in any country, that's for sure. You'll see. Iran will be like this, or Afghanistan, in ten— or twenty-years' time if they run things. People will live like cutthroats and bandits, and beggars will be running the streets."

They rode through the boulevard in a bright blue motorized rickshaw. How traffic flowed, intense and chaotic without any hint of regulation, defied logic.

"It's amazing how the exorbitantly-priced restaurants are just mashed in with the cheap bun and kabob vendors." Vartan shook his head in wonder.

"You can live as well as a king here or as poor as a pauper, depending on your cash flow. Same as back home," she said.

"Back home is still better."

"We are a little biased, perhaps, but I don't disagree."

"There it is." Vartan pointed. "The Pakistan Air Force Museum."

"Drop us here, please," Jaleh said in English.

The rickshaw driver pulled to a stop, and she handed him a fistful of Rupees. They walked the very long runway preceding the entrance to the gates of the museum.

"Why would your guy want to meet us here?" said Vartan.

"It's public, it's open, and therefore difficult to hide and do surveillance. And it's a military museum, so they probably figured you'd enjoy it."

"How thoughtful," he said.

She enjoyed his sarcasm, even though she acted like she did not. He was one of the rare few who could make her laugh despite herself.

They paid for their tickets and entered the museum. Right away, the planes drew Vartan with youthful delight. The first one he came to read—*Shenyang F-6*.

"We can look around later." She prodded him to keep moving. "We are supposed to rendezvous inside."

They walked past many planes on display. Vartan tried to take them all in, like a kid being dragged through a candy store by the arm. Arriving at a large, beige hangar, they followed a few wandering tourists in through the oversized doors. Inside, only the odd muffled chatter disturbed the quiet.

The place had far fewer planes within than the size would suggest, but they were well spaced and well maintained. Vartan walked over to a sleek silver plane shaped like a bullet, resting off the ground on three steel poles. Jaleh followed close behind him.

"A Folland Gnat," said Vartan, with a bit of awe in his voice.

A man in a light gray suit and bowler hat stood enjoying the display as well. "You know, this plane landed in Pasur during the Indo-Pakistani War of 1965 and was captured." He looked at Vartan as he spoke. "Very neat that they still have it. So much is lost during wars."

"Only just under 500 of these were ever built," said Vartan, with increased excitement for having found a fellow connoisseur.

"449, to be exact. Levi," said the man, extending a hand. "Ari Levi, at your service."

A very thin man, Ari had a large, hooked nose and a snow-white ring of hair around a bald spot so perfect it looked as though he had shaved it that way.

"Good to meet you," Vartan said, offering his hand in return.

"The pleasure is mine. I'm already acquainted with your wife here."

Vartan looked like he would protest the title but changed his mind. Jaleh cracked a smile, finding it amusing that the idea still got him so nervous.

"So what have you got for us, Mr. Levi?" Vartan's eye continued to rove back and forth between the man and the plane.

"Ari, please," he said, handing him a heavy shoulder bag. "Here is everything you need to get you started. Cash, IDs, passports, weapons, and your first joint assignment, which is right here in Karachi."

Vartan took the bag and hefted it onto his shoulder.

"What's the job?" Jaleh said while they all stared as if to admire another plane.

"An Iranian national who is training and sending troops to support the new regime. The Israeli government has agreed, unofficially, to work with the remnants of the Shah's supporters to undermine the Mullahs in any way we can. This will make up the bulk of your assignments."

"That is fine with me," Vartan said.

"The instructions for contact and dead drops are all in there. Read them. Memorize them. Destroy them. All as per usual, etc, etc."

"Thank you, Ari," Jaleh said.

"I'll be in touch. Enjoy the museum," Ari said with a casual two-finger salute before leaving.

"You have unusual friends," Vartan said to Jaleh with a smile.

"Yeah… Look at you, for example."

"We are friends now? Wow. Our relationship is really blooming."

"Don't push your luck. You can just as quickly be demoted."

CHAPTER FIFTEEN

Paris, France
July 21, 1980

Fear was the blood in the water that brought out the shark in him. Some killers loved the thrill of the fight, but he preferred the excitement of the chase—that moment the prey believes himself to be defeated and his flight instinct takes over. The mindless dash to find safety, the pleas and the loss of body control before the final twinkle of understanding passes the eyes. Often his job called for the element of surprise, which negated his pleasure to a great extent. The inevitable need to make up for it with a target of his own he found difficult to ignore.

He had become known as the agent called Rostem, but he had worn so many faces over the years that sometimes he was not quite sure which one was real. He could transform from old and decrepit to young and virile. He could be a woman, a priest, a beggar, or a businessman. The fluidity with which he alternated between identities made it almost impossible for his enemies to avoid death when the time came to deal with them.

The man running from him now emanated fear like pheromones. He zigzagged between the thin tall birches, snapping twigs and branches. Rostem followed at a leisurely pace. The direction he ran would come to a dead end. Then an inevitable, soul-crushing realization would dawn on him when he came out at the lake, and he would try to double back.

The bodyguard he brought with him on his daily jog had been inept, despite his size. Rostem had made short work of him with his small paring knife. He had bled out in a slow and silent stream. He could have had them in the same stroke, but that would not have been as enjoyable. He inhaled the fear in the air, closing his eyes to bask in it.

Looking at the trail on the ground, Rostem guessed that the good General Farbod by now realized the severity of his predicament. A life-long soldier, of course he would make a valiant attempt to defend himself if he could not escape. But that would come to nothing, as it always did. He made a left and walked parallel to the beaten running path. He detected no sign of any other presence, as per usual for that time of day.

He heard crashing through the underbrush, like a moose being chased by a mountain lion. Rostem ducked behind a fallen tree that offered a wide cover and drew his blade again. As the general ran past in a panic, Rostem cut him in the leg, just below the knee and to the back, severing a tendon. Screaming, Farbod tumbled and rolled in the leaves and dirt.

Rostem rose and stalked toward the bleeding general. Somehow, the man had found the strength to raise himself and limp down a small path between the trees.

He really doesn't want to die.

Rather than give chase, Rostem walked in the same direction, confident that there was nowhere for him to go. Farbod could not get far with his injury anyway.

He came to a little creek where two tributaries met in a junction. Crouching by the water's edge, he noticed the blood trail ended on a stone several feet out. *He must have gone into the—*

A reflection in the clear pool caught his eye. He pivoted off of his right foot, spinning around just in time to avoid the large branch being swung at his head.

Farbod had given the swing all of his strength and commitment, sending him sprawling into the water. He fluttered and sputtered like a dying fish. Rostem pulled him out by the hair, tossing him on the ground like a dishrag, gagging and coughing. His dark beard, thick with mud and leaves, clung to his face, large water droplets falling from it.

Rostem dug his knife into the general's other leg, causing renewed screaming. He waited for that to die down a bit before addressing the doomed man.

"You are a traitor to your country." His words seemed to take some of the fear from Farbod's eyes. Rostem did not like that.

"I am a patriot. I served my country for longer than you've been alive."

"You are a traitor, and you have been sentenced to death." He leaned in and jabbed the blade into the man's side. The fear returned.

"Long live the Royal family. Long live the Shah."

"But not long for you now, eh? I'll tell you a secret. They paid me a small fortune to kill you, but I would have killed you for free."

"I will see you in hell."

"You will be waiting a long time, I'm afraid. I have so many more of your compatriots to kill before I die. But I've sent a few ahead of you so don't worry, you won't be alone." Rostem drove the knife into Farbod's neck, holding the back of his head with his other hand. He stayed with the Shah's favorite general until the last trickle of life ebbed from his black coal eyes.

He wiped the blood off his knife on the man's shirt and stood. Sweat poured off his forehead and his breath came out ragged from the exertion of holding him down, but it had been well worth the effort.

He kicked leaves over the body until the pile concealed it well enough for him to be long gone before it was discovered.

CHAPTER SIXTEEN

Karachi, Pakistan
July 22, 1980

Vartan checked his watch for the hundredth time. 10:46pm. Jaleh was still as late as she had been a half hour ago, only more so.

He sat alone at the table in his tuxedo, throwing awkward smiles at the people next to him. They sent him the odd pitying glance in return.

Mehrdad Gobadi, the target of the evening, danced the night away with his wife Shireen, oblivious to the pending danger. Vartan feared they would soon tire and leave.

Many politicians and men in uniform were present, as well as high-profile businessmen. A set of fancy invitations had been included in the bag of goodies Ari had given them.

Jaleh had bought a dress the day of the event and left Vartan to practice the dance steps she had painstakingly tried to impart on him, to get her hair done. She was supposed to meet him at their table.

He fended off yet another look of pity from an older Pakistani dignitary as the current song ended, running his finger under his collar to let some air in. He looked at his watch again, noting a full two minutes had passed. He turned to look toward the door unprepared for what he saw.

The woman in the doorway looked like a storm compressed into a perfect, form-fitting burgundy dress. Vartan couldn't think of a more apt description than that. A perfect and beautiful storm. Her thick, bountiful, hair—the color of a raven's wings—spilled over her bare shoulders. Her arms were bare down to the matching gold-hoop bracelets sparkling on each wrist, complementing the wedding and engagement rings on her finger. Her onyx eyes dominated her flawless face. She had high but subtle cheekbones and her full, pouting lips held a hint of silver gloss. Her skin was like cinnamon and olive oil. She was not tall, even in her black stilettos, but well-proportioned from her head to her sculpted, bare legs.

Vartan looked around at the other tables to see if any of the guests were as awestruck as he, perhaps even feeling a slight bit of...jealousy? *No. Protectiveness.*

Everyone had their eyes glued to Jaleh as she approached the table, anxious to see who the fortunate recipient of her attention would be.

Vartan stood and took her hand, kissing it before pulling out a chair for her. Her subtle perfume floated toward him causing a moment of mind-numbing intoxication.

"You look...uh...amazing." He made the comment as his undercover persona, but he did not have to act at all.

Jaleh's blush at his stuttering words was a rare treat.

"Sorry I'm late," she said. Not for the first time, Vartan noted how soft and musical her voice could be when she was not yelling at him.

"Are you? I didn't even notice the time." The memory of his discomfort moments ago was lost in the hazy trance she conjured over him.

"I'm sure," she said with a smile.

The waiter brought champagne to their table. Even though alcohol was banned in the country for Muslims, it flowed freely at political events without raising an eyebrow.

The ethereal string tremolo of Strauss started up, and the Gobadis were the first to step back onto the floor. It happened to be a waltz—the only dance he had practiced. He gulped and turned to Jaleh.

"Care to dance, lovely lady?" He extended his hand and rose.

"I thought you'd never ask."

They walked onto the dance floor hand in hand. She rested her free hand on his chest. He took hold of her lower back and began to move.

One-two-three, one-two-three, dip-sway-three, turn-two-three. He counted in his head, but he must have moved his lips for she giggled under her breath.

"What?" he said.

"You don't need to count. Just relax and let your feet carry you."

"My feet will carry me back to the table if I don't count."

She laughed again, a little louder. The sound was better than the music that played. He could have danced to that for the rest of his life. For just a moment, they were a real couple, enjoying a real affection, and not just two spooks about to end someone's life. It was magic.

Before he had a chance to wonder if she too felt the magic, he realized he was being led closer to the target. She did it while still giving the appearance that he was in control. Jaleh had a real knack for that. And he did not mind it as much as he probably should have.

With the gradual crescendo of the Blue Danube, they swayed over to the dancing couple. Mehrdad Gobadi expertly guided his wife over the shiny surface as if she was a featherlight chess piece moving across a board.

The song ended and the two couples, along with several others, applauded the orchestra.

"You both dance so well," Jaleh said in Farsi to Mrs. Gobadi. "We could barely keep up with you."

"Oh, you are Persian. How nice," she said, looking delighted. Mehrdad, on the other hand, looked a little suspicious.

"Fellow Iranians, that is wonderful," he said. "What brings you to Pakistan?"

"Mehrdad, where are your manners? Don't interrogate them. Please forgive my husband. He means well but he is very direct."

"Not at all, we're here to secure a cement contract for our construction company in Canada. I'm Ali and this is my wife Darya," Vartan said, as per the false IDs they carried.

"Very interesting. A pleasure to meet you. I'm Mehrdad and this is my wife, Shireen. Please, join us."

"Oh no, we couldn't intrude," said Jaleh.

"Nonsense, I insist," Mehrdad said, snapping his fingers at the waiter to bring chairs.

"Thank you, that's so kind." Jaleh smiled and took Vartan's hand to follow.

"This is Mr. Ardashir Najafi and his lovely wife, Arezoo." Merdad pointed at a middle-aged couple seated at the table who rose at their approach.

They exchanged greetings and Vartan noted that Arezoo Najafi was the only woman in the place wearing a headscarf.

"Pleasure to meet you." Vartan gave a little bow.

"Mr. Najafi is visiting us from back home," said Gobadi. "He is the Minister of Trade."

"Please, call me Ardashir." The minister extended a hand.

"Ali here is in the cement business in Canada." Gobadi gestured toward Vartan with a smile.

"Oh? That's a great country," Ardashir said. "Lots of Persians there. I visited my cousin there once, years ago. Where are you living? Montreal? Toronto?"

"No, just outside of Toronto in a city called Guelph." Vartan smiled—details were essential.

"I see. Very nice." Ardashir picked up his drink and took a long sip, then lit a cigarette.

The waiters provided service for two more and then brought the entrees. Only Mr. Gobadi seemed to throw in the odd question to test their story every once in a while during their pleasant conversation. Vartan deflected them with little effort, as he had rehearsed the story enough times. And if there were any problems, he would just shoot him at the table and leave. Not ideal, and not something that would please his fictional wife, but he kept the option open.

The real wonder of the evening was Jaleh. She charmed them all with her quick and masterful weaving of intricate and fascinating stories. She had the entire table hanging on her every word—Vartan included. He could have listened to her talk forever and was reluctant to let it end—but end, it must.

The others protested when Vartan stood to take his leave. Alas, he had an early meeting with cement exporters.

"We are leaving as well. It was indeed a wonderful pleasure, and we hope to see you again," Mehrdad said.

They extended hands and everyone exchanged shakes. Jaleh reached for Merdad's hand—her ring turned around in her palm to inject the polonium-210 that would cause him to die of acute radiation syndrome—but he pulled his hand away and placed it on his heart instead. He bowed and thanked her for the pleasure of her company.

Jaleh spared a glance at Vartan, and they left the table together.

"This just got complicated," he said.

"Who knew he wouldn't shake my hand?" Jaleh's annoyance bordered on anger.

"He's one of those that thinks westernized women are dirty."

"Westernized? I grew up in Iran."

"Yeah, but you're a modern Iranian woman, not one of those relics stuck in the 8th century. Don't take it personally."

"Doesn't bother me one bit, but it does throw a damper on our plans."

"Well, we have a contingency plan," he said, grinning.

"What would that be?"

"I pinned a tracker to the bottom of his jacket."

"I didn't see you do that." Jaleh furrowed her eyebrows.

"What can I tell you? I'm like a god."

"Only in your own mind."

The valet returned their car and they drove down the block, pulling over to wait for the Gobadis to leave.

"Well, if our intel is right and he does meet with the mercenaries tonight to deliver funds, we can follow him and take out the mercs too," Vartan said.

"We don't know what we will be walking into."

"True. But worst-case scenario, we hang back and then get him as he drives home."

"I guess we don't have much of a choice." Jaleh frowned and leaned her head back on the seat, crossing her arms. She did not like improvisation.

"That's the spirit," he said, but his humor went unnoticed.

Vartan pulled out a receiver from a duffel bag in the back seat. The black box had a series of buttons and a green screen. He pulled the antenna out and found the signal beeping and moving.

"They are already on the move."

"Here, take this and tell me where to go. Unless I'm wrong about him, he will drop his wife at home before he does any business."

"Chauvinist pig."

"Hey, I'm just telling you what I think he's thinking."

"Not you, him. Guilty conscience?"

"Are you watching the screen?" he said.

"Yes. Turn here."

"Crap. A little sooner next time, please." Vartan cranked the steering wheel hard to the left. Jaleh slid on the seat closer to him.

"Stop talking to me, then." She pushed herself back to her side and sighed. "Too bad this hair and dress were all for nothing."

"I don't think it was for nothing," Vartan said, keeping his eyes on the road.

"What do you mean? We didn't get the job done."

"I mean it wasn't wasted. You looked…you know…good." The words were more difficult to produce when he was not in character.

"Mr. Vartanian, are you complimenting me?"

"Watch the screen," he said, avoiding the question. "Where to?"

"There. That's his car." Jaleh pointed to a vehicle in the distance.

"He is pulling into that complex."

The car pulled into a security gate of a posh townhouse complex and disappeared inside. Vartan pulled over, grateful that the conversation had been diverted. He cringed in anticipation of a revival, but it never came.

A good twenty minutes passed before the blip of the receiver box began to move again. They watched him drive by alone before following at a good distance.

Vartan had to be even more careful once Gobadi got off the freeway about a half hour later. Driving into a less populated, industrial area, he slowed down and hung back a fair distance, turning off his headlights.

The BMW pulled into a large, empty lot where a dozen or more bulldozers and excavators were parked side by side. Another car sat waiting and a signal of flashing lights was exchanged before Gobadi's car came to a stop, facing it.

"Wait here," said Vartan.

"No way. I'm coming too."

"Your shoes," he said, pointing. "It's all mud."

"Damn."

Vartan left the car and kept to the edge of the fence, his movement swift and quiet. At a row of heavy machinery, he navigated the gaps between them, remaining unseen. He had his six-shot Colt Python drawn, pointed upward.

At the last bulldozer, he peered around the edge of the large, rusted blade. Two men stood beside Gobadi. He did not see anyone else in the cars. They wore heavy jackets despite the warm weather, their bulkiness telling him they were armed. A large hockey bag rested on the ground between them. He would have to shoot the Kurds first since they were facing his direction.

Vartan straightened and fired, walking out from the machine as he did. The first bullet struck one merc right in the forehead. The second caught the other square in the chest. He fired an extra round to make sure he stayed down. This took precious time, and Gobadi was quick. He drew and fired, forcing Vartan to drop to the mud and roll out of the way.

Back behind the Bulldozer blade, two more shots sent sparks over his head. He returned fire, hitting the tire of a car. Gobadi ran, firing blindly behind him. Vartan jumped up and gave chase, following him as he disappeared between two rows of large tool sheds.

Damn, he is fast for his age. He checked his gun while he ran. Two shots left and no time to reload.

Rounding a corner, Vartan saw no sign of his target. He slowed and walked with caution. The only light came from a thin post at the end of the row.

Where the hell is he?

As if in response to his silent question, Goabdi leapt from a crevice between the sheds and brought a shovel down on Vartan's gun arm. The weapon skidded across the gravel. Blinded by the pain, he could not react fast enough. Gobadi swung the tool again, delivering a solid strike to Vartan's chin.

Dropping to the ground, Vartan rolled toward his attacker in a desperate move, taking his legs out from under him. The two men rolled in the mud and dirt, exchanging punches and trying to get the upper hand. Gobadi forced a handful of gravel into Vartan's eyes. He followed up with a series of punches while Vartan struggled to clear his vision. He was losing. Gobadi got on top of him and picked up the fallen shovel. Vartan cleared his eyes in time to see the blade raised up, poised to strike.

A loud shot rang out and his assailant was flung off him like a sack of grain. The hole where his face used to be told Vartan the man was no longer a threat.

"I found your gun," Jaleh said.

"So I see."

Barefoot in the mud and stones, she shifted from one leg to the other, Vartan's smoking pistol in her hand.

"Agh, I just got a pedicure. What a night."

"I'm glad you didn't listen to me," he said, wiping dirt and blood out of his eyes.

"Remember that the next time I don't listen to you."

"Here." Laughing, Vartan pulled off the dead man's penny

loafers and tossed them at her feet. “Put these on until we get back to the car.”

“That’s so gross.”

“Better than walking back on all those stones. Look, your foot’s bleeding.”

She grimaced but slipped them on. “Ew, they are still warm. And they are too big.”

“Complaints department is closed.”

Somehow, she managed to laugh and groan at the same time. They walked back to the car, stopping only to pick up the hockey bag. As expected, it was full of cash. Vartan guessed about two-million American.

“What are you going to do with all that?”

“Well, it would be a shame to let this go to waste. I’m going to pay for you to get another pedicure.”

PART 3

CHAPTER SEVENTEEN

Berlin, Germany
July 24th, 1980

The militant Islamic students *in Iran that stormed the US Embassy in the capital, Tehran, on November 4th, and took more than 90 people hostage, have demanded that the Shah of Iran, who fled the country in January 1979, be extradited from the US, where he is currently receiving medical treatment for cancer, to stand trial in Iran.*

It is reported that revolutionary guards and police did nothing to stop the take-over, and Iranian television has indicated its support for the action by broadcasting live pictures of the siege.

The Ayatollah, who assumed control of Iran in February of 1979, has also voiced his support for the occupation.

Supporters of the siege, many of them children, have gathered outside the embassy. Some have set fire to American flags and have posted anti-American messages around the building.

"Can you believe these animals?" Vartan yelled at the little black and white television sitting on a wooden dresser table in their rented flat. He gave the beanbag chair a half-hearted kick and continued his relentless pacing for a few more turns across the green shag carpet.

"What are they thinking? Who storms an embassy? And

how have they held it for so long?" Jaleh said, shaking her head in disbelief.

"The embassy wasn't stormed. This was a very organized and controlled attack. They are doing this because the Shah is in a US hospital, and they want to get him back and execute him."

"They can't even leave a sick man alone." With two wine glasses in her hand, she pulled a wine bottle from the rack.

"We should be there. *I* should be there." He stood and shut off the television.

"We can't follow them everywhere. The work we are doing is important. We are still fighting to bring him back home." She put his glass of wine on the table and took a sip of hers.

She had a point, of course, but he could not help but think the Shah would be in danger no matter where he went. Would his skills have best been served next to him and the Queen?

He came close to regretting his decision to leave them in the first place, until he looked at Jaleh. She sat on the crushed velvet chair, her long black hair cascading over her shoulders and her legs crossed. He realized he could never regret it fully.

"It won't mean much if they find a way to kill him on the operating table." He struggled to keep his temper in check, not wanting her to see him succumb to his baser emotions.

"He has good people with him. You said your friend Abbas is there." She offered one of her relaxed smiles that always soothed him, as though she knew how calming they were to his tormented mind.

"I suppose so." He had too many doubts of his own to try and sound convincing. "But Abbas is an intelligence agent, and so is not always with the royal family." He sighed and walked over to the small wooden table to continue his preparations for the next day. Jaleh refilled her glass and leaned in to watch.

He took an empty soda can, cleaned out with soap and

water, and cut it in half using a sharp pair of scissors. Once done, he ran potassium powder through a sifter in order to break up any clumps until satisfied.

"You look like you've made this before," said Jaleh with amusement in her voice.

"Well, not with such basic supplies, but it will do the same job. I hope."

He measured out his ingredients, adding about three parts potassium nitrate for every two parts sugar, putting them in small bowls on the table.

"What are you going to use to ignite it, a shoelace?" she said, grinning.

"Are you making fun of me?"

"No, just your Fanta can of doom."

"I resent your lack of faith."

"I apologize," she said with a giggle. The sound, like music, made him feel better.

Vartan moved from the small living area, with its two chairs and a small sofa which he slept on, to the kitchen. The bright orange paint on the walls reminded him of a renaissance painting. Cracks covered the entirety of the coated surface, to the extent it seemed to be done on purpose. He placed an empty pan on the gas stove-top burner, adding his ingredients once he deemed the pan hot enough.

"For your information, if you must know, I'll be using a timed igniter," he yelled back in the direction of the living room until he realized she had followed him with her glass of wine in hand. With a spoon, he mixed in slow, careful circles. He continued the constant stirring motion until the mixture dissolved into a clear liquid. "I could use a wick, but I won't be able to light it without being noticed."

"Good thinking. Do we have any more of those?"

"I have a box full in the closet." Vartan motioned with his

chin to the small closet set into the space between the kitchen and the bedroom Jaleh occupied—a luxury compared to the spring-loaded sofa, but he did not mind.

Using an oven mitt, he grabbed the pan and poured the liquefied solution into the bottom half of the severed can.

"What now, Mad Doctor?"

"Now, it goes in the fridge until it hardens. Once that happens, I push the igniter in, tape the top half of the can back on, and voila—boom."

"Boom?"

"Boom."

"I wonder," she said, with a mischievous grin.

"Wonder what?"

"I wonder what you would have been in another lifetime."

"I already know."

"Oh really? Do tell."

"Isn't it obvious?" He closed the refrigerator door, leaving his creation to chill. "I'd either be a model or a movie star. Probably both."

"How could I have missed that?"

"I don't know," he said with his most sincere face.

She laughed and he wanted to tell her to never stop doing that, but he kept it to himself. Still, somehow, he suspected she was able to read his mind.

CHAPTER EIGHTEEN

Berlin, Germany
July 25, 1980

Dressed as a blind beggar, Vartan shook his tin cup. The few coins inside jingled, calling attention to his need for funds. A passerby in a fedora dropped another coin in with the rest. No conversation was exchanged—no small talk.

One of the many things that made Berlin so authentic had to be people's lack of interest in anyone else's business. No one liked or cared for tourists and foreigners. In this, the city resembled what he had heard about New York, but with culture. In such a city one could disappear—blend in without raising an eyebrow.

He wandered back and forth along the boulevard, rattling his cup and ignoring conversations. Being blind, he did not take any overt notice of the four dark-skinned men in business suits, trying to blend in as well as possible outside the Cafe Edelweiss, even though they were surrounded by conspicuous men in sunglasses. He gave their conversation equal indifference, spoken in Farsi as it was.

"I hate this country. Everything about it. The food. The people." The man in the white shirt sneered at the bustling scene around him from his seat at the outdoor cafe's patio.

"I know what you mean, my friend. Look at these women,

for example. They all dress like whores. I get a new one every night," said a second man, bald-headed and smoking an over-sized cigar with a smug look on his face.

"Those ones actually are whores," said the third man at the table.

"What do you know, Arash?" Baldy said, the smugness turning to annoyance.

"I know you borrow my money to pay for them. When are you planning to pay me back, by the way?"

Baldy ignored the question by pretending to be preoccupied with reigniting the half-smoked cigar hanging from his thick lips.

"Well back home isn't exactly a paradise right now. Otherwise, we wouldn't be stuck here," Arash said, changing the subject.

The large man in the white shirt, the buttons barely holding in his large stomach, flung an angry look at the fourth man who had said nothing so far."We were cheated." He pounded the table, making the cups jump and coffee spill. Spit foamed at the corners of his mouth. "We were promised positions, and we were cheated."

"Yes, we did everything that was asked of us. Now we are hiding like dogs," said Baldy. "And we are running out of money. Our US accounts have been frozen."

The fourth man, Darius, who had until now been smoking his cigarettes in silence gave a stern glance to each of his three companions. "Gentlemen. Brothers. No one has been cheated. Revolutions are messy. Things can get…complicated. Unforeseen problems arise. Everyone gets his due, in due time. As for money, that is no issue. There is more than enough to go around." He produced a large manila envelope filled nearly to the breaking point and placed it on the table. No one reached for it.

"When can we go back?" said Baldy.

"Soon. I'm working on the details," said Darius.

"When? This is ridiculous." Arash sneered and spat on the ground.

"Listen to me. Yes, we have won the country, but the snake still has teeth. You expose yourself to unnecessary risk by even calling this meeting in public." Darius emptied his coffee cup and waved to the waiter for another.

"Bah," said Arash. "Look at these men that follow me everywhere. I have more bodyguards than the prince. I want what is coming to me. We all do."

The blind beggar approached the table next to them, feeling his way along with his white probing cane. He raised his cup and rattled it. "*Bitte, ersparen sie sich etwas kleingeld,*" he said, asking in German for spare change.

After collecting a few marks from the reluctant patrons, he turned to the four at the table. The bodyguards moved in to intercept, knocking the sightless man down.

"Stop! What is wrong with you? Can't you see this beggar is blind, you bastards?" Darius stooped to help him back up. "And whatever wealth you spend on them, Allah will know of it." He reached into his pocket and placed a roll of bills in the beggar's hand. "Forgive these animals, sir."

"Thank you, young man." The blind beggar pocketed his windfall and walked off.

The man sat back down with his comrade, shaking his head at the bodyguards. "Wait, how did he know to call me young?"

A loud hissing sound interrupted his wondering.

"What the hell is that?" Baldy slid his chair back and looked around.

Streaks of smoke erupted out from under the table, engulfing everyone on the patio in a fast-moving fog. Women screamed. People coughed and gagged. Tables were overturned and glassware broken. The smoke rolled onto the street, causing a vehicle to collide into the one in front of it. Horns blared and curses were exchanged between unseen faces.

When the smoke finally cleared, the bodyguards had their guns drawn while rubbing their burning eyes. Their attention turned to the four men they had been tasked to protect. They sat slumped in their chairs in various positions, their throats cut from ear to ear, the blood collecting in one large pool under their table. Also, the envelope was gone.

Screams and panic ensued. Patrons ran in every direction, ignoring the bewildered guards.

The blind beggar peeled his face away, replacing it with Vartan's trademark grin. He discarded his glasses and cane and walked away from the chaos with a casual stride. The air smelled of petrol and cut grass, yet it might have been jasmine. He took a deep breath of it and strolled along at his leisure, enjoying the coolness of the autumn breeze while stopping at a fruit stand for some fresh fruits, like pomegranates. Vartan so loved pomegranates. Jaleh, not so much. She complained about the lack of fruit for so much work and that the other half of the seed was too crunchy. Perhaps it was an Armenian thing.

A few more city blocks took him to a park, where Jaleh sat in the sun reading a book, shaded by an oversized straw hat. The sirens in the distance were too far to be really noticeable.

He sat next to her and chewed on his red seeds.

"What are you reading?"

"The Name of the Rose, by Umberto Eco."

"Is it good?"

"So far. How was your errand?" She looked up.

"It went well. I managed to get some fruit. Would you like some?"

"You know I don't like that. Or did you forget?"

"No. I remember. You like peaches," he said, pulling a large peach from the brown paper bag.

Her smile was the most wondrous sight in the world. He would do anything to see it, yet all he had to do was something as simple as bringing her a peach.

"Well, Vartan Vartanian, you do surprise me from time to time," she said.

"I surprise you all the time."

"I'm not surprised that you think so."

CHAPTER NINETEEN

Munich, Germany
July 27, 1980

The man at the next table would not take his eyes off Jaleh, staring as if looking at a steak after a two-week fast. She allowed no more than a casual glance in return and otherwise ignored him.

The light breeze took hold of her coiffed hair, making it dance playfully in the sun. She continued to study the contents of a folder in front of her. The warmth of the day caressed her, and the streets teemed with way too many people for a Monday in Munich. She closed her eyes and sighed, the sunlight glimmering off her tanned skin.

She crossed her smooth, bare legs, careful to keep her short skirt from riding up any higher than necessary. Her subtle movement made her observer shift in his chair. She imagined this was what fishing in a stocked pond must be like.

It irked her that men, especially men like Bijan Hashemi, would have women cover themselves up from head to toe but were easily swayed with just the slightest hint of skin or hair. She presumed those two facts were inextricably tied together, but in the end, it was much easier to blame women for their weakness and depravity than to control themselves.

She blew her bangs out of her face and put on an expression of helpless exasperation. Hook, line, and sinker, Hashemi stood from his chair and walked over in ridiculously tight pants that splayed out at the bottom over high-heeled leather boots. She was not sure if the wide-open silk chemise he wore was exposing his chest hair or an angora sweater underneath. From his swagger, one could assume he had not gotten the memo that fashion had changed, and the seventies were now over. Jaleh suppressed a laugh and returned her eyes to her papers.

"Excuse me, do you mind if I follow you around?" Hashemi said in a smooth voice.

"I beg your pardon?"

"Oh, sorry. My parents always told me to follow my dreams."

Her laugh came out genuine and loud, but part of her wanted to vomit. Hashemi, of course, took it as a sign that he should sit.

"Does that ever work for you?" she said, toning down the sarcasm as much as she could.

"I will let you know in the morning."

"Wow. You are a breath of air, aren't you?" *Foul air.*

"You look like something is bothering you. Anything I can help you with?" He offered a wide grin and a wink.

"No, it's nothing. Just looking over some legal forms for a property I'm hoping to buy and I'm afraid I don't really understand them all."

"No problem, let me take a look. I was a lawyer back home."

Is that what they are calling murderous traitors these days? "Oh, I don't want to trouble you," she said instead.

"No, it's no trouble at all. A beautiful woman like you shouldn't have to concern her mind with such things."

"Well thank you," she said, trying to sound grateful. "Mr…?"

"Call me BeeJay."

"BeeJay," she said with a laugh. "Okay. Thank you BeeJay."

He flagged the waiter to replenish their drinks and made a show of putting it on his tab.

Jaleh watched his face with amusement as he tried to decipher the German documents and wondered if he would be able to understand a word of it even if they were in Farsi. She doubted it. He was a blunt instrument. A byproduct of an illegitimate government.

"Is it difficult to understand, BeeJay?"

"Oh, no not at all. Just looking at the fine details. Everything seems to be in order here."

"Oh, that's so good to hear. I didn't want to have to bring it to a lawyer and spend more money on such a small property."

"Yes, yes, everything is good here." He took a sip of his newly arrived beverage.

"Hey, BeeJay. Maybe you can help me with another problem I'm having."

"Sure, baby. What can BeeJay do to help?"

"Well, I'm trying to buy a cologne for my brother who is coming to stay from Paris, and I can't decide which to get. I have a sample of one that he might like, and I would love your opinion."

"Of course. Beejay knows colognes."

"Oh, would you? That's so sweet of you. I don't even know how to repay you for your kindness."

"Well now that you mention it…"

"It's new. It's called VX." She pulled a small spray bottle out from her brown leather handbag.

"VX. Okay, let's have a little…"

She put the bottle close to his face and sprayed it pointblank, tilting her head back as far as possible. He gagged.

"What does it smell like to you?" She covered her mouth and nose with her napkin as she asked him the question.

He coughed and wiped his face with his silk sleeve. "Jesus, are you trying to drown me?"

"I'm so sorry."

"Yeah, it's good. A little tangy for my taste but I'm sure your brother will love it." He went into a coughing fit, his eyes reddened and watery.

"Oh, that's wonderful. He's so hard to shop for."

"So what do you say we get out of here and go to my place?" he said, trying to compose himself.

"Well I would love to, but I have to meet my brother at the bus terminal. How about I give you my number and you pick me up at the Hilton tonight?"

"Sure, that will be great," he said, still coughing.

Jaleh scribbled on a napkin and handed it over to him. The color of his face fluctuated from green to yellow and sweat gathered in large droplets above his thick eyebrows.

"Are you okay? You don't look well."

"I'm fine." He coughed again. "It's this German food. Not as good as back home, you know."

"I'll bet. Well thank you again, and I'll see you soon, Mr. Hashemi." She rose from the table.

"Hey, I never told you my name was…" He trailed off into a violent series of coughs and gasps. He grabbed the napkin she had written on and unfolded it on the table.

To the traitor Bijan Hashemi
Compliments of The Persian

He tried to rise and grab her but fell back onto his chair, frothing at the mouth.

"Help! Someone help!" she cried out to the waiting staff. "I think he is having a heart attack. He was complaining of chest pains just now."

Without another word, she slipped away from the gathering crowd under the cover of the commotion. She walked down the sidewalk like nothing had happened of any more significance than a spilled cup of water.

"Hey Beautiful," a man called from a blue Renault with the windows down. "Need a ride?"

"Are you following me or are you following your dreams?" she said with a giggle.

"Lovely lady, I have no dreams to follow. They have all come true."

"Haha. Not bad." She stepped into Vartan's rental car. "Not bad at...all." Something caught her eye. A headline glared at her from the newspaper dispenser. "Wait." She got out of the car, walked over and put a coin in the box. She grabbed a paper and her jaw dropped at the words in large, bold print.

"What is it? What's wrong?"

"The Shah. He's dead.

CHAPTER TWENTY

Berlin, Germany
July 29, 1980

Rostem did not enjoy using bombs. He found them loud, unpredictable, and most of all, distasteful. But if blowing up a city block was the only way to get his man, he would do it in a unique and spectacular fashion.

He had spent several days extracting enough glycerin from laundry soap—a crude and rigorous process. However, it would not raise any red flags or force him to make contact with suppliers that may or may not be under surveillance. He did not need much.

Once he had achieved the desired amount, he poured the volatile chemical into a small gel-like container with a gentle hand. He took care to place the filled vessel into an empty cigarette package. After some final adjustments to the receiver, he put that into another empty cigarette pack and placed it next to the other.

The doorbell rang. Rostem draped a bath towel over his entire workspace with care. Wrapped in a towel himself, he rose and went to the door.

"*Wer ist es?*" he said, keeping to the side to avoid any bullets that might come through the door.

"Room service." The voice sounded muffled behind the

solid wood door of his hotel room.

He examined the rounded image of the server up and down through the peephole until satisfied no surprises would be forthcoming. He opened the door.

"Come in," he said.

"Good morning, sir. How are you this morning?"

"Well, the bed is a little soft for my taste, but otherwise I am great."

"I apologize, sir. I can have someone look into a different mattress for you if you like."

"No, no, that's fine. I'm only here for a short time. I'm sure I can endure."

"Very good, sir. I hope the breakfast is to your liking."

"I have no doubt," said Rostem, handing the man a generous tip.

Once the server cleared out of the room, Rostem double locked it again, placing a door-wedge under the door for extra resistance.

Sitting down to breakfast, he read his newspaper while he ate, until a check of his watch told him it was almost time. Finishing up, he had a cigarette on the balcony then took a shower and put on a black cashmere jacket over a white silk shirt and gray slacks. Double checking his work one more time, he pocketed the items and left the room.

He strolled the six blocks to the Adlon Hotel, right next to the Brandenburg gate, smoking and watching people along the way. He loved watching people. They were so much like little sheep going about their daily lives, oblivious to the goings-on and harsh realities being played out right under their noses—life and death struggles for power and money being fought while they worried about their coffee orders. Billions made and spent like drops of water while they worried about paying their rent on time. The idea both amused and annoyed him with simultaneous vigor. They were insignificant, as they contributed nothing to the real world. Still, he liked watching them.

He crushed a butt with the sole of his patent leather shoe before walking into the lobby of the large, historic hotel. How fitting that this would happen here. It would be long remembered.

A row of payphones lined the far wall of the richly carpeted lobby. He walked over to them. Far too many people milled about. The risk was extreme, but this had always been how he liked it.

Leaning against the barrier that separated his chosen telephone from the next, he used his body to cover his busy hands. He unscrewed the cap on the receiver and took out the electronics inside. A little sizzle sparked as he severed the live wire. Careful not to shock himself, he attached the detonator to that same wire and grounded it on a little screw inside.

He cast a quick glance about him. No one seemed to notice his activities so far. He stuffed in the explosive with expert care, closed the cap, and hung up the receiver. Over the coin slot, he placed a pre-taped card indicating the phone was out of order.

Nonchalant, he made his way to the elevator and took it to the second level, which overlooked the first. He found a quiet corner and pulled out his brick-shaped cellular phone and made a call. An uncertain voice answered the line on the first ring.

"Hello?"

"Mr. Sadeghi."

"Who is this?"

"Listen very carefully. Your life is in danger. You need to go down to the lobby and stand by the pay phones. Pick up the one that rings for further instructions."

"Who the hell is this?"

Click.

Now he just had to wait for his prey to come to him. He did not have to wait very long. The Shah's former Minister of Foreign Affairs walked out onto the lobby floor, his rotund mass flanked by more than a dozen bodyguards. He marched toward the phones in the same cocky manner Rostem had expected of the man. His face held a defiant scowl, visible even from his high vantage point.

He rubbed his grubby hands together while his security team staked out every inch of the place, hands on the weapons hidden in their blazers.

"Come and get me, you bastards," he yelled in the middle of the lobby, arms raised in the air.

Onlookers slowed and hushed, staring at the mad Middle Easterner yelling at no one in particular.

Rostem let him wait a full minute, the rage building to a boil, then he dialed the payphone number from his Motorola 3300.

The former minister walked to the ringing phone and snatched it from its cradle, bringing it to his ear.

"What do you want? Come out and show yourself!"

Rostem pressed the button on a small transmitter in his pocket. The explosion, loud yet controlled, echoed through the lobby. It sounded like a tire popping.

After the initial pause of silence, the screams erupted. Parents covered the eyes of their children to shield them from the gore. Some even fainted at the sight of the headless body sinking to the ground like a deflated balloon, his head now a misty red spray floating in the air above him.

"Sorry, wrong number," Rostem said into his phone before walking away.

CHAPTER TWENTY-ONE

Cairo, Egypt
July 30, 1980

Vartan sat high on the rooftop of the Cairo Citadel—an ancient building of much historical significance. One of many in Egypt. He watched the procession of the state funeral of the Shah of Iran.

"There must be thousands of people following him," said Vartan, referring to the casket draped in the Iranian Imperial flag being pulled by two horses. A contingent of Egyptian soldiers marched behind.

"Civilian population. His Majesty was well loved," said Reza, a former Iranian army general, scanning the crowd with high-powered binoculars. Reza, along with Vartan, had been assigned security oversight of the event. The queen hoped that a strong Persian presence would make the family more at ease and had requested them both specifically. Abbas would remain at her side, leaving her in good hands.

"Who else is here?" Vartan had not received the guest list in his briefing, but his main focus was the queen and her children anyway.

"Besides the Pahlavi royal family? President Sadat,

President Nixon, King Constantine and Queen Anne-Marie of Greece, Prince Victor Emmanuel of Savoy, the ambassadors of the US, West Germany and France, the new ambassador of Israel and the Chargé d'affaires of Britain, to name a few."

"No other Arabs?" Vartan didn't anticipate there would be many.

"The only other Arab country represented here is Morocco. That guy in the blue silk suit." Reza pointed to the left.

"Who is he?"

"King Hassan sent one of his lesser relatives, Moullay Hafid Alaoui."

"But no other world leaders could be bothered to attend the funeral of the man who had ruled Iran for thirty-seven years. Quite disgusting." Vartan tasted the bitterness rising in him at the poor treatment his king had endured during his final days.

"Good point. No argument here. There are no friends in politics."

"Except for Sadat," said Vartan. "He didn't conveniently forget who his friends were when it got uncomfortable."

"Another good point." Reza nodded

Vartan looked into the scope of his rifle again, scanning the crowd.

"Like my father always said, never forget who your friends are. If you leave your friends when they need you most, they may miss you for a while, but their aim will improve."

"Your dad said that?" Vartan looked over at the skinny, dark-skinned man.

"I'm paraphrasing."

The procession rolled down the large thoroughfare toward the Al Rifa'I Mosque. The Shah was to be laid to rest within its magnificent marble walls. The last king of Iran would lay near his former brother-in-law, the last king of Egypt.

Crowds of the King's supporters followed behind the VIP mourners. Vartan caught glimpses of the innumerable security operatives on the ground trying to manage the logistical nightmare. He spotted his old friend Abbas, several feet behind the queen, scanning the crowds himself for any sign of problems. It was good to see him looking well, if stressed, given the occasion. Every rooftop had a sniper, and soldiers were everywhere on the ground with fingers not far from their triggers.

"Do you want to see her majesty later?" Reza asked.

"No. I don't want to distract or interrupt her from her grief. I'm quite content to stay behind the scenes."

"I'm sure she—"

"Hey, what's that guy up to?" Vartan squinted, looking back into his scope.

"Which one?" Reza raised his binoculars in the direction indicated.

"Blue button-down shirt and straw hat, four o'clock."

"He's walking."

"Yes, but he's walking the wrong way," Vartan said, finger near the trigger. "The crowds are coming from the other direction. That's a restricted area."

"Maybe he is lost."

"Too bad for him," Vartan said, removing his walkie-talkie from his belt. "Echo team we have an unauthorized person on your six coming in. Take him down quietly and carefully. Status unknown."

"Roger that."

"Our friend looks like he has a little extra weight on him," said Reza.

Vartan looked back into his scope. The man was indeed too bulky and sweating profusely through his clothes, marking the outline of a vest.

"I think you are right, brother. Good eye."

"I'm not just another pretty face."

"I never had any doubt," Vartan said, grabbing his radio again. "Echo team, be aware, target may be rigged with an IED."

The ground team swept in and arrested the man, grabbing his arms and retrieving an object from his hand before he could react.

"Echo to Delta. Suspect in custody."

"Set him up for interrogation, right after the ceremony."

"Roger that."

"Oh, and captain."

"Yes, sir?"

Vartan's tone went cold. "Bring me the checkpoint guard responsible for letting him pass."

"Roger that."

The casket made its way up the stairs of the mosque followed by the family, friends and dignitaries, while a profound sadness crept into Vartan's chest.

"He was the only one who could have saved us from this," he told Reza. "May he rest in peace. What a mess." He bowed his head.

The ceremony ended in less than an hour. With the crowds dispersed and the dignitaries whisked away in armored vehicles, Vartan came down from his perch with Reza. He handed off his rifle to a soldier who ran up to him. Other soldiers ran about dismantling their temporary posts for the event. He wiped the dust from the roof off his shirt and slacks. The captain of Echo team approached him.

"We have the suspect in the tent at the command center waiting for you. He was carrying this."

The soldier held up a green military tactical vest loaded with charges and wiring.

"Detonator?"

"He had it in his hand. We were lucky to have caught him off guard, and somehow he didn't press the button. Half the people there would have been dead for sure with the amount of C4 in here."

"This is military grade."

"Yes, sir."

Vartan followed the captain to the command center tent with Reza in tow. The prisoner sat in a chair with his hands and feet cuffed. The soldiers on either side of him had guns at the ready. Another soldier sat in a chair to the side. Vartan glared at the checkpoint guard in question, watching him shiver with fear.

"Leave us," the captain ordered, and the room was cleared.

Vartan walked up to the prisoner, examining him. He was dark skinned from exposure to the sun and his arms and face were covered in thick, black, fur-like hair. His hat had been removed, revealing a balding sun-burnt head. His face wore the scowl of a man consumed by hate.

"Who sent you?" Vartan said in Farsi.

"You know who sent me, traitor."

"I need you to tell me how many more operatives are on the ground in Cairo and what their targets are."

"There is nothing you can do that hasn't already been done to me. I'm not telling you anything, you bastard."

Vartan pulled his revolver with such speed, surprise did not even register on the man's face before he blew off the front part of his foot through his tennis shoes. The man screamed and thrashed, rolling off the chair onto the muddy ground. He screamed again, helpless due to his restraints.

Vartan noted that both the captain and Reza were about to interject but seemed to reconsider. The guard in the chair, watching in horror, had made a puddle on the ground beneath his seat. Vartan waited with a calm patience for the screams to subside.

"I don't think you've had that done to you yet. Now, how many more of your filthy operatives are there on the ground in Cairo, and what are their targets?"

A string of exclusively Iranian expletives rang out in the tent, accented by spittle and vitriol.

"He has training." Vartan turned to the men behind him. "He won't talk."

"My men will loosen his tongue when—"

Bang.

"No," Vartan said, putting his smoking gun back in its holster, standing beside the now quiet body. "That won't be necessary. But this guy is ready to tell you everything you need to know." He pointed to the now wet and sobbing guard.

The two men said not a word as Vartan walked past them and out of the tent.

CHAPTER TWENTY-TWO

Paris, France
August 2, 1980

Jaleh loved the open markets of Paris. They were a part of the fabric of Parisian life. Merchants came early in the morning from all over France and offered the best specialties—fresh vegetables, fruits, flowers, breads, pastries, olive oils, jams, wines, meats and more. She preferred the non-tourist areas because of the quality, and the prices were reasonable.

For a week now, she had been staying in a small bed-and-breakfast. She found she loved to search for the perfect ingredients for the evening meal and could find almost everything she needed—from salads to fully prepared and roasted chickens. She could even find an endless selection of foreign desserts she could not pronounce. But Vartan was coming home in a few days. She wanted to practice cooking a few Persian dishes for him. His favorite, she had discovered, was *ghormeh sabzi*—which consisted of parsley, red kidney beans, and beef.

The furthest thing from a domesticated woman, she had sworn at an early age that she would never be tamed into submission by any man. She had never wanted to cook and slave like her mother had, so the urge to do this came as a big surprise. But Vartan was no ordinary man. More often than not, he was the one who cooked and washed. He insisted on it under the pretense that he thought he could do a better job. Now she wanted to do something for him. And, truth be told, she missed the smell of her mother's kitchen back home. She needed this for herself as well.

The day she arrived she had been fortunate enough to discover a small, Persian-owned grocery store—a booth really—that had all the ingredients in one place. From a security standpoint, going there might not have been the wisest move on her part. Jaleh needed to stay away from Iranian people as much as possible for her line of work. However, she could not resist a taste of back home, especially on the occasion of Vartan's return. She would surprise him with fresh *barbari* bread and also some Armenian *lavash* bread—the really thin kind.

Jaleh stood in the back, waiting for the baker to wrap her breads. She heard muffled voices in Farsi coming from behind the closed door next to her. One word stood out to her—*tofang*—gun. She bent down to adjust her shoe strap and get a better listen, but she could not hear much else.

"Ma'am, your bread?" The baker stared down at her, his expression tinged with suspicion, holding out the warm bag.

"Ah, great! Thank you so much." She took the bread and went to the checkout counter.

While she paid for her groceries, two men emerged from the back room. Both rough-looking characters wore black jackets that were way too warm for the summer weather. She thanked the woman at the cash and walked out, heading across the street to the cafe for tea.

On the patio, she waited almost twenty minutes for the two men to exit. They both walked to a car parked in front of the store. One climbed into the vehicle and handed the other a medium-sized paper bag before closing the door.

Jaleh snapped several photos from a small camera in her palm but doubted they would be of much use from that distance. She left a few francs on the table and rose to follow the one man who set off on foot, hurrying as he turned right onto the next street.

She cursed her choice of footwear, high heels, and longed for a good pair of sneakers. The paper grocery bag in her hand did not make it any easier. Turning the corner, she found her target crossing the street. She did the same but stopped at a store window to look at some dresses while the man continued on for a bit.

She followed again, staying on her tip-toes to reduce the clopping sound her shoes made on the cobblestone sidewalks. He turned left into an alley between the City Bank and a law office. She sped up to follow but by the time she reached the corner, he had vanished.

Down at the end of the alley, the paper bag lay, discarded on the rubbish-strewn pavement. Approaching it with caution, she crouched to pick it up. Empty, of course. She smelled nothing inside. She inhaled again but felt the muzzle of a gun touch the back of her head. She froze.

"Why are you following me, bitch?"

"What are you talking about? I was just walking home."

"I saw you from the store," the angry voice shouted. The muzzle pushed harder against her skull. "Now, hurry up and tell me who you work for and what you want before I spill your brains all over that pretty white blouse."

"Well, that wouldn't be very nice. I just bought this yesterday."

"I'd be happy to take it off for you so that it doesn't get…"

Jaleh spun around with blinding speed, dropping her groceries and snatching the gun right out of his hand. She miscalculated a little because the gun had a long suppressor attached. Her slight fumble gave the man time to react. He lashed out at her, clamping down on her wrist with one hand and grabbing her throat in the other. In his ironclad grip Jaleh's leg just about buckled from the pain.

Summoning her strength, she launched several knee-strikes to the groin of her opponent. His unexpected resilience annoyed her, but on the fourth strike his grip on her windpipe loosened. She used her free hand and punched him in the throat as hard as she could. His trachea split under the impact with a satisfying crunch.

His hands flew to his neck. He gurgled and sputtered, his eyes growing wide. She had turned his own pistol on him. Two bullets in the head later he lay face up in a Parisian alleyway, thousands of miles from home.

Jaleh rubbed her sore throat and straightened her hair. *That was too close.* She should have been more careful, but she had allowed him to get the drop on her. That would not happen again. She checked the man for ID, finding nothing but cigarettes and cash—a lot of cash. She relieved him of it. Vartan's dinner was now paid for, compliments of the Islamic Republic of Iran, no doubt.

She put the gun, along with the two warm ejected cartridges, back in its original bag and picked up her fallen groceries.

The *lavash* had gotten dirty, but the rest was okay. Well, she would make it up to Vartan by grabbing some wine on the way home.

PART 4

CHAPTER TWENTY-THREE

Paris, France
August 5, 1980

Among the crowd, his prey were but two raindrops in the ocean. Each person on the busy street, Rue de Passy, moved as if unseen hands dragged them this way and that, pulling their narrow collective focus to one thing and then another. They responded in predictable ways, each of them with a self-important goal to achieve for the day. Underneath it all was the illusion of free will, the ability to direct their own path.

Sometimes Rostem would engage people in small conversations, just to wake up the part of them that might be capable of taking charge, making choices. But no sooner would he disengage, then they were off, back on auto-pilot—the most dangerous mode a human being could slip into.

The world was but an ant-farm, and he, the fascinated observer. He took the occasional pleasure in shuffling the deck for the occupants, snuffing a few out to see how they reacted within this ongoing experiment called life.

Speaking of snuffing out ants, the Persian had certainly been busy. He had taken great pains to clear the chessboard in this deadly game they played. Rostem was impressed. He had been well trained. Better than the average SAVAK or Mossad agent, to be sure.

He had to admire the man's work. The smokescreen assassination in Berlin had been a brilliant piece of craft. The only witness a blind beggar—nowhere to be found. The London underground "suicide" he considered a true work of art. Not a trace of foul play had been left behind. Heart attacks, car accidents, lightning strikes, death had become a canvas for the master's brush strokes. Still, he remained just another, more dangerous, ant.

Now it was his turn. Rostem could not pass up this chance to paint his own masterpiece on the canvas before him. He did not prescribe to the elaborate and meticulous details his counterpart seemed to enjoy, but none could deny the effectiveness of his methods. And this time he was not going for pawns. Instead, he would take out the two knights, crippling the resistance.

He stepped out of the Hotel Les Hauts De Passy, onto the narrow street. The sun looked pale and distant in the hazy sky while he ignored the February afternoon chill seeping into his bones. Across the street, the four-man hit team they had provided for him sat parked, two to a car. Though they looked over at him for a sign, he ignored them. They were brutes, blunt, and tactless as hammers. Perhaps they were better than the last hit team, but they had no concept of the game either, with its subtle, blood-drenched beauty. He had no need for backup teams, but they would not stop sending them.

Rostem checked his watch. It showed a quarter to one on the dot. Walking, he snatched up a newspaper from a stall and dropped the appropriate coinage with hardly a break in stride. His light brown, wool overcoat left unbuttoned, flapped in the occasional wind gust—as did his burgundy tie.

His shoes made loud clip-clops on the sidewalk. He could have opted for soft soles, as many in his profession did, but he found the sound pleasing. Good shoes were meant to be heard, as well as seen. There could be no substitute for style.

Like clockwork, the good General Gholam and his brother stepped out of the restaurant they would patronize as a matter of daily routine. Habit was a deadly thing to be a slave to in times of war. But humans were creatures of such, and therefore all too easy to exploit.

The noise of his footfall elicited no more than a casual glance over the general's shoulder. He could detect no apparent concern from the brief view of his clean-shaven face. Arrogance or ignorance, Rostem could not tell which failure of character allowed them to drop their guard in a time such as this. Nor did he care to know. He drew his pistol from under his coat, holding it low. None of the ants noticed, going about their business without a care.

Catching up to his two targets, he spotted the hit team rushing out of the vehicle. Their panic at his lack of adherence to their plan was obvious in their mad scramble. Rostem, almost right on his targets, stopped and raised his weapon in a double-handed grip, letting off two loud shots in quick succession.

The echo, swallowed by the thickness of flesh, hair, and bone, came out as deadened thumps. Terrified ants were awakened from their habitual activities. They screamed, threw hands over their heads, crouched to the ground, or, for those not caught in the headlights, ran in random directions. The bodies had already dropped to the ground in a tangled heap of bloodied flesh.

To Rostem, the passage of time slowed, the sights and sounds as if underwater. Aside from the beating of his heart, he heard none of the myriad of sounds he knew there must have been around him. That pounding sensation beat a rhythm inside him like music to the execution. The warm steel in his hand pulsed as though alive. The thrill of sudden death coursed through him, his drug of choice bringing him to ecstasy.

Dropping the gun to his side, he moved. The sounds all came back to him at once, assaulting his senses. He cringed but walked on, glancing down at the bodies. Once so charismatic in life, they lay frozen, eyes open, mouths slack, both heads twisted in an unnatural fashion from the impact and fall. In particular, the general's eyes held his gaze. In that fraction of a second, he thought he caught a faint light before it vanished—and with it, all of the last vestiges of hope for the monarchy in Iran.

CHAPTER TWENTY-FOUR

Paris, France
August 6, 1980

Vartan had never been to Paris. He had only ever seen it in pictures. The city of romance, of kings and of revolution—it was a haven of poetry and art, trodden upon by the heavy boots of triumphant armies and the soft soles of scholars. In such a place of legend, the very air of history encompassed him from the moment he arrived to reunite with his not so blushing bride.

Jaleh did not seem as smitten with the city, having traveled here with her parents in her youth. She had gotten lost in the Louvre and found the Parisians less than helpful or willing to try to communicate in anything but French. He resolved to take her back to the Louvre to change that lasting first impression.

Riding in the back seat of the taxi together, the day seemed postcard perfect. Ancient architecture mixed with modern skyscrapers shone silver in the afternoon sun, and the sky was an unbroken backdrop of blue. Commuters walked like shoals of fish in a myriad of directions upon the cobblestones, oblivious to their role in the overall image projected. Vartan stopped himself more than once from blurting out his excitement at things that caught his eye, afraid he might come across as childish. Their cab brought them from the airport to Rue de Ravoli. The car stopped in front of a little baroque style house. A woman in a gray pantsuit stood waiting for them on the stoop.

"Mr. and Mrs. Vartanian," she said in a cheery, almost squeaky voice as they stepped out of the vehicle.

"That's us," Jaleh said without hesitation.

"Very nice to meet you both. Kaliope Oge. I see that you are coming straight from the airport." She glanced behind them at the luggage the cab driver was unloading.

"Yes, the room we had been renting was getting a little crowded, so we decided to get a hotel room after our appointment," Vartan said.

"That's not a problem. You can put them into my trunk while we look at the properties on our list." She walked to the car parked in front of the cab and opened the boot.

"Very kind of you. Thank you." Vartan piled the luggage on himself like a professional bellboy and brought it to her car before following the agent and Jaleh up the stoop.

"As you can see there are two separate entrances. The upstairs is rented to a doctor and his wife. They are very quiet. The ground floor unit," she said unlocking the door, "has a large bedroom, a guest room, a small study, kitchen, and bathroom. Basement laundry is shared—alternating days seems to work."

Vartan hoped Jaleh caught all that because his French was not the best and the woman spoke fast. He stepped over to the bay window overlooking the quiet street. He could not see it from here, but he was within running distance of her majesty's apartment building. Also, the private layout provided ample ability to observe anyone approaching. They would be able to detect any suspicious movement near the safe house due to the inactivity on the street. The location also provided easy access to transportation and had very few neighbors—cutting down on the chances that some might be nosy.

The heavy curtains on the windows and thick walls were a plus. What they needed most was to appear ordinary, and this quaint yet nondescript residence fit the bill.

Jaleh seemed to approve and, switching to Farsi, she confirmed that notion.

"We'll take it," she told the agent.

"Oh. You don't want to see the other places on the list?" Kaliope said.

"That won't be necessary." Vartan smiled at the agent's reaction.

"Okay. Uh…perfect. When would you like to sign the paperwork and when are you planning to move in?"

"How about now?"

"Now? Like today now?" Her eyes widened.

"Well, there is no one here, so why not?"

"Oh, I…now. Okay. Let me make a phone call." Kaliope wandered away to call on her portable phone.

"I think it's good for our purposes," said Jaleh, looking pleased.

He liked that look. "It's great. I'll take the study, you take the bedroom."

"How very gentlemanly of you."

"You realize we don't have any beds." Vartan pointed to the bare floors.

"Hmm. I forgot about that. Let's go out and buy something to sleep on."

"Let's go eat first. I'm starving."

"You are always starving."

The Realtor came back into the room with a wide smile on

her face. "Well, everything is settled. The owner says as long as you pay the deposit, the keys are yours."

"No problem." Vartan counted out the proper amount from his thick roll of bills and handed it to her.

"Well. Okay then. Here are the keys, and I will be by in the morning with the papers to sign."

Evening was falling by the time Jaleh and Vartan finished dinner at an overly expensive French restaurant where they tried snails for the very first time along with more wine than usual.

The orange and red blotches of dying light in the sky framed the Eiffel tower as if it were hand painted on a giant canvas. It was beautiful, and for a moment as Jaleh unconsciously took his arm, the idea of a life in exile did not seem like such a dire sentence.

CHAPTER TWENTY-FIVE

Paris, France
February 11, 1981

Jaleh noticed Vartan had not smoked in a while. From almost the moment she told him that it gave her a headache, he had stopped cold turkey. It could not have been easy for a guy who could chain-smoke his way around the great wall of China, yet she also knew he was not smoking outside the house. She could tell the difference when she walked out of her room in the morning. The gushing tidal wave of nicotine odor that used to assault her senses was no longer there. He had even gone as far as to wash by hand the sofa cushions on which he slept.

He was a strange one, this Armenian. A far cry from the thoughtless brutes she had come to know. He had a depth to him, even an innocence, as far as that was possible from a professional killer. He could get under her skin too. Jaleh could not tell half the time if she was annoyed or intrigued by it, so she went with annoyed.

"I need some newsprint. Also, a paper bag, if you can find one," she said.

He sat in a chair beside her night table, playing with an

unlit cigarette from the last pack he had ever purchased, as though considering lighting it right there.

"How about one of my shirts?" He lifted the cigarette to his mouth and let it dangle from his lips, a smirk on his face.

"No. I don't want fibers on this pistol. I thought you quit that disgusting habit."

"I did. My mouth just doesn't know it yet."

"Well, you certainly smell better these last few days."

He put the smoke down on the table. "Thanks," he said with a little laugh. "I'll see what I can find."

He got up and left the bedroom, closing the door behind him. She took out the gun she had retrieved from her would-be assailant and unscrewed the suppressor.

Vartan reentered the room and handed her yesterday's Persian newspaper and a brown paper MacDonald's bag. He sat next to her—drink in hand—leaning over but keeping enough distance to be respectable.

Always the gentleman, I'll give him that. Jaleh spread the newspaper on the bed, picked up the gun, and pushed the magazine release button. With a soft click, it slid from the grip.

"You really need to clean his gun? You already used it." Vartan picked up his cigarette again from the table.

"No, not really. I'm just taking it apart."

Vartan flicked his lighter open and closed, producing a flame each time. Jaleh pulled back the slide, caught the cartridge that popped out of the gun's ejection port, and put it in the paper bag. Holding the weapon over the newspaper, she disassembled it.

"You think you'll find something?" Vartan put his smoke back down, then picked it up again. "Or is this just for practice?"

"Both."

"You don't smile as much as you should, you know?" He

gave her a little nudge on her shoulder, which she did not react to.

"I don't come across all that many reasons to smile."

"We need to remedy that."

"Let me guess, my smile would make me look even prettier."

"No, just less ugly."

Stunned, Jaleh looked up at him. He wore a straight face, but he could not keep it for very long. He burst out laughing, quite impressed with himself. She picked up a pillow and threw it at his head. When it dropped, the cigarette hung between his lips, broken in half, dangling by a thread. She laughed before she could stop herself.

"Walking on thin ice, Mr. Vartanian." She turned her attention back to her task, forcing the smile to fade from her lips.

She held up the suppressor. It looked like machined steel, but the outer layer felt like fiberglass. She unscrewed the adapter fitted onto the barrel and peered inside—glass wool mufflers around a perforated titanium barrel. Professional job, probably more expensive than the pistol itself.

Vartan cocked his head. "I can tell by your face that you found something interesting."

"You are a professional face reader now? I'm just admiring the suppressor. Since when did you start watching every move I make?"

"When did I not?"

His comment made Jaleh blush. "Since you asked, this is very high-end work. Not some home-made kit. Whoever this guy worked for, he had access to some very good hardware."

"That doesn't narrow it down much. There are plenty of big players in Paris," Vartan said.

"Yeah, but how many will supply Iranian hitmen when they get here?"

"Anyone who wants to make a quick buck. The regime has the money printer now." Vartan tossed his broken cigarette into the trash bin.

"I guess so. Well, I better report it. Let everyone know what we are up against here."

"Finished?" he asked.

"Yes. I can't take it apart any more than this unless I unfasten the grip screws. I'll get rid of it in the morning."

"Maybe we should keep the suppressor."

"For what?"

"I'll use it on my gun."

"But you use a revolver."

"Revolvers can't be suppressed?"

"Seriously? You're pulling my leg."

"What?"

"Ugh. Here." She reached her hand out to him. "Give me your gun. I'll show you."

Vartan reached into his holster and put the rubber grip of his pistol in her palm. She took his hand and guided his fingers over the revolver. They were incredibly soft for someone so rugged. She had noticed before but realized it anew. Why did she notice at all?

"Now what?" He interrupted her thoughts, which annoyed her more.

"The cylinder where the bullets are stored. When fired, the sound of the tiny explosion that propels the bullet radiates out from here, so a suppressor on the barrel won't make much of a difference." She handed him the grip of the automatic. "This pistol has a hollow grip with bullets in a magazine that has a spring that pushes the bullets to the barrel." She held up the barrel, not wanting to touch his hands again. "The gases from the tiny explosion form a pressured cloud that follows the bullet through the barrel and comes..." She looked at his face.

The corners of his mouth were quivering. He was laughing!

She snatched the gun grip from his hand and wiped his fingerprints from it. "Bastard," she muttered.

Vartan chuckled, trying to hold it back. "Hey, don't stop. I was waiting for you to get to the part about how suppressors best work with subsonic bullets because regular ones break the sound barrier."

"Damn it! I knew you knew this. How could you not? Ugh. I fell for that?"

His laughter annoyed her and Jaleh swung at his chest with a closed fist, but it felt like hitting velvet-covered marble.

He rubbed his large pec and laughed harder. "Okay," he conceded. "Okay. I'm sorry."

"You should be."

"But just to be clear," he said, still choking on his laughter. "Which end do the bullets come out?"

She battered him with several more punches to the chest. It only made him laugh harder until there were tears in his eyes.

"You hit like a girl," he said through his laughing heaves.

That was the final straw. She launched herself at him, knocking him back into the pillows and pinning him down. She thought she would head-butt the bridge of his nose as instinct demanded, but she found herself kissing him. *What the hell does he think he's doing? What the hell am I doing?*

His riotous laughter abated, Vartan seemed to hesitate for a second before becoming lost in the moment. Despite herself, she was lost in it too.

CHAPTER TWENTY-SIX

Paris, France
February 23, 1981

Vartan's eyes flew open like two wolf traps being set off at the same time. The hairs on the back of his neck rose and not due to the cold air seeping through the poorly sealed window on the other side of the room that needed replacing.

It was just after dawn. He did not need to glance past Jaleh's body to the clock on the night-table to know that. He had a very keen internal clock, but he also saw a sliver of orange and red heralding the rising sun in the eastern sky.

Though the colors seemed richer this morning, his eyes remained focused on the other side of that window, seeking the source of the sound that came from beyond.

Even on winter mornings, the sounds from outside were consistent. People walking their dogs, neighbors shoveling their driveways or scraping their car windows. Most of them never triggered an alarm in his mind and so were ignored, but this sound had a different aura to it. A car moved at a very slow pace down the snow-crusted road in front of the house.

Get out of bed, urged a silent voice but he remained inert. Holding his breath, he listened. Not one car. Two. They inched their way closer, then stopped. Their engines went still.

Do something, said the voice, more urgent now. He thought of the shotgun under the bed, but his body did not want to move, other than to turn his head toward Jaleh. She continued to sleep, oblivious to what he heard, unaware of the thoughts that held him there against her warmth.

Watching the swirl of her long dark hair touched by a dusting of sunlight, he heard the stealthy click of car doors. First one, then a second. There might be even more doors opening in careful silence, guided by hands trained in covert operations.

A patch of Jaleh's dark shoulder showed through the tangle of her hair. He would have touched it if he had not feared to wake her, but he did not want that. If something terrible was about to happen, he did not want her in the thick of it—not in her condition. And in the thick of it, she would be. He had no doubts about that. She was not like anyone else.

The careful footsteps coming toward the house made only the occasional crunch on the snow, but his time with the intelligence branch of SAVAK had trained Vartan's ears well. The house was being surrounded. His shotgun would not do much good against the five or six people he guessed were outside. But listening closer, he realized firepower would not be called for. The people out there were not intent on violence.

A soft knock came at the front door. He slipped from under the thick down cover, pulled on jeans, and left the bedroom. In seconds, he was down the hall and through the living room. Not bothering with a light, he pulled the door open before another knock came. Abbas's hand hung in the air, poised. A large, toothy grin spread across his face.

"Don't you own a shirt?"

"Times are tough," Vartan said, smiling back.

He embraced his old friend and partner. It had been too long. Then Vartan directed him to the living room, taking a quick look at the men remaining outside before he shut the door.

"What's with the army of silent killers?" Vartan gestured for him to sit across from him on the recliner.

"Yeah, sorry about that. A man in my position can't be too careful when traveling in Paris. You know how it is."

"Ah yes, I've heard about your promotion. Right there with the top brass of the resistance."

"Well, what can I say? The generals know talent when they see it." Abbas laughed, his face betraying the toll of years.

"I feel like I'm seeing the ghost of Christmas past."

"I wish that were the case, brother—that one was more pleasant. I'm afraid I am the ghost of Christmas future, and it's pretty bleak unless we can remove the problem."

"Right to business then. Okay, who is this problem?"

Abbas drew a manila folder from his briefcase and dropped it onto the glass tabletop. Vartan opened it. The two-page document also had a blurry photograph, taken at either a bus station or an airport. He couldn't tell which.

"Is this all you have? Or is this just a teaser?"

"He is…elusive, to say the least."

"Who is he?"

"We are not sure, but we think he might be ex-Mukhabarat—infiltrated his majesty's department of defense, now working for the RG."

"Iraqi Intelligence?" Vartan let out a long whistle.

"That's the theory. This guy is as much an enigma as you are. IIS guys don't fool around. Trained from birth. Made to steal food for their meals and forced to kill their own dogs. Really hardcore stuff."

"I think that was the Spartans, but I'm sure it's as bad as all that." Vartan scratched his head. "So who is he?"

"We code-named him Babylon. We think he is the one that

also goes by the alias Rostem, but it is not confirmed.

"That's Rostem?" Vartan stared at the smudge of pixels purported to be the infamous hitman. "I didn't think he was Iraqi."

"We don't know for sure."

"So what do you want from me?"

"Liquidation."

"Why me?"

"We know how busy you have been for the cause. I was surprised to learn the extent of it when I got the promotion. There is no one better—except me and I'm busy—so it should be you. Besides, the generals ordered me to reach out to you. Chatter has it that you are on his to-do list as well, and it is only a matter of time before he makes you."

"Where can I find him? There is nothing in this file."

"He is here in Paris, as far as we know. That picture was taken at Charles De Gaulle last Thursday."

"It's crap. His face is a blur. Could be anyone."

"We were lucky to even get that. It's like he knew where every single camera was and when to turn his face or cover it with his hat. The only reason we got a ping—his passport rang an alarm. And I doubt that was by accident either. He is calling us out."

"What was the alias on the passport?" Vartan rubbed his eyes, a sudden urge to crawl back under the sheets with Jaleh hitting him hard.

"Farzad Hossein, but the trail went cold immediately."

"Why didn't they detain him at the airport?"

"It's what we call a White Alert," said Abbas. "It only comes to us. We didn't want the locals involved. If they detained him, they'd have to question him, and that would be a whole different can of worms. We just need him gone. The Jews are in the loop too, of course."

"Besides me, do we have a list of potential targets?"

"Other than the obvious, here are the possibilities we know of." Abbas handed him another manila folder. It had one page with names running down both sides.

"All these people are here? Christ, it's like a government in exile." Vartan flipped the page and scanned the names, many of which he recognized. He did not see Jaleh on the list and breathed a heavy sigh.

"Except that most of them are running scared. That hit on the general really sent a clear message."

"That was him too, eh?"

"Same M.O.—brazen, careless, and very public, then gone like a ghost through a wall. We need to eliminate this threat, and soon before he wipes our people out entirely, or, God forbid…" Abbas could not even finish that sentence.

"Well, If I do this, I must charge my usual fee, of course." Vartan smiled.

"Way ahead of you, brother," His friend said with a smile, pulling out a large bag of pistachios and dropping them on the table.

"Ha! You remembered. Is this from back home, or that Turkish crap?"

"Vartan-jan, you injure me," he said, hand on his heart, making a show of his hurt feelings.

"Let me make you some Armenian coffee. I know you love that stuff."

"I'm afraid I can't stay. Duty calls."

The two men stood and shook hands.

"Yes, you're a big shot now. My regards to her majesty." Vartan had not seen her in far too long, other than from a distance.

"I will relay them. You'll receive the usual implements and any new intel. The resistance thanks you for your service."

"No thanks necessary. But after we get this guy, I think I might just retire. I wouldn't mind settling down. Somewhere close to the empress to keep an eye on her, but still settled down." Vartan meant it.

Abbas's eyes made an almost imperceptible turn in the direction of the bedroom and back, his smile even wider than usual. "They won't hear it from me, old friend."

"We are that, aren't we?" It was not a question. He embraced his comrade-in-arms with a hard slap on the back to seal it. Then Abbas was gone.

"Did you catch all that?" he asked the empty room.

"I couldn't have avoided hearing it if I tried. Together you two are as loud as an Anzio 20mm." Jaleh came around the corner in her bathrobe, the bump of a tummy hanging out. Her long charcoal hair fell like dripping honey onto her shoulders. It reminded him of a shampoo commercial and made him smile. He noticed the gun in her hand, held down to her side. That made him smile even more.

"Looks like I have some planning to do," he said.

"Looks like we do."

CHAPTER TWENTY-SEVEN

Paris, France
March 20, 1981

The wounded sky bled rain upon the city, the black clouds dying above them in a slew of lightning. The downpour washed away the vestiges of snow from the ancient streets. Rostem stood in the doorway of a long-defunct shoe store, the collar of his long coat up and shielding his neck and face from the rebounds of angry droplets. He caught a glimpse of himself in the dirty glass of the store, his face yet again unrecognizable—even to himself. Scanning the streets in both directions, he waited. The breadcrumbs he had left the Persian in the last few months would lead him here.

The radio squawked in his ear, causing him to grimace in annoyance. *Why do they insist on sending me these fools?*

"No one yet," said the voice of the dumb ogre on the rooftop across the street with a sniper rifle.

"Tell me when he is here, you idiot, instead of when he is not."

"You got it, boss."

"Remember to hold your fire. You are only here as backup." *And I don't need backup.*

"Got it."

Idiot.

He did not have to wait long. The Persian appeared in the rain like a wraith from a bad dream. Always a cautious killer, he kept his distance, his face obscured with that antiquated fedora and a long beige trench coat with the collar pulled up.

The man was truly a relic, but a dangerous one. Rostem doubted such a basic trap would catch someone of the Persian's caliber. Such an inglorious death would not be acceptable for this class of assassin. He needed to look the man in the eye and see the surprise, the pain, the fear if he could find any. Somehow, he doubted he would.

The buffoons in his assigned hit squad had not spotted the target yet. The radio remained silent. Thankful for their incompetence for once, he smiled with relief. The last thing he wanted was a stray bullet putting an anticlimactic end to years of scheming and plotting before he could plunge his hungry blade between his foe's ribs. Even this simple trap took unbelievable effort. One of his own men, Mansour, had gone missing while tailing the target and was presumed dead.

Acting like a man waiting for a ride in the rain, the Persian paced back and forth, but he did not approach the target zone. No doubt he must be aware of its location to come this close. The clues Rostem had spread for him, though subtle in the extreme, could not be missed by such a man. The harsh pang of regret flooded through Rostem for the events about to transpire. He could not be turned, that much was certain. The Persian was loyal, and loyalty was predictable.

The die had been cast, but the delay proved a gradual annoyance. What was he waiting for? No sooner had the question entered his mind than the target turned, stepping onto the street. A slow passing bus interrupted his view just long enough, leaving an empty spot where the Persian had stood moments ago. Rostem cursed out loud.

Where could he have gone? Rostem scanned the area with

his monocular but found nothing, as though he had seen an illusion. *The man is a ghost!*

"I've got something. Thirty degrees north by northeast, near the gray Datsun. Target is in play."

Rostem turned a full hundred and eighty degrees to see what his sniper had located.

"Hold your fire," he said into the radio. "Let him come to us."

"I have a clear shot," the sniper said in his earpiece.

"Negative. I repeat, hold your fire."

Now the Persian circled—just as Rostem would do in his place—walking the grid to draw out potential enemies by forcing them to change their angles of observation.

Come to me. Just a little closer. Rostem held him in his line of sight but could not see the face of his old enemy—the angle and the rain saw to that.

Lightning flashed, and soon after, thunder rolled in with force. Like clockwork, another bus passed. Again, the assassin vanished.

"He's gone!" said the buffoon.

"Yes, I can see that. He's just faster than you. He will reappear. Keep your eyes on the street so that he doesn't end up behind you." Adjusting his microphone, Rostem spat on the ground and scanned the street again. "What are you playing at here, Mr. Persian? Are you trying to draw me out, or just poking to check for a trap?"

"I see him. He is on the south side now. How the hell did he get there?"

"Don't take your eyes off him."

"I have a clean shot."

"No."

"We are going to lose him again."

"I said no. He's mine," Rostem said.

"He's on the move."

"Hold your fire." Rostem was almost shouting into the com.

The target turned, his face pointing back in the direction from which he had arrived. With a slow yet purposeful gait, he walked away.

"He's leaving."

"Forget it," said Rostem. "Let him leave. Abort."

"What the hell? Are you kidding me? Months of effort went into this setup."

"I said abort, you idiot. That's an order."

"I take my orders from higher up."

"If you take that shot…" But his threat went unfinished.

Bang.

The report went off with an echo, sounding to the untrained ear like another clap of thunder, so it garnered no attention at all. From his vantage point, the fallen body appeared as clear as day in the lens of his scope.

"You stupid donkey. What have you done?"

"I completed the mission."

Rostem spat again, anger bubbling like froth upon his lips. "Piruz, go check the body."

"Copy that."

True to Parisian fashion, the crumpled, wet corpse that lay slumped by the brick wall of a Paris Bank went unnoticed by all passersby scrambling to get out of the rainstorm—just another homeless man by the wayside.

Rostem held his scope up to watch Piruz emerge from his position behind a dumpster and skulk over to the body. Without ceremony, he pushed the dead man over. Its lifeless arms flailed to the concrete, and he bent to get a better look.

"Oh, my God," he heard in his earpiece.

"What is it?" Rostem asked the question, but he already

knew the answer.

"It's Mansour." Piruz fell atop his friend like lovers in a tryst, the echo of thunder fading in the air.

Rostem smiled. *You never fail to disappoint.* The Persian had played him like a toy, failing only in drawing out the real enemy.

CHAPTER TWENTY-EIGHT

Paris, France
May 30, 1981

"That's the car I saw leaving the scene," said Vartan, pointing to a red Fiat.

"Are you sure?" Jaleh stretched her neck to see. It was difficult, sitting in the passenger seat of their car, to even lean forward with all that roundness.

"Absolutely. The dent is on the same side of the bumper. Plates are different. They changed them."

Vartan had waited in the rain for an hour to catch his enemies departing after they had tried to kill him. The thought filled Jaleh with rage and dread. If the Fiat had been the only vehicle that had stood out in his mind, it must be the target. Her husband was never wrong about these things. She pulled her handgun from the glove box and rummaged around for the suppressor.

"What are you doing?" he said, his eyes going wide.

"Well, we can't let him go." She found the suppressor and screwed it onto the nozzle.

"What about the hospital?" He smiled in a way that she could not tell if he was impressed or amused. "Did you forget that you are in labor?"

"It's not something you can forget," she said, unable to keep the irritation out of her voice. "There's plenty of time."

Shifting her hips in the seat, she leaned her aching back against the backrest. Vartan, in his wisdom, kept quiet. He stepped on the gas, but with a gentle touch. She noticed that everything he did was so gentle when it came to her pregnancy.

The Fiat had gained significant distance, but Vartan wove in and out of the traffic with the smoothness of a painter's brush and was soon right behind it. Traffic came to a halt at a red light.

Jaleh reached for her door handle. The sooner this was done the better.

"Where are you going?" Vartan's eyes went even wider.

"I'll finish him off and do a quick search before the light changes."

"No. Too many witnesses. I'll get beside him at the next intersection."

She released the handle, taking deep breaths as another contraction came on. She had forgotten to time them.

Traffic moved again at its hurried Parisian pace. Vartan waited for an opening on the left and took it with a sharp jerk of the wheel when it came, reaching his hand out protectively as he did. He looked to see if she was okay. She nodded.

The next intersection was coming up. Jaleh cocked her weapon, placing the barrel on the door frame. She rolled the window down just as the cars lined up. The lone driver, a middle-aged, dark-skinned man with glasses, came into view. He had both hands on the wheel, eyes focused dead ahead.

She took aim and reached for the trigger. Her abdomen cramped as though an electric current ran through her. The weapon jerked up and the bullet went wide, shattering the driver's window but missing his head.

He turned in her direction. Their eyes met, fear and

understanding erupting across his face. Tires squealed, smoke billowing from behind. The frightened driver bolted through the traffic crossing in front of him, clipping the bumper of an oncoming Beetle. Horns blared.

"Damn it!" She clutched her sides. "Go. Go."

"Hold on." Vartan slammed the gas, the tires screeching in response. The lights had already turned green so he ripped through without any obstacles.

The motion made her want to vomit. She clutched the armrests with white knuckles. The backache increased, working itself into a slow rhythm. It dawned on her now that the baby might have no intention of waiting until they reached the hospital.

The Fiat swerved through traffic with reckless disregard while Vartan did his best to catch up, despite the handicap of having to be careful.

"Don't lose him," she shouted, sensing he might be about to cut their losses and not take any further risks.

"He's not worth it," he said as if reading her mind.

She grunted. Vartan sighed and took a sudden left into a back alley.

"What are you doing?"

"I'm going to cut him off."

He tore through the alleyway, garbage cans and boxes flying in every direction. He reached over and took the gun from her hand as the end of the alley approached. By then, the backache had become a boa constrictor, coiling itself around her. She could do nothing but pant and whimper, the steady grinding of gears and the churning engine dampening her moaning.

Vartan took a sharp left, then another into a shorter alley. In seconds they emerged out onto the street, brakes screaming to a halt. He did not have time to roll down his window. He fired three shots right through the glass, then accelerated again into the adjacent alley, moving out of the way of the careening Fiat just in time. The sound of it crashing into the parked cars on the side thundered in her ears.

Coming to a stop, he touched her arm. "Are you okay?"

"Go." She nodded, eyes closed, and head arched back.

Vartan did as she demanded.

She wriggled out of the undergarment beneath her dress, pulling back a bloody hand. The leather seat under her was soaked. The pain increased into waves of cramping agony that left her gasping for breath, over and over. She did not want to push, but it pushed all by itself.

She could not tell how long the pain continued. Everything around her seemed hazy. She heard Vartan's voice and felt the seat go back. She heard herself scream. She grabbed his arm and dug her nails in so hard that she felt one break. He did not even try to pull free.

As fast as it had come, the boa released its grip on her and slid away. The pain remained but had been vanquished to the back of her mind as the newborn cries erupted in the darkened alleyway. Her eyes cleared and she saw Vartan wrapping a bundle in his shirt.

"He's okay. I'm going to get you to the hospital. We're not far. Hang in there, my love."

"He?"

"Yes. A strong, healthy boy."

"Armik," she said, breathing as if she had run a marathon.

"Armik? After my father." Vartan looked at her with a smile. "It's a good Armenian name."

"Armik-*jan*," he said, looking at the bundle. "Welcome to the fire, my son."

CHAPTER TWENTY-NINE

Southern France
June 6, 1981

Vartan hated leaving his wife and newborn son so soon. He had hoped to retire after eliminating Rostem but that trail had vanished after their failed attempt to eliminate him.

On top of that, something about this particular piece of work seemed off. The alarm bells had rung in Vartan's head the moment he received the intel package. What would a high-value target such as Farid Almasi be doing in Paris? He was, after all, the regime's top general. His fast-rising star had ripped through the Middle East like a dirty little tornado. A man personally responsible for countless murders would not venture into a western country where he would be so vulnerable. Even Jaleh, now home with Armik, had warned against this mission.

After the murder of General Gholam, the well-oiled machine of the resistance would be chaotic at the very least. A sudden disruption of leadership always came with problems. He could no longer even be certain the resistance still existed in any significant form. But if it proved to be true that Almasi was here, an opportunity such as this would not come along again. The elimination of this monster would cause similar chaos within the burgeoning network from Syria to Egypt. With this in mind, and with much reluctance, Vartan kissed his family goodbye, packed his tools of the trade and drove south.

The information packet pinpointed the target in a seaside villa in Saint Tropez owned by a low-key Iranian expatriate. Dressed for the beach, Vartan wore knee-length shorts and a loose-fitting button-down gray silk shirt, topped off with a straw fedora and dark sunglasses. He had also shaved his face for the occasion, just to change his appearance, much to Jaleh's amusement.

The bustle of the city had long since given way to the open space of the southern countryside. Having never explored this part of the county, Vartan gawked at the beauty of it all. The portrait-like greenery was decorated by the backdrop of rocks, sand, and sea—the rough and the smooth. The brightest of blues contrasted with the soft white-golds and grays. Jaleh would love it. He made a mental note to bring her and Armik here when not on assignment. They were well overdue for a vacation.

Driving straight for the water, he took the wide streets at a relaxed pace, blending in with the local and tourist traffic that swarmed the sunlit cobblestones between the cottage-like white buildings with red tiled rooftops. He pulled his rental into a parking spot next to the marina, the church bell calling high twelve at a distance.

The entire area, alive with music from many radios and people loading and unloading their boats, seemed an easy place to get lost—or found, depending on the situation. A tingle of unease crept into Vartan's chest. He cocked his pistol and stuffed it into his paper lunch bag before stepping out of the vehicle.

From the trunk, he produced a long, thin shoulder bag that

contained his sniper rifle. He locked his doors and climbed onto the boardwalk. With each step, grains of fine sand scraped beneath his rubber-soled shoes against the smooth wooden planks. Vartan navigated the opposing currents of human traffic, looking for dock 628. There he found a small boat tied to the moss-covered mooring.

The boat could have come straight out of a child's picture book. Painted in stripes of blue, red, and white, it might have once been part of a small fishing fleet that launched from a pebbled beach. The single mast poked into the clear morning sky, the sail hanging loose to the deck. The large white auxiliary motor had already been fired up and rumbled in preparation for departure.

A man stepped off the medium-sized craft and walked toward Vartan. His appearance looked at odds with the other boaters around, as if he and his life's ambitions had departed on separate paths some time ago—though who gave up on who first was anyone's guess. His weathered face betrayed his age, with a salt and pepper two-day growth across a strong chin. He walked like his bones were just loosely connected, shoulders moving like potatoes in a sack with every heavy footfall. The dirt on his fitted clothes stood out, even from a distance. His eyes never left Vartan.

"Rick?" said Vartan.

"You must be Steve?" Rick said, mumbling in an American accent, really more spat than spoken, with the smell of whiskey spewing forth.

"Yes, I'm Steve."

"Great. She's all yours." Rick stepped aside, gesturing for Vartan to board.

"Wait, you're not taking me? That wasn't the arrangement."

Rick's eyes made an almost imperceptible flicker. "That's what I was told. It's easy. Follow the shoreline southeast for six miles. Look for the villa with the dark blue trim."

Vartan looked at the boat, then turned his gaze back to the now agitated boater.

"Is there a problem?"

"Yes, Rick. There is a problem." Vartan placed his right hand inside his paper lunch bag and kept it there, pointing the bottom at the man. "But don't worry. You're coming with me to solve it."

"I can't…I…I have to go…" Fear grew in Rick's beady eyes.

"I'm afraid I have to insist."

"What? You're not going to shoot me in front of all these people."

"I will empty every last bullet from this gun into you in front of all these people, dance over your body, and then walk away. The choice is yours, but you're out of time." Vartan raised the bag.

Rick's body quivered and he boarded the boat ahead of Vartan, who sat on the protruding deck bench while the man unfastened the moorings and took his seat by the motor. In moments, they were off, the engine roaring and white water spraying in their wake.

Vartan went to work, unzipping his shoulder bag and piecing his rifle together, his lunch bag within easy reach in the event that Rick decided to be brave. By the time he put his scope in place, the target location came into view around a bend of villa-specked shoreline. His driver appeared to be even more nervous than at the outset. He needed no more confirmation—the mission had been compromised.

"Stop here," Vartan yelled over the noise.

Rick cut the engine. All went quiet.

"You plan to make the shot from here?"

"There is no shot, is there?"

"What do you mean?"

"What exactly was supposed to happen here today, Rick?"

"How should I know? I'm just a guy with a boat."

Vartan set the gun on the deck and with one deft leap brought Rick down. The man's face slammed against the fiberglass bottom with a satisfying thud. He produced a knife from his pocket and snapped the blade open, pressing the sharp point against the stubbly face.

"Let's try this again. What was the plan here, Rick?"

"I…I swear, I don't know."

"Well, if you had to guess…"

"I was only told to give you the boat and not to go with you. I'd say you were not supposed to come back from this. And neither was the boat."

"Damn." Vartan drove the blade into Rick's neck, holding his head down while his knees kept him pinned.

The lifeblood came spurting out of him like a pig, the struggling movements coming to a gradual end. Taking a quick pulse check, Vartan took his knife out and wiped it across the man's shirt. He stood—his own shirt covered in warm, sticky blood. He removed it and tossed it aside.

He scanned the boat, trying to think of what might have been waiting for him. If he were conducting this operation, a bomb would be his weapon of choice. Nice and loud, yet sure to destroy any evidence on board. His gaze came to rest on the life vest storage bin under the bench on which he had just been sitting. With a slow hand, he lifted the lid.

Although expecting to see some sort of incendiary device, the size and scale of the trap came as a surprise. Someone wanted him dead several times over. There had to be a bit of flattery in there somewhere. The explosive apparatus had been fabricated in an improvised manner, but with an obvious degree of professionalism. The composition, familiar and typical, included a power source, lots of colorful wires attached to electronic circuitry, an explosive initiator, and a whole bunch of explosive charges with shrapnel products to increase fragmentation.

Vartan traced the thick black wire to a trigger mechanism that had a receiver that could have been from a child's toy. The range would not be very far. Perhaps the signal would come from another boat. If fireworks were what they wanted, he would gladly oblige.

With haste, he packed his rifle and secured the bag around him. He stepped over the lifeless body that had been Rick and went to the motor, which came to life on the second pull. Vartan moved the vessel so that the nose pointed to the target villa, then pulled off one of Rick's filthy sneakers. He jammed it between the throttle and the boat so that it would not turn. He produced a bit of duct tape from his bag.

Jaleh always laughed at him for carrying duct tape everywhere, but no other product served so well in so many situations. Cranking the throttle, he secured it in the maximum position with several layers of the silver tape. The boat lurched toward its final destination.

Vartan took a run and dove off the side, the coldness of the water raking his skin like claws of ice. Full of curses, he breached the surface. Treading water, he kept his eye on the fast-moving boat, already a receding dot in the distance.

The explosion came only about a mile from shore, the hot wave of energy sweeping across the surface of the water and slapping him in the face. The ensuing waves rippled out from the inferno, rocking the other boats on the water. Vartan made for the nearest shoreline. It would be a long swim.

"I really need a vacation."

CHAPTER THIRTY

Paris, France
August 2, 1980

Entering the cruise terminal, they were directed to go through an airport-style security screening. Despite Jaleh's reassurances, Vartan did little to disguise his uneasiness. She had long been aware of his particular dislike for crowds—a dislike she shared but to a lesser extent. Large groups of people were hard to predict. With their newborn son Armik along, she understood why his protective instincts were high—even for his standards.

He tossed their baggage onto the conveyor belt to be screened. They also had to walk through a metal detector, so they came unarmed. Unlike an airport, they were also asked to fill out a health questionnaire. Vartan was already grumbling about the whole process, and they had not even boarded the ship yet.

Jaleh kept touching his arm in a preemptive move to calm him. It was not working quite as well as it would under normal circumstances. She felt bad for him. The vacation had been his idea. The cruise had been hers. Vartan had suggested the south of France, where assassins unknown had tried to blow him to pieces. Somehow that did not seem so appealing.

After checking in, they were sent to a waiting area until the ship was ready to receive passengers. The wait was not a long one, and they were soon called to the gangway to board. But by this time Jaleh could tell that Vartan had become quite overwhelmed.

The ship's photographers offered to take their photo in front of a scenic background. Both her and Vartan declined in tandem. Photos were not something people in their line of work wanted. Random photos lurking on unknown memory cards could be detrimental.

Armik seemed excited by the commotion and let out a series of cheery coos from the comfort of his oversized red stroller.

Vartan had never taken a vacation before, other than the occasional road trip from Tehran to Ramsar to enjoy the Caspian Sea. She had traveled with her parents, but never like this. The whole thing seemed exciting to her, despite her husband's trepidation.

Most of the people stayed on deck to wait for the ship's departure but Jaleh worried that the blast from the ship's horn would be too loud for the baby. Going straight to their cabin, Vartan scanned the massive crowds nonstop, as per his habit. She wondered if he would ever be able to relax at all. Then again, she wondered the same about herself.

Their modest suite came with one soft-looking queen bed and a small crib provided. In the corner sat a mini bar and a phone, as well as a small table for two. The portal turned out to be smaller than she had expected, but still offered a nice view of the docks.

The ship departed about fifteen minutes late. By that time hunger had ravaged her. Deciding to get something to eat, they headed over to the restaurant. Vartan still appeared uncomfortable, with his wide eyes and flushed skin. For a spook, he was not that great at hiding his feelings—at least not from her. She liked that he dropped his guard around her as much as he did.

"You aren't going to stay in defense mode the entire trip, are you?"

"I don't have any other modes." He tried to make it sound like a joke, despite being quite true.

"Well, you need to find some. This is our first vacation together. What's bothering you?"

"Besides the thousands of possible threats and the complete lack of escape routes or weapons. Nothing."

"It will be fine. Besides, we did everything carefully and properly. No one knows we are here. I just want to forget who we are for a few days. Do you think you can do that?"

"Of course, my love. Though I wouldn't say no one knows. I'm pretty sure Mossad sent people to see what we're up to. I caught a whiff of one earlier."

"A whiff, you say?"

"Yeah. A whiff. I get whiffs. Anyway, don't worry. I'll get into it more once we are out to sea and I've had a few boat drinks in me." Vartan offered his best winning grin.

"That's the spirit."

Armik giggled his agreement.

The waiter poured a small amount of wine in the glass in front of Vartan. He gave the waiter a strange look. "I'm not a kid, I can have a full glass."

"Would *monsieur* not like to taste it first?" the waiter asked with practiced patience.

Jaleh covered her smile with her napkin and turned away. The embarrassed look on Vartan's face was priceless, as he was not easily flustered. He took a small sip and nodded. The waiter finished pouring.

"What do you think he is going to turn out like?" Jaleh

said, nodding toward Armik. The boy was content at the moment with a warm bottle of milk.

"Hopefully like his mother," Vartan said without hesitation.

"I'm sure he will have plenty of you."

"I hope not. I was a terrible kid."

"Oh? Do tell."

"Every new year in our house an Armenian priest would come and give us a blessing. He would walk around and bless the food on the table and the rooms etc. An old Armenian tradition. One new year, when I was about twelve, my mother had to go out to buy something for the large feast we always had on that occasion, and the priest hadn't arrived yet, so she left ten tumons on the table for him. The usual payment, I guess."

He took a bite of the appetizer the waiter brought out. "Now the priest also moonlighted as a taxi driver and he arrived after she left, pulling up in his cab. He knocked on the door and asked if my parents were home. I told him no, so he turned around and walked back to his cab and drove off. Somehow I ended up with the ten tumons."

"Somehow, eh?"

"It was a lot of money back then."

"It was. That's terrible." She laughed.

"Always felt guilty about it, so hopefully he's a little better than that."

"I'll know not to leave money around, just in case."

They both laughed. She watched Vartan playing with the baby and felt content. He had already become as good a father as he was a husband, despite his unusual vocation.

A few bottles of wine later, he seemed much more relaxed. It was going to be a good vacation, and she hoped it would be one of many. Still, even through the haze of alcohol, she could see his keen eyes did not miss a thing. He had an extremely high tolerance though he often pretended otherwise. He remained as sharp as a razor at all times. They were safe with him, come what may.

CHAPTER THIRTY-ONE

The Persian seemed not to notice anything. Rostem assumed he would be extremely vigilant and on guard but watching him drink and laugh with his Jew wife and play with his kid, Rostem was surprised to find him so negligent. Or perhaps he only acted so. Either way, the cat and mouse game they played had become something of a distraction.

The Islamic Republic wanted him dead and kept sending hit teams who failed time and again. Truth be told, Rostem did not want to kill him. He merely enjoyed seeing him kill everything that came at him. It was beautiful, like a bloody art display. Besides, Rostem got paid for every attempt, passing the blame of failure on the idiots they sent. The whole thing was quite lucrative, yet in this relaxed and seemingly safe atmosphere killing the Persian might be easier than anticipated. He might actually die this time. That would be a shame. There were many things he could be useful for.

Rostem came disguised as an old, fragile man with a beard and mustache as white as the hair on his head. He even added the touch of a bald spot. No one paid any attention to him. He counted at least three operatives on board, besides his own two. Mossad, most likely. The Persian was a high-value target, so they could not afford to let him out of their sight. For the sake of appearances—and entertainment—he would need to level the playing field.

When he, at last, decided to end him, Rostem wanted to make him run—to find the fear buried deep inside him. He doubted he would get that satisfaction unless he turned his attention to the family on which the Persian seemed so focused. Strange how a man who killed so many people without mercy could turn into such a devoted father. The world was not so black and white after all. Either way, the outcome would be interesting.

Looking at the reflection in his soup spoon, Rostem saw two agents arriving to dine behind him. One woman and one man, obviously posing as a married couple. They seemed immersed in their conversation, as if newlyweds, but they observed their surroundings with great care. The man was average height with a lean, athletic build. The woman was quite attractive and also had the body of an athlete, though she distracted from it by wearing loose-fitting clothes and a large hat.

They would have to be disposed of with extreme caution. Any hint of a problem would send the Persian into a defensive mode. That would be very dangerous but having babysitters around just would not do.

A green plastic keychain protruded from the back pocket of the man's gaudy-looking, Hawaiian-style shorts. An invitation that seemed all too easy. Rostem never ceased to find himself disappointed by the lack of attention to detail, common in foreign intelligence agents. The love of the craft had become a rare thing indeed. Such inattention could, and often did, have fatal consequences. This would be one of those cases.

Resting his weight on his cane, Rostem arched his back into a most uncomfortable and contorted angle. He hobbled forward, his old man persona in full effect. The couple, focused on their target, seemed oblivious to his presence up until the very moment he was upon them, leaning over their table with his best toothless smile.

He noted their startled reaction, each making a reflexive but stifled move for weapons that were not there. Both displayed an obvious embarrassment from having been caught unaware while relieved that no threat presented itself in the elderly gentleman that grinned like a fool over their steak and shrimp.

"Two young lovers," he said to them, his voice ancient-sounding and shaky. "I remember those days. Enjoy every minute while you can. Time...time is so fleeting."

"Thank you, sir," said the woman, a kind smile playing across full lips. "Is your wife here with you?"

"Alas, she passed away many, many years ago. We used to take a cruise together every year. Now I take it alone." He let a long sigh pass from him to add to the effect of his saddened face.

"I'm so sorry to hear that," said the woman.

"Well, life goes on." He perked up and gawked at their meal again. "That steak sure looks good. If only I still had the teeth to chew it. He gave out a little laugh, then stood there staring until the moment became awkward.

"Well, I don't want to keep you from your own lunch, sir," said the man, unable to hide his annoyance at the interruption.

"You have a wonderful time. Enjoy your meal." Rostem tipped his hat and turned to go.

"Aww, thank you. You too." The blond beauty smiled again.

He took several steps before catching his cane in the leg of the chair. Tumbling over, he snatched the key chain from the man's back pocket. It came away in his palm and disappeared in his sleeve with the smoothness of new whipped butter before he hit the ground with a thud. He let out a dramatic groan. The couple sprang to their feet to offer assistance as the other patrons looked on with concern.

The commotion attracted too much attention for his liking, but the prize had been worth the small inconvenience. Offering profuse thanks to his would-be rescuers, he declined assistance, not wanting anyone to feel the lean muscle that lay under his loose-fitting clothing. He hoisted himself onto his walking stick, keeping his back contorted.

The spectacle ended and, already forgotten, he walked out of the dining area and made his way to the elevators. Glancing at the key in his palm, he pressed the button for the eighth deck.

The hallway stood empty as he stepped between the sliding metal doors. Not having to walk with a bent back any longer, he located the couple's cabin door in short order. He waited for the passing maid pushing her trolley to turn the corner before entering the room.

As expected, nothing about the suite belied the true vocation of its occupants. The two large suitcases he found were filled with clothing, a pair of Belgian passports for Mr. And Mrs. Aaldenberg, some field glasses, and an ornithologist handbook resting on the nightstand. Other than the big wad of cash stuffed in among Mrs. Aaldenberg's vast collection of bikinis, he saw nothing out of the ordinary that would suggest what his instincts already assured him.

Availing himself of the cash, he put the rest of the couple's belongings back the way he found them and wiped his prints off all the handles. Then, taking out a small pocket knife, he pulled the mattress aside and flipped the wooden box-spring over. He cut it open with one slice down the middle and two across each end so that the material opened like French doors. A sturdy beam running down the middle supported the wood slats beneath the mattresses, but the underside of the box had been constructed hollow. Flipped over and cut open, the queen-sized box made for a perfect set of temporary coffins he could cover with the mattress.

His keen ear picked up the sound of a muffled discussion down the hall. Wedging himself behind the wardrobe, Rostem waited.

"How could you be so careless?" The voice of the model-faced Mrs. Aaldenberg had lost its smooth and compassionate tone, now sounding angry.

"I…I don't know. I had it in my back pocket. I must have dropped it somewhere."

"What if someone took it?"

"No one took it. We had eyes on the subject the whole time," said the male voice as the lock turned.

"Christ. This is all we need." The door opened and her voice became clear.

"Just relax. Someone probably turned it in by now. I'll go up to customer service and…" Mr. Aaldenburg's last words trailed off into a gurgle from Rostem's fist slamming into his throat.

The man crumpled like a house of cards in the wind. Rostem lashed out at the female partner without hesitation. Her training and reflexes saved her from the same immediate fate with a skilled block. She kicked out at him, her sandal flying off when he sidestepped the strike. She pressed her attack with a series of blows, the power and speed surprising him.

Rostem stepped back and found himself on the discarded mattress, his footing compromised. The woman leapt forward, driving her knee into his thigh while her elbow slammed into the side of his face. He responded with a hard roundhouse kick that sent her crashing into the nightstand.

He smiled and wiped the blood off his lips with his forearm.

A look of recognition spread onto her face, soon replaced by anger. Rostem's amusement put him off guard for a moment, realizing too late she had retrieved his walking stick.

Her attack rained down on him like a relentless hailstorm. His arm took the brunt of the assault until he felt the bone crack. The cane broke striking just above his elbow at the same time. He grunted, the pain intense. Taking advantage of his injury, Mrs. Aaldenberg drove the jagged end of the now broken stick into his stomach, tearing into him. He stopped her with a head-butt before she could shove it into his internal organs.

Her turn to grunt, she staggered back, her nose covered in her blood. In a heartbeat, Rostem threw himself at her, the piece of bloodied cane falling to the floor. Toppling over, she rolled onto all fours to push herself back to her feet. He came down on top of her, the pain in his arm sending blinding white lights behind his eyes. His functioning arm slipped around her throat. With his shoulder, he drove her face into the carpet. The bone of his undamaged forearm squeezed her larynx with all the strength he could muster until he heard the crack.

For good measure, he held her in his embrace of death for several minutes, listening for any sounds that would indicate their scuffle had raised alarms. Also, the sheer exhaustion and agony of his broken arm and torn stomach made movement unappealing.

He should have known better than to underestimate the woman. The lesson had come close to costing him his life. In no position to eliminate the Persian, he had a painful excuse to leave it to the clowns he had with him. He would send Laylah to try—and Laylah would fail, of course. But first, he would have to get Kurosh to clean up the room before room service came to turn down the beds.

CHAPTER THIRTY-TWO

Valletta, Malta
August 5, 1981

On the third day, the ship landed at Valletta in Malta, beginning a multiple-night stay at this port of call. Being an early riser, Vartan went off to the shoreline on his own while Jaleh took full advantage of Armik's restful state to catch up on her sleep.

The warm salt water stung his eyes, but he still enjoyed the swim. Rising out of the sea, he looked up at the cloudless blue sky, his mind restful and at ease. Looking down at his abdomen, he noted that drinking beer had begun to obscure the lines that were once so distinct. They were still visible but would not be for long if he did not take care.

Overcome with a bout of self-consciousness, he shrugged it off with a chuckle and sucked in his stomach. Vartan closed his eyes, allowing himself to absorb the much-needed rays of sunlight while being lulled by the soothing sounds encircling him. He took a deep breath, allowing the moist, salty air to fill his lungs. He could not remember a moment of such peace since he was a child playing in the Caspian Sea.

The soft, smooth sand beneath his feet was so much finer

than his beloved Caspian, though still not as beautiful in his mind. Yet the same seagulls above him squawked, waiting for someone to drop food.

He looked for his towel in a sea of towels and recognized his blue beer cooler. Walking over, he did a careful scan to take in all of his surroundings. He saw middle-aged people resting on their beach blankets, children creating sandcastles or frolicking in the ocean, and young couples holding hands while walking along the shoreline.

He had no doubt he was being watched. His guess would be Mossad but he had to remain open to the possibility that they were not the only ones. Jaleh had not mentioned it, but of course she must have been just as aware and alert. She had a keener eye than he did.

One woman in particular seemed to be paying close attention to him while he toweled himself off. She smiled and he turned his head away. She was trouble. Curiosity made him wonder just how much trouble.

His stomach called out for breakfast. He left his belongings on the beach and headed over to the row of huts on the other side of the boardwalk housing the cafes and snack shops. Vartan stopped at a sunglasses vendor en route to look at a few pairs.

The reflection in the lenses told him the woman had made her way in his general direction, walking with a slow, casual stride. She stopped to pet a dog, fix her hair in the reflection of the shops, and look at some bikinis. He smiled to himself, walked across the street to the nearest patio, and took a seat.

"*Bongu,*" said a young, black-haired waitress.

"*Bongu,*" he said, the Maltese good morning. "*Hobz Malti u kafe, Jekk Joghgbok.*"

The waitress nodded at his request for Maltese bread and coffee and left.

"You speak like a native," said a sultry voice.

He squinted, the sun in his eyes as he looked up at the brown-haired woman from the beach.

"Picked up a few words here and there. Enough not to go hungry." Vartan smiled and shrugged.

"Is anyone sitting here?"

"Please," Vartan said, gesturing to one of the empty metal chairs. He detected a whiff of a Persian accent that had been hidden away.

"So you are here on business?"

"Something like that." Vartan gave her a wide, mischievous grin.

"Oh, a man of mystery. I like that." She sat back and flung her long curly hair back over her shoulders.

"How about you, miss…?"

"Well, I'm going through a bit of a rough patch actually. My boyfriend and I just broke up—fiancée actually." She gave a bit of a pout, a thick lower lip protruding in his direction.

"Sorry to hear that."

"Thanks. Yeah, so I thought, what better way to get my head clear than to take a vacation?"

"Well, I think that's a great plan." The waiter came by and placed his order on the table. "What are you having…"

"Jane. Sorry. I'll have what you're having."

"*I-Istess ordni ghall-mara,*" he told the waitress, pointing to his breakfast. "Rubik's the name, by the way. Like the cube."

"Nice to meet you, Rubik," she said, putting out a hand.

Vartan took it. It was soft but he detected a trace of calluses that indicated training.

"So, Rubik. Is that Russian?"

"You're very close. It's Armenian."

"Where is that?"

"It's a little dot between Turkey and the USSR. You won't

find it on most maps, but it is there."

The waiter brought her order out and she took a piece of bread and popped it into her mouth. Vartan followed suit. He noticed two agents at a cafe a couple of stores down seated in a position to keep watch. He did not recognize them from the ship, guessing they might have been sent here ahead of them.

In one clumsy-looking move, Jane knocked her open purse from the table. The contents spilled all over the patio stones.

Vartan, ever the gentleman, bent to help pick it up. He found little of note, aside from a lipstick, a wallet with some American cash and an American passport—fake, no doubt. What he did find interesting was the move she made above the table, slipping something into his coffee. Vartan smiled and lifted himself back up with her purse intact.

"Thank you so much. I'm such a klutz—always have been." She let out an innocent giggle and shrugged.

"Don't mention it." He threw a quick glance over at the agents, who did not seem to have caught her move—or at least they did not react. If they were Mossad, they would have moved in to help had they seen it, assuming he remained in their good books.

He waved the waitress over again and asked for a glass of water.

"So, listen. I hope this isn't too forward, but a few of the people I met here are having a beach party tonight. Would you like to join us? Me?"

Vartan made a show of considering it. "That sounds like a plan."

The waitress came by with the water. Vartan nudged the lipstick he had kept under his foot from Jane's purse into the waitress's path, making her stumble. He made a show of trying to assist her but made sure the arm with the water was shoved in Jane's direction.

In the Chaos, Vartan switched the drinks with the skill and speed of a magician, even impressing himself.

"I'm so sorry. I don't know…" The waitress looked down and saw the lipstick. "Oh, I slipped on this," she said, picking it up.

Sopping wet, Jane looked about to come unhinged, but made a great effort to compose herself. She wiped her face down with a napkin.

"Are you alright?" Vartan said, trying hard not to crack into a laugh.

"Yes, yes, I'm okay. Thank you. No problem, accidents happen. It's just water anyway, and we are on the beach."

"That is true," he said, taking a sip from his coffee cup.

"Cheers," she said, holding up her own cup.

Vartan finished off his coffee. She did the same. He tore a piece of the delicious Maltese bread off and jammed it into his mouth, smiling at Jane. They chatted for another ten or fifteen minutes. All the while, she watched him with great intent, waiting. He noticed a few extra beads of perspiration appear on her forehead, though she complained of the coolness for this time of year.

"Well," he said, shifting forward in his seat, "I have to say, it was really enjoyable meeting and chatting with you, Jane." He dropped a few dollars on the table.

"Oh here, let me," she said, going for her purse.

"Oh no, my treat. I insist."

"Well thank you, kind sir," her voice faltered a little.

"My pleasure. So I'll see you tonight?" He grinned even broader.

"Around seven. We can meet right here." She coughed, a confused look on her face.

"Perfect. Unless of course, you are not feeling well," he said.

"What do you mean?"

"Well, you are looking a little green around the gills. Feeling a little feverish?"

"No, I..."

"Me, I feel great. The coffee here really agrees with me."

Her eyes widened. He chuckled, flashing his pearly white teeth at her.

"I...uh...I have to go." She stood so fast she almost upended the table.

"Are you sure you're okay, Jane? Should I call you a cab? A doctor?"

"No...thank you...I..." She grabbed her purse off the table and left.

Vartan snatched the last of the bread and finished it off, observing the way she staggered away on uncertain legs.

Yes, she definitely was trouble. He laughed and checked his watch. Jaleh would be up by now and getting ready. The time had come to go get his family and continue his vacation. He did not want to ruin it for her if he could help it, but they would have to be careful. Their enemies had found them.

CHAPTER THIRTY-THREE

Being the cautious person he was, Vartan shoved a rubber door stopper under the door inside the room as an extra measure. He did this even at home at night, despite his high-tech security system that rendered it redundant.

"You look like you're a million miles away," Jaleh said, her observation accurate as ever.

"Me? No. I'm just thinking about how much fun we are having."

"Of course." She shook her head at him.

He sat on the bed with his son, who lay on his tummy playing with a squeaky toy hammer he enjoyed.

"Armik-*jan*, are you having fun? Baba loves you, *joonam, azizam.*"

"Terrible about that young girl they found dead on the beach."

Somehow Jaleh never missed anything. "Terrible thing, yes," he said, his attention on Armik.

"In some public bathroom on the main strip, the cruise director was saying. Apparently, she was also on a cruise, vacationing alone."

"Terrible thing." Vartan focused on Armik, avoiding eye contact like a dog who had chewed something he was not supposed to.

"From our ship, incidentally." She folded her arms, which had never been a good sign.

"A terrible shame."

"Some kind of fast-acting poison."

"Wow," Vartan said. "Can never be too careful these days." He squeaked the rubber hammer and Armik's eyes lit up.

"Do you think there are any more?"

He paused from his playing and looked up at her at last. He could not hold back a smile at her perceptiveness. "Not sure, but that one wasn't much of a threat."

"She was no match for your charms, I suppose."

He smiled an extra wide one for her. "No one is."

"Lucky me. So I've made arrangements to switch ships at the next port of call."

"I figured you might," he said. "Is that going to ruin the trip for you?"

"Turned out better actually. We get to stop in Barcelona."

"Did you hear that, Armik-jan? We will get to watch a bullfight together."

Armik spat out a laugh as Vartan tickled him. Jaleh slipped on a cotton nightshirt and began her facial routine.

"Are you coming to bed?" She said with a casual glance.

"I think I'm going to take a little walk around. See what I can see."

"Right. Okay. Be careful. I'll put the door stopper back in when you leave, just knock lightly and I'll open up for you."

She was almost as much a light sleeper as he was and would hear him coming down the corridor on the carpet in stocking feet. Vartan kissed his boy and his wife, slipped on a light jacket, and left the room. He waited to hear the sound of the latch and the door jamb sliding in place before making his way to the stairwell. He did not come across many other passengers—not anyone unusual, anyway. He took the stairs down to the main deck and headed to the bar.

"What can I get you, sir." A young bartender with dark skin and light dreadlocks offered him a pleasant smile.

"Give me a good cognac."

"Kelt XO okay?" The bartender held up a bottle.

"Neat, please."

He took his glass and went out on deck to take a stroll. Warm air fluttered against his skin, mixed with the cool breeze blowing in from the ocean. The clear sky appeared dotted by more stars than he had ever seen. He put the glass to his lip, realizing that the bartender had put an ice cube in despite his request. He shook his head and caught the barest hint of a movement to his left. He turned to look. A few couples walked farther down the deck but nothing unusual.

He spun to his right, smashing his glass into the face of a man trying to inject him with a syringe. The attacker cried out—the sound cut short by an elbow under his chin. The man gurgled and grabbed his throat. Vartan got a quick look at him before he ducked and caught his pant legs with two hands. The next move had him up and over the railing, striking his head against the metal deck before careening into the dark water below.

Vartan tried to follow him down with his eyes, but something slipped around his neck from behind. He managed, just barely, to get two fingers into the loop before the second assailant yanked it tight. He flung his head back to bash his attacker's face, but the grip held firm. A knee went into his back, pulling the loop even tighter.

The lights were going out fast. Vartan could not hold on. He sank to the ground, the attacker pressing his advantage and forcing him down until his head touched the wooden deck.

Something sharp pierced the flesh of his face. The pain

stopped him from succumbing to the darkness just yet. A shimmer from glass shards came into view. The remnants of the cognac tumbler he had smashed moments ago. With his free hand, Vartan picked up the closest fragment and slashed at the hands that held the wire. It took several tries, but the grip loosened enough for him to roll himself back and lash out with a kick.

He struggled to get air back into his screaming lungs. His throat ached with the pain of being crushed, but self-soothing would have to wait. Kicked in the ribs, Vartan rolled with it and managed to get up on one knee before the assassin sprang on him again. The silver flash of a blade only gave him enough time to raise a hand, the slash cutting into his forearm. His injured limb followed the momentum of the strike, despite the pain. He moved his wrist in a quick circular motion, sending the blade clattering onto the deck.

Vartan threw a solid punch to the groin. Hearing the sharp expulsion of air, he followed up with another, then launched himself up and forward, with an elbow to the face. It caused enough of a distraction for him to get behind the man and put on a chokehold of his own. He held it there for a long while, even after the body went limp. Looking around, he could find no sign of any civilians who might have ventured close enough to notice two men struggling in the dark. He made sure the coast was clear before lifting the unconscious body to the railing and sending it over to join its companion.

His arm bled like a fountain through his clothing, and he cursed out loud. A blood trail back to his room would not do. He removed his jacket and used the sleeve to tie off the wound, then draped the rest of it over his arm like a waiter would a towel and made his way back.

Jaleh would not be happy about this at all.

PART 5

CHAPTER THIRTY-FOUR

Paris, France
August 6th, 1991

At around 5:00pm, Rostem, accompanied by Vakili Rad and Azadi, drove his BMW to the former Prime Minister's home. The location had long since changed after the first botched attempt on Bakhtiar's life. Having learned his lesson, he insisted on an Iranian-only hit team this time, and only those who were former intelligence.

"What do you intend to do about the Persian?" Avadi sat, watching the comings and goings around the former Iranian Prime Minister's secured building while Valki Rad listened to his Walkman.

"Nothing." Rostem, now sporting platinum blond hair and a goat-tee, took a long drag of his cigarette.

"Nothing? They won't like that back home," said Azadi. "They want him dead in a bad way. He's killed a dozen of our agents."

"More. But who cares about 'back home' and what they don't like? They keep sending me useless mutts from God knows where, and they expect me to somehow wipe out a legend?"

"I don't get why you just don't set a bomb and—"

"Of course you don't get it." Rostem spat and lit another

cigarette. "I don't expect you to get it. Where is the sport in just blowing up someone like that?"

"It's not supposed to be a sport."

"This is why you are who you are and I am who I am. This tedious life is nothing if not a sport."

"If you say so." Avadi scanned the street again. "So, are you sure Bakhtiar's staff will be gone?"

"The housekeeper and the gardener are on vacation. I heard them discussing it several times, and I saw it on his personal daily planner."

"How did you manage to get in there?"

"Even an exiled Prime Minister needs a light bulb changed every once in a while. I just made myself available for odd jobs. Aside from his personal secretary and the French policemen who guard his house, Bakhtiar will be alone and suspects nothing. Also, unlike last time, he is actually expecting us and will welcome us with open arms, thinking you two are big investors."

"That's amazing."

"I'm happy you're impressed. Let's get this over with." Rostem opened the car door.

He and his two hitmen walked across the street. They were clad in suits and black ties as a token of respect for the former prime minister. The man was still grieving the death of his good friend, Boroumand.

"You follow my lead," he told them, "or they will find you next to his body. I don't need a repeat of the last time."

Azadi nodded his agreement without raising an eyebrow. He stood a good deal larger than most men with the build of a professional wrestler and hands like bulldozer blades, but he knew who he was dealing with. Vakili nodded also. Rostem thought him dimwitted right from the get-go, but still a far cry better than anyone on his last team.

The gate had no less than half a dozen tactical police officers standing with fingers near the triggers of their submachine guns. They were not taking any chances either. The Boroumand assassination had the entire country on edge, just where Rostem liked them. There would be no storming in, guns ablaze like last time.

Like any other visitors, the three men showed their IDs to the guards and stepped in, passing through the metal detector set up in front of the house without a single beep. They were more than happy to submit to being frisked and did so without incident.

They handed over their fake passports to the policeman with the clipboard and were guided by a plain-clothed officer to the elevators. The escort took them all the way up to a room where two uniformed police stood guard in front of the door. They looked the visitors up and down but said nothing. They were escorted in and announced to the secretary, Hamid Eghbali.

Bakhtiar was on the phone, as was his usual state, but he ushered the three men to join him in his living room. Shortly thereafter, he hung up and rose from his chair.

"My apologies, gentlemen. Things are quite hectic as always."

"Don't apologize, *Agha* Bakhtiar, we are just honored to be able to sit with you. We brought you a small token. It's from back home," said Rostem. He motioned to Azadi, who presented him with a picture frame with a lavish openwork border and gold finish that they brought as a gift. Framed inside was a velvet back-drop with Persian words painted in gold calligraphy.

"Ah, the Ghazals of Hafez," he said with delight. Looking at the frame but reciting from memory he began almost musically.

"This is the kind of friend you are.
Without making me realize
My soul's sordid history,
You slip into my house at night,
And while I am sleeping,
You silently carry off.
All my suffering and sordid past
In your beautiful hands.

This is wonderful, thank you. Poetry is one of my great loves," Bakhtiar said, signaling his secretary for tea to be served.

"I am told that you have committed to memory over ten thousand verses of poetry," said Vakili with the look of someone awestruck. Rostem thought him a decent actor.

The secretary poured tea into a very ornate set of glassware with gold and pearl inlay from an antique teapot of hammered copper then left them alone, heading out to the kitchen terrace.

Rostem slipped a subtle eye to Vakili. He joined the man outside under the pretense of needing fresh air.

"Well, I've lost count of how many verses I know. Perhaps it's an exaggeration to say ten thousand. Perhaps not."

"We would be honored if you would recite something for us."

"Oh, I don't know..."

"Perhaps the rest of the piece from the frame," Rostem said.

"Of course, if you insist." Bakhtiar cleared his throat.

The moment he raised his chin to begin, Rostem struck his throat hard with the ridge of his hand, ending the recital before it began. He could neither cry out nor breathe, his windpipe collapsed.

"There are knives in the kitchen," he told Azadi, as the

Prime Minister lay dying on the sofa. He stood and went over to the glass sliding door of the terrace and opened it. "You better come quickly. The Prime Minister is not well!"

Eghbali rushed in like the loyal vassal he was, looking frantic at the sight of his boss withering on the sofa. He did not see Rostem's swift hand either as he met the same fate.

"Finish it up quickly," Rostem said to Azadi who returned with several serrated knives.

He closed the curtains of the outside balcony window, then walked over to the phone on the large oak desk and took it off the hook before heading over to the front door to wait.

Minutes later Vakili and Azadi were finished, their clothes covered in blood. They went into the powder room and used the guest linen to scrub off whatever they could from their garments.

"We can't get it off. They are going to see it right away," said Vakili.

"No. They won't. Don't worry about it. They are so incompetent they wouldn't notice if we rolled the bodies up in a Persian rug and carried them out."

"Here," said Azadi, handing Rostem a gold Rolex watch. "He won't be needing it anymore."

Rostem smiled. He was impressed by the honesty. Most people would have pocketed a fifty-thousand US dollar watch.

"You keep it," he said, tossing it back to the large man, whose eyes lit up.

The assassins exited the house by 6:00pm. As Rostem had predicted, the guards noticed nothing out of the ordinary, despite the bloodstains on the two killers' clothing. The three men drove off and headed straight out of Paris proper, pulling over only when they reached the Bois de Boulogne Park.

Vakili and Azadi changed into clean clothes, tossed their bloody garments in a trash receptacle, and discarded all three false Iranian passports after tearing them up. They grabbed a new set of Turkish ones from the trunk of the car, along with some cash.

"You will proceed to Annecy, near the Swiss border. The instructions are in the envelopes with your new IDs. Remember to switch trains in Lyon. There, you will phone the number on the paper. Memorize and destroy it. On the Swiss side, you will be taken home. Good job."

Rostem took them to the nearest train station before abandoning his now bloodied vehicle in the Iranian emigré neighborhood known as Téhéran-sur-Seine. He figured it would sit there undisturbed for a few days before someone took notice of a BMW in Persian town.

CHAPTER THIRTY-FIVE

Paris, France
September 18, 1991

"How do you even know how to do that?" Kaveh asked.

Armik shrugged, then twisted the copper wire around the seat several times. He connected the end of it to the guts of one of his toy cars. "My dad wires stuff all the time. Light switches. Washing machines. Car radios. I watch. It's pretty easy."

"I watch my dad drive a car every day. You don't see me driving around the neighborhood," said Bobbak.

"That's because your dad doesn't really know how to drive. Have you seen him park?" Kaveh laughed.

"Shut up." Bobbak did not refute the statement but offered a scowl.

"You know that he's going to kill you if he finds out you did this, don't you?" Kaveh handed Armik a pair of pliers.

"He tries to kill me every day. Why should today be any different?" Armik twisted the copper wire taut against the metal frame of the chair. "Besides, it's going to be funny."

"Funny until he kills you. How does this work, anyway?" Bobbak seemed fascinated by the endeavor.

"Simple. When I add the battery, this thing will be live. All he has to do is sit on the chair. It has four screws on the seat. As soon as his legs press down on the wire, it will close the circuit and send a current up into all of them plus the metal back. He is going to feel…unhappy."

"He's going to kill you." Kaveh smiled from ear to ear.

"Hurry, someone's coming." Bobbak snatched the tools and shoved them in his backpack.

The three boys scrambled to their seats and sat with hands folded across their desks just as a group of girls walked in. The rest of the class, along with the teacher, Monsieur LeBeau, filed in after them.

Bruno, the largest kid in fifth grade, walked in a few minutes after the bell, as he always did. He walked to his desk and put his book bag down. Armik cringed, watching his bottom being lowered to the seat.

"Bruno, you are late. Again."

Bruno froze, hovering inches above his chair. "Sorry, Monsieur Lebeau. I missed my bus this morning and my dad—"

"Bruno, I don't really care why you were late. Whatever you have to do to make sure you are not late again, do it."

"Yes, Monsieur Lebeau." Bruno sat. He let out a loud scream, followed by a series of vulgarities that kids his age should not know, even though they all did.

"Bruno! Go to the office."

"Monsieur Lebeau. My chair… It wasn't—"

"Now," Lebeau yelled.

The entire class went from stunned silence to laughter. Bruno's face became as red as his rear end would have to be. His direct glare of doom fell upon Armik.

"You…," he yelled, pointing.

Armik shrugged in protest of his innocence, certain it must have seemed less than convincing.

"Now, Bruno."

He left but Armik knew the stage had been set. He sighed. *It was so worth it.*

They did not see big Bruno for the rest of the day, even when the bell rang at the end of classes. It looked like Armik had earned a reprieve.

"I don't see him anywhere," said Kaveh, looking out the window of the northernmost exit of the school while the others sat by the stairwell.

"He'll be there," said Bobbak.

"All three of us can take him," said Kaveh, his statement sounding more like a question. "Besides, we're all Persian. Mess with one of us, you mess with all, bitches." He threw a few shadow punches in the air for effect.

Armik laughed. "What are you guys worried about? His hands are so fat, his punches feel like a massage."

"If that's true, why don't you ever beat him back instead of just standing there and letting him pummel you?" said Kaveh.

"Because, unlike his, my father's hands are as hard as steel. And I don't want to find out what he'll do if he finds out I've been fighting."

"What makes you think he will do anything?" said Kaveh.

"Because he told me, 'You don't want to know what I will do if I find out you've been fighting.'"

"Oh. Well that's pretty specific."

"Please, your dad never hits you. My dad hit me on the head so hard last week I had to pull my socks down to eat," Bobbak said.

They all laughed, despite the ring of truth to it. Bobbak's dad was a known drinker and a brute. Armik's dad did not like him going over to their house at all.

"Come on guys," Armik said, "this is stupid. Let's go."

With vocalized reluctance, they followed him out. Finding

no one in sight, they began their walk home.

"There you are, you little coward. Did you think I wouldn't find you?" Bruno's booming voice materialized from thin air.

Armik turned around to find him standing with several of his only slightly smaller friends, there to goad him on.

"Nothing wrong with hoping," he said.

"Shut up. I'm going to smash your face in for that stunt."

"No idea what you are talking about."

"Shut up, camel-jockey. You're a little sissy. Just like your dad, the dressmaker." The other boys laughed.

"Really? Because I have a half-brother that looks a lot like your mom."

The bigger boy shoved Armik hard in the chest. He stumbled back, dropping his backpack but did not raise his hands.

"Look at this little sissy boy. He's too scared to fight back. What's the matter, Camel Boy? You gonna cry for your belly dancing whore of a mom?"

Armik's vision went black. No longer in control of his hands, he pummeled Bruno's face several times. The surprised boy tumbled backward. Armik kicked out at his ankle, sweeping his leg up and causing him to fall onto the asphalt. A large hand grabbed Armik's wrist before he could continue the barrage. He swung at the owner of the hand but was lifted up until his arm hurt.

"That's more than enough, Mr. Vartanian. This is not how we behave in school, or out. To the office, now."

CHAPTER THIRTY-SIX

Paris, France

Vartan always got a little nostalgic around schools, and even more so walking into this one. His leather shoes made loud taps on the polished floor, walking past rows of multi-colored lockers and walls decked out in art projects.

He had left for his mandatory two-year army commitment right after finishing high school with the intention of going to university afterward and becoming a doctor as his father had expected. Instead, he had been recruited right out of basic training to join SAVAK.

His excellence with firearms and hand-to-hand combat had caught the right—or wrong—person's attention. He found himself in a grueling special operations training program that eventually landed him on the queen's own personal security detail as an agent of the king's secret police.

How far he had come and how much things had changed. Here he was, being called into the school because his son got into an altercation, quite reminiscent of his own school days. His father had paid more than one visit to the principal's office.

He walked into the door of the main office and was ushered right in through the large brown door at the back. A tall woman with graying blond hair rose to greet him upon entering, reaching out a hand. In front of her sat an over-sized kid next to an over-sized man. They both looked to Vartan like they had just come off a construction site. He took a seat in the empty chair next to Armik.

"Mr. Vartanian, I'm glad you could come on such short notice."

"Of course. It sounded as if I had little choice."

"Well, the situation was quite urgent. Armik got into a fight after school with Bruno here and punched him in the face several times. It resulted in a bloody nose and blackened eyes, as you can see. Now, I'm sure you can appreciate that we have a zero-tolerance policy for bullying in our school."

Vartan looked over at the child in question. Slumped in his seat next to his scowling father, he held a wet paper towel to his nose. The boy, thick and large for his age, stood twice the weight of his son, and easily a full head taller. He looked over at Armik, who sat with his head down.

"So, Madame Simard, you are telling me that my son has gone out of his way to bully this boy right here?"

"Well, Mr. Vartanian, there are, of course, always two sides to the story, but when we weigh the evidence, it would suggest that is the case."

"If we are going by weight here, Madame Simard, I believe that your conclusion doesn't add up. Why would a kid this small attack another twice his size?"

"Are you calling my son a liar?" the big man said.

"I'm calling your son large."

"Look, little man. Maybe these things are done back home in Pakistan—"

"I'm from Iran."

"Same difference. Maybe that's how you people behave, but over here we respect other people."

"Yes, I can see that." Vartan smiled, showing teeth.

"Gentlemen, please. We are here to resolve this."

"Very well," said Vartan. "What is the resolution for this situation?"

"He should apologize for hitting my kid for starters, then get suspended." The large man scowled.

"Well, I don't know that we have to go that far," Madame Simard said. "But an apology is in order, and maybe a week of detention...and no Volleyball."

At this, Armik looked up, but his face did not betray any emotion.

"This all seems a little one-sided," said Vartan.

"Armik here is not the one with the bloody nose," said Madame Simard.

"Armik. Why did you hit this boy? Tell the truth." Vartan looked at his son.

Armik hesitated for a moment, but a nod from his father told him to speak. "He pushed me to the ground. Then he said I was a camel-jockey. That my father was a terrorist and a sissy dressmaker, and that my mother was a belly dancer and a whore."

A little giggle came from the boy's father. Vartan turned and eyed him.

"And this is acceptable to you?" he said to the principal sitting back in her leather chair behind her desk.

"Words, Mr. Vartanian. Words never justify violence. Sticks and stones and all that. Besides, Bruno has already said he uttered no such thing. It's his word against Armik's, but the bloodied nose can't be denied."

"Sticks and stones," Vartan repeated quietly to himself, mulling it over. "Armik, are you sorry you hit this boy?"

"No, Baba."

"I'm afraid he is not sorry. I can't ask him to lie."

"Then I'm afraid I have no choice but to suspend him for a

week." Madame Simard picked up her pen and scribbled onto her notepad.

Vartan looked from his son to the boy and his father, who both looked quite pleased with themselves. "No," he said, turning to the principal again.

"I beg your pardon?"

"No," said Vartan. "One week is too short. Make it two."

"I don't understand." Madame Simard looked perplexed.

"We are going to Orlando for an overdue vacation. Universal Studios. Thank you for your time." He stood and Armik followed suit.

The other three people in the room looked stunned. Vartan and his son walked out of the school and to the car. Armik remained quiet. Vartan looked at him as they reached his vehicle.

"Are you okay, son?"

"Yes, Baba. Are you mad at me?"

"Of course not. But I am disappointed."

"Why Baba?"

"You let them see you."

"What do you mean?"

"You were seen hitting him. Unless you have no choice, never let them catch you. If you feel that you absolutely have to fight with idiots like that, the best way is to follow him when he goes to the urinal, and no one is around. Then you teach him a lesson and wash his mouth out in the bowl. Do you understand?"

"Yes, Baba." Armik could not suppress his smile.

"Don't tell your mother I said that." Vartan ruffled the boy's hair with affection. He was a good kid.

"Will she be mad that I hit someone?"

"She'll be mad that you didn't hit him twice as many times. Now get in the car. Let's go home." In the midst of opening the door for the boy, he heard a voice shouting at him.

"Hey, tough guy. Why don't you go back to whatever desert hole you came from? We don't need your type around here."

The large boy and his even larger father stood at their SUV, glaring at them.

"Armik, get in the car and wait for me."

The boy complied, jumping in.

Vartan walked toward the man who had heckled him. He could see the larger man's face lose some of his resolve right away. It was obvious the big, blond-haired bruiser had been used to getting his way because of his intimidating size and girth. The trait appeared to have been passed on genetically. However, like most men of his size and mindset, lack of fear confused them. Vartan had none.

"I'm sorry," said Vartan, hands raised in the air in a show of harmlessness, "but years of fighting on loud battlefields has not been good for my hearing, I'm afraid. Can you repeat what you said?"

"I..." He hesitated for a moment, then straightened himself to his full height. "I said go back to your terrorist country and take your—"

Vartan had him by the wrist in a flash. He squeezed and found a very uncomfortable spot by the elbow with his free hand. From any distance, it would have looked as if they were engaged in a handshake, but the big man had trouble staying on his feet through the pain, his knees buckling beneath him.

Vartan turned to the boy who stood with eyes wide with terror at the sight of his giant father being brought to heel.

"Now here's what I'm going to do, kid. I'm going to let your old man keep his fat arm today, but every time you see my son and you don't treat him like your new best friend, I will come back and break one of your dad's bones. He only has 206, so don't take too long to figure it out. Nod if you understand."

The boy nodded. He released the man, who winced, clutching his arm. A mixture of fear and newfound appreciation appeared across his face. The men now understood each other.

They drove home in silence. Vartan could not tell how his son had taken the events that just passed. He was hopeful a lesson had been learned, but he could not be sure.

"You know, fighting is still the stupidest way to solve this kind of problem," said Vartan, breaking the silence. "You didn't use your head."

"But you said—"

"I said if you have to. Sometimes you have no choice in these matters but there is usually a smarter solution."

"But you just fought his dad, isn't that the same thing?"

"No, I didn't fight him. I took his power."

"I don't understand, Baba."

"It's like this. If I wanted to, I could have smashed him in the face and hurt him badly, but that would have only made him want to come back and hurt me badly. On and on it goes. What I did was break the power he had over himself. I broke his self-confidence and his arrogance and, more importantly, I made him small in front of his son—and that can't be fixed. His power is broken—therefore he can't hold it over anyone. Power is a fragile thing, but it can't easily be beaten, it needs to be broken. This is how you deal with bullies. Understand now?"

"Yes, I think so." Armik looked thoughtful, as if taking it all in. "Baba?"

"*Jan-am.* What is it?"

"It's just… Well. Why did you choose to be a tailor?"

"What's wrong with being a tailor?"

"Nothing."

"People need clothes, don't they?" said Vartan. "You wear

clothes, don't you?"

"Yeah, I guess."

"So what's wrong with it?"

"Nothing. It's just…"

"What? Because that fat kid said it was gay? Or because Timothy's dad is a banker, and your old man isn't as cool?" Vartan laughed a little, even though he felt wounded by the idea.

"I don't know."

"Bobbak's dad is a hair cutter and Kaveh's dad delivers pizza. How about that? Huh?"

"Yeah, but Bobbak's dad says he was a doctor back home, and Kaveh's dad was an engineer and built bridges."

"First of all, no one would trust Kaveh's dad to build a tower out of Lego blocks, let alone a real bridge. He was delivering kabob back home instead of pizza, so this is an upgrade for him, believe me. Secondly, everyone says they were something special back home because no one can check. If Bobbak's dad was a doctor, I was the pope."

"So what were you back home, Baba?"

A thousand memories came flooding into his mind. The empress, his majesty, bullets, and blood. "I was just a soldier in the Shah's army, son. That was an important thing to be."

"Well, that is cooler than a kabob delivery guy, I guess."

Vartan burst out laughing, despite himself. "It's a little cooler, yes. You have your mother's sense of humor. Don't ever lose it."

"Did you ever meet the Shah?"

"Yes."

"Really? What was he like?"

Vartan thought for a moment. He had so much he could say about the king. "He was… He was a very strong man who had a very heavy burden placed on him at an early age. He was a dreamer and a chaser of dreams. He loved his country."

"Bobbak's dad says he wasn't a good king."

"What does Bobbak's dad know about being a king? He can barely run his barber shop."

"Okay, Baba."

"Don't think too much about it, son. Save room in your head for math and science homework. And Universal Studios." He tousled his son's hair again and they drove home.

CHAPTER THIRTY-SEVEN

Milan, Italy
September 19, 1991

Jaleh sat on the bed of her impersonal but lavish hotel room listening to her son through the phone.

"You did what?" She choked on her swallow of coffee. *Gone only one day!*

"It wasn't my fault Mama. Ask Baba," said Armik.

"I'm sure it wasn't. And your father had to go see the principal?"

"Yes," Armik said with hesitation.

Vartan's voice came through in the background, telling him not to bother her with the details right now—a bad sign.

"Then what happened?" She pressed the beige phone receiver against her ear even harder.

"They suspended me, then Baba beat up the boy's dad. It was great, Mama. You should have seen it."

Vartan groaned in the background. She could imagine him pacing and pulling at his hair. Jaleh shook her head and sighed.

"That's not something to be happy about, is it?"

"Sorry, Mama."

"Well, don't worry about it for now. We will talk about it when I get home, okay, Armik-*jan*? Mama loves you."

"I love you, Mama"

"Now, let me talk to your father." She heard some muttering between them before Vartan came on.

"The number you have reached is no longer in service..." said Vartan in a robotic voice, trying to be cute.

"Nice try. What happened? You both beat up someone today?"

"It's a pretty long story. The kid said you were a belly dancer. He deserved it."

"I would make a great belly dancer." She tried to keep the amusement out of her voice.

"That's only for me to know. I've beaten men for less."

"Do you two tough guys think you can restrain yourselves at least until I get back from my trip?"

"It's worth a try," he said in his usual non-serious manner. "How is that going anyway? Your trip, that is."

"So far, so good. The show has some amazing things this year. I've already spent too much."

"Good," said Vartan.

"Although, for the money, I really didn't get all that much."

"Well," he said, "we are just a small tailor shop."

"But I did find the odd wonder I just had to bring back for our customers, like squid-based biomaterials, and some graphene based 'Smart' textiles. There are endless new trends for weddings, which I think will be the bulk of our business this year."

"I can't stand altering tuxes, but it sounds like it was worth the trip."

"I hate being away from you guys like this every year, but the MMV is amazing. There is always something new to be found. I hope to wrap up shortly and come home." Jaleh missed her boys.

"I like the sound of that. Come home soon before we end up

burning the whole place down. Nothing works right without you here."

"I know." She chuckled.

"Good. Stay safe."

"You too." She hung up first because she knew he never would.

He was still a kid in the way he loved her. She could never fault him for it. It was the only pure thing this world had to offer her—he and Armik. *I am a lucky woman.*

Buttoning her blouse, she finished her coffee, checked her hair, and exited the room. Once outside, she looked around to make sure no one was watching her before she produced a roll of scotch tape from her handbag. She placed two pieces of the clear tape across the crack of the door, one at the top and one at the bottom. If someone entered her room before she returned, she would know.

Putting the tape away, she hurried down to the lobby. Making her way across the fine marble tiled floor, her every step echoed but became lost in the din created by patrons coming and going. A massive chandelier made rainbow colors dance across the luxurious space. Embroidered silk sofas surrounded a large television. She passed the service desk of amber-colored wood and a green granite top, slowing to glimpse at the exquisite paintings hanging from the rich, red walls. The domed ceiling must have been a hundred feet high. The twin doors leading out of the lobby were pristine white with golden handles. Even the hinges were engraved with swirls and elegant designs.

Jaleh went through the doors, opened by a doorman in a red and gold uniform. She slipped a folded bill into his hand as she passed.

"*Ringraziamo, Signora. Buona serata.*" He offered a smile and a slight bow.

"*Grazie mille.*" Jaleh stepped off the curb and crossed the street. A block down Via Uberto di Modrone stood a cafe called Taveggia—the perfect place to meet her contact from Israel, who also happened to be the famous designer, Dafna Gould. Upon pulling the cafe door open, a booming voice greeted her. All heads turned in her direction.

"Jaleh, darling! Look at you. You must sleep in the freezer at night. You haven't aged a day since I last saw you," said the flamboyant, middle-aged woman in a dazzling, sheer golden dress. It left so little to the imagination Jaleh had to imagine her covered up.

"Dafna, how are you?" The two women embraced over the small table. "And look who's talking, with skin smooth like fine China."

"Oh, please. My plastic surgeon is an artistic genius."

Laughing, Jaleh sat beside her to order. "So, what do you think of the Moda Milano Voga this year?"

"Wonderful trade fair, as always, darling. It's still the only place to be for fashion and connections—all the top designers are here. And, of course, that makes it a celebrity hot spot. In fact, I hear Iran's newly appointed foreign minister, Nasser Javodi, just arrived in Rome to meet his good friend Ali Roshani, the Iranian Ambassador to Italy. No doubt they will be attending. They are well known to have a taste for models and movie stars alike."

"That is so interesting," Jaleh said with a show of enthusiasm. "How exciting."

"That it is, darling. That it is."

"So, what magnificent new trend are you starting this season?" Jaleh took a sip of her cappuccino.

Dafna leaned in and whispered, placing a dainty hand on Jaleh's sleeve. "It's all about intelligent fabric bringing natural fabrics to the next level. I am combining the magic and beauty of nature with the technology and performance of synthetic material, marrying synthetic yarns to natural ones, combining ecologically friendly fibers with performance materials. Ah, look at me. I'm pitching. But anyway, darling, it's all beautiful. I'll send you a bunch of samples in your size. Thirty-six, twenty-four, thirty-two?"

"Haha. You've always had an eye."

"An eye for beauty, yes. And that you are. How is that husband of yours? And your precious little boy? I want to squeeze his cheeks."

"They are very well, thank you."

"Speaking of beauty," Dafna said, laying a manila envelope on the table. "This right here is a thing of beauty. It's a two for one deal. The two men are responsible for that situation in Delhi."

The news had shocked Jaleh. An Israeli diplomat had been the victim of a car bombing in Delhi India—along with his wife. Everyone knew Iran was responsible but to have confirmation of the people involved was a gift.

"Well, I'll see to it that it gets sewn up nice and neat."

"I have no doubt."

Their conversation went on for another hour. Jaleh found genuine joy in the other's company—like an injection of sunshine on any somber day. Afterward, Jaleh headed back to her hotel.

The tape on the door remained intact. After scanning the place for cameras or listening devices, she ordered dinner to her room. She took her time, studying the faces in the photographs provided while she dined on minestrone, veal parmigiana, and an assortment of cannoli.

CHAPTER THIRTY-EIGHT

Milan, Italy
September 24, 1991

Humans could be so disgusting. If Jaleh had not had her faith in them renewed by Vartan, she would likely have written off the entire species altogether. The petty weakness of flesh had been the ruin of so many lives. She found it disturbing, yet it remained the most useful and dependable tool in her line of work.

The two men she eyed from across the room were a prime example of that weakness. Their hands, like hungry squids, groped and prodded at the bevy of attractive women that surrounded them, like so many seagulls circling spilled fries at the beach. The women pretended not to notice stray hands wandering into forbidden crevices or bumps.

These men had limitless financial resources at their disposal, as well as diplomatic immunity. The combination made the options for debauchery wide open for them, and high-profile fashion events such as this one were the best places to indulge in those opportunities.

Jaleh also sought an illicit opportunity. She sat at the bar eying the two Iranian diplomats molesting the young models with relentless enthusiasm over giggles and a steady flow of champagne.

"What can I get you, miss?" The bartender asked.

"Whiskey sour."

"Sure thing."

She shifted in her tight dress. She hated the limited mobility and the constant effort involved in avoiding spillage of her ample assets, but it had already garnered her the attention she wanted. Her two targets nudged each other and pointed her out. They beckoned her over, but she turned away, ignoring them.

"Thank you," she said at the drink placed in front of her on a coaster.

"Compliments of those gentlemen over there," he said, pointing to the veritable orgy happening in the private lounge in the corner.

"Tell them thanks, but I can buy my own drinks," she said with an annoyance she did not have to fake.

"Of course."

She pretended not to watch the bartender walk over to the men on the large white sofa, with obvious trepidation, and render her answer to them. She could tell from out of the corner of her eye that they were not pleased by it either. She smiled a little to herself. One of them stood and left his small party to walk over to her. She looked in the opposite direction.

"When someone buys you a drink, it's not polite to refuse," said a voice in a thick Persian accent.

With a bored scowl, Jaleh turned and looked at the man. He wore a shiny gray silk suit with butterfly collars and a shirt opened to the navel, exposing a thick nest of hair.

"Save your money," she said. "You seem to have a lot of little girls there who want it."

"There is plenty of money to go around, baby."

"I'm not your baby, and I'm not interested."

"Hey, now. Why so uptight? We can be friends."

"I'm not looking for a friend," she said with hostility. Her lack of interest seemed new to him and was driving him crazy. The thrill of the chase dilated his pupils even more than they already were. His nostrils flared.

Hook, line, and sinker.

"So what are you looking for? I can show you a good time. What is it you like? Nice jewels, fast cars? I got it all, baby. Want some herb? Some blow? Ah...you like the blow."

Jaleh made a less than subtle change in body language at his last suggestion.

"Well, I could always go for a line or two, if you're carrying."

"Of course, of course, baby. Let's go to the restroom."

She looked around as if to see if anyone was watching, then gave a wry smile. "Lead the way."

The man's face lit up and he turned toward the corridor just off the end of the bar. The hallway led to a series of single, unisex restrooms. He opened the door to one marked vacant and held it open like the true gentleman he pictured himself to be. She walked in and sat on the warm radiator, looking at him.

He devoured her with his eyes, glazed over by intoxicants and lust. He pulled a little packet out of his coat pocket, wiggling it in front of her like bait. He poured some white powder onto the marble countertop next to the sink, then took out a credit card and with it arranged the powder into several neat rows. Next, he produced a hundred dollar American bill, making sure she saw it, and rolled it into a small tube. He held it out to her.

"Ladies first." His smile exposed several gold teeth.

"Show me how it's done, Mr. High Roller," she said with a bit of tease in her voice.

"Don't trust anyone, eh? Smart girl, but the stuff I get is the best."

He flashed his golden smile and turned away from Jaleh, placing the rolled-up bill in his nose. Like a vacuum hose, he sucked up an entire line. By the time he had sucked in half of his second line, the contents of his skull were spattered onto the countertop. Blood oozed through the snow-white powder and poured down into the sink.

Jaleh put the pistol with the silencer back into her purse.

"One down, one to go," she said to the man who could no longer hear her.

She looked in the mirror for any stray spatter, straightened her blonde wig, and checked her teeth for lipstick, then opened the door.

His partner stood just outside. The look of shock on his face quickly turned to anger. His hands clamped on Jaleh's throat. She had not been ready for him to be there—a bad mistake. Her head slammed hard against the bathroom wall. Her one arm tried to purchase relief from the two-handed grip, the other dug into her purse.

He had no intention of letting her off so easily. He pinned her arms with his shoulder and kept choking her. She batted at his solid arms and tried throwing a knee to the groin, but found her leg pinned by his hip.

Running out of light fast, she still fumbled with her right hand in her purse. She grasped her pistol but couldn't draw it out. She grunted, the lack of choices dawning on her. Flicking the safety off with her thumb, she fired through the handbag, saying goodbye to a $4000 Fendi.

Her assailant staggered back—the bullet having torn through his thigh. Jaleh's struggle to pull the gun out lasted just long enough for him to turn and run out of the restroom.

Damn. So much for being discreet.

She took a moment to adjust herself and went after the wounded beast, pistol drawn. The man did not get far. Bleeding like a fountain, he limped down the short corridor to the bar area. A woman in the hallway screamed at the sight of the gun. The screams multiplied as soon as she stepped into the crowded barroom. The music came to an abrupt stop.

Two bodyguards reached for weapons in their jackets. She shot them down before they could draw. People scrambled to leave the bar in what became a stampede of high heels and business suits. Jaleh followed the wounded victim right up to the large window overlooking Milan. He reached the glass and, having nowhere else to go, turned to her with horror in his eyes.

"Please, don't kill me. I have money. Lots of money."

"So your friend kept telling me."

"Whatever amount they are paying you I—"

"I paid them to let me do it. I was going to do a car bomb to make it fair, but this is so much more intimate, isn't it?"

"No, Please I…"

His head snapped back from the impact of her bullet. His body shattered the glass behind him and tumbled to the ground twelve stories below.

The time had come for her to leave. Though impeded by her tight dress, she made it back into the corridor. She pushed through the stairwell doors, moving as fast as she could in her heels.

Two levels down, an open door led her to a darkened office floor. Jaleh moved down the hallway to a specific door, which she opened with a key and walked in. There, she changed her clothes, dawning a maintenance uniform. Replacing her wig with a hat, she grabbed a mop bucket pre-filled with dirty water, suds, and a huge amount of bleach. She dropped her wig and discarded clothes into the bucket, along with the gun and the ruined purse, pushing them down with a mop.

Heading for the elevators she made her way to the lobby and past the large group of *Carabinieri,* the Italian police. One checked the ID on her lapel.

"What floor are you coming from?" The officer compared the photo on the ID to her face. It matched, of course.

"Cipolone Law offices."

"Okay. Don't go back upstairs, for now. There is a police investigation," he said.

"Yes, officer. Thank you."

She rolled her bucket to the front doors and walked right out with the panicked crowd. She was back at her hotel well before midnight.

CHAPTER THIRTY-NINE

Paris, France
October 9, 1991

"You're not going to drink that, are you, camel boy?"

"I guess not." Armik had barely returned from his two-week vacation and trip to Florida with his father, yet Bruno's bravado had already revitalized.

"Good." Bruno grabbed the chocolate milk carton off the table. "And I'll take this too. Thanks." He snatched the large chocolate bar nestled in Armik's lunch container.

He made a small gesture of protest but said nothing as the large boy and his friends walked away.

"I'm surprised he didn't learn his lesson after that beating you gave him," said Kaveh.

"Yeah." Bobbak said. "You beat him good, but he is still at it. What's his problem?"

"You can't beat it out of him, you have to break it," said Armik, much calmer than he felt.

"What does that even mean?" Bobbak tossed him half of his chocolate bar.

"Nothing. Something my dad told me. Today we are going to fix this problem, once and for all. I'm going to need your help."

"No problem." Kaveh lit up like a Roman candle. "What do you want us to do?"

"Did you bring me that duct tape I asked for?"

"Yes." Kaveh patted his rucksack.

"Six rolls?" Armik raised a skeptical eyebrow.

"I only had four at home."

"It's okay." Armik smiled, satisfied he had been correct about his friend's reliability. "I have a roll too. That's more than enough."

"Enough for what?" Bobbak's curiosity seemed piqued as usual.

"I'll show you now. And why does your dad have so much duct-tape anyway?"

"No idea," said Kaveh. "He keeps it next to his bottles of chloroform." This made everyone laugh hard.

They were good friends. Maybe not the bravest—but always willing to help cause chaos.

"You guys ready?" Armik stood, ignoring the rest of his plundered lunch.

Armik's two good buddies nodded, and at Armik's instructions Bobbak ran off, leaving him and Kaveh to begin their work.

His dad, Vartan the tailor, had been right. Power was fragile and could be broken. Bruno had to be broken. And so Armik found himself duct-taping toilet seats on a Wednesday afternoon, three days after his return to school.

It had shaken Bruno to see his dad being taken down a notch, but it had not broken him. He clung to his power in desperation, stepping up his bullying to an intolerable level. Kicking Armik's chair every time he found a pretense to walk by. Stealing his chocolate milk off his lunch tray and guzzling it. Though Armik did notice the large boy avoided insulting his parents.

"Armo, you in here?" Kaveh's voice echoed in the empty bathroom.

"In the third stall." Armik checked the toilet lid to see that it had been secured.

"Done." Kaveh's head popped through the stall door, his cheeks flushed from running.

"You got them all?"

"Every one—I used a lot of tape. No one is going to use those anytime soon."

"Did you get the girls' room too?" Armik added another piece of tape for good measure.

"Yeah. I almost got caught. Now Cossette thinks I'm a pervert."

"She's not entirely wrong."

"Shut up," said Kaveh, laughing. "Why are we taping shut every toilet seat in the school anyway? What's this brilliant plan?"

"We are breaking Bruno." Armik stood, brushed himself off, and moved to the next stall.

"How? By disrupting the bathroom schedule of an entire school?"

"No, only his." Armik handed Kaveh one of the tape rolls.

"We are disrupting Bruno's bathroom schedule?"

"Yes. That's exactly what we are doing. Now hurry and finish, we don't have long. Bruno is going to come running soon." Armik wrapped the toilet in the stall so that it would take a half-hour with scissors to undo.

"How do you know that?"

"Simple. For the last few days, this mutt has been helping himself to my chocolate milk at lunch. Today he did the same, but this time I added something special."

"Oh yeah. What?"

"A laxative."

"What's that?" Kaveh struggled to find the edge of his tape roll.

"It makes you want to crap really bad," Armik said, laughing.

"Oh… Ha! Are you sure it's going to work?"

"Yeah, I'm pretty sure it will. But I wanted to be absolutely certain, so I bought a laxative chocolate bar too and, of course, he snatched that up. That works really fast. I tested it on my neighbor. He was running to the washroom within minutes, crying."

"How do you come up with this stuff?" said Kaveh.

Armik shrugged, finishing up the last toilet. He had no idea.

The door of the bathroom burst open and Bobbak rushed in, panting. "He's coming, and he is not looking happy."

"Quick, everyone, take a urinal." Armik hid the tape in his bag and flung it on his shoulders. The three of them scurried to take their positions at the urinals.

The door burst open again, a sweating, groaning Bruno smashing through. He did not even seem to notice he had company, pushing his way into the nearest stall.

"What the hell. Come on!" His voice had a distinct note of desperation in it. He ran out and went into the next one. "What the damn sh… Come on. No. Come on."

He had the same luck with the other three stalls. He came out of the last one and came face to face with Armik and his friends. A look of realization grew in his eyes as he stared at his three tormentors. Bruno's bowels rumbled so loud it sounded like a lawn mower engine starting up, leaving him unable to utter his usual array of threats. He turned tail and ran out of the bathroom. The three friends followed.

"Bruno, are you okay? Where are you going?" Armik yelled, getting the attention of the other kids around.

"Yeah, Bruno. Come back. What's the matter?" Kaveh said.

They ran after Bruno. The bully had broken into a light jog with an awkward limp. His innards still growled with a loud intensity, the overdose of laxatives running afoul of his intestinal workings.

"Bruno, slow down. Let's talk."

"Go away."

"What's wrong? Are you okay?" Kaveh cracked as he tried to hold in his laughter.

Ignoring them, Bruno ran to the boys' bathroom on the other side of the school. They followed him in, now pursued by other kids who had their curiosity aroused by the commotion. A sizable crowd had gathered to watch by the time Bruno came out of the last stall, realizing these toilets had also been incapacitated.

Bruno bulldozed his way through the kids gathered in the doorway, tears streaking down his face, and ran into the girls' bathroom just next to them. The kids laughed and jeered, but he did not care. Girls that were already in the bathroom screamed. The result was the same. Bruno burst out of there hobbling, his legs squeezed together. His hands clutched his bottom as if, somehow, he could hold back the oncoming storm. He ran bent, doubled over in pain as he made his way to the nearby staff washroom.

"Did you get that one too?" Kaveh whispered.

"Better, I broke the lock so that it won't open."

"No, please, no. Why God? No." Bruno's voice sounded pathetic. The boy banged on the locked door before him.

Several teachers arrived, along with what seemed to be the entire school. They were quick to ascertain the gist of the problem. One male teacher tried to get the door open with his shoulder to no avail.

All went quiet at the gurgling surge of dark liquid that

erupted from Bruno's light-colored pants. He wept, loud sobs, his chest heaving. In front of everyone he knew, many of them long-suffering victims of his torment, he stood in a brown puddle, the foulness of the odor the only thing that diminished the laughter.

Armik had taken his power, leaving Bruno broken.

PART 6

CHAPTER FORTY

Paris, France
June 16, 1999

Armik had a low tolerance for the partying scene but enjoyed the occasional drink with his friends, perhaps more to keep Kaveh out of trouble than anything else. He suspected that Bobbak's reasoning ran along the same lines, since they found themselves in the same district more nights than they cared to. Oberkampf, the Parisian byword for boisterous nights out, had among its many vibes, an indie rock feel. There were classy dive bars and wine bars opening up all the time along the strip, but most establishments looked as though they had been thrown together by impoverished art students during a drunken weekend.

Armik had no love for the hustle and bustle of these popular areas, but Kaveh's preferred haunt, La P'tit Coq Bendy, stood right on rue Oberkampf, between the Ménilmontant and Parmentier métro stations.

"Do we really need to come here all the time?" Armik said over the barrage of loud music, voices, flashing lights, and the release of mist from a fog machine. "It's so loud we can't even talk."

"What?" Kaveh danced next to the bar as though no one

was watching.

"It's so loud we can't even talk." Armik repeated in his ear.

"Okay, so don't talk. What do you want to talk about? I've seen you every day for twenty years." Kaveh laughed and ordered another round of beers with the twirl of a finger.

"Then what's the point of coming here?"

"That's the point." Kaveh smiled and gestured to a group of girls in scanty outfits dancing nearby.

Armik rolled his eyes. "Do you ever think about anything else?"

"He thinks about money a lot," Bobbak said, waving to the girls.

"Yes, that is true." Kaveh laughed.

"They look Persian," Armik said, pointing his chin toward the girls while the thumping music tore into his eardrums.

"So? What's wrong with Persian girls?" Bobbak said.

"Besides being half-dressed and drunk, you mean?"

"Still not seeing a negative here, Armo."

"Their moms probably know your mom," Armik said. "It's a small community."

Bobbak laughed. "My mom only says nice things about me."

"That's because she doesn't know you like we do." Kaveh clinked his beer bottle against Armik's for approval.

"Thank God." Bobbak seemed to wither at the thought.

"Anyway, boys," said Kaveh, moving off. "Let me show you how it's done, Persian style."

"Hey, be careful Romeo. Where there is a dancing Persian girl, there is always a jealous Persian ex-boyfriend lurking nearby."

"You worry too much, Armo. Bobbak, tell him he worries too much."

"You do worry a lot."

"Watch and learn, kids." Kaveh sauntered over to the girls.

Armik and Bobbak leaned against the bar and watched their friend, Kaveh the Hunter, as he often liked to call himself, move in on his hapless prey.

"You think he will get anywhere?" Bobbak downed the rest of his beer.

"Well, none of them have slapped him—yet." Armik shook his head and leaned back against the bar to watch the show.

"That's because they haven't heard him speak yet."

"Oh. Look. One of them is dancing with him."

"Or despite him," said Bobbak.

"That's probably it." Armik had to laugh

"He's whispering to her."

"He's saying 'Baby, do you believe in love at first sight, or should I walk by again?'" Armik did his best Kaveh impersonation over the din.

"Nah, he's not that clever. Hey, they are walking over to the bar together."

Kaveh turned to his friends and shot them a wink, but a group of young men in the far corner caught Armik's attention.

"See those guys over there?" He said to Bobbak, who took a second to find them.

"Uh oh, there is the jealous ex you warned him about. He looks none too pleased and is staring daggers at them."

"Yup. I have a feeling it's not going to end well. I count seven." Armik moved off the bar, ready to run over.

"There are more guys over there watching." Bobbak nodded to their left. "At least six more. What should we do?"

"Hang tight for a second and see how it plays out. Look, one of them is going over. Must be the ex."

"Crap, he is big," said Bobbak.

"Kaveh can handle him. He's tough enough."

The large individual approached the bar and inserted himself between the would-be couple. As expected, Kaveh became incensed and got off his bar stool. Several of the man's friends made their approach while words were exchanged.

"And it begins." Bobbak sighed, gripping his beer bottle by the neck like a cudgel.

"Let's go," Armik said.

They walked toward the group now gathered. A heated discussion in Farsi was in progress between Kaveh and the boyfriend.

"I don't see a ring on her finger, buddy."

"I don't need to put a ring on her finger, *buddy*. She's mine."

"I'm not yours, Hushang," The girl inserted herself between them, hands on her hips. "I'm not anyone's, so get lost."

"You heard the lady," said Kaveh. "Get lost."

"Hey guys, we are all Persian here," Armik said, stepping in between them. "I'm sure it was just a misunderstanding."

"Yes, and I'm going to make your little friend here understand," said the boyfriend.

"Let me buy you guys a round and we will laugh about it," Armik said, trying again.

"Yeah, like that time I was with your sister, and we laughed while we talked about you," said Kaveh.

Armik had only a moment to glare at his friend before the bigger foe swung a fist. Kaveh shoved Armik out of the way and connected with one of his own, dropping the boyfriend to his knees.

The girl screamed and moved aside. Two of his friends came in hot with fists raised. Armik spun out of range of a wayward punch and caught another tall Iranian by the back of the head. He guided his forehead to the brass rail running along the length of the bar, the contact making a gong sound that could be heard over the music.

Bobbak smashed his bottle over the second attacker's head, beer and glass flying everywhere. He was ready to follow up with a punch to the face when they were overwhelmed with the club's security team. Keeping fists from flying and holding back newcomers from joining the fray, the big bouncers separated everyone. They escorted the whole lot of them to the back door and urged them to walk away in separate directions through the alley behind the building.

"Well, that went south pretty quickly," Bobbak said, the obvious adrenaline rush still flowing through him.

"You sure have a way with people." Armik scrubbed at the blood now staining the sleeve of his white shirt.

"It's my extreme manliness," said Kaveh. "It threatens people. What can I do?"

"Well, you can stop telling people you slept with their sisters, for starters." Bobbak gave Kaveh a punch in the shoulder.

"Ow. Given the odds, it's probably true in most cases."

Armik shook his head but laughed along with his friends. They had another story to tell when they were older.

Exiting the end of the alley onto the main street, they took a second to get their bearings.

"Where did we park?" said Bobbak.

"Are you drunk?" Armik scanned the street for their car.

"A little."

"Just off of Parmentier," said Kaveh, "a block from the metro."

"That's in the other direction. The direction those guys went." Armik groaned.

"Yeah, so what?" Kaveh smirked. "If we see them, we can teach them some manners."

"They outnumber us three to one," Bobbak said.

"My kind of odds."

"You're insane." Bobbak shook his head.

"Bobbak is right. It's a bit much, even for Kaveh the Hunter. Let's take a parallel road, we've had enough trouble for one night."

"Well the guy you cracked against the bar with his face sure had enough," Kaveh said and they all laughed.

"It's only 10:00pm." Bobbak looked at his watch. "Why don't we head over to Chez Papa. Never any trouble there."

"Chez Papa sounds good to me," said Armik. "Some jazz and some drinks."

They walked up the street and turned onto Rue Saint-Bientot. They were about halfway to the Jazz club when the same group of young men turned the corner and stopped in front of them, half a block away.

"Your friends seem to have found us," said Armik.

Bobbak cracked his knuckles. "Just when things were getting quiet."

"Run or fight?" Kaveh turned to his friends.

"Running might be better," Armik said, trying to be the voice of reason. "I'm counting twenty."

"I'm too drunk to run—or count," said Bobbak.

"Me too." Kaveh smirked again

Armik resigned himself with another sigh, longing for their childhood days when these two did not have the stomach for fighting. "Fight it is. Hit whoever is nearest and keep back-to-back."

The three of them walked toward the group. This action alone seemed to take the wind out of their opponent's sails, despite their numerical advantage.

"How's your face?" Armik said to the one he had smashed. His eye had swollen shut, his lower lip bloody.

"We were looking all over for you guys," said Kaveh. He

walked up to his nemesis and threw a direct punch to his face.

"Straight to business as always," Armik said. He grabbed the closest opponent by the wrist and twisted, bending him down low enough for a knee to the head. Bobbak jumped into the mix, arms swinging like jackhammers. Despite being the smallest of the three and having a hatred of fighting, he had the heart of a lion when the moment arose. And there was no shortage of moments with Kaveh.

An all-out brawl erupted, a tangle of swinging limbs that moved into the middle of the street. Traffic came to a halt. Horns blared. Armik kicked the legs out from under someone taking a swing at Kaveh. Kaveh smiled back at him, teeth bloodied, and moved on to someone else, until the knife came out.

Everyone stepped back, as if taking a break. The boyfriend charged at Kaveh.

Though he did not flinch, Armik moved in to intercept. One hand caught the wrist holding the blade, the other reached up and grabbed the opposite side of his chin. With a quick twist, the knife-wielder dropped to the ground. The sound of a snap seemed to mute all other sounds.

Sirens and flashing lights shook everyone from their disbelief. Everyone scattered in different directions at once, leaving Armik surrounded by police.

CHAPTER FORTY-ONE

Paris, France
June 18, 1999

The ceiling fan whirled in the large office—the only sound in the otherwise silent room. It looked to Vartan like it could have been a judge's chambers, with all the dark wood, cushy seats, and shelves piled with volumes of legal books.

Ari Levi had somehow managed to get Armik out of the holding cells in the basement of the courthouse and up to this room with no guards or cuffs—quite an impressive feat in itself. It would have been easy to walk out and disappear, which Vartan considered as a viable option at this point.

"I have a lot of pull in Paris." Ari puffed on a thick cigar. "But I'm afraid I don't have that much pull, my friends. If this were Jerusalem or Tel Aviv, we wouldn't even need to think twice, but we are all foreigners here." Vartan sat between Jaleh and Armik across the table from their long-time handler.

"The kid didn't die. Plus, he had a knife. Why are there even charges? This is ridiculous," Vartan said, not bothering to hide his frustration.

"That's just the way things work, unfortunately. The winner usually takes the brunt of the charges. No, he didn't die, but he may very well never walk again."

"So the only way Armik wouldn't have been charged is if he had been stabbed?" said Jaleh, sounding distraught.

"That sums it up quite well, I'm afraid." Ari rekindled his cigar, a cloud of smoke hanging above him.

"That's the stupidest thing I have ever heard." Vartan waved the smoke away, causing Ari to extinguish it. "What do we know about this guy? This Hushang Mohammadi."

"We looked into him. His dad is a high-ranking government official in Iran. Ali Mohammadi. Corrupt as they come and they have money spread all over the place, including here. The kid drives a Ferrari and lives in a four-million-dollar condo on the Champs, and he doesn't have a job." With a casual swipe, Ari pocketed several more cigars from a gilded cigar box on the desk.

Vartan looked over at Armik. He had his head down, remaining silent thus far. He wanted to be angry at his son but found he could not. He had trained his boy to fight since he could walk, paying for all sorts of martial arts classes. What had it all been for if not to come out of a knife attack alive?

No, he held no anger, only relief. But now they had a mess to deal with, and he was not about to let his boy go to jail. He would whisk him out of the country before that happened—today and from here if necessary.

"So what is the maximum jail sentence we are looking at?" Vartan looked over at his wife and saw her wince at the question. He hated to see her suffer like this.

"Ten to fifteen for assault with intent," said Ari.

"Can we beat it?" Vartan stared at his handler.

"Maybe. There is a decent chance. It will depend on eyewitness testimony mostly. Maybe some CCTV camera footage, if we can get it. And we will, of course, provide you with one of our best lawyers. But if we go that way, the deal is off the table."

"Two years of military service." Jaleh winced again.

Ari shrugged. "That's right."

"And the charges get dropped?" said Vartan.

"Completely. It's a decent deal. One impossible to obtain without our...connections. Besides, he is young, athletic, and obviously an above-average fighter. How many fights has that been in the last two years? Six?"

"Five," said Armik, looking up

"Let's call it seven." Vartan glared at his son and he put his head back down.

"Right. This will be a walk in the park for him. It's a good deal. A great deal. Unheard of. And there are lots of opportunities that the armed forces can provide. It might be just the thing to set him on a good career path."

"Like what?" said Armik.

"There are endless training programs available that can apply to the real world. You could become a pilot, maybe an avionics technician. Dentistry, security, intelligence."

The last option made Vartan cringe. "Okay. What do you think, Armik-*jan*?"

"I'm sorry, Babba. It wasn't my fault. We tried to avoid it. They followed us. He had a knife."

"I'm not asking about that. I'd rather we be here discussing this than me identifying your body. I would have done the same—or worse. Now we have to deal with the options we have. So what do you think?"

"I guess the military doesn't sound so bad. It's not like France is at war with anyone."

"Don't fool yourself, Armik-*jan*," said Jaleh. "We are always at war with someone."

"Then it is settled, yes?" said Ari, standing. "Armik will do two years of military service for his country and come out a clean-cut, educated young man."

Vartan looked over at Armik and then they both turned to Jaleh. Obvious distress was etched on her tired face. She looked at her son for a long moment, then with a sigh she nodded.

"I accept the deal, Mr. Levi," Armik said to Ari. "Thank you for securing it for me, I know that could not have been easy."

"No, it wasn't easy, but I am more than happy that I was able to do it for you. Your family and I have a long history." Ari passed a paper across the desk and indicated where Armik should sign. The signature affixed, he stood and offered a hand to Armik, who accepted it.

"So what now?" Vartan said, standing and taking Ari's hand. The man seemed no older than he had the first time they had met him. He had been a timeless constant in their lives, for better or worse.

"Now, he's free to go. I will square it with the judge. This little incident never happened. With a few small conditions."

"What conditions?" asked Jaleh.

"There is to be no contact with the so-called victim. Ever. Also, Armik will report to the recruitment office no later than Friday of next week. Oh, and try not to hit anyone until hand-to-hand combat training."

"I think I can manage that."

"Good, then you are a free man. That is until next week when you will belong to the French government," Ari said and left the room.

Jaleh hugged her son, then she cupped his face in her hands. "I'm going to kill you myself."

"I love you too, Mama." He received another hug. "So who is Mr. Levi, and what kind of favors did you have to call in to get this miracle to happen, Baba?"

"I had to sell one of my livers."

"You only have one liver."

"Exactly, so don't mess this up."

"Thanks, Baba."

"Don't thank me. They are going to kick your ass in basic training."

CHAPTER FORTY-TWO

Perpignan, France
October 1, 1999

Face down in the mud, Armik could only think of his father. The cold ooze permeated his fatigues with impunity, and so much had entered his nose and mouth that his teeth and throat maintained a sandy coating.

"Goddamn it, Vartanian, this isn't a mud spa. Move your ass." The drill sergeant somehow managed to keep his shiny black boots spotless as he lorded over the soldiers in the sludge.

The sun, no more than an orange gap on the horizon when he and four others were roused from their bunks, now cast everything in a soft light without any warmth. The three senior officers fired weapons in the air and several smoke canisters had been tossed at them to simulate combat. The purpose of this unscheduled torture of only the five of them had not been disclosed. Such was life at the Centre d'entraînement à la Guerre Spéciale. Though how he ended up here, he had no idea.

At least now crawling through the muck, amid yelling, smoke, and gunfire, his father's description of his time in the army made sense. The words in the latest letter rang in his mind.

In the army back home, we would each have to carry a donkey on our backs up the side of a mountain made of broken glass in our bare feet each morning just to eat breakfast, which was a single grain of rice. Then, the hard part would begin.

Or something to that effect. It lost a little in the translation. The letters did, in fairness, include some expressions of pride along with bits of sage advice on how to navigate the shark-infested waters of basic training.

A man of few words, his father wrote to him with uncharacteristic frequency since he had left home—even more than his mother did. Less surprising, the letters were all in Armenian, done with the knowledge that his son had some difficulty reading in that language.

Typical.

He would give you love, but made you work for it—like a seal that clapped for a small fish—that was Vartan the Tailor. Still, better some small fish than no fish at all.

Reaching the end of the mud field, the gunfire ceased but the ringing in his ears remained. Armik pulled himself out of the slime and broke into a run, following Louis, the one soldier who managed to get ahead of him. The sixty pounds of gear in the backpack made the straps sink into his shoulders and the mud on his hands made his rifle slippery.

Armik tried to imagine Vartan covered in mud and running through the woods but could not conjure up the image. His father's time in the military in Iran remained pretty much a mystery, other than him being a soldier, and a good one. Armik always suspected that he had some higher military training but discussions on that part of his life had always been rare.

"Why do you think they've singled us out?" said Louis, his breathing less labored than Armik's.

"It's either because we are the top of the class or because

they hate us." Armik pushed to keep up the pace with Louis. The other three soldiers languished a few meters behind.

"Sure feels like they hate us."

"Come on, you camel-jockey," the sergeant said, his voice booming in Armik's deafened ears. "Shut your mouth and move that butterscotch-candy-ass of yours before I make a flying carpet out of your greasy skin."

Somehow, he managed to say it all in one breath. Armik had learned to take the racist taunts as terms of endearment. Besides, he found them more amusing than insulting, as he had never even seen a camel.

Armik lost track of the distance by the time they ran out of path, the gravel beneath their boots coming to an abrupt stop at the water's edge. The agitated waves lapped the eroding shoreline, the cold air blowing off the surface penetrating his wet clothes. His teeth chattered.

"Okay, you three pussies can stay," the sergeant said, addressing Armik, Louis, and Frank, who had taken a significant lead over the other two. "The rest of you, back to the barracks."

"What's this all about, sarg?" said Frank when the stragglers had gone.

"That's need-to-know, private. Understand?"

"Sir. Yes, sir."

"Good. Now, for this portion of this morning's special treat, you will each complete a five-hundred-meter swim in ten minutes or less. That's the distance between the two red buoys. Should any of you fail to complete the distance, Sergeant Dion is out in the motorboat to haul your carcass out. Your packs and rifles will be waiting for you on the other side, as will I."

The firing of a pistol sent Armik running. He hit the water just ahead of Frank and Louis, the icy water ripping into his body like the claws of a demon. He screamed but lost the sound to the crashing waves. In defiance of his body's desire to shut down and sink, he forced his failing limbs to make the swim out to the first floating red ball. He caught a glimpse of someone swimming beside him and spurred himself on.

The agony subsided after the first few minutes, and he soon found his stride. Reaching the buoy ahead of the others, he was turned back to shore by a flag-waving Sergeant Dion. He touched the sand and dropped, his waterlogged boots and uniform weighing him down. Louis dropped next to him. Frank did not appear. Looking up, Armik saw Frank in Dion's boat being motored away.

"Now," yelled the sarg, "ninety more push-ups and sit-ups. You have two minutes each." He made a show of pulling out his stopwatch. "Then give me thirty chin-ups on those bars over there. Then get ready for another fun run. You girls hear me say take a break?"

By the time they were done, he and Louis could no longer speak. They dropped in the sand, gasping for air like two fish out of water. Armik had never prayed in his life, but he prayed now that no one would ask him to move.

"Grab some chow, boys," said Sergeant Dion. "I'm not entirely disappointed in you."

"That," said Louis, coughing and struggling for air, "was the best compliment he's ever given anyone."

"He sounds like my dad." Armik tried to raise his head, but it would not move.

CHAPTER FORTY-THREE

Paris, France
October 5, 1999

On most days, with work done and his tailor shop locked tight, Vartan drove the long way home, stopping in front of the queen's apartment. He did this whether or not her Majesty was in residence, as she divided her time between Paris and her home in the United States. On days when Jaleh dropped by the shop, she came along for the ride.

"I don't like this place," he said of the gray-stoned, neoclassical building, from which he had parked several blocks down. "From a security standpoint."

"So you've told me—many times," Jaleh said in that patient and not-at-all-condescending way she had.

"Have I?"

"Yes. Even though the place is crawling with plained clothed and uniformed French Sûreté, French intelligence, and a slew of loyal SAVAK operatives, including your good friend Abbas on occasion."

"It's much too open. No gates. No kill-zone between the entrance and the front door. No watchtower. If I had it my way, they would fortify Versailles and have the royal family live there."

But you have to concede that a secure location has never stopped the Iranian Death Squad from finding a way to get to someone when they really want to. They assassinated the Shah's own nephew in broad daylight, in the same area that houses consulates."

"Good point."

Shariar had been a military hero of the resistance and Vartan still lamented that event. It had signaled the death of hope for many, including him.

"Hey, do you see that?" She pointed to the apartment opposite the Queen's. It was not quite as tall and newer, but architecturally similar.

"No. What is it?"

"That tiny flash of light from the top floor. The far-left window."

They waited together in silence for a few moments and sure enough it appeared again. The movement of the reflected light signaled the possible presence of a telescope or a large camera lens.

Vartan pulled out his trusty monocular scope from the glove box and tried to get a better look, but he could not see much. The windows were closed with a slight gap in the curtains. He did detect some movement in the fabric.

"Someone is watching. Maybe." He brought his spyglass down and put it away.

"There is only one way to find out." Jaleh had her game face on, and he loved it.

"I was hoping you'd say that," Vartan said, retrieving a pistol from under the seat. He pulled back the slider to check it, then put it behind his back in his waistband, adjusting his jacket over it.

"You want to wait here and let me go?" She said with a smile.

"And let you have all the fun?"

"Fine, let's go. Armik is supposed to call after dinner."

They exited the vehicle and hurried in a direction away from the building. She grabbed his hand as they crossed the street. Her touch still excited him after all these years and it also made for a good cover. What mischief could two old lovebirds be up to anyway?

Once out of view of the east face of the building, they doubled back and around to the other side. They got to the back door just as someone else came out. Vartan smiled and slipped past with Jaleh.

The large lobby had a high ceiling, but the scanty decorations made the place appear cheaper than if they had left it bare. Vartan moved to the nearest stairwell. He would clear an escape route, while Jaleh took the elevator.

Taking the steps two at a time, he reached the top just after Jaleh. He was in great shape for his age, and the great pains he took to keep it that way seemed to pay off more and more often.

She was already heading to the door of the apartment on the north side of the building. She had her ear to it by the time he ran up to her. His chest heaved a little but he tried his best to slow it so Jaleh would not notice. She shook her head, indicating she could not hear any sounds from the flat. She ran her hand around the lock mechanism.

"Deadbolt," she whispered.

"Too noisy to pick and too hard to kick." He smiled at his clever accidental rhyme. Jaleh rolled her eyes and knocked on the door.

Vartan drew his gun and pressed his back flat to the wall.

A few seconds later a muffled voice called out to her.

"*Qui es la?*"

"*Martin, es que c'est toi?*"

"*Non, Desole.*"

She knocked again, harder.

"*Martin!*" she yelled. "*Martin, c'est Marie.*"

There was no answer, just the shadow on the viewer hole. She banged on the door with a closed fist even harder and louder. Vartan hoped no neighbors would come out. The lock clicked and the door opened slightly, the chain still on.

"Look, lady, I told you already—"

Vartan did not even have a chance to spin around before Jaleh kicked the door open with the force of a mule. The chain snapped with a loud thwack and the door's edge connected with the face of the person behind it. In a flash she had subdued the half-conscious, bleeding man. Vartan never ceased to be astonished by her skills.

He leapt into the apartment, weapon poised, looking for whoever else might be inside. He closed the door with his foot and ventured about, clearing the space room by room.

"Clear. Who have we got here?"

"Middle eastern male, mid-twenties." She applied pressure with her foot on the back of his neck and bent his arm against the shoulder joint. He gave a stifled cry.

"Mr. Norouzi, Bahman. Born in Iran. Didn't even bother to change that part," said Vartan, examining the passport which had laid on the coffee table in the sparsely furnished room.

"They are letting just about anyone in these days."

"You've been busy, Mr. Norouzi," Vartan said, referring to the photographic equipment with more than one high-powered lens. He walked over to the camera and flipped through the photos. "Several of the queen coming and leaving the apartment and a few of her in her sitting room chatting with a woman, probably a journalist or writer. There are a few of the prince coming to visit."

"Vartan," Jaleh said, getting his attention.

He looked up and spotted the large folder on a bookshelf that she pointed to. Inside, he found it filled with black and white surveillance photos, enlarged to 8x11.

"More of the queen and other staff, and family coming and going. Looks like he has been keeping tabs for a few months at least. Wait. Oh, Jesus." His jaw dropped.

"What is it?"

Vartan held up a photo of Armik on the street and one of himself at the tailor shop. He found none of Jaleh.

Her eyes widened at the sight of her son in a spy photo. She stepped harder on the man under her boot.

"Wait," he said. "Let me talk to him first."

He crossed the room and grabbed the man by the collar. He picked him up as he might a child's toy and slammed him against the drywall, putting a dent in it. "Who do you work for? Why are you watching us?"

"I'm a journalist—here doing a story about the old regime players."

"None of us were players. Why do you have my son's photo?"

Jaleh lifted the top of the coffee table and pulled out two handguns, raising them in the air. "There is a sniper rifle in here as well."

"Journalist, eh? How about I give you one chance to revise your story?" Rage boiled in Vartan's blood—a rare occurrence.

"Hey, I was just doing my job."

"Who hired you?"

"I don't know. They never gave me a name. Paid cash and sent me to this address. I didn't ask any questions."

"How long have you been tailing us?" Vartan fought to control himself.

"Four months." The man's voice had risen to almost a squeal.

"Do you know who we are?"

"No idea. I was just told to follow you when the queen wasn't in France."

"How did you deliver the information?" said Jaleh.

"Dead drop."

"Where?" Vartan put pressure on the man's joints, and they popped.

"They'll kill me if I tell you anything."

"You have bigger problems right now." Jaleh pressed the muzzle of one of the handguns to his eye.

"Alright, alright. Grand Mosque. Southwest corner. There's a loose brick. Chalk mark arrow on the green—upright means delivered."

"Now what should we do with him, dear?" Vartan already knew what he wanted to do.

"We could just let him go…off the balcony."

"No, please!" The teary-eyed spy let out a series of sobs.

"That would attract the police too quickly," said Vartan.

"Can't really shoot him here. Too noisy and we didn't bring a silencer."

"Knife?" He had one in his back pocket that would work.

"Messy," said Jaleh.

"Are you two serious? Listen, let me go and I'll disappear."

Vartan looked at his wife. She shook her head. He broke the man's neck with a quick twist of the head as if he was trying to spin a large top. Only it did not spin but rather dropped onto the floor with the torso in a crumpled heap.

"Good enough?" he said, straightening his clothes.

"Crude, but effective."

"Hey, I'm old school." Vartan flashed a smile.

The two of them quickly and quietly went about searching the entire residence. When they finished, they had a large cache of weapons, several ounces of cocaine, a bag of marijuana, and a large gym bag full of cash.

"Need some money for a vacation?" said Jaleh, holding up the bag.

"Well, he won't be needing it anymore."

"Cruise?"

"Noo!" Vartan laughed and cringed at the same time. "Let's stick to land."

"You're no fun." She teased.

Vartan packed several handguns and ammunition into the bag with the money. He dumped the drugs in the toilet. "Call your Jewish cleaner friends. Make it like he was never here. Tell them we'll pay cash."

CHAPTER FORTY-FOUR

Kabul, Afghanistan
January 7, 2000

Before leaving, Armik had been given a description of Afghanistan. 'Imagine the Old Testament. Now, give everybody white Toyota trucks.' Upon arrival, he noted how perfectly accurate that statement was.

Basra looked reduced to little more than a pile of rubble around some flat-roofed adobe buildings—a dirty, dangerous, backward place, even by third-world standards.

The barracks at their base sat close to the runway that had F18s constantly taking off within 500 meters of where they worked. The noise was so loud Armik wore earplugs all the time rather than risk losing his hearing.

The constant attacks only added to the sound pollution. The enemy was very dependable when it came to those. They fired rockets at them once or twice a week. The location of the rocket could easily be determined once fired and a unit would invariably be sent out. The enemy knew this and looked for ways to make certain they had enough time to be far away before the soldiers arrived.

One of their best ideas was to dig a hole in the ground and put the rocket on a rail. They were very resourceful, rigging up timers out of scraps. Most commonly, they took a bag of ice and put the fuse across it. As the ice melted, it would eventually hit the contact and send the rocket screaming toward the base. The amount of time it took for the ice to melt was how long they had to get away. *Pretty ingenious.*

One of these rocket launches was the first time Armik ever actually came under fire. He would never forget it. The weapon came so close he could see the shrapnel bouncing off the dirt, making it fly everywhere.

"Your friends are at it again," said Private Thomas Leduc. Another rocket blew over their head like fireworks in Times Square.

"Shut up. I told you, I'm Persian, not Arab," Armik said, tired of the common misconception that they were one and the same.

"Well, what's the difference?"

"We actually eat our goats." Armik gave him a wide grin.

"Lucky thing for the goats."

"What's wrong with Gaunthier?" Armik said, noticing one of his fellow soldiers shaking uncontrollably.

"Ah, he gets nervous around loud noises," said Leduc. "Hey, Gaunthier, you know this is no place for a woman, right?"

Laughter rolled through the ranks, but Gaunthier did not really seem to register it.

"Easy there, Flintstone. Your Neanderthal is showing," said the loud female voice of their commanding officer, Josette Fortier. "Let's go boys. We're off in five. Get your gear."

The trucks rolled out after five minutes as promised and took them further into the city. Signs of life were everywhere among the ruins, conducting business as usual, making the best of utter destitution. The people were resilient, Armik had to give them that. Seeing their suffering, he could not help but think of the stories regarding the Armenian Genocide.

They drove around the city, street by street, gunners on mounted cannons atop every vehicle. The radios were abuzz with chatter exchanging information and drone scout reports. Often, Armik would see the US Marines go from one side of a clearing to the other. The videographers that followed them around taking footage would certainly make them look heroic.

"Look at them," said Leduc. "They are like movie stars."

"Well, I feel better having them here than not. The Taliban would rather shoot at them than us." Armik chuckled but there was truth to his words.

A yell of "stop" brought the entire motorcade to an abrupt halt in the middle of the street. Armik jumped off the truck and raised his rifle to the ready, looking to see what had caused the delay. A small object stuck out of the dirt-covered asphalt. He walked to it with extreme caution, scanning the rooftops for any signs that hell was about to rain down on them.

"IED," Armik said.

"Okay, let's get Disposal out here. Cobert, you guys stay with this until they get here. Meanwhile, the rest of us will go around it carefully and look out for more."

Armik got back into the truck, and they were on the road again, cutting into a Taliban stronghold area of the city. They arrived at a small F.O.B. or Forward Operating Base. They parked their trucks behind some trees and disembarked to head out on a foot patrol.

Another French infantry unit was already there. They walked together into a large field of grape rows that looked like mud walls about five feet high with grapes growing on them.

"For a country that doesn't drink, they sure have a lot of wine grapes. I wonder why that is?"

"Ask Armo here, they're his people."

"Hi. Did I mention I was Armenian, not Arab? We invented

drinking."

"I thought you were Persian."

"Persian/Armenian/Jewish actually—and I was born in Paris so..."

"So you're as messed up as the rest of us."

"Basically."

Through a break in the grape rows Armik saw a wide-open poppy field—a sea of green, dotted by little pink flowers.

"Now I could use some of that with my wine," said Leduc.

"It would make you whine even more than you do now." Armik laughed at his own joke.

The two crops were separated by a large ditch cutting across the entire length, which ran further than Armik's eyes could see. Someone saw wires coming out of the ground, so they were told to take a knee. Everybody went down and the first infantry unit went up to make sure it was not an IED.

"These people can't build a toaster, but they can put bombs everywhere."

"Well, at least they are not shooting at us."

A ringing struck Armik's ears, then everything else went silent. An explosion had occurred right next to them. Hit with an RPG shock wave, the projectile struck one of the grape rows and a large pile of dirt. The dark, eye-stinging cloud took minutes to dissipate.

They returned shots, and the firefight began. Bullets streaked across the dirty air like low falling stars. The enemy seemed to be attacking from all sides, but Armik could not see any of them. The craggy, rocky hills that one sees in news footage of Afghanistan, with a turbaned shepherd standing in the wide-open landscape, was nothing like the Afghanistan he was in. The lush green vegetation and countless trees were reminiscent of a tropical country. Endless opportunities for the enemy to find cover abounded.

"I can't even tell where the bullets are coming from." Armik fired in bursts, his aim random.

"This is crazy, we are just fighting blind." Gauthier shook without control, his rifle firing more by accident than on purpose.

"Just return fire or send some grenades wherever you see movement." Armik focused his mind, reverting to his training. He lobbed two grenades as far from him as he could. Seconds later they blew, and he heard screams.

After that, it quieted down to an occasional shot. The air was clearing but they still could not get a visual on the enemy.

"They must be holding down at the edge of that fence line on the other side of the poppy field." Leduc put another clip in his rifle.

"Look where my grenades landed," said Armik, pointing to a large, blackened patch in the middle of a sea of four-foot tall poppies. "It must have been their nest."

"Lucky hit, Armo."

"Tell me about it."

"Hey, where the hell is Gauthier going? Gauthier! Come back here, you crazy son of a bitch." Leduc tried to go after him but Gauthier grabbed his backpack.

Gauthier had shed his pack, running unarmed into the field. The fear seemed to have gotten the best of him, causing legs to just carry him in a random direction.

"He's lost it. He's going to get himself killed."

"We need cover fire," Armik yelled. "But don't hit him.

The men all fired toward the foliage, not knowing where their enemies were hiding or if they had decided to run away already.

It came with no immediate reaction. They had fired off a good many rounds and all was quiet but for a screaming Gauthier, getting smaller by the second. Armik rose to retrieve him when an explosion sounded again.

He could not tell up from down. His eyes closed. How long he remained that way he had no idea. It could have been a second—it could have been an hour. When his senses returned at last, he found himself down on his belly. Propping himself up on his elbow, he could now make out the enemies' muzzle flashes in the distance. Gauthier lay on the ground.

"Gauthier, stay down." Armik ran toward his fallen comrade, his steps off balance from the explosion. The others immediately offered more cover fire.

The field was wide open but with the poppies so high it was hard to see where he was going. He only hoped he was going in the right direction to reach Gauthier.

A few bullets whizzed by his head. He dropped to his stomach again and started crawling. When he looked back, he saw several of their gun trucks laying down a good amount of fire into the field. .50 caliber machine guns mounted on those things sprayed the field as if they were fire hoses.

He could not hear a thing. Something was wrong. He heard only ringing but he knew they were laying rounds down, so he concentrated on Gauthier.

Crawling again, Armik felt something skim over his shoulder, taking a chunk off his body armor. He knew he had been shot, but not to what extent.

They were putting a lot of lead downrange, so he just crawled a little further to where Gauthier lay in a small ditch in the middle of the field. He could have gotten up and run at any time. He felt no pain at all, except for a slight burning in his shoulder. Perhaps it had just been a graze or a flesh wound. He did not want to reach up and touch it, in case he discovered that he was, in fact, badly hit. It might distract him from his goal to extract Gauthier. The man lay on his back in the grass, groaning.

"What the hell were you thinking? You will get yourself killed quickly out here if you can't keep it together."

"Help me." He moaned. "I don't want to die. I have a kid at home." Armik's hearing had come back enough to make out his words.

"Okay, okay, shut up. Your kid won't be an orphan today."

Gauthier groaned even more. The cover fire continued in spurts. They were firing higher now, in the likely event that the enemy had retreated. But they had not all retreated. Armik saw the grass and poppies moving not far from them. He cupped Gauthier's mouth with his hand, quieting him. He drew his sidearm.

"Someone's coming," he whispered. "Don't make a sound."

Armik kept low in the grass and moved toward the rustling, going wide enough to flank whoever was coming. He stopped just as a leg passed inches away from him. There were two. They were moving in a cautious manner, their rifles trained ahead of them. He rose once they passed, put his gun near the back of the first man's skull, and pulled the trigger. The body lurched forward and dropped. By the time he had turned his pistol to his left, the second man was staring right at him.

The man dropped his rifle to the ground and raised his arms in an apparent surrender. But in the blink of an eye, he grabbed Armik's wrist, pushing it up to escape the line of fire. His strength surprised Armik. With the other hand, he produced a long knife that could have been a short sword. He slashed once, still holding the wrist.

Armik caught the man's knife arm on the second slash, pushing it toward his body. He leaned in hard and fast, ramming his forehead into the enemy's nose. The crunch echoed in his still ringing ears.

His foe went down on both knees, his iron grip released. His hands went up again in surrender—for real this time. Armik re-aimed his pistol and took the shot without hesitation.

Leduc and a few others came upon his position moments later, just in time to see him standing over two dead Taliban soldiers.

"You planning on killing them all yourself, Armo, or do you care to share the action?" Leduc said with a grin.

"If I waited for you, the war would be over by the time I got a shot off."

"Ha. The war is never over, my brother."

They went back to see how Gauthier was holding up. He still lay on his back in the field. The barrage of cannon fire had stopped, signaling the enemy had fled the scene—or died. It was hard to tell which, but either would do.

"You're hit," Leduc pointed out.

Armik had forgotten. "Seems to be no big deal," he said, examining his wound for the first time. "Looks like it just skimmed over my shoulder. It opened me up pretty good though. A few stitches for sure, but it doesn't look like it caused any permanent damage."

"You'll probably need to have a skin graft done. Maybe some skin from your ass to cover the gash, but I don't think it's going to hurt your golfing arm any."

"I play soccer anyway, so I'm okay with it."

"What the hell kind of sport is soccer? That's not a sport." Leduc gave a smile, respect now in his eyes.

"Yeah, that would mean you had to think and run at the same time. I can see why that wouldn't work for you."

After about twenty minutes, the adrenaline had begun to wear off and Armik started to feel the sting. It did not bother him so much, knowing the alternative.

On the way back to base, he remained lost in his thoughts. He had just taken two lives, and the only thing that bothered him was he was not bothered at all.

CHAPTER FORTY-FIVE

Jaleh held the photo up to the sunlight. Her son's image, marred by a slight blur, spoke of the distance from which the photographer had stood to capture it. This was not an accidental shot. Whoever the interested parties were, they were interested in Armik. But why? Some sort of revenge plot? They had been so careful over the years. Only a handful of trusted handlers knew anything about them. Then again, this was a game where anything was possible—even probable.

With an outstretched arm, she held the photograph up against the edge of the rooftop overlooking the street where their tailor shop was located. This had to be the spot, no doubt. In the distance, the exact location her son had been standing loomed before her, and a sense of dread sent shivers through her body. She searched the rooftop of the modern building for any clues that may have been left behind and was not disappointed. While obvious evidence had been cleared out, the habitual flicking of cigarettes had left behind ashes of a moment in time. They were concentrated in the crevice between the roof and the ledge, where the wind could not clear it away.

While she could not be certain the ashes were from the photographer, the buildup spoke of a person who had been stationed in one particular spot for an extended period of time rather than a smoker who came out to the roof to have a short break now and again. A disgusting habit that was not only bad for you, but also gave away clandestine intentions. Jaleh now appreciated Vartan even more for letting go of the dreadful addiction years ago.

She pulled out her burner phone and called her husband on his.

"I was just thinking about you," he said, answering in a cheery voice.

"Oh really? And just what were you thinking about me, exactly?"

"I was thinking it's been over an hour since we spoke. Surely you must be missing me by now. Then my phone rang."

"I'm always amazed at how well you know me."

"I'd like to think so."

"I know you do. Anyway, the other reason for my call. I found the spot."

"Anything interesting?"

"It's cold. At least a day or two. But the person who was snapping photos was someone other than our friend. Or, perhaps, they were together. In any case, it was not a solo act. Our guy was not a smoker."

"You always did have a good nose for that."

"Why, thank you." Movement from the top of the building across the street caught her attention.

"Why don't you come home, and we can discuss our next moves. I made lunch."

An uneasiness came over her—trusted instincts warning her something was not right. "Lunch sounds good. I'm just going to look around a bit more, then head home."

"You have company?" Vartan read her better than she ever would admit, even after all these years. "Stay put. I'll be right—"

"Negative. It's a small problem if anything. Might be nothing."

Vartan sighed, experience having taught him not to bother arguing. "Call me when it's resolved. And be safe."

"Always." She kissed the phone and hung up.

Lowering her head, she pretended to be looking for something, but her eyes strained upward to get a discreet view of the roof across the street. The man was dressed as some sort of caretaker, with white coveralls and a painter's hat. He fiddled with a long wood-handled tool, raking at the gutters with casual movements. But even from that distance, he stood out. He was too…clean for the type of work he was doing.

Alarm bells went off in her mind. She could not see from her position, but she would bet a handful of euros that he had on shoes that were much too comfortable and expensive for his disguise. It was a fatal flaw that most operatives never deprived themselves of—sensible footwear. She needed a closer look.

Showing no notice of his presence, she turned and went back to the door that led downstairs. She pocketed the photos and reached into her purse, flipping the safety on her small pistol to the off position.

She exited the building and crossed the street without looking up, moving away from her target. She walked past a bakery and feigned interest in the window display. As if on a whim, she entered the shop, inhaling its sweet warm aroma. She walked past the counter and into the kitchen. The staff, too stunned to protest, stared at her with wide eyes.

"Short cut. Big rush. Sorry," she said without slowing her pace.

Out the door, she doubled back and hurried to the building where the man had been. The back door opened just as she arrived. A woman came out. Jaleh grabbed the handle before it shut. The woman gave her a backward glance but did not seem to care much.

One thing she had learned in her years as an operative was that as long as you acted like you belong somewhere, very few people ever questioned your presence. It was a rule that had served her well. Vartan was a master at acting like he owned every room he walked into. People always let him walk right in, like the lady who had opened the door for her.

Moving with speed up the stairs, she heard footsteps coming toward her from above. On the eighth landing, she opened the door and went into the hallway. She pressed her back against the wall and waited. Fortunately, none of the residents were about.

Once enough time had passed, she opened the door with a cautious push. She did not have time to register the displaced air around her and only the edge of the open door prevented the strike of a wooden broom handle from connecting with her head.

A piece of it broke off in splinters. She sprang back into the hallway and jabbed her hand into her purse, but the man, large and lean like an athlete, lunged for her. He tackled her down like a football player. *American.* The thought whizzed through her mind as she hit the ground hard.

With her shooting arm pinned, she could not pull her weapon free from her purse.

Before she could lower her chin, a thick forearm landed across her throat. The immense pressure closed off her air passage. Jaleh bucked, trying to get the heavy man off, or at least free the gun. But he was too strong, and it had been years since she had been in hand-to-hand combat. Through blurring eyes, she tried to get a look at the face of her attacker. Young, pockmarked, a scar, the blond-haired opponent showed no sign of emotion or exertion. A professional, but for who?

The view became dimmer under the increasing pressure on her neck. Another futile thrust of her hips failed to save her. Time slowed and she thought of Vartan and Armik. They still needed her. Her finger found the cold trigger. She squeezed it, unable to tell where the barrel was pointing. With barely the strength to fire, she heard the pop. The forearm lifted and she gasped, cool air rushing back into her lungs. Jaleh made a blind roll to get some distance. The man cursed in English. *American.*

The sound of apartment doors opening reached her ears. She staggered to her feet. The man was gone. *Damn.*

She shook her head to clear her vision. "Police," she said with a croak. "Get back in your homes."

The sound of immediate slamming doors confirmed compliance. Taking a deep breath, Jaleh ran out to the stairwell after her prey, gun in hand this time. It took only a second to see the blood droplets that told her he had gone down the stairs. He had only been grazed, judging by the amount of red liquid he left behind. It had been enough to save her life though.

She took the stairs two at a time and arrived at the door to find it smeared with blood too. She took a pause and another breath before shouldering it open, her firearm pointed up in a two-handed grip.

He was nowhere in sight. She looked for more of his trail, but that had vanished too. Her handbag hung open at her side. A dark-rimmed hole the size of a coin allowed her to see right through it.

Ugh. Not again. I loved this purse.

Tucking the weapon away, she headed back to the bakery. Her hand went to her throat. It was sore and probably bruised. Vartan was not going to be happy. The staff of the bakery again allowed her through unhindered. This time they seemed stunned by what must have been a drastic change in her appearance. She caught a glimpse of herself in the door glass and smoothed her disheveled hair before walking out.

"There you are." A worried-looking Vartan stood before her.

CHAPTER FORTY-SIX

Kabul, Afghanistan
February 6, 2000

After a few days' stay in the hospital, Armik received a summons to a nondescript building way over on the southwest corner of the base. The level of security covering the building surprised him. He had never noticed it before.

The minute he entered he was relieved of his sidearm and ushered to a large office on the third floor by an MP who may as well have been a mute. Inside, a dark walnut bookcase lined the entire left-hand wall. Next to that sat a leather sofa with a fur rug over the back and an Indian blanket draped over the arm. The far wall had a large gas fireplace and mantle dominating the center, with bookshelves lining it on either side. On the mantle rested two antique clocks and a painting of three jazz musicians. There was a television on the shelf to the right. In front of the shelf stood an upright piano and bench in dark walnut. Hanging on the wall above the piano hung another abstract painting of jazz musicians.

The door opened behind Armik, interrupting his mental tour.

"Mr. Vartanian," said Colonel Cartier, his medals sparkling off the chest of his uniform. He walked in with another man behind him.

The man's massive bulk forced him to step sideways to get into the room. He wore jeans and a brown plaid button down shirt. His large Stetson cowboy hat and belt buckle stood out as accents to his pointed-toe cowboy boots.

"Sir. Yes, sir." Armik saluted, not knowing the man's rank.

"At ease, soldier."

Armik relaxed and placed his hands behind his back. "You wanted to see me, sir?"

"Yes. This is Jack Smith, Director of National Intelligence from Langley."

Smith stuck a slick palm out and Armik gave it a hard shake.

"Pleasure to meet you, Armik. I've heard only great things."

"Langley, sir? I'm not sure I understand. Why is the CIA—"

"That understanding is above your security clearance, son."

"Yes, sir."

"Suffice it to say, the US and France have certain interests in common and work together from time to time. This would be one of those times."

Armik nodded, but his reeling head tried to anticipate what they could want with him. His instincts told him it could not be anything good. Smith had a perpetual leering look about him. His pale, sweaty skin gave the impression he would pass out from the heat at any moment, but something in his eyes looked sharp. And the way he stared…as if he recognized Armik from somewhere and was simply waiting for him to remember.

"I see here you scored the highest in your class in everything," said the colonel.

"I'm not sure, sir."

"What do you mean?"

"I never asked how anyone else did, sir."

"Well, Goddamnit, if I say you scored the highest, you better Goddamn believe it, soldier," the commander shouted.

"Sir. Yes, sir." He snapped back to attention.

"At ease."

Armik complied. "I appreciate you letting me know, sir."

"Well you swim faster, run further, fight better, and shoot straighter than anyone since…well hell… Me."

"Thank you, sir."

"Why did you join the military, son?"

"My father wanted to keep me out of trouble, sir."

"What does your father do?"

"He's a tailor, sir."

"Well, that's why he knows damn all about the military. See, here, we throw you right into trouble, headfirst. Do you want to be thrown into trouble headfirst for your country, son?"

"Sir. Yes, sir."

"Good. I have some good news and some bad news. The bad news is that you are no longer going to be with your platoon. The good news is that you will not have to wander around this hell hole looking for rice cooker bombs anymore. You have been assigned to a special mission."

"Special mission, sir?"

"Goddamnit, did I stutter, son?"

"No, sir."

"How is your Farsi?"

"Passable, sir."

"Good. You leave at 0800 hours by helicopter tomorrow to complete a short, specialized training and get right into the field. Mr. Smith here will be there to brief you when you arrive at your next destination. There is a war going on, son.

There is always a war going on. We need men. Good men. Men of substance. Are you such a man, soldier?"

"Sir. Yes, sir."

"Get a shower, some grub. Pack your kit and get a good night's rest. Wings up at 0800."

"Yes, sir." He saluted, did an about-face, and went for the door.

"Oh, and soldier."

Armik turned back to the commander, hand on the doorknob.

"Sir?"

"From here on in, everything you hear, see, and do, you've neither heard, seen, or done. Your training is now classified. That means not a word to your comrades or to your Sergeant. And as far as your dad, the tailor, and any girl you may have left behind, your deployment hasn't changed. Is that understood?"

"Yes, sir," he said.

Armik walked out the door, closing it behind him. His head spun. What had he gotten into? What was he going to tell his parents? The speed of events boggled his mind.

He headed down to the mess hall to grab a bite. They were serving some kind of mystery meat, like a hybrid of ham and salami in one big slice. It was hard to swallow, much like this whole special mission business. What did that even mean?

Dumping the rest of his inedible dinner into the garbage can, he walked over to his dorm. Packing up his kit, he realized he did not enjoy being unable to see his future with clarity.

CHAPTER FORTY-SEVEN

The atmosphere was thick with dust. The wind tossed the tiny rough particles about, striking Rostem's face and bouncing off his sunglasses like hail on a windshield.

Upon his arrival at the Kabul International Airport, he was whisked away by a Lincoln waiting just beyond the terminal doors. The driver had held up a sign that read Rahimi, the name he used while dealing with the French and American intelligence agencies.

The old Town Car passed multiple checkpoints without even slowing down. They drove toward the outskirts of the city nestled in a valley, the Hindu Kush mountains looming in the distance. Three thousand years of history stood before him, but Rostem did not care for such things. He would just as soon blow it all to dust.

Traffic, as bad or worse than Tehran, abated once they pulled onto the Kabul Bagram Airport Road. Hardly a vehicle could be seen on the long, straight highway.

The scenery was a blur of browns and beiges, with hills of all sizes. The monotony reminded Rostem that he had not slept in days. He closed his eyes halfway, resting but not asleep. His driver remained silent, which pleased him.

An hour and a half later, the car sped through into Bagram Airfield, pausing only to let the gates open. They sped across the base, passing soldiers in formation among several large airstrips, watchtowers, and numerous hangars and support buildings. At last, they came to a dusty stop in front of a plain warehouse style structure.

Through his dark sunglasses, Rostem made note of the numerous cameras pointing in his direction. He kept his head down to avoid offering a clear shot despite his disguise being sufficient to hide his identity. He was taken up three flights of stairs and directed to a large brown door in the center of the hall.

He walked into the commander's office without knocking, turning to watch a soldier walk out of the administrative office. The kid looked young, but he had shoulders like a quarterback and the same swagger. Rostem wore an elegant silk suit, his hair dyed a shade lighter, and his mustache like a pencil across his lip. He spoke in a thick accent for the men in the room.

"I assume that was the soldier." Rostem put on the act, knowing full well what the son of the Persian looked like.

"Yeah, that was him. Vartanian, as requested." Colonel Cartier seemed annoyed, as he always did.

"He looks formidable. What did he say?" Rostem said.

"What do you mean, what did he say?" The colonel scoffed at the question.

"Did he accept?"

"There is nothing to accept. This isn't a ballet academy where he gets to accept the role of Prima Ballerina. This is the military. We tell our soldiers what to do."

"Point taken. How did he seem to take the news?"

"I didn't care to look."

"I see." The colonel's insolence made Rostem want to slit the man's throat here and now. Only the bigger picture prevented him from acting on that impulse. "As long as the thing is done, it doesn't really matter." Rostem smiled.

"Do you think he will be the right fit for this, Smith? He's good and has a killer's instinct, but he is still wet behind the ears." The colonel reached behind his desk and pulled out a whiskey bottle and three tumblers, filling each with a dark brown liquid.

"You said yourself that he was top tier," said Smith. "What are you worried about?"

"He's just a kid. I'm all for snatching up prodigies, but he's fresh out of basic—not even done his first tour." Without bothering to hand over the other glasses, Cartier picked up one and downed it.

"Is this your usual drinking time, colonel?" Smith took one and handed the other to Rostem.

"No. I'm a half-hour late."

Smith chuckled and took a small sip of his drink. "This one is unique, trust me. He's already up for commendations. The kid's a hero."

"Don't you Americans have your own soldiers to choose from, or did you run out?" The Colonel tightened his perpetual scowl.

"It's next to impossible to find someone with all his criteria as well as the right ethnic background and family connections. I'm telling you—this kid is important."

"Alright, Smith, I hope you know what you're doing. You can have him after his first round of training. But get him back to us in one piece. We have our own ops to run here too."

The big cowboy, splayed out on the leather sofa like a piece of whale meat, turned to Rostem. "I assume, Mr. Rahimi, that plans on your end are in order."

"Of course, Mr. Smith. We are ready and waiting." Rostem set the glass down on the desk without drinking it.

"And of course, the new government, under your leadership, will cooperate with both American and French interests?" Smith's voice took a more serious tone, even with his comical southern drawl.

"As discussed, we will be partners in a mutually beneficial arrangement."

"Okay, good. We had similar arrangements with the Shah, his father, and his successor. Eventually, they each became suddenly afflicted by delusions of grandeur and we had to step in to…affect changes, shall we say. Frankly, I need a win here."

"I assure you, Mr. Smith," said Rostem. "The new Democratic Republic of Iran will play ball with its western neighbors. You will get all the oil you need. I do not harbor any of the delusions of the leaders in the past or present. I am a practical man. You help me get into power—I will give you what you want."

"And this insane plan of yours," said Cartier, "all hinges on one young, simple, soldier?"

"Oh colonel, he is so much more than that. But he is only the first piece of the puzzle." Rostem could not help the smile that grew across his face, stretching his mustache.

"And the other pieces?" said Cartier.

"When Vartanian is in play, the other pieces will come."

PART 7

CHAPTER FORTY-EIGHT

Tehran, Iran
July 14, 2000

With a firm chokehold in place, Armik cranked the man's neck, squeezing his windpipe and compressing his carotid artery.

"Who sent you to follow me?"

As expected, he made no attempt to answer. By this time, his pursuer's vision would be going black, making him aware of his pending loss of consciousness. His only saving grace being he would no longer have to suffer the agony of his broken arm.

The good arm went limp, and the futile struggle came to an end. Armik let the body drop to the dirt-crusted ceramic floor of the public washroom. The victim's drooping head scraped against the filthy stall wall. He checked for a pulse and found a weak one. A quick search of the pockets produced a sharp, military-style boot knife, some gum, and a roll of Iranian currency—all of which he took. Without identification, cell phone, or clues, Armik could not tell what team the man played for. He had the black hair and tanned skin of a local, much like his own complexion, however that meant very little.

With one down, he had one more to go. Armik locked the

stall door from the inside as someone entered the restroom to use the urinal. He listened for the occupant to finish. It took only a minute before he heard the flush and the door open and close again. He did not even wash his hands. *Disgusting.*

Crawling out from under the stall, Armik made certain to give his hands a thorough scrub and rinse before exiting. It did not take long to spot his second tail. The man in a blue New York Yankees baseball cap had taken a covert interest in him just after he had noticed the first man. Perhaps he had picked up the tails at the airport, despite his attempt to be cautious.

Outside, unwholesome vapors of polluted air blanketed the chaotic jumble of concrete and insane traffic. He found Tehran to be a strange but wonderful place. The vast size and sheer intensity of this modern city stunned him. Armik, having never traveled anywhere but Cuba, Florida, and the Bahamas had not been prepared for the shock of culture—even if he shared that culture. This led him to wonder, and not for the first time, why he had been chosen for this assignment.

He had managed to pass customs on arrival without issue. The fake passport provided by Jack Smith garnered no attention at all. He went through unmolested.

The thought of being in his parents' country for the first time did distract him somewhat. He had come here on an assignment fraught with serious risks, but he could not help the surge of curiosity flowing through him. He wished his dad could be here with him to experience it.

Thousands of people plodded through the colliding sounds of incessant horns and loud voices. Mixed scents of exotic fruits, spices, perfumes, and diesel fuel choked the senses, but awakened the soul. Ghosts of thousands of years past strode without a sound and without notice in the wake of modern footsteps.

People kept singling him out as a foreigner. Being approached by so many random locals he found just a little unnerving. He had no idea that people could be so friendly to strangers. The number of invitations he declined with regret seemed unbelievable. He promised himself that he would have to come back again as a real tourist, if he ever made it out this time around.

The man in the cap stopped to look at postcards while Armik tied his shoe. He inspected his pursuer in the reflection of a small, busy pastry shop. Young, clean-shaven, well built, and well trained. A friend, perhaps—or a foe. He had no way to tell for sure. An accident down the street caused the man to turn and look. Armik stole the opportunity, slipping into the bakery.

Trying to blend in with the other customers, he kept watch out the window while picking a few walnut cookies to snack on. Sure enough, the man passed the store looking frantic, his earbud hanging down the collar of his shirt. Armik lingered a little longer, then paid for his cookies. Before leaving, he took off his reversible shirt and flipped it inside out, so that it went from blue to white. Placing a cap on his head, he stepped back out into the sunshine.

The man had gone, so he continued the short distance to his destination. The instruction packet told him to take a cab from the airport, drop his bags at the hotel, then go into the city center. There he was to change cabs before heading to the north of the city. In Shemiran he would buy a ticket to the Niavaran Palace Museum, home of the last Shah of Iran before the Islamic Revolution.

The palace compound loomed high, nestled at the southern foothills of the snow-capped Alborz mountains. It was a beautiful part of the city. A surprising number of people stopped him along the way, eager to offer him directions or random invitations to tea. One lady even went as far as to walk him to the entrance gates.

"Ma'am, really. It's very kind of you, but there's no need to walk me all the way there," Armik said, his Farsi more than passable, if a little rusty.

"Nonsense. You are a guest in our country. You should not have to wander around alone, God forbid."

The elderly woman had her white hair tied back under a dark, fringed headscarf, which she wore high and loose above her hairline. Her weather-beaten face held two black orbs for eyes. Stooped over from the burden of her many years, she still walked with the vitality of someone half her age.

At the entrance, Armik paid for his ticket and thanked the old lady. She told the museum security that he was a foreigner and a good boy and to help him if he needed it. They, in turn, agreed to do so with eagerness and curiosity.

"You are too kind, ma'am. Thank you again."

"Please, don't mention it at all. Make sure you go see the cars, young man."

"Cars? Sure, I will…"

"The cars." The woman grabbed his arm with a surprising firmness and lowered her voice, giving it a more serious tone. "Make sure you go see them. First."

She walked away quicker than an old lady ought. In seconds, she rounded a corner and vanished out of sight.

Past the main entrance gate stood a large billboard indicating what he could expect to see on the property. His reading of the language did not come back to him with the same eloquence as the spoken word.

"Ah, okay I hope that's the right place," he said to himself. "I guess I should ask someone."

A man sweeping the grounds pointed him in the direction of a large warehouse type building. People strolled about the property, moving in and out of the structure, taking photos for posterity.

Armik stepped in and his mouth opened, finding himself amid the most wonderful car collection he had ever seen. A 1974 Lamborghini Countach, a rare 1971 Lamborghini Miura SVJ, a 1950s bronze C30 Chrysler coupe. He came close to losing his mind.

"That's a very nice one, don't you think?" said a voice behind him.

Armik spun around. Caught by surprise, he almost took a man's head off, but stopped himself in time.

"Yes, sir," the man said, acting undaunted by his startled reflexes, "these cars are something else. That Countach was given to the crown prince by his aunt for passing his driving test. And that C30? That was bought by the Shah for his second wife, Soraya Esfandiary, at the Geneva motor show. It has a pure gold dashboard, refrigerator, record player, and air conditioning. They sure lived the good life back then."

"And the leaders now? They've taken a vow of poverty, have they?" His father's words were now coming out of his mouth.

"Careful, kid." The man chuckled, taking a nervous look around. "Words like that will get you in trouble here. This isn't Paris."

"Duly noted. Thanks." The man had said Paris, revealing himself as the contact.

"This is for you." He pointed to a burlap rucksack resting on the ground between them. "Everything you need is in there. I'm your man in town. There's a phone if you need me. Number three on the speed dial."

"Why three?" Armik said.

"What?" The man looked puzzled.

"Why three and not one or two?"

"What the hell difference does it make?"

"None." Armik smiled.

"Okay then. Call only if you need something. There is cash, as well as a hotel key with directions. Don't go back to the one you're booked in. Your luggage has already been moved. It's not the Hilton, but it's not a dump either. Green Mercedes in the parking lot is yours. Gassed up. Bring it back gassed up."

"Got it."

"Good luck, kid," he said, turning to leave.

"Hey, what's your name?"

"Oh, yeah. Right. It's…uh…Boris."

"Boris? What kind of Persian name is Boris?"

"What the hell difference does it make?" He called out walking away.

CHAPTER FORTY-NINE

Tehran, Iran
July 14, 2000

As night fell, the blue haze of day lifted to reveal the stars. The city seemed to come to life, making the transition from a hurried survival mode to a more relaxed, enjoyable atmosphere. Bright neon lights came on everywhere, and men, women and children intermingled around a host of street musicians and vendors of the most aromatic food. Some of the familiar scents reminded Armik of his mother's cooking.

Taking pains to shake any tails he might have acquired along the way, Armik did not inspect the contents of the envelope until he reached his hotel, the Persian Kowsar. Boris was right, it was no Hilton, but cozy enough with its royal red curtains and yellow walls. It was also clean as could be expected, and he had a decent view of the river from his balcony.

The Mercedes had been another experience altogether. A relic from the early nineties, the little box-shaped, light metallic green thing had a dent on every door and a large crack across the windshield. The stick shift refused to go into third, so he had to rev it high and go from second to fourth every time—not quite the low-key mode of transportation he had envisioned. Driving among maniacal drivers had been hard enough on its own.

He poured the contents of the envelope out on the tightly made queen bed. A large wad of American cash fell out along with a cell phone—also from the nineties—and a nine-millimeter semi-automatic handgun. A passport, Italian, also came with the bundle. A sticky note with his new name, Giovanni Aquila, clung to the red cover.

In the back pages of the passport, he found a photo. It appeared to be a surveillance still—taken from a distance but zoomed in to make the image clear enough to see even the moles on the man's skin.

Armik flipped the photo over. On the back were a few typed words—an address, a main intersection, a name, Doctor Benjamin Barron, and the words target and liquidate.

What the hell? That can't be right.

This was supposed to be an intel-gathering mission. He picked up the phone, opened the flap and pressed three.

A sleepy voice answered after several rings. "Yes?"

"Boris?"

"Who?" The person at the other end cleared his throat.

"Boris, I'm looking for Boris."

"Yeah, yeah, Boris. That's me. What is it?"

"Hey, I think there's been a mistake with my mission parameters."

"No. No mistake." The sound of a cigarette being lit followed.

"Yeah, this was not part of the plans I was given."

"Plans change. We change with them. Cogs in the wheel and all that. What can I tell you, kid? Call me if you need me. Good luck."

"No. Wait. Boris. Boris. Damn it." Armik tossed the phone back on the bed.

Who the hell is this doctor and why am I supposed to kill him?

He stood, grabbed his keys, and walked out, heading for the business office off of the lobby. There he found an unused computer with a large, old-style monitor. He opened the search portal and typed in the doctor's name.

He opened the first link that came up, an Al Jazeera news file:

Israeli Nuclear Physicist Missing, Thought Dead.

Was he kidnapped and taken here? Or was he here of his own free will. His head spun and his empty stomach churned, but he realized he did not have that much of a choice. They had trained him to kill, and here he was in a hostile country, with a target. He would have to do it, or risk becoming a target himself. But before deciding, he wanted to do a little reconnaissance.

He grabbed a few kabobs in barbari bread to-go and drove to the address, according to the map. He opted to leave his gun in the hotel room on the off chance he might be pulled over. The directions took him to a posh neighborhood, not far from the location of his new hotel, in the Niavaran District.

The North, as in most cities in the world, was where the upper class lived. The districts were nestled into the mountains, the architecture having a more European feel than Persian. Besides well maintained streets, the area had a noticeable upgrade in air quality when compared to the lower areas of Tehran he had driven through.

The target residence ended up being quite large, connected to a massive front lawn that boasted a fountain and a roundabout driveway. Darkness had set in by the time he arrived, so the house's myriad of pot lights lit up the place like a Christmas display, casting well orchestrated shadows in every direction.

He saw no security to speak of but for several sensor lights and the flashing red light by the door indicating an alarm. The "Beware of Dog" sign on the low stone wall around the yard stood out, yet he saw no dog in sight, no bones, no bowls. A sign was less expensive than a dog.

There were no bodyguards as far as he could tell, though he wished he had binoculars with him to get a better look.

Two beams of lights from the other side of the hill heralded the approach of a vehicle. Armik slumped in his seat as it broke the horizon line. Once it passed without slowing, he straightened back up to look. A black Rolls Royce pulled into the round driveway and stopped in front of the large double doors. Two men got out. One had gray, straggly hair like the photo of the doctor. The other looked like a plain clothed revolutionary guard. He detected no sign of coercion or fear suggested in his movements.

Traitor.

A little burst of anger took hold of him, but he reminded himself that he could not make this personal just because of his mother's Jewish background. Still, it helped harden his resolve to complete his mission. On the surface, it looked easy enough. He noted the time of the target's arrival. He would watch for a few more nights to establish a pattern before making his move.

CHAPTER FIFTY

Tehran, Iran
July 22, 2000

Armik hung back within the cluster of trees in the center of the boulevard. Dusk had already settled on the street, the dying embers of sunlight fading fast. Cars turned on their headlights and a trickle of the night time crowd hustled toward the restaurants for their evening meals.

He had been diligent in his surveillance for several nights. His target ran on a precise schedule, his handler whisking him back and forth on the hour. Armik followed them twice from the house to a large, nondescript building complex in the city's business district.

According to Boris, the address belonged to an Iranian tech company's research and development installation, but the thirteenth floor and above housed the State nuclear development program facility. The country's worst kept secret, it would seem. Boris had offered his professional opinion on the matter, stating a hit in that building would be impossible. The security, according to his informants, could only be described as impenetrable.

Examining the car with a pair of cheap binoculars he had acquired at a bazaar, he guessed it to be an armored vehicle.

With that option off the table as well, not many choices remained. He could strike either on the driveway or in the house.

Hitting him on the driveway coming out of his car would be ideal, but no nesting spot in the immediate vicinity offered an optimal position for a clean shot. The house became the only viable option by default. But getting into the home posed a problem as well. With no plausible ideas materializing, he decided his best option would be to follow the one person who had access to it all. He went after the driver.

Like his employer, the uniformed chauffeur followed a set-in-stone agenda that wavered neither in content nor substance. After the drop-off, he drove down the street to a little theater where he watched the same movie three times, sleeping through most of it. An hour before pick-up, he attended the same restaurant. He ordered the same meal of saffron chicken with an oversized plate of rice upon which he poured a vast quantity of yogurt with dill and cucumber. He also drank the same number of beers, provided discreetly to him in repurposed coke cans, before paying and leaving. He drove back to the building, scanned his card, and drove to the back door to wait for his fare. In less than five minutes, they were on their way.

Like clockwork, the Rolls sped up to the curb, taking its usual parking space next to the theater. Armik flicked off the safety of the gun clutched in his pocket. The chauffeur got out and walked. He had no spring in his step, as if the monotony of his vocation seemed to have diminished him.

For the third evening in a row, he followed his target at a distance. Having already purchased his movie ticket in advance, Armik walked in while the man paid for his own. He had already settled in the near empty theater by the time the driver walked in with a large drink and a bag of pistachios, taking his usual seat.

The feature had changed, now showing a comedy about a prisoner who escapes by taking the clothes of a Muslim cleric. The prisoner is then forced to keep up the pretense of being the cleric in a mosque of the nearby village, hiding out until he can procure a forged passport. While the driver snored, Armik laughed and enjoyed the movie.

Right at the best part of the film, the man got up to use the restroom. Armik cursed under his breath and got up a few seconds later to follow.

After locking the washroom door, he joined the man, broad-shouldered and a half foot taller, at the urinals.

"Good movie, right? I mean, that scene at the mosque."

The man looked livid at being addressed while conducting his personal business. "Hey, man, are you from Qazvin or something? You want me to step back so you can get a better look?"

"Qazvin. Isn't that the city where the birds fly overusing only one wing? I think I met your dad there."

"You keep talking, I'm going to make you fly with one wing."

"Here, let me show you mine first." Armik stepped back, exposing the pistol where his privates should have been.

The driver did not flinch. He just turned back to the urinal and zipped himself up. Armik was not sure what to make of it.

The driver's sudden spin knocked the weapon from his grasp. Unwashed hands were at his throat, giving him no time to react. A knee to the groin drove the point home.

Seeing stars, Armik went down thinking he was going to die. But the driver had no intention of letting him off so soon. He pummeled Armik in the head with relentless fury.

On his knees, Armik grabbed the closest body part, the

man's ankle. He yanked with two hands, flinging the driver back. His head hit the porcelain with a hollow thunk.

The man's legs lashed out, catching Armik on the right cheek. He fell back and smashed into an unused stall door, his body laying halfway inside. The furious driver sprang on top of him again. A thick forearm crushing his throat, pressing his airway shut. Armik raised his knee with as much force as he could muster in between the legs straddling him, but it had no effect at all.

What the hell kind of chauffeur is this?

With his vision dimming fast, he noticed the driver's head was next to the frame of the stall door. Grabbing the door with his free arm, he slammed it into the man's temple. Then again. The man's grip loosened enough that Armik could hip-thrust his opponent off him. He staggered to his feet, gasping for air.

The driver got up too, now brandishing a knife in his hand. He slashed out, slicing Armik's shirt. His stony, bearded face broke into a smile. He slashed again with a lunge.

Armik sidestepped and caught the offending hand with both arms, but the other man's free arm wrapped around his throat in another chokehold.

Battling for life, Armik staggered back and forth across the bronze-colored tiles, trying to keep the knife at bay. The pressure on his windpipe continued to grow. He shoved the driver back into the hand-dryer hard. The air nozzle broke off with a clatter and a loud gush of air sounded.

From his periphery, Armik saw that the broken nozzle's bright red heating coil had become exposed. He forced the knife hand in that direction with all his might as the grip tightened around his neck.

On the brink of collapse, he kept pushing. Consciousness slipped from him in a steady stream, his legs all but ready to buckle.

At the sound of a sizzle and a scream, the scent of burnt flesh gushed into his lungs past the loosening chokehold. The knife dropped. Armik dropped. His hand touched the knife. With a last surge of effort, he grabbed the handle and delivered the knife back to the driver, blade first. For added force, he pushed with his other hand.

The knife lodged deep into the solar plexus of his maddened assailant. He gurgled and spat, looking no less angry as he died and slumped down the wall.

"Note to self. Don't piss them off first next time." Armik pulled himself up, using the sink counter to help him.

He relieved the man of his keys, wallet, and keycard and took up the hat that had fallen during the fight. Moving to the sink, he cleaned himself off, giving his hands a thorough wash. There was a lot of blood. His lip bore a nice gash, his cheek was swollen like a grapefruit. He wiped his prints off the sink and door handles before leaving, heading out the front door of the theater.

He jumped into the Rolls, donned the hat, and took off with squealing tires, hoping to be gone before anyone discovered the body and all hell broke loose in the area.

Moments after he pulled up to the research lab. Two men entered the vehicle without a word, sitting in the back seat. The windows were tinted, just like the partition that separated the passengers from the driver. It had no opening, only a speaker, which Armik had already turned on while disabling the light in the back that would indicate so.

He drove out of the secure area after scanning his card to open the sliding steel gates. He took the same route the now dead driver had taken every day—keeping the same speed and driving style so as not to raise any red flags. He considered pulling over and killing them there. But leaving the bodies in the house would give him more time to get away. Besides, the conversation was informative.

"What's the matter, my good doctor? You look quite out of sorts today," the dark bearded handler said.

"What do you expect?" Dr. Barron's voice had an edge to it that sounded like spite and regret. "You people keep me working seven days a week for twelve-hour days. Something has to give. I didn't work half of that in Tel Aviv."

"You didn't get paid half of what we are paying you either, doctor. You are going to be a rich man with a new identity when this is done. Then you can retire, maybe live someplace warm, and never have to work again."

"Yes, about that. I have not received the rest of the funds. I was promised the full amount. I'm feeling less and less comfortable with this arrangement."

"Let me talk to my superiors and find out what the delay is. We wouldn't want our Jewish savior to feel...uncomfortable in any way." The doctor's hard swallow came through the speaker with a chill and menace to those words that Armik could sense even through the barrier.

"Of course," said Dr. Barron. The confidence in his tone had diminished. "I'd appreciate that very much."

"I will keep you posted."

"So, when are you expecting this device to be functional?"

"Let's not talk about this here, doctor. The walls have ears everywhere in my country. You just worry about your part of the task."

Armik's curiosity spiked. He would have to interrogate the good doctor to find out more about this device before he eliminated him.

The conversation ended, silence prevailing for the duration of the drive. When the Rolls reached the top of the hill, the house came into view. Armik pulled up to the door. The handler jumped out as always, offering to assist Dr. Barron. He ignored the gesture.

They passed the driver door, which Armik held ajar. Gun in hand, he sprung out right behind the two men, his weapon just inches away from the handler's head.

"Alright, gentlemen. Looks like we have some business to discuss. Shall we step into your office for a drink?"

"Alcohol is illegal here Mr…I didn't quite catch your name." The man had his hands in the air yet seemed unfazed by the sight of the pistol.

Isn't anyone in this country afraid of guns?

"Yes, that's right. No booze. I guess it will have to be a sober discussion. Let's go. One wrong move, one bullet."

The doctor, moving slow and steady, extended his hand to the keypad and punched in the lock code. The door buzzed open.

"You are making a big mistake." The handler seemed amused.

"Get in." The moment Armik stepped inside the large anteroom behind the men, the door clicked shut behind him. It had indeed been a mistake.

Instinct made him drop to one knee. A hail of bullets tore past his head and into the wood paneling behind him. The doctor and his handler took off, but he was too busy rolling for cover to fire at them.

He came out of the roll in a large sitting room, taking cover behind a wooden China cabinet—the only object in the room offering any cover. The door at the far end of the room burst open. Armik fired two rounds in the general direction, hoping for an opportunity to dive through the large bay window. It would be a tight fit between the framework, but he might have a chance as long as the glass was not bulletproof. Armik fired

Damn.

"You are surrounded. Throw your weapon on the floor and put your hands on your head. If you comply, you will not be harmed...much."

"Tell you what. We'll both drop our weapons on the count of three and pretend this little incident never happened. One, two…" He peered from the corner to find a half dozen men in tactical gear, weapons raised. He fired, able to hit two before he emptied his clip.

Damn.

The men fired back, weapons on automatic. The cabinet was ripped to shreds around him. He sank lower and lower to the ground, yet no bullets hit him. They could have killed him many times over, but it seemed they wanted him alive. Given the circumstances and location, being kept alive would be the worst option. The deafening barrage gave way to an eerie silence, but for the ringing in his ear.

"Do you give up?" Armik asked.

The thunderous noise began again, stopping what seemed like minutes later.

"Come out, Mr. Vartanian. There is nowhere to go from here. If we wanted you dead, you would have been dead when you landed at the airport."

"That's comforting." *They know who I am. I've been set up. Damn. Damn.*

"This is your last chance, Mr. Vartanian. We won't miss again." The voice was that of the handler from the car. He saw no other play here—surrounded, out of time, out of bullets.

"Looks like you got me there, black beard." He tossed his spent weapon on the Persian rug in the center of the room and rose from his demolished hiding place with his hands on his head. The room was full of soldiers and police. "So. Take me to your pirate ship."

"You have a big mouth, foreigner. I'm going to enjoy plugging it for you."

"Oh, crap. You're from Qazvin too?" Armik gave one of his

signature smirks.

The response won him a hard hit to the back of the head with a rifle. He had some other clever remark to add but it slipped his mind, his vision going dark.

CHAPTER FIFTY-ONE

Paris, France
July 26, 2000

The streets were quiet, only a few people here and there walked past the tailor shop on Rue Charlot. Quiet was bad for business but it was nice to have a break from time to time. Besides, wedding season was in full swing and alterations had been flooding in non-stop.

He played no music in his shop, only the sounds of work. The click-clack of the sewing machine was enough and more than a little therapeutic for Vartan. It did, after all, drown out the sounds of the city around him, helping him focus. The only thing in the world at that moment was the stitches in front of him. No covert operations, no politics, sometimes he would even ignore his phone. This was as far from the ghosts of his past that he could get. He still had a gun hidden under a loose floorboard behind the counter and also in the back room. Old habits made dying harder.

The winter coat lining he sewed at that moment was a work of art for him. It was useful rather than destructive. He derived great pleasure from being useful.

The door of Vartan's tailor shop opened, awakening the little bell hanging above the top rail. He took the two men in with a glance, summed them up, and went back to his stitching.

One was obviously military. The silver and gold alternating stripes on his uniform said lieutenant-colonel—already a red flag. The way he held his hat tucked under his elbow confirmed they had news, but why would they send a high-ranking officer?

The other guy was a bit of a puzzle. Civilian, in his mid-thirties. Quite tall and well muscled with a thin waistline—a bodybuilder no doubt. He wore soft soled shoes that looked well-worn along with an ill-fitting suit. Vartan noticed a small tear in the bottom lining. *French Intelligence? No. CIA. Why is he here?*

He took a glance over at the floorboard where he kept his gun, grabbing it first in his mind in case his body was called upon to react as such.

"Gentlemen, what can I do for you?" said Vartan in his genial customer service voice, pushing back the mounting dread.

"Mr. Vartanian?" The man in uniform extended his hand.

"Yes, that's me."

"I'm Lieutenant Colonel Pierre Valois and this is Anthony Fuller. You are the father of Armik Vartanian?"

His stomach churned and he wanted to vomit right there, but he held his composure with a strength he did not know he possessed.

"That's right. Did something happen to my son?"

"Oh no, no, Mr. Vartanian." The suit raised his hands in assurance. "We have no reason to believe that anything has happened to Armik just yet."

"Just yet?" Vartan glared at the men.

"Well at the moment he is simply…unaccounted for."

"Unaccounted for, as in missing in action from a combat search and rescue mission or as in AWOL?"

"I'm afraid I don't have any details as his mission status is classified," said Valois.

"Classified? A CSAR mission classified?"

"I'm afraid so. Has he contacted you at all?"

"Not since he was deployed to Kandahar. I think the last letter was a month ago."

"You're sure?" Mr. Fuller had a disrespectful air about him. Vartan made a mental note of it.

"What are you not telling me? What's a lieutenant colonel and a...whatever you are...doing bringing me news that two grunts could have delivered?"

"I'm the US military attaché. Just observing the goings-on," Mr. Fuller said in barely adequate French. "You have a military background, Mr. Vartanian?"

"Mandatory two years in my country. I want to know where my son is. Is he, at least, still in Kandahar?"

"I'm afraid I can't even tell you that, Mr. Vartanian. As I mentioned, his mission status is—"

"Yes, classified—I got that part. Anything else I should know?" Vartan's surging temper made him consider killing the two men right there and then, but he held it in check. Losing his mind would not help him help Armik. He offered a forced smile instead.

"That's really all I can tell you, sir."

"I understand. You will keep me posted if you find him?"

"Absolutely. And please call me at my office immediately if he does make contact with you." Valois handed Vartan a business card.

He knows where Armik is. This is just a front to find out if he told me anything regarding his mission. Vartan could tell by the agent's smug look.

"Of course," he said. "Before you go, at least let me take care of that." Vartan stepped from behind the counter, pointing to the nearly invisible tear in the man's jacket lining.

"What's that?" Fuller looked confused.

"This tear caught my eye. I've been a tailor much too long, I'm afraid."

"Oh, don't worry about it. Thank you. It's an old—"

"Nonsense, it will take me two seconds and it's on the house. The least I can do for the trouble you took to come here and tell me about my son."

"I..."

Vartan helped the large, flustered man remove his jacket, ignoring the firearm he carried in a shoulder holster. He took it over to one of his sewing tables and picked out matching thread before loading it. All the while the man insisted that it was absolutely unnecessary.

A couple of quick stitches later and the hole was gone as if it had never been torn. The muscular man admired the handiwork and thanked him profusely, offering to pay.

"Nonsense. Thank you for coming gentlemen." Vartan extended his hand.

Handshakes dispensed, he watched the men leave his shop, the brass bell hailing their departure.

They were lying and he had to find Armik. The tracker in the CIA man's coat would help with that. Now, how to tell Jaleh that their only son was missing? All his training and experience could not have prepared him for that.

CHAPTER FIFTY-TWO

Tehran, Iran
July 25, 2000
Evin Prison

Dark. Empty. Cold. The room stood silent at the end of the dank corridor. Filth-covered fluorescent lights flickered. The walls screamed out in pain. The reek of feces and wasted humans floated in the air while lifeless, shadowed figures curled up in the corners of the cell, whispering their demented secrets.

His robust captors had dragged his feet across the rough concrete floor. The baggy blue uniform hanging from his bruised body was pierced with holes and stained with blood—both his and its last owner's. The beating had been his introduction to the prison system. They had not even asked him any questions. Though they seemed to have held back, letting him off rather easy, it was still the most excruciating ordeal of his young life.

A day later, they returned and picked up one of the little shadows in the corner. The man came to life when the guard put handcuffs on him. His skeletal fingers clutched the cell bars trying to resist what he must have known would be more torture. He screeched, rattling the bars, throwing himself around, shouting about the conspiracy. He kicked and threw punches at the guards. They subdued him with little effort, their batons ever eager to be used.

If Armik had any notion that they would not dare treat foreign citizens in the same manner as the other prisoners, he was disabused of it by the morning of his second day at Evin. That day they took the American journalist, Don Ashton, from their shared cell to the interrogation room.

When the guards unlocked the chains at Don's feet, he had been in such a state of terror he lost control of his bowels. Sweat poured from his face, tears from his eyes. Armik felt terrible for him.

They extracted his fingernails one by one until he confessed to an entire buffet of crimes. He returned with seven, indicating it did not take long to convince him. But when they brought him back, he could barely stand, let alone walk. His muscles seemed to have seized up. He tripped over his own feet, relentless in his sobbing. The shame in his averted face was obvious.

Armik could not dwell on the other man for long. His turn came next. Unchained and pulled to his feet without ceremony, his guards led him back along the same corridor past a chamber full of odd-looking instruments. Even though he walked without resisting, they still felt it necessary to push him forward until they yanked him to a stop.

They deposited him into a windowless room lit by a single, dangling electric light. On the other side of a stainless-steel table sat a very mild looking man in unadorned military fatigues. At his right hand sat a cleric in a white turban and brown robes—his last rites, perhaps.

To his surprise, a guard pulled a chair out for him at the slight gesture from the military man. Armik sank on it with less relief than expected. His muscles were not used to sitting anymore and the low seat caused his legs to cramp at once. Armik clamped his teeth together to keep from crying out, while he tried to shake the spasm from his limbs.

During the entire procedure, the military man and the cleric stared at him without the slightest flicker of emotion. The guards, who stood just inside the door, made some crack to one another in a relaxed tone. Then, all went quiet. He waited.

"What is your name?" the soldier asked.

Armik pulled himself together, having had enough time to think about what he would say to this inevitable question. "My name is Giovanni Aquila. I am an Italian Citizen. I demand to be allowed to contact the Italian Embassy." It sounded decisive and self-confident—if only his sweating body and spasming legs had not betrayed him.

Even so, there came evident amusement and mockery from behind the table.

The soldier raised his eyebrows and turned to the cleric. The cleric leaned forward and whispered in Farsi loud enough for Armik to hear, but he showed no semblance of understanding.

The Soldier turned back to Armik. "You are saying, you are not Armik Vartanian?"

"Never heard of him."

"Who sent you after Dr. Barron?"

"Never heard of him."

"And you are planning to stick with that story, even though you are caught with a gun in your hand?"

"A misunderstanding. I want to speak to my embassy."

"I see. Your request has been noted. I will pass it on to my superiors. For now, your absolute cooperation in this grave matter is requested. I am certain that voluntary assistance will be noted with favor by both your own country and mine.

You are aware of the seriousness of a charge of espionage in this country, are you not?"

"Espionage? I don't know what you're talking about."

"And besides those injured during your capture, there is the matter of the homicide at the theater. What can you tell me about that, Mr. Vartanian?"

"I don't know anything about a homicide either. Look. You're obviously looking for a different guy. My passport—"

"This passport?" The cleric held up his forged Italian Passport, dangling it from his fingertips as though it was something dirty.

"Looks like mine from here."

"I see. If you admit the truth, your stay here will be much less uncomfortable." The soldier gave a nod and the two goons swept Armik out of his seat, a black hood placed over his head.

He hardly touched the ground, carried at a pace too fast to keep his bearings. When the hood came off, he recognized the room. It was the same one he had first come to for a beating. As before, his arms were shackled to the wall, though, this time, he stood facing the dirty brick.

The flogging began without any pause. He soon lost track of how many hits he had taken, or how long he had taken them. He tried not to cry out but his back soon became one large, mushy nerve center and the sounds came out of him.

They stopped just before he reached the point of passing out and dumped a bucket of what he thought must have been salt water on him. Then the goons left him alone.

CHAPTER FIFTY-THREE

Paris, France

Sitting in the dark, Vartan blended in with the shadows. He could scarcely believe that anyone in the spy game could be so lax regarding their own home security. He had bypassed the door alarm with ease and had disarmed the main panel. His own home was full of unseen surprises for anyone unfortunate enough to break in. This was almost disappointing.

He sat on a dining room chair sipping on a glass of scotch, waiting for this spook to return from his long day of causing havoc in the world. Headlights from an approaching car swept across his face as it pulled into the driveway. One door opened—one door closed. He was alone. The arming of the car alarm sounded, followed by a key turning in the front door lock. A light in the vestibule came on.

As expected, the silhouette made its way directly to the safe in the living room. *446622.* Vartan had already cracked the code. It took him just under five minutes. The figure deposited his firearm after removing the clip.

So careful.

He looked even larger in the dark—like a Viking. Only

missing the furs and sword, he had the swagger. He walked to the fridge. Yes, he was a beer man. That would explain the cheap scotch. After the sound of an airtight can being opened, he downed the beer in one long swig and grabbed another.

"Are you thirsty or stressed?"

With a yelp, the startled man dropped the beer.

"What the hell?" He went for the light switch. "Mr. Vartanian? What the hell are… How did…?"

"You look surprised," he said. "You didn't really think that farce of a conversation was going to satisfy me, did you, Mr. Fuller?"

"Hey, listen. I told you everything I was able to but breaking into my house is not acceptable. I'm going to have to call the cops, you understand? This is extremely serious."

"Go ahead. But one way or another, you and I are going to revisit the conversation regarding my son. Now, you can save yourself a lot of unpleasantness and tell me exactly where he is, and why he is there, or I can take it out of you piece by piece."

"Listen, old man. I don't know who the hell you think you are, but this has gone far enough. I'm calling the… What the f…" He held up his cell phone and realized there was no service.

"Yeah, sorry about that. I took the liberty of jamming your cell signal." Vartan finished his scotch and stood slowly. "That stuff is garbage by the way. Oh, I also cut your alarm and landline."

"Who the hell are you?" the burly man said, his hand reaching for the kitchen drawer. He pulled a pistol out and aimed it at the intruder.

"I'm just a father, concerned for his son. A father that will do anything to keep his son safe." Vartan walked toward the barrel of the gun.

Click. Click. Click. The gun was empty.

"What the…"

"Yeah, I also took your bullets out of that." Vartan ducked to his left, dodging the gun flung at his head with ease. The metal object hit the cabinet behind him with a loud smash. The bigger man took the opportunity to lunge forward, going for a takedown from the waist.

Vartan twisted to the side and brought the ridge of his left hand up and into the Adam's apple of the attacker. A loud gurgling sound burst forth with a mist of spit. Fuller stumbled back, hand to his throat. The surprise and fear registered with clarity on his face, but he was well trained. He lashed out with a kick despite the lack of air. Vartan was already out of the way. He replied with a kick of his own to the side of the knee. Fuller staggered and grabbed the marble counter for support. Vartan followed up with another kick, this time to the groin, which caused a squeal in response. He finished the move with a hard strike to the side of the man's head. The legs buckled and the muscle-bound shell hit the linoleum floor with a thud.

Vartan rubbed his hands. That had hurt more than he remembered. There could be no doubt he had slowed down in his old age. A few more years and these young mutts might be able to get the drop on him. He shuddered at the thought.

Producing a large roll of silver duct tape, he bent over the limp body. He noted just how huge Fuller's arms were. *Must be a juice monkey.* He guessed him to be easily 270lbs. He made thorough work of taping the wrists together, using nearly half the roll. Then he did the same to the ankles.

He went to the fridge to see what there was to eat. The man had a lot of eggs. Also, the shelves were filled with Tupperware containers full of pre-prepped meals. How do people live like this? He found half a tuna sandwich on brown bread and took that. He was almost done with his snack when he heard movement.

The angry man moaned and grabbed for his head, started to find his hands bound together. "What the hell!"

"Oh, good. You're back. You really need to get some food in this house. How do you expect to feed your guests?"

A string of curses filled the air. "I'm going to kill you."

"Well, we'll get to all that in a moment."

"Where is my son?"

"I told you all I know. It's classified. I don't have clearance."

"You have a level six clearance. You are CIA. You are the station chief in Paris. I checked. Now tell me what I need to know."

"I don't know what you're talking about."

Vartan grabbed one of the kitchen knives from the wooden knife holder. He kicked the thick man over on his stomach and cut open his shirt. Then he cut a line down his back from the nape of his neck to the base of his spine. His scream was loud, but the house was large, and the neighbors would not hear.

"So, one of two things will happen tonight," he said to Fuller once the scream had died down to muttered threats. "Scenario one is you will supply me with enough information to find my son and bring him home safely. Then I will kill you quickly and painlessly. Scenario two, I will cut off all of your skin while you are alive and take it home with me. There, I will dry it and cure it, and cut it into little square strips. With your large size, I calculate I will be able to wipe my ass with you for at least four or five weeks."

More curses went flying. Vartan stepped on the squirming man's head, pressing his face to the floor. He cut a horizontal line across from shoulder to shoulder. The man screamed again, which became even louder and more frantic when Vartan dug his fingers in and began peeling back the skin.

"Okay. Okay! Goddamnit. He's in Iran. Your son is in Iran."

"Why?"

"I don't know. Ahhh!"

Vartan pulled at the skin again. "Why?"

"He was recruited to infiltrate the Iranian Nuclear Program and find out how far they have gotten toward making a nuclear weapon."

"Where is he now?"

At Fuller's pause, Vartan's hand moved toward the bloody gash on his back.

"Evin," he cried out. "He's being held in Evin Prison in Tehran. Please don't kill me. I have money. Cash in my—"

"In your safe. Yes, I saw. You sent my son there?"

"He was Iranian. He had already been recruited by the French. It was a freelance job."

"You sent my son there." It was not a question.

"No, not me personally. He was already there when I was briefed. Come on. You got what you wanted."

"So where did the order come from?"

"It came from well above my pay grade. Highly classified. That's all I know. Please let me go." Fuller sobbed into the kitchen floor.

Vartan pulled out his pistol and then a suppressor which he screwed onto the barrel. He pulled the trigger twice. The room went silent.

A few minutes later the doorbell rang. Vartan looked through the keyhole. He opened the door.

"I'm told you are in need of a cleaner," said a man in a long coat with a red baseball cap and thick glasses.

"You have good timing."

"I saw a muzzle flash. I figured you were done."

"Come in," Vartan said. "The mess is in the kitchen."

CHAPTER FIFTY-FOUR

Paris, France
July 27, 2000

The swishing of his windshield wipers lulled Vartan into a bit of a dream state. He thought of Armik languishing in a cold cell—the beatings, the ceaseless harassment. He had to shake his head to get the images out. Jaleh put her hand on his while he shifted gears. She held a strong front, but there could be no doubt she did so for his sake. Inside she had to be dying the way he was.

The figures on the sidewalks appeared isolated in the rain, their expressions as downcast as the evening sky. They hurried rather than strolled through the streets, absorbed in their own thoughts. The umbrellas shielded them not just from the rain, but also from other passers-by.

Vartan pulled to the curb, scanning all his mirrors for signs that he had been followed. They could not afford to be followed. Not to this meeting.

"Relax," said Jaleh. "We didn't pick up any tails."

"I don't want to get careless in my old age."

"You are many things, my love, but you are not careless."

"That's because I have you to look after me." He offered his signature grin but could not muster it to its full strength.

“Yes, that’s true.” His wife of so many years smiled back at him.

Only the dark shadow of stress and fear betrayed the hollowness of the gesture. She was still beautiful and still a mystery to him. He had never allowed himself to fail her, and he would not fail her now. He would not let their son die. He would bring Armik home.

Vartan removed his gun from his holster and put it in the glove box. He would not need it. Then he kissed Jaleh and got out of the car.

He walked at a casual pace but with purpose, as one might stroll after a meal. It took a block and a half to get to Darvish Restaurant. He circled it twice to make sure. He spotted cars up and down the street that he recognized as security detail. They had the place locked down tighter than a military base. A man in a black suit with dark glasses, despite the lack of sun, met him at the entrance and patted him down before stepping to the side.

Vartan removed his wet overcoat and walked in, finding the restaurant empty, devoid even of staff. Soft Persian music played over speakers, the singer lamenting over times long past and loves long lost. Half-eaten plates of Kabobs and rice with grilled tomatoes lay abandoned on saffron tablecloths throughout, as if everyone had left in a hurry.

She still commanded much respect. The thought made him smile. As if conjured by his thoughts, she appeared from the kitchen entrance and walked toward him. He could not help but be awestruck even after all these years.

So much time had passed since he had seen the queen up close, yet she had lost none of her regal beauty and grace. She looked no less majestic and stood no less proud than when she had been next to the Peacock Throne. A lump formed in Vartan’s throat.

"Your majesty," he said, bowing low. She stopped him with a hand on his shoulder.

"Vartan, my old friend, it's so good to see you," she said, the pleasure in her voice genuine.

"I've never been far, majesty, only out of sight." Vartan saw the shadows of her security team lingering out of sight but just close enough, as he had done so often for her in his youth.

"I know," she said. "And I have felt safer for it all these years."

"Now, I'm afraid I must go...back home. They have...they have my son." Vartan struggled to hold his composure.

"This I know also." Her hand squeezed his shoulder in the motherly fashion she had always exuded.

"I feel like I am abandoning my post, but—"

"Nonsense," she said, her brows furrowing in admonishment. "You have been a loyal soldier all these years, even when it was no longer expected of you. I am well aware of the sacrifices you and your wife have made for our country...and for me. Now you must go to your son and bring him back safe."

"It was my duty, your majesty. And my honor."

"The honor was mine, Vartan-*jan.* Go with my blessing. My son has made some arrangements for you." She handed him a small envelope. "This will get you set up for whatever you need to do over there. God watch over you and your son."

"Thank you, your majesty. I don't know what to say."

"There is nothing to say. We are family, and we must help each other in any way we can. Come back safely to us. We need you. There are so few of us left now." A little sadness crept into the sparkle in her dark eyes.

Vartan bowed again. "One more thing, your majesty. I wanted to return this to you."

He handed her a little velvet pouch. The bracelet she had

given him, what seemed like a lifetime ago, lay tucked inside. She recognized the item without opening it.

"This was to help you in your time of need. You should have used it." Her face was stern, but she held the pouch close to her heart.

"The gesture was more help to me than all the money in the world, majesty. I thank you."

The empress of Iran smiled and nodded. For a moment, he saw the young queen as she had been and would remain in his mind. She left with the same silent abruptness with which she had come, yet she might as well have been heralded by trumpets for the grace of her presence.

Her detail had vanished like mist in the night by the time he exited the restaurant.

CHAPTER FIFTY-FIVE

Tehran, Iran
July 28, 2000

He had acquired a covert tail already. Vartan had not even been in the country for four hours, but he had no doubt. He could not pinpoint what triggered the suspicion, yet he knew enough to trust his intuition. He had only his instincts to depend on now.

A reoccurring glance, a pair of legs in a crowd with the wrong gait, a car color that passed his field of vision more than it should have. It could have been any one of these things or a number of them. After so many years, it all happened at a subconscious level, but he was sure. What he was not sure of, was who.

His return to Iran after so many years had been something of a shock to Vartan's system. So many things were the same, while everything had changed. For one, the insane traffic had become even busier. It was all but impossible for someone to cross unless they were used to it. A tourist could be stuck on a street corner for a week. Vartan was now a tourist in his own country. The thought saddened him a little.

He noted that all the women's heads were covered to varying degrees. That had not been tolerated in the Shah's time. His father, Reza Shah, was particularly opposed to it and was very much an advocate for women to play a higher role in Iranian society. So much so, he had sent soldiers on horseback to rip the headscarves off women's heads, ridding the country of what many considered a sign of oppression.

Vartan made several circles before entering the city's marketplace in an effort to shake his pursuer. The bazaar's covered stores still lined a stretch of more than ten kilometers of lanes with several different entrances. He entered the central artery using the main entrance facing the square Sabzeh Medyan. The warren of people and goods made it a city within a city, and included banks, a fire station, and several mosques.

Most lanes specialized in a particular commodity—copper, paper, gold, spices, and carpets, among others. The carpet, nut, and spice bazaars were his favorite, awash with the colors of the ancient world. Those lanes took him back to his childhood days and stood in stark contrast to the lane of stores selling items such as fake designer labels—not even the clothes, but just the labels.

Vartan wandered the labyrinth of streets and alleys at leisure, taking whichever turn he fancied and going with the flow in the hope that he would draw out whoever was following him. He was intercepted at a stall by a carpet vendor who would not be ignored.

"*Bebakhshid, Agha.* You look like the type of person with an eye for beautiful things. Look at my carpets. They are beautiful, are they not?"

"They are beautiful, but I don't really need a carpet at the moment."

"No problem, no problem. I will help you find whatever you need. Homayun knows everybody. Everybody knows Homayun. If they don't know Homayun, they are not anybody."

"Thank you, that's not—"

"Trust Homayun, you need my help," he whispered, then upped his volume again. "Tell Homayun what it is you need, *Agha*! We'll find it and then come back to my place for tea."

Vartan understood and followed the large, jolly man through the maze of stalls. He was quick for his roundness and short legs. They reached a sheer gallery of hanging carpets, obscuring them from the sight of the rest of the bazaar. Vartan was ready for anything, tugging gently at the knife hidden in his sleeve. Homayun turned to him.

"You've been picked up. Two on your tail."

"Who are they?"

"As far as I can tell they are not ours."

"RG?"

"Ah, don't worry. They tagged you because you were traveling alone. They practically tag everyone and their mother these days. I'll buy you some time. Here. You'll need this." Homayun handed him an envelope full of Iranian currency and a 9mm handgun in a belt holster.

"Thank you." Vartan tucked the weapon away and pocketed the cash.

"Don't thank me yet. That was the easy part. Take my keys. The car is just on the other side of this wall. A beige taxi. The address to your safe house is in the glove box. Go there, leave the keys under the mat. Don't scratch it, I'm still paying for it."

"Right."

"*Javid Shah.*" Long live the king.

Homayun ushered Vartan into a small space in the adobe wall behind a mountain of rugs through which he had to duck to pass. The cab was there as promised. He looked around and saw no one following, so he opened the door and got in. He drove off, merging with the mad traffic flow.

It had been so long he was not sure if he could navigate with all the changes. But when he took the paper from the glovebox, he recognized the address well. It was a block away from his old high school.

The drive took him over an hour, but he finally arrived. He left the keys as instructed. His old and tired back ached from the journey, and he was anxious to lie down. *I'm too old for this spy stuff.* He gave a half-hearted laugh.

He walked for about half a block until a long series of brick townhomes came into view. He approached the first one, took another look around and knocked on the blue door. After a few seconds, the viewing hole darkened and then the door opened.

"Goddamnit, they let just about anyone into the country these days."

"Abbas! You old bastard! What are you doing here?"

The two men stepped in quickly and exchanged kisses on each cheek.

"You don't think I am about to let my oldest friend go into enemy territory alone, do you?"

"But how—"

"Her majesty sent me to make sure you had every resource possible at your disposal. Mossad doesn't have the network they once had here, but we still have a trick or two. We'll get your son back."

Vartan's head dropped. "They took my boy."

"I know. I was sorry to hear. Don't worry, my people tell me he is still alive."

"But for how long?"

"Long enough for us to get him out."

CHAPTER FIFTY-SIX

Tehran, Iran
July 29, 2000

She found the wearing of the burka akin to being in a coffin with a peephole. The fundamentalists Jews had something similar, but it was rare to see. Breathing came with difficulty in the claustrophobia-inducing garment. She had worn it for the duration of the five-hour flight from Paris to Tehran without a word. Only her frequent trips to the bathroom to remove the mask offered any relief.

The diplomatic aircraft, a private Gulfstream G550 jet, touched down at the Imam Khomeini International Airport with a smooth landing. When it came to rest about a half a kilometer from the main terminal, the entourage was ushered onto the tarmac. The group included His Excellency, Shahriar Iranshaad, charge d'affaires of the Islamic Republic, his sister, mother, and a slew of attaché and assistants. Jaleh exited behind them, carrying all the belongings she had brought in a single rucksack slung over her shoulder.

Each had expressed some concern over the unscheduled return to Iran, to which Iranshaad had offered only a simple "Classified." This abated any further discussions on the matter. Jaleh had called in a big favor, choosing to use this way to get into the country on the chance that her husband did not make it through. Someone had to get Armik out of Evin.

She had remained silent throughout the flight to avoid revealing her identity, which only the charge d'affaires was privy to. To everyone else, she was his wife, Rayhoneh. His mother seemed to have more than a strong suspicion, the eighty-eight-year old having eyed her with a look of distrust much like she was doing now. To her credit, she said nothing despite her motherly instinct.

Iranshaad approached her at the bottom of the steps just as two limousines and four security vehicles pulled up. He held a passport in his hand.

"Take this. Only show it if they ask. They cannot search you or your belongings even if they suspect you—technically. Just don't let this fall into anyone's hands. If this comes back to me, I'll lose more than my job."

"I know. I'll be careful. I owe you."

"Forget it. Anything for the cause."

A chauffeur came around and opened the door for them. Jaleh and the charge d'affaires took the lead car while his family climbed into the one behind. The fleet of diplomatic limousines tore across the open tarmac at breakneck speeds. The lead security car sped toward the checkpoint at the southernmost gate with no intention of stopping. Machine-gun-toting soldiers crowded around the guardhouse and gate, their demeanor alert and tense.

"Sir, the barricade is up," said the driver.

"So honk." Iranshaad looked at Jaleh, panic appearing just under the surface.

The driver honked. A guard stepped forward and waved a hand, indicating that they should stop.

"Is this normal?" Jaleh knew the answer. Reaching under her long drape, she clutched the gun in her waistband.

"They never stop us."

"Don't worry. Just stay calm." *Not good.*

They rolled to a stop and were surrounded in an instant, curious eyes squinting into every tinted pane of glass. The driver rolled down each window at once and a bearded soldier, the one in command judging by his inordinate collection of chevrons, stuck his head all the way into the car. Jaleh half expected the man to kiss the driver on the lips. But he turned his head to the back, looking first at Iranshaad, then Jaleh.

"This is a diplomatic vehicle, colonel. Did you not see the plates?"

"I saw them." He kept his gaze fixed on her, his face unreadable.

Jaleh thumbed the safety off beneath her black attire, prepared to shoot her way out. If they could only make it past the gates and far enough for her to jump out unseen, she might be able to escape into the surrounding forested area. Odds were slim she would get far, but slim was better than none.

"What is it you are looking for, colonel?"

"Funny thing about these burkas. You could pretty much hide anyone under them, could you not."

"What are you suggesting?"

"Perhaps we should take a look just to be sure."

"You have no authority."

"Technically."

"Colonel, let me remind you of the verses. 'And tell the believing women that they must lower their gazes and guard their private parts, and must not expose their adornment, except that which appears thereof, and must wrap their bosoms with their shawls, and must not expose their adornment, except to their husbands or their fathers or the fathers of their husbands, or to their sons or the sons of their husbands, or to their brothers or the sons of their brothers or the sons of their sisters, or to—"

"Okay, okay." The colonel pulled his head out and waved for the gates to open.

When the windows were back up and the tires were in motion, Jaleh, the driver, and Iranshaad all let out their breaths at the same time.

"Let's never do that again."

"Agreed," said Jaleh.

After a few kilometers, they pulled off the narrow side road and onto the main thoroughfare. Light traffic helped them make good time getting to the city center. The driver's eyes focused more on the rearview mirror than the road for the duration. A look of concern showed in his creased brow.

"Looks like our caravan has picked up two extra cars, sir," he said.

Iranshaad looked back and then nodded at Jaleh. "Thank you, Kevon. Looks like the delay was just so they could get a tail on us."

"Head to Shahyad Tower." Jaleh pulled her suffocating headdress up to catch a breath. "Get on the roundabout."

The noontime traffic had gotten thick and slow, making progress difficult. The pursuing vehicles stuck to them without trying to be discreet. The driver turned into Azadi Square and entered the inner roundabout as instructed, the tail still on them.

"We must have been betrayed," said Iranshaad.

"It may just be that your unscheduled return set off the exact red flags that someone was looking for. Once I'm in the wind, you'll have nothing to worry about." Jaleh handed him back the passport.

They had just entered their third turn on the roundabout when Jaleh spotted her opportunity. On her command, the vehicle made a sudden sharp turn onto a smaller street and pulled to the curb. The abrupt stop set off a chain reaction of horns and squealing tires. She pulled her hood back down and jumped out, making a mad dash across the street before the rest of the caravan was able to catch up to the lead car.

She did not wait to confirm whether or not she had been seen, moving with haste down the street, but not running. She took the next left and found herself in an area full of small shops. She needed to circle back and get to Almahdi Park, where her contact would be waiting at a preset rendezvous point.

The buildings, landmarks, and street names had all changed. Any similarities to the image she had retained in her mind had all but vanished. The cars were different, the people were different—even the air was different. But her memory of a city she had not returned to in decades surprised her. She could navigate the streets with a blindfold on.

Jaleh stopped at the large window of an electronics store and took her time looking at the various items on display. The reflection caught a man walking at a slow pace on the opposite side of the street. The thin man wore a blue plaid shirt over a t-shirt and jeans. His bushy mustache hovered over a set of thick lips, and he had eyebrows to match. He happened to throw one too many casual glances in her direction, sending her instincts into defensive mode. Jaleh entered the busy shop, squeezing past the customers to get up to the counter.

"Miss, can I use your restroom?"

"Through the doors and to the left, ma'am."

Jaleh followed the directions and entered a small, clean washroom. She pulled off her burka, sucking the ammonia-filled air around her as if she had been holding her breath until now. She splashed cold water on her face and reversed the burka, with now a light blue side showing. She put it back on.

Instead of going back the way she came, she headed further into the store. The staff, busy with the frantic pace of their tasks, did not seem to notice. She walked straight out the back door and into a narrow laneway. In a few minutes, she returned to the main street and continued her stroll toward the park, careful to alter her gait.

Despite the complications, she arrived at the rendezvous point a half-hour earlier than scheduled. She took a seat on a gaudy looking sundial made up of concrete and random stones. She produced a piece of chalk from her pocket and, checking to be sure no one was watching, drew a long blue line on the black metal gnomon. She then sat on the rounded edge, taking advantage of her covered face to scan her surroundings.

"Excuse me, ma'am. What's the best way to the train station?"

At hearing a man's voice behind her speak the code phrase, Jaleh responded without turning. "You could walk, but it's about ten blocks."

"That's fine, I could use the exercise. Thank you."

He had not mentioned the built-in abort phrase, a streetcar, to signal he believed them to be under surveillance. She turned around. To her surprise, the man that she had seen in the bakery window stood before her, one hand holding a takeout coffee cup, the other holding a cigarette. He put the cup down on the dial plate and bent to tie his shoe before walking away, leaving his coffee behind. When the man had disappeared from view, Jaleh picked up the cup. Lifting the lid off, she found the address to a safe house.

Keep strong, Armik-jan. Mama is coming for you.

CHAPTER FIFTY-SEVEN

The Alborz Mountain range rose before him like white-tipped pillars holding up a dusty looking blue ceiling. Until now, Vartan had not realized how much he missed the sight of those peaks. Though he had made a great life for himself with his family in Paris, he had always hoped to return with the royal family when the prince took his rightful place upon the Peacock Throne. Only then could he retire. Only then would his mission be truly complete.

But now his new mission—his top priority—had become the rescue of his son. If he could not save his boy, it would have all been for nothing. That thought alone almost broke him.

So many buildings had sprung up since he last set eyes on the area. The city seemed poised to swallow the mountain. Leaving the northern part of the capital under a sky hazy with pollution, he and Abbas spent much time in bumper-to-bumper traffic, staring at the murals lining the highway. It had taken more than an hour to just pass the Bazaar and wind their way through the maze of Darvazeh Ghar's tiny streets to even get to the freeway.

Finally, they approached the old section, filled with orchards and gardens of ancient houses. Lush vegetation overhung high stone walls all around them, and he saw more potted plants on windowsills and balconies than ever before.

Abbas pulled the rickety beige Pontiac to the side of the road in the northern part of the neighborhood, where the amount of greenery made a significant decline. He turned off the engine and looked at Vartan, handing him a tactical semi-automatic pistol with a Red Dot Sight package and two clips.

"Are we storming a maximum security prison or robbing a liquor store?"

"There are no liquor stores here anymore. And 'storming' might be a little strong. If we walk in there with RPGs and a Howitzer, we won't make it very far. Here, clip this on." Abbas handed him a plastic security tag to clip on the prison guard uniform he wore. "You really think it's still there after all these years?"

"It wasn't known to many people," said Vartan. "Just a handful."

"That may be, but it's been twenty years."

"If it's not there, we'll have to come up with another plan, but it's worth a try. Get a hostage if we have to. The warden or a guard. Grab my son and be in and out before they figure out where we went. What could possibly go wrong?"

"Famous last words," said Abbas, tucking away his pistol. "Let's do this."

"Hey." Vartan stopped his old friend before he stepped out of the car. "You don't have to do this. He's my son and this is not—"

"Shut up. You'd do the same for me."

"Break into the most notorious prison in the country? I don't know about that." Vartan laughed.

"If you're trying to talk me out of it, it's working."

Vartan checked his gun before hopping out of the car. They took a trail, now overgrown with weeds and brush, that led partway up the mountainside behind the gray prison walls below them. Crouching low to keep out of sight of the guard towers, they arrived where the brown rocky cliffs made a v-shaped crevasse that sank downward, back toward the valley. Facing the northernmost wall, Vartan could see the little gray specks of prison guards pacing the length of the yard beneath them.

"It was around here somewhere." Vartan looked around, puzzled. "I never actually came out this way myself. Look for a big rock. There should be a small metal door."

"The whole place is made up of big rocks."

"There." Vartan pointed to what he hoped was the right spot.

Abbas followed him to the six-foot boulder. After clearing away the thorny brush covering the ground, the door appeared. Rusted with brown flakes of paint peeling off in strips, the door had a small metal wheel protruding from the center. Vartan grabbed it and yanked, He groaned under the effort, but it did not budge.

As an escape tunnel, the door was meant to be easier to open from the inside. Installed at the insistence of the Shah, just for peace of mind, it had never been intended as an entrance.

"Give me a hand," he said.

Abbas took hold of the other side. They both tugged but it did not give so much as a creak. A loud pop of a rifle echoed all around them. They released the wheel and dropped to their bellies.

"Damn. We've been made." Abbas pulled out his weapon.

"Why would they even be watching this place? It's far enough out of their kill zone."

"How would I know? We'd better split up. I'll meet you back at the car. Or if not, the safe house."

"Sounds like a plan." Vartan took his pistol from his waistband.

Another shot struck the dirt to their left and the sound of

shouting mixed with the barking of dogs floated up from lower down.

With a nod, Vartan took off at a run in the opposite direction from Abbas, tracing the path they had taken on the way up. He took care not to break an ankle on the uneven terrain, which slowed his progress. The barking dogs seemed to be getting louder. He cursed himself for slacking off from his daily runs, swearing he would step up his regimen when he got home—if he got home.

The whistle of a bullet by his ear sent him tumbling. He rolled off the gravel path and into the thick brush, thorns, and branches scraping at his face and body. Springing to his feet, he kept going in the direction he had fallen, tearing through everything in his way.

At last, he arrived at the road. Abbas was not there. He did not want to lead the pursuers to the car. Abbas might have a chance if he distracted them, so he kept running. He took wild turns through the streets, trying to find someplace he could duck into. Distant police sirens grew louder, and the rumbling of a helicopter overhead almost drowned out the barking dogs.

Vartan came to an overpass looking down on the tracks, one that he was familiar with. A long cargo train had just gone under. He took hold of the metal rail, placing a foot on the concrete barrier. He expected a hail of bullets. He would have to make a blind jump. Only a fool would do it, but only a bigger fool would follow.

Being less of a fool than he was twenty years ago, he stood down. A guard with a revolver ran up behind him, yelling for him to raise his hands. Vartan complied. The moment the guard touched him, he spun and slammed the man's wrist with his forearm. The bone snapped and the weapon tumbled off the overpass.

By then the train had passed, and he was surrounded.

CHAPTER FIFTY-EIGHT

Tehran, Iran
August 1, 2000

Jaleh thought Saed, the prison guard, to be a caricature of a man. Tall and lanky, his arms hung so far down his body his knuckles nearly touched the ground. He possessed a face that appeared neither awake nor asleep, but somewhere in between. A creature of habit, he was chronically lazy and as slow as a sloth in a tar pit. Yet he seemed only about half as intelligent. Still, someone thought it a good idea to give him a security pass to the most notorious prison in the country.

He walked six-and-a-half minutes to work each day, stopping at a stall for hot tea a block from the prison. He could not be bothered to walk back home for his hour long lunch break, so his burka wearing wife would run it over in bags every day at exactly 12:15pm. He would come out a side fire door and snatch it without a word.

At 7:10pm every night he left the prison from that same door, walking the same route home, with a stop at the corner store to buy cigarettes. He would enter his house where his wife would greet him with slippers and a prepared meal much too large for one. His wife and daughters always ate earlier. Only his prepubescent son would join him for dinner.

His son is the key. He is the weakness.

Jaleh watched his house for three days, from early morning to well into the night, following him along his route. She memorized his every step, every pause, every sideways glance. It was a long time to leave her family locked away, but she had to be certain.

Following someone, even someone as predictable as this prison guard was a lot harder now that she was older. She could no longer dive into a doorway or flip over a fence, and she certainly could not run as fast as she used to if her target discovered her and wanted to confront her. It had been just as long since she had knocked someone out cold too. *Could I still?*

The only real advantage was her ability to wear a black burka. It still amazed her how invisible a woman was completely covered up to the eyeballs. But then, that was the point of the outfit. They liked their women invisible.

Like clockwork, he left work and walked with long Neanderthalian strides, heading for his cigarette purchase. That being done, he walked straight home, his head down, without a care in the world.

Saed entered his front door and went to dinner. Jaleh went to the back door that led to a large mudroom. The area looked darkened and empty. Before going to the door, she cut the phone line running from a post in the backyard. It dangled in a sloppy manner across to the roof where someone had stapled it along the aluminum siding, making no effort to hide it. She put her cutters away and took out her bump key.

The use of a bump key was a very old technique for opening a deadbolt, and though Jaleh had not broken into a house for a very long time, she was happy to see that the locks had not improved—at least, as far as this prison guard's home was concerned.

The key's low peaks and wide valleys were not designed

to properly align with the lock's pins. Instead, it ensured that under force the pins could merely be impacted. She inserted it into the lock until one notch remained between it and full insertion.

She produced a small rubber mallet and applied an impact force to push the key deeper into the lock. This caused the key pins to jar and the driver pins to jump. Now aligned for a fraction of a second, she quickly turned the core and opened the lock. The rubber kept the sound to a minimum, but she paused for a second before opening the door, just to make sure.

Jaleh stepped into the mudroom and removed her burka. She drew her revolver. The door opened quietly enough but she kept her back against the wall. She made her way through a long, narrow hallway to the kitchen and peered through a half-closed sliding door. Saed had his back turned, eating in silence with his son. The girls were always in their rooms at this time and did not come out again. *The wife…?* Jaleh realized she could not see the wife. The thought came too late. The door slid open, and the surprised woman stepped into the hall—right into Jaleh.

A quick strike to the temple stifled a scream. Not hard, just hard enough. Jaleh spun behind her and wrapped her arms around her neck, cutting off her airway.

The woman's strength and determination surprised her. It took a lot to maintain the hold, but soon her arms dropped to her side. Jaleh kept the pressure on just a little longer to make sure she was asleep, then lowered her to the floor. She dropped down beside her, winded. *I'm too old for this,* she thought, sweating and panting.

Once recovered enough, she took a quick check of the woman's pulse, confirming her to be alive. She stood and walked into the kitchen with her gun pointing. The son jumped up with a start, knocking his orange juice over, but said nothing.

Saed turned, coming face to face with the nozzle of Jaleh's 9mm semi-automatic. While his surprise registered, she took out a small pocket flashlight and clicked the button several times, pointing it out the kitchen window.

His surprise turned to annoyance. Whether it was the gun pointing at his head or the fact that a woman pointed it she could not be sure, but she suspected a bit of both.

"What do you want?" he said.

"Saed Naghashi. I'm afraid I'm going to need your help."

"This is how you ask for help? What kind of help?"

"You have something of mine. Two people actually. They are locked up in your little prison over there, and you are going to help me get them out."

"Don't be stupid. I'm not going to help you, you crazy bitch. Now get out of here before I take that gun and…"

She turned the gun toward his son, whose wide eyes became even wider.

"I'm afraid you have no choice," she said.

A moment later a team of three Mossad agents entered the room in full tactical gear, weapons at the ready.

CHAPTER FIFTY-NINE

Tehran, Iran
August 2, 2000

His head whirled like a top that would not stop spinning, his thoughts wandering in different directions. Had they beaten a hole in his brain that allowed them to escape? Pain surged through his old bones. He had bruises layered upon bruises in so many places that Vartan could not pinpoint where it hurt. But he would not give them the satisfaction, so he concentrated his energy on the muscles around his mouth, forcing his lips into a perpetual grin.

They are smart. By keeping him separated from his son he had no idea what was happening to him. The possibilities were left to the worst of his imagination. It was a form of control, and one he would have employed were he in their place. Knowing the why, unfortunately, did not make it any better, but it was something. Understanding their mindset gave him an advantage over them.

These strategies came from above—the top guys, the policymakers. They were the ones that thought things out, figured out the whys and the hows. The guards just enforced those ideas. They were stupid and lazy. Now, this—this he could exploit.

One guard, in particular, he found irksome and stupid to perfection. His name tag said, "Naghashi."

He liked the power afforded by the uniform. He liked the torture and the humiliation. It was the only time Vartan saw him come alive. Otherwise, he was just another brain-dead drone benefiting from the sudden need of blunt instruments after the revolution. Vartan spat at the thought of it, but Naghashi was one that he could get to. For, where there was stupidity, there was greed.

"Hey," said a voice from behind the bright light shining in his eyes. A hand slapped him in the face, pulling him from his thoughts. "Hey, are you paying attention?"

Vartan, his left eye swollen shut and his lip split in two places, sat shackled to a metal table by a long chain. He grunted at the slaps.

"I find you completely boring, donkey. You lost me about an hour ago."

A fist struck his already pummeled face, splitting his lip a third time. Or was it a reopening of a previous split? He had lost count. He spat more blood.

"You want to be a funny guy, huh? I'm happy to do this all day and night."

"If you are happy, donkey, then why such a long face?" He laughed at his own joke even though two more punches arrived in succession.

"Let's start again. Who are you? Who do you work for? What are you doing here in Iran?"

"I told you a thousand times."

"Tell us again."

"Okay. Okay. My name is Charles Aznavour. I'm a singer from Paris. You must have heard of me. I'm here because I made a wrong turn from your mother's house and got lost."

A flurry of punches hit him from all sides. He almost

lost consciousness. He was kicked so hard in the chest that his flimsy chair flipped over. Only his head hitting the floor prevented him from registering the pain of at least a few broken ribs. He saw white dots behind his eyelids.

"Pick him up," The donkey motioned to the guards on either side of him. They straightened his chair and deposited him back into it. He squinted again into the light.

"If you don't believe me, name a song and I'll sing it for you." He tried to laugh, but it hurt too much.

The donkey slapped a file folder in front of him and opened it to the first page where a photograph was held fast to the top corner by a paperclip.

"Is this you?"

Vartan strained to see the picture. "Are you going to show me a picture of every guy your sister slept with until I confess to being one of them?"

A punch amplified the pain of his broken ribs, throwing him off his seat once more. When he was redeposited on his chair, he spat more blood.

"You are Vartan Gharabian. You are a former SAVAK agent. The one they call 'the Persian.' But you are no Persian. You are a collaborator with the criminal regime and the Israeli government. You are a traitor here to spy on your own country."

"Sorry, I'm not familiar with that song. But if you hum it, I might pick it up."

The two guards moved toward him again. He braced for an even harder beating, uncertain if he could take another.

The door opened, and the face of Naghasi appeared. "Take a break," he said.

"But—"

"Leave him. We need him alive, or heads will roll. How much do you think this old man can take?"

"Skinny donkey!" Vartan called out in a cheerful tone with a mouth full of blood. "You're just in time." His head wobbled a bit, fighting off the urge to pass out. The pain was tremendous.

"Shut up, you. Everybody out."

The three guards left the room in a hurry and closed the door behind them. Naghashi shut off the recorder and sat on the desk in front of Vartan.

"You have some very crazy friends. They are, at this moment, pointing guns at my children's heads. So I'm going to get you and your son out the door. But just know that when I get you back here…and I will get you back here…I will kill you myself, along with that crazy bitch."

So, Jaleh had exploited the same weak link. She had come through. He was not surprised at all. Vartan was not able to come up with a suitable quip—a shame because it was a great moment for one. He spat more blood and grinned again.

"We have to be quick. There are very few windows of opportunity. You will do exactly what I tell you, and don't do anything stupid if you want to make it out. Can you walk?"

Vartan nodded, though he was not so sure he could.

"Good. If I am caught, I'll hang from the nearest tree. But not before I put a bullet in your head. Be ready. I will come for you after the guards change."

PART 8

CHAPTER SIXTY

"Not the balls again guys, come on."

"But this is my favorite game," said the shorter guard.

Armik had no idea that there were so many ways to hurt a man's testicles, but he was learning. Their favorite method, thus far, was to place them in a piece of soft leather and rub them slowly between both hands. The savage pain from this simple, almost effortless action often made him pass out.

As they had done for days, two large brutes pinned his legs down and a third brought out the leather.

"I'm never spending another vacation in this country again." He cried out in torment.

"What's your real name, traitor?"

"If you had come by your mother's room last night you would have heard her call it out more than once," Armik said through a mixture of tears and laughter.

The guard shook his head in disbelief. "If we didn't already know he was related to the other one, we would have figured it out. They are exactly the same," he said to the other two holding Armik's legs.

The guard gave another few passes at his family jewels. Armik cried out and then his head rolled forward as he lost consciousness.

An overpowering and disgusting smell cut into his nostrils

and pulled him back to the light. The guard was waving smelling salts under his nose. Armik turned his head away.

"Let's try this again. Who are you? Who do you work for? What are you doing here in Iran?"

"I already told you. I'm an Italian here on a—"

"I am aware of what you told me. I think, however, that shortly you will tell me something different."

"I want a lawyer."

"And I want less hair on my back and more on my head, but you see, God often conspires against us." Shorty pulled a pair of needle nose pliers from a toolbox on the window ledge.

Armik looked down at his fingernails and shivered at the thought of his cell mate's hands.

"Look, this is just a huge misunderstanding. If you let me call the Italian embassy I'm certain that we can—"

"Your father was born in Iran?"

"No, my father was born in Rome."

"Right."

"What does my father have to do with anything?"

"Who is your handler here in Tehran?"

"Handler? What does that mean? My team supervisor is Richard Nevaro. He can vouch for me."

The soldier wrote something in his notepad. "Yes, we will have a discussion with your Mr. Nevaro. I mean your CIA handler."

"CIA? What are you talking about? Come on, you can't be serious."

"I am afraid this is very serious, Mr. Vartanian. But I assure you, if this is a mistake, we will get to the bottom of it. In the meantime, please enjoy the full hospitality of our humble prison." He snapped his fingers and the men who had brought Armik to the room now grabbed him. One wrapped an arm across his neck and the other forced his arm down on the table, pinning his wrist and palm down onto the cold metal.

"My manicurist is going to kill you." Armik fought to keep the bravado going.

Shorty sighed, fatigue in his expression. He had been working hard. Armik wondered how his father was holding up. The poor man had come to bail him out and had gotten himself arrested in the process. The guilt from that fact alone tore through him worse than the torture.

"Don't you want to go home?" said Shorty, frustrated. "Don't you want your father to go home? Just answer a few simple questions and we will let you both go. How long do you want to keep doing this?"

"I don't know," he said, coughing. "How long do you plan on playing with my balls?"

The man sighed again and set the pliers down. "Afsheen, go get the water table."

"Now you're talking. I was a little disappointed in your lack of imagination for a moment there, if I'm being honest."

"We'll see if you still feel so clever after drowning for a few hours."

Afsheen stood to leave. He pulled the latch aside and opened the door but was flung back into the small, bricked room. He fell to the floor, making gurgling noises.

"Baba." Armik could not stop himself from crying out at the sight of his father standing at the door. A tall prison guard stood next to him.

His tormentors turned their heads in surprise. Armik took full advantage of the diversion to kick out at Shorty, the one who had hurt him the most. The impact snapped his balding head back so hard it came with a loud crack. He crumpled to the ground. His father fired one shot into each of the other guards. Armik could not believe his eyes.

"Are you trying to alert the whole prison?" the tall guard said.

"These walls are soundproof. Besides, you want them alive to say that you helped us?"

"Let's go. We don't have much time." The guard unshackled Armik.

"What are you doing here, Baba?"

"Getting you out of trouble, what else?"

"I had it all under control," said Armik, rubbing his arms and reaching for his pants.

"Yes, I can see it was going so well—with your nuts hanging out and all."

A loud crash made Armik and his father spin around. Saed the guard had smashed a chair over the head of one of his fallen colleagues. He shrugged at the two men staring at him.

"What?" he said. "He was still alive."

"Friend of yours?" said Armik to his father.

"No, I think mom invited him to the party." Vartan smiled at him.

"Mom's here?" Armik's eyes grew wide. "Christ, it's a family reunion."

"Watch your language."

"Seriously?"

"Hey," Saed yelled. "Sorry to interrupt this…whatever this is…but if you don't want all of us to be hanging off of cranes by morning, we need to get you the hell out of here."

Armik and his father relieved the guards of their uniform shirts and hats, dawning the ill fitting garbs with haste. One had a gun, which Vartan took. Saed checked to see that all was clear before they ventured out the door and into the corridor. They walked at a casual pace down the halls in full view of the security cameras.

Out of the corner of his eye, Armik watched his father. He

had taken a severe beating and struggled to walk, holding his ribs with his forearm as he went, but he was not slowed down at all. His old man was still as tough as ever. He felt the same admiration for him as he had when he had beaten that bully's father.

"We will use the guard exit," said Saed, "but you'll have to do what I tell you. Now pull your hats down and keep your eyes on the floor. Don't say a word."

The three followed in single file through the narrow corridor until they reached a glass partition. Saed looked up at the camera and hit the buzzer. He made a gesture with his two fingers that he was going out to smoke. The door buzzed and the bolt moved. They pushed through. There was another long corridor on the other side, with an emergency exit at the end. The light of day spilled in through the space around the door, a sight Armik had been certain he would never see again.

"What's the plan," he asked.

"When we get outside, your people will be waiting for you. Look for a silver corolla. I expect my family will be unharmed and your agents out of my house when I get home."

"Sounds about right," said Vartan.

They were almost at the door—only ten meters away and seconds from freedom—when it opened and two guards came walking in.

"Saed-*khan, Koja rafti*?" Where are you going?

With the sun to their backs, the two guards approached as silhouettes.

"Just taking these new trainees out for a cigarette"

"What? When did we get new—"

A single bullet took both guards down. Smoke billowed from Vartan's gun.

"We need to go now," Vartan yelled.

"Wait," Saed called out. "Shoot me."

"What?" said Armik in surprise. "Are you—"

"Shoot me or they will think I—"

Bang.

"You're welcome," said Vartan, turning and grabbing his son by the arm.

"Aghh. Goddamn you! Not in the knee, you bastard. I meant in the thigh or something." Saed's screams and moans followed them out the door.

Gunfire greeted them, striking the asphalt at their feet. Another shot rang out from across the street. A body fell from the roof. A silver Corolla rolled up with a screech. Jaleh jumped out from the driver's seat, firing just behind them.

"Well, come on. Get in," she said.

"Mom?"

"I'll drive," Vartan yelled over the gunshots.

"Not a chance."

CHAPTER SIXTY-ONE

"Mom, how is it you are here? And firing a gun! When did you even learn to fire a gun? What's going on?" The shots still rang in Armik's ears.

"You obviously have a lot of questions," his mother said, squeezing his hand in her usual motherly-non-gun-firing way.

A huge explosion went off behind them as they put distance between themselves and the prison. Armik turned to look back, unable to imagine what might have caused it. At least their pursuers would have something to preoccupy them while his family escaped.

"A lot of questions? First, my dad shows up in a prison in Iran that I'm being held in…himself a prisoner. He breaks me out of there by killing five guards…"

"You killed five guards?" his mother said.

"It was four actually," Vartan corrected.

"…and then my mother is waiting outside with guns blazing to drive the getaway car—probably stolen."

"Borrowed," said Vartan.

"And I'm pretty sure I spotted another carload of shooters behind us giving cover fire. Who were they? What am I missing here? Who are you people?"

"I should be asking the questions here." His mom grew furious, slapping Armik hard on the shoulder. "What are you doing in Iran? Who are you working for? CIA? French intelligence?"

"I can't tell you that stuff—that's classified. You don't have clearance, do you?"

"I've got your clearance right here." Vartan made a fist, but his face winced at the gesture.

"You're in no shape to clear anyone, Babba. Momma, we have to get him to a hospital. He may be bleeding internally."

"No hospitals." Vartan shook his head.

"We'll get him to a safe house and have someone come and take a look at him." Jaleh reached out to touch her husband's ribs. He winced again.

"Safe-house? What are you?"

"Can't tell you—it's classified," said Jaleh.

"I don't believe this."

"Relax, Armik-*jan.* We'll figure this out. First, we need to get out of the country." Jaleh made a sharp turn.

"Out of the country? I can't leave. I have a mission."

"What mission?"

"I can't tell you, It's..."

"Let me guess—it's classified." His mother's angry look had not abated.

"As a matter of fact—"

"We know you're here to assassinate Dr. Benjamin Barron—a nuclear physicist and a traitor." Vartan gave his son a knowing wink.

"What? Baba, how do you even—"

"And how is that working out for you..." Jaleh hit him again.

"It was going well, for a while."

"I think you're going to have to abort."

"No, Baba. I can't. You don't understand."

"I do understand, but we are compromised. Besides, why

you?"

"What do you mean?"

"Why you? Of all the people to do this, why did they choose a young, inexperienced operative to pull off such a difficult and dangerous mission alone? Mossad is on the ground here. It makes no sense at all. Something is off."

"He's a fresh face," said Jaleh. "It wouldn't be the first time they called in a pinch hitter from out of town. If he gets caught, he knows nothing. If he dies, they've lost nothing."

"No. Something is not right. Plus, he was compromised too fast. It's like they were waiting for him. They lured him here." Vartan's brow furrowed.

"What? Do you know how crazy that sounds? Mom, talk to him."

"No, your father is right. If he smells a rat, it's a rat. If there is one thing I learned after all these years, it's that your father can read a situation better than anyone."

Armik sat back, stunned by the revelations. His parents were some kind of agents, working for who knows who. His mom drove like a professional race car driver, cutting between cars so closely that he could almost feel the metal brush against his bruised cheek. His life had just been turned upside down.

The sun, thick and heavy, hung low in the reddening sky like an Armenian Christmas ornament. It painted the vast mountain range in the distance with its glow. They exited the freeway and took a sharp turn, pulling into a newly erected underpass currently under construction. He saw no one around but spotted an old, gray Mercedes parked close to the concrete wall waiting for them. They hurried to swap out the vehicles.

While he helped his reluctant father into the car, his mother retrieved a gas canister from the trunk. When the getaway car was engulfed in black smoke and flames, she joined them, taking the driver's seat. They sped off, leaving a dust cloud and a bonfire behind them.

Like his father, Armik's body had suffered much trauma. His testicles ached so much he could barely breathe. They were likely swollen to the size of grapefruits by now, but he had no intention of complaining about it to his mother or father. He would wait and pull the medic aside when he came to look at his dad.

A thick, battered hand, the hand of Vartan the tailor—or whoever he might be—rested on Armik's shoulder from the back seat. "I'm glad you're okay, kid."

"Thanks, Baba."

"Don't mention it."

"No, I mean it. I don't know how much more I could…" he trailed off, choking a little. "So, yeah. Thanks."

"You're my son. I'd kill a thousand guards to get you back. But let's not do that again anytime soon. I have an entire wedding party worth of tuxes to hem back at the shop. Jesus Christ."

"You too, Mom. Thanks."

"I'm your mother. I came because I wanted to be the one to kill you for coming here."

They all laughed, then Vartan groaned. They drove in silence the rest of the way.

CHAPTER SIXTY-TWO

The warmth of the day had risen off the asphalt like a blurry mist, and a chill now rode the wind. Armik shut his window and sat back, his mother navigating their winding route into the inner city.

The safe house turned out to be in a small apartment complex at the southern end of Tehran, the neighborhood less than picturesque. Each building seemed as derelict and nondescript as the next. Homeless individuals populated the nooks and crannies. Bonfires in oil drums spread out like church candles, keeping the darkness at bay.

The shiny Mercedes attracted the odd head turn along the way, but no one followed. Jaleh circled the block several times before pulling to a stop along the curb. They all got out, following her into the building and up the stairs to the third floor.

She banged on a door at the end of the hall. It opened and a clean-shaven man in thick, horned-rimmed glasses, no taller than Vartan, stood before them. He wore no pants, just a pair of boxers to compliment his tank top. A heavy gold chain resting in a bush of chest hair was his only accessory. He blinked but said nothing, beckoning them into the tiny apartment. He closed the door and turned several locks, taking another glance into the peephole. The soft glow of a TV shone from another room in the otherwise dark space.

"I'm Salman," he said, turning to them. "You must be hungry. Come. Let's eat while we talk."

Salman flipped on some lights, and they all took a seat at a kitchen table. Armik went for the chair that would have his back to the wall facing the entrance. His dad had the same idea and shoved him out of the way to get it. They both groaned, their injuries agitated. Armik smiled and rolled his eyes. Jaleh gave them both a warning glare.

Salman set three plates down and served warm rice off the stove with *tadik* and *khoresh gheimeh*, a beef, and split pea stew. He brought them cold bottles of coke and put tea on while they ate. During Armik's short stay in prison, the absence of food had been almost as difficult to bear as the torture. He tore into the magnificent feast. His father did the same while Jaleh looked on, pity in her eyes.

"My poor boys. They starved you in there. They always starve you in that place. I remember it well." Jaleh looked off into space as if her mind was flooded by her own memories.

"You've been in there?" Surprise diminished for Armik with each new revelation.

"It's how I met your father," she said, smiling and placing a hand on Vartan's forearm as if recounting a beautiful moment. His dad nodded and continued to chew.

"Wow, that sounds like something straight out of a romance novel—wait. I thought you told me you met in University."

Vartan laughed and Jaleh followed suit.

"Yes," his father said. "Evin prison was nicknamed Evin University due to the number of intellectuals housed there."

"Oh my God." Armik shook his head in disbelief.

Salman returned to the kitchen with pants on and a handful of files and papers clutched in his fist. Pushing some plates aside, he laid them on the table. Jaleh picked up one of the files and leafed through.

"This is what we know about some of the key players in this situation." Salman selected a photo from the pile and held it up for them to see. "This is Jack Smith. He was section chief in Tehran in 1978. Now he is stationed in Islamabad, but he has been spending a lot of time here and seems to be able to move about with impunity, meaning he is in good with the higher-ups. He arrived from Afghanistan a few days ago and is staying at the Espinas Hotel, his usual haunt."

"That's the guy that showed up at the base when they recruited me." Armik took the surveillance photo and examined it—the large man in a cowboy hat getting into a limo.

"He is also believed to have been instrumental in arranging certain events that contributed to the overthrow of the Shah."

"And now he is here to do what?" said Jaleh.

"We don't know. But whatever it is, it can't be good." Salman took out another photo.

"We had a hit on the phantom spook Rostem. We got a ping on him arriving in the country a few days ago from Afghanistan—probably because he wanted us to. His face is obscured but we managed to track a phone he carried using the man-in-the-middle attack. It led us to Nasim Park, District 1. Then we lost the signal."

"He's sending a message." Vartan snatched the photo. "This is worse than the last one I saw of him, but it's as good a place to start as any. I'll head there tomorrow after sunset."

"Whoa, whoa. What are you talking about, Baba? We need to get you to a hospital and out of the country. Both of you."

"You said it yourself. We can't just leave, Armik-*jan*. We have to finish this."

"I said me, not you!"

"Listen to me. Our enemies know us. They know us so well that they played us all. There is no going back. We will never be left alone until we put an end to this. We kept the truth of what we were from you all these years because we didn't want this for you. But here you are, right in the middle of it. So we need to finish the game."

Armik sighed and looked at his mother, who nodded but said nothing. His father was right. With all that they knew, there would be no way any of them would be left alive to tell the tale.

"Okay, so what's the plan?" Armik slipped a piece of rock sugar into his mouth and sipped the hot tea he had just been served.

"I'll deal with Smith," said Jaleh. "We get rid of him, that sets the regime back. He is obviously working his own agenda as much as that of the US. Then I'll take care of Barron so that your mission is completed. I don't want you on a hit list because you abandoned that. Your father will try to flush out Rostem, and you will stay here until we can get you out of the country."

Armik shook his head. He still could not wrap his mind around his mother being an assassin, despite seeing her firing a gun a few hours earlier. But that fact did not change anything, he needed to complete his mission on his own—not just as a matter of pride, but also that of practicality. He had been the one who had watched the doctor. He knew his movements, habits, and safety protocol—even if he had botched it on the first try. They would be expecting him to run, not to try again.

"No, Mama. I have to get Barron myself."

"This is not up for debate."

"I'm not a kid anymore. I'm a soldier. I have the training, and I can do this. Besides, getting to him will take too much time for you. I've already done all the groundwork. I know all

I need to know to get to him. It has to be me."

"You got caught last time."

"They knew I was coming. They won't be expecting me now, with all this heat. Come on, mama. You know it's the only option that makes any sense."

Jaleh looked at her son, then at Vartan. He seemed even more reluctant but also resigned to it. She let out a long breath.

"So it's settled then," said Armik.

"Do we call for backup from your side? Or I can reach out to Abbas," said Vartan, going for another helping of *gheimeh.*

"No." Jaleh had a strange uneasiness about her. "Let's leave everyone out of it for now. There has to be a mole somewhere. They knew we were coming. The less people that know our next moves, the better."

"And how are you going to find this Rostem, Baba?"

"Easy. I'll let him find me." Vartan smiled, his mouth full of food.

There came a knock on the door and Salman stood. "The doctor is here."

CHAPTER SIXTY-THREE

Tehran, Iran
August 3, 2000

There was no way he could get a gun or even a knife into the building. Instead, Armik had ground a large piece of hard plastic down to as fine an edge as he could without making it flimsy. It ended up being surprisingly sharp and could even slice paper. It was the best he could do on such short notice.

Now, he needed a way in.

Under heavily armed guards, the good doctor had already been shuttled by an armored car and deposited into his place of employment. Nestled right in the center of District 6 in the charming and quaint Iranshahr, the building stood hidden in plain sight in an area bustling with students.

Armik saw nowhere to hide to get a shot at the doctor while going in. Inside the lab seemed to be the only place he could get to his target, which, according to his mother's Mossad intel, was situated on the thirteenth floor.

He sat at a cafe across the street, sipping hot tea and reading a novel while watching the comings and goings. The lunchtime hour had many of the staff stopping by to pick up coffee or pastries. Several came in groups, young men wearing ties without jackets. Their security passes around their necks dangled like badges of honor. Most of the passes had a green stripe, but the odd few had a red one. Armik wanted a red one.

One of the groups that came in to order had a young man with just such a pass among them. Vartan stood and moved next to him. When the man's steaming hot order was placed on the counter, Armik reached for it.

"Hey, uh…I think that's my coffee."

"Mmm, no I think that's my tea," said Armik, letting a small amount of clear liquid pour into the steaming beverage from his cupped palm.

"Yeah… I don't think so, pal. It says Jamsheed right there, and I'm Jamsheed."

"What? You're Jamsheed? I'm Jamsheed too. What are the odds?"

"Pretty good actually, but…"

"Hey, my apologies. You're right, this is coffee."

"Yeah, okay. No problem."

Armik watched the young man take his coffee and sit. He returned to his chair and flipped through his book again, keeping his periphery on the show that would unfold next to him. It had a gradual start—a few tummy rumbles, a look of discomfort. When the weapons-grade laxative took effect, the man could not get to the restroom fast enough, just about overturning his table along with his friends' drinks.

Armik waited about a minute before following. He cringed at the assault on his senses upon opening the door. He spotted clear evidence that the man did not make it to the stall on time. The sedative he combined with the laxative must have worked a little faster than anticipated because the tall door was ajar. The coffee drinker was on his back with his pants barely unbuckled.

Armik checked his pulse. Still alive. Then he relieved him of his security pass. He slipped it around his own neck, washed his hands, and put on a pair of fake spectacles before walking out of the bathroom and straight out the door. He headed across the street and into the building, past the security guards, through the metal detector, which did not beep at all, and into the lobby.

He was in. Now he had another problem. His security pass would get him on the restricted elevator, but only as far as the twelfth floor. After that, he needed a restricted zone pass. Armik scanned the lobby floor for someone who had one. He found her—a young woman in a lab coat with a red headscarf. She shuffled over to the lift, her eyes focused on a document in her hand. Armik felt a little bad about what he had to do.

"Nice day," he said to her as they both approached the lift. She looked at him but made no reply. He scanned his card first and pressed the button. The doors opened and a group people exited. Armik gestured for the woman to go ahead of him. She went in but said nothing.

What a real ray of sunshine, this one is.

He pressed for the 12th floor and up they went. With the elevator moving fast, he did not have much time. He pulled a small plastic bottle from his sleeve and was about to give it a squeeze when the elevator bell rang, indicating a stop. And they were on the 9th floor.

Damn.

Two revolutionary guards stepped in. They pressed for the 11th floor.

Damn.

He made himself busy, cleaning his glasses, keeping his face down and to the left. They did not seem to be alarmed by his presence, but they were jeopardizing his plan. He would need time for the aerosol to take effect.

Not a moment too soon, the elevator stopped, and the two armed soldiers stepped out on their floor. Armik wasted no time, stretching his arms as if yawning while squeezing the bottle as near to her face as he dared. So focused on her documents, she did not seem to notice.

The tasteless, odorless spray hit the mark. She lost her balance and fell, spilling her papers. Armik caught her and eased her to the floor just as the door opened on twelve. A young woman with several packages in her arms was about to step in when she saw the scene.

"Hurry," Armik said. "She fainted. Call for an ambulance."

The woman dropped her packages and ran off. Armik snatched the card from the sleeping woman's neck, swiped it, and hit the 13th-floor button. The light went green and the doors closed.

Hopefully, no one saw that, or I won't have much time.

The doors opened again, and he came face to face with a crowd of shocked people.

"What happened?" someone asked.

"Is that Farnoush?" said another.

"She passed out. Someone call a doctor," Armik said with as much panic as he could muster. The crowd entered the elevator in a rush to help. He slipped away unnoticed and made his way down to the lab, according to the map his mother had provided. He had in his grasp a handful of the unconscious woman's papers.

The passkey granted him access to the first three doors. The fourth, the one he needed to get into, was guarded by two security men with holstered sidearms.

Damn. Looks like it's going to be the hard way.

The hallway was empty but for the two men at the end. Armik made his way toward them, looking down at his document. When he got to the door, one of the guards stopped him with a hand on his shoulder.

"You can't go in here with that card, Dr..." The mustached

man lifted the card to get a look at it. Realization crept across his face. Armik did not resemble the woman in the photo, but by the time he looked up, he was dying. Armik sprung forward and twisted the man's neck to an impossible degree while slipping the thin plastic blade into it.

His shocked partner froze, unable to react before Armik's hard kick struck his knee. As the guard toppled, he pulled the blade out from one and jabbed it into the other's neck. He released his first victim and took hold of the back of the second man's head while he died, careful to avoid being drenched in blood. The struggle was brief, and they both expired with quiet gurgles. He helped himself to a pistol, several rounds of ammunition, and a blood-covered passkey.

The door opened before him, and he ran ina look . The first person he saw was a man with thinning gray hair and a silver goatee carrying a tray of empty Petri dishes. Armik aimed his pistol at him.

"Dr. Benjamin Barron?" he said.

The man's eyes widened, and he dropped the tray. "Th... there," he said, pointing to a closed door across from them.

A loud, resonating alarm sounded. The doors were being locked down. He had a few seconds at best. He kicked the door just beneath the knob and it burst open.

"Dr. Benjamin Barron."

"Yes? What is this?" The man sat at a desk, his back to a large picture window overlooking the city. He looked more annoyed than frightened until he recognized Armik's face. "You!"

"Israel says hello, traitor."

The gun went off twice in quick succession. The first hit him square in the forehead knocking him over. The second hit the lifeless body in the chest.

Well, that's off the to-do list. Armik turned back to the

door swinging half on its hinges. He peered out. Soldiers in tactical gear and policemen were already gathered together at the point from where he had just entered. He looked left and saw more hallways and corridors. All with no exits.

Think, think, think.

He ran around to his victim. His arms were splayed out like a scarecrow. A gaping hole had replaced where his face should have been, and blood was spattered everywhere. Armik fired into the window. It took three shots to shatter. Tossing his glasses, he stripped the good doctor of his lab coat and security pass. He picked him up like a barbell and tossed him out the shattered window. Putting the gun in his waistband, he went to squat in the corner, his head between his knees.

The door burst open a second later, red laser-sights on automatic machine guns swept the room from side to side, with yells of adrenalized men right behind. They all trained on Armik, who slowly put his hands up and pointed out the window.

"He jumped out the window," he said, pointing with a shaking hand.

Two guards hauled him up to his feet.

"Sir, it's not safe. We have to get you out of here now. Let's go."

Whisked away toward the stairwell, Armik kept his head down and they did not look at him. They passed by the man who he had pointed the gun at moments earlier. Police were asking him questions, so he was not facing their direction.

Don't turn around. Don't turn.

The man was too focused on recounting his near death experience to notice Armik being carried off the scene. They pulled him nonstop all the way down the thirteen flights to the bottom. The emergency exit at the end would not open because of the lockdown, so the soldier shot it open while the other called for a car from his radio. The car came from around the corner in under thirty seconds, coming to a screeching halt in front of them. They threw Armik in the back like a duffel bag, and one guard hopped into the front. The other ran back into the building.

"Are you okay, sir?" said another soldier. "Are you injured?"

"No. No, I'm fine. Where are we going?"

"I'm to take you to the airbase until we get this all sorted out."

"What are we waiting for?" Armik expected them to realize he was not the man they thought he was, but they did not.

As he had hoped, the security protocols for evacuating Dr. Barron out of the building had never been activated until now, so none of them had ever seen him. Finally, some good luck.

"Your assistant is being brought out as well, so I'm told."

Crap.

A few seconds later they brought out a young woman with a red headscarf—the woman from the elevator.

Crap. Crap.

She had regained consciousness, though she still looked slightly off balanced the way she held the soldier's arm. She would have a massive headache soon.

The soldiers pushed her into the car next to Armik and the tires burned out before the door fully closed. It took a moment, but she finally looked up at him. Recognition crossed her face, then came a look of rage. Armik readied his hand to draw the weapon in his waistband. She sizzled for a bit, but as the wick burned the explosion never came. She turned her eyes forward and said nothing, clutching her head to ease what must have been a massive migraine.

Armik smiled a little. Okay, this is interesting.

They were about two blocks away when several military vehicles raced past them. And Sirens could still be heard in the distance.

"Wait," Armik said. "Stop the car."

"We can't, sir. Orders."

"Stop the car, you idiot. I'm going to be sick."

The vehicle slowed and came to a stop at the curb. Armik slammed the butt of his gun into the driver's temple. He slumped down against the window. The nozzle was already pointing at the other guard's head by the time he tried to react.

"This is not going to end well for you," said the man, his surprise turning to anger.

"Turn around."

"You don't know who you're deal…"

Armik put him to sleep in the same fashion as his partner, only this one took several hard strikes until he became still. He turned to the angry woman, who looked more annoyed now than distressed.

"Hey, sorry about that whole elevator scenario." He offered her his famous Vartanian smile.

"Who are you with? CIA?" She crossed her arms and glared.

"Why do Persians blame the CIA for everything?"

"Because they are always to blame for everything. Goddamnit, you are, aren't you?"

"Not exactly. More like French intelligence. So I'm guessing you are not really a physicist's assistant."

"MI6. And you took out my target."

"Hey, If I had known that you were here for the same reason, I would have let you do it."

"We'd better go."

"My car is right here," Armik said, pointing to the old, beat up, blue Mercedes next to them. "Need a lift?"

"Drop me off at the British Embassy. My work here is done."

"You're welcome."

"Shut up."

With haste, they switched vehicles, pulling away from the scene with a screech of rubber against the road.

"So what was your plan?" said Armik.

"For what?"

"To rid us of the doctor."

"Lab accident."

"How was that coming along?" He smiled at his own question.

"Smartass. I admit there was a bit of a hiccup. He hardly set foot out of that office. And when he did, his two guards would escort him down to his waiting armored car."

"My plan was more direct."

"Your plan was no plan at all. It was a suicide mission."

"Why do you say that?"

"Because the soldiers that got you out of there, who obviously had mistaken you for Dr. Barron, were not even his regular extraction team. It was only because of the lockdown protocol that the nearest soldiers were dispatched and therefore they didn't recognize you. That was just luck."

"No such thing as luck. I planned it to the letter."

"Sure you did."

"Oh, now you're just hurting my feelings." Armik put his hand on his heart as if he was injured.

"You're a tough guy. You can take it."

Armik stopped the car on the side of the street and stared at her for a moment. Strands of her auburn hair had slipped out from the headscarf, framing her face. She had a perfect set of eyebrows above two of the blackest eyes he had ever seen, accented with long, curled eyelashes. He had not seen it right away since he had to knock her out—that was not a good start—but she was beautiful. And she was a spook.

“So much going on in that head of yours?”

“Nah, it’s nothing too complicated.”

“I’ll bet.” She smiled and he liked it.

“This is you,” he said, pointing to the embassy building across the street.

“Thanks.” She stared for an extra second before opening the door. Then she turned to him one more time. “So what do I call you.”

“James.” He had always liked that name.

“Thanks, James.”

“What do I call you?”

“You don’t.” She laughed and closed the door.

CHAPTER SIXTY-FOUR

When Jaleh walked into the restaurant of the Espinas Hotel in Tehran all heads turned toward her. Even at her age, with her barely-there headscarf, she was still a stunning woman. She had learned long ago how to weaponize beauty, and she was no less adept at it now.

The maitre d' gawked but did not question her. Striding with purpose, she moved right past the entrance and into the crowded restaurant. In an instant, she identified two tables that were agents for sure, and one other was most likely.

Tableware clinked and wine glasses touched while murmurs of polite conversations drifted together into one musical rumble. Dim lighting and a three-piece ensemble in the corner stage helped complete the elegant ambiance. How she would love to bring Vartan here sometime, though he was never really all that fond of anything pompous. He preferred a good grilled kubideh with rice over any fancy meal, but he never complained and indulged her more refined tastes. He was a good man. A rare specimen.

One restaurant patron stood out among the others. He was not engaged in merriment or discussions, but rather dined alone at a specially placed table next to the emergency exit. The comb over on his balding head looked so haphazard it seemed deliberate. His bulbous nose held up a thin pair of glasses. His days-old white mustache danced upon his lip as he chewed the food he shoveled into his mouth.

Being an obese man, his small chair seemed precarious beneath the immense weight. On the chair next to him lay the cowboy hat that would crown his adipose head. A denim jacket hung on the back of his seat and his sleeves were rolled up for the gargantuan task of dispensing with all the food before him.

Jaleh went straight for his table as if he expected her. She noted the faces of the agents at the other tables becoming alarmed, some even gestured toward their weapons.

"My Goodness. I thought it was you."

"I'm sorry, ma'am. Have we met?" He wiped his greasy mouth with a napkin.

"Well, of course we have, in a sense. I'm surprised you don't remember. Mind if I join you?"

"Well actually I—"

"Perfect. Thank you." She moved to stand across from him and a waiter appeared behind her with a chair. "Some tea, please," she said. She made herself comfortable while the man watched her with an astonished expression. She noticed his casual motion for his agents to stand down. "Don't you miss being able to have wine in a restaurant out in the open? I certainly couldn't stand it for very long."

"Forgive me," he said. "But who are you, and what is it you want?"

"Well, let's see. You recruited my son and delivered him to VEKAK so that they could lure my husband to the country because they think he is the former SAVAK operative known as The Persian. You facilitated the kidnapping of an Israeli nuclear Physicist for the purpose of pushing this country into the age of nuclear weapons, and you were complicit, along with other rogue CIA elements, in the illegal surveillance and attempted assassination of members of the Iranian Royal family. So, what do I want? I'd really like your head, for one thing. But how about we start with some answers. Who paid you to betray your country and mine? Who wants The Persian so badly? And what's the main objective here?"

"Yikes, sweetheart," he said with a thick southern drawl, "that sure was a mouthful. So, you are the famous Mossad operative that caused so much trouble for the new regime. Interesting. I should be asking you questions. Such as, what makes you think I will ever let you leave this restaurant?"

"Well, perhaps you didn't notice that red laser dot on your shirt."

He looked down to find the tiny red circle hovering over the center of his chest.

"The second I see you signal those agents that are watching us right now, I will sit back and drink my tea while I watch you bleed on this nice tablecloth." She could see the anger burning in his face. "So, again, who orchestrated this?"

"Impressive, little lady. Very impressive. You have a pair of brass ones—I'll give you that. It doesn't matter now. It's all done."

"It's being undone as we speak. By the time you pay your bill, everything you've worked for will be unraveled. The evidence I've gathered about you will wipe you out. Even your Cayman accounts will be forfeited. The question is, will you point me in the right direction and make it easier, or will you be a casualty of the clean up?"

"What can I say? Your husband...and you...wiped out most of the new Regime's best operatives right from the get-go. They hold grudges. What did you expect? Rostem is the man behind it all, but even I don't know who he is."

"Another lie."

"It's the truth. I've never seen his face. We always used

intermediaries. This was all off the books because the regime didn't want to make waves and risk further sanctions."

"So what's the endgame here? To take Israel off the map?"

"Or to at least be able to—that's not news though."

Jaleh contemplated his words. The man would not reveal anything she did not already know. She had not expected him to—at least not on purpose. She finished her tea and stood.

"I thank you for your time. You've been most helpful, Mr. Smith."

"You think you can work against the CIA and get off unscathed?"

She stopped at his chair and leaned close to whisper. "Who says I'm working against them?"

She strutted out of the restaurant, past the agents who watched her closely. She thanked the maitre d' and headed out, where she hailed a cab. A waiter ran up to her.

"Ma'am, what should I do with this?" he said, holding up a laser pointer on a key ring.

"Keep it, as a souvenir." She replied with a smile that was still effective after all these years. She handed the young man a few American twenty-dollar bills. "For your trouble."

"Thank you, ma'am." He gave a grateful bow of his head.

She entered her cab and drove out of sight, her part of the mission nearly complete.

"Where to, ma'am?" said the driver.

"Shahyad Tower."

"You know, it's not called that anymore." The elderly driver smiled at her through the rearview mirror.

"Yes, I know. How sad." Jaleh smiled back, taking the phone from her pocket.

Hitting the speed dial, she put it to her ear and waited. It rang four times before Jack Smith's angry voice answered.

"Who is this?"

"Hello, chief," she said

"Oh, that's cute, slipping a phone into my pocket. You think the theatrics are going to frighten me? Listen, you crazy bitch. This time you've done kicked the wrong hornet's nest. You'll never leave Iran alive."

The unhappy agent's voice must have been loud enough for the driver to hear. He looked at her in the rearview mirror with curious eyes. She gave him another smile.

"Try not to give yourself a heart attack. I have a message for you, chief."

"Message from who?"

"Check the text." She could hear him fumble with the phone and imagined him struggling to handle the small device with his pudgy hands.

"What the…The Persian. That's a cute little trick. That's your message?"

"No. This is." Jaleh pressed the star key twice on her phone.

A second later a loud bang sounded, followed by static. She folded her phone and put it away, shrugging at the still curious driver. The Persian would be the last thing Jack Smith ever saw before the small, concentrated explosion cast him into the darkness forever.

CHAPTER SIXTY-FIVE

Vartan had not set foot on the grounds of the Royal Palace or its immediate area in decades, yet a vivid memory remained as though it had been only yesterday. From Nasim Park, just across Darabad street from the north-facing side, he could see the upper half of the private mansion. The silhouette of its flat, overhanging roof was distinct in the waning light. The rest of the building remained obscured by foliage, as some of the trees had been old even back when he was not.

An uneasy blue dusk washed over everything, like a spotlight in a sad stage play scene waiting for the drama to unfold. Seated on a cold, metal park bench, he checked his holstered weapon, then took a casual sip of his coffee. His eyes swept the surroundings for any signs of movement. A dog barking in the distance broke the quiet swishing of passing cars and the buzz of the electric lamps. Vartan breathed in the cool air.

How had time taken him from here only to bring him back again? He had imagined visiting the palace—now a museum—with his family. In his mind, he pictured all he would show them, like a tour guide with knowledge more intimate than most. But he never imagined returning here under these circumstances.

A shadow flickered among the trees. Careful not to tip off

his observer, Vartan brought a hand closer to his weapon. The shadow moved again, this time without any regard for stealth. The outline of a man against the light of the street ran in the opposite direction. He headed straight out of the park, crossed the street, and made a dash toward the thick stone wall that surrounded the palace. Once there, he was again obscured by trees.

So he wants to end it in there? This guy is really sentimental.

Vartan rose, tossing his coffee cup into a trash bin. Sighing, he drew his gun and took off after the shadow. Arriving at the wall, he found no one. With the barrel of his gun, he scanned the length of the ancient brick structure. He looked up, the top of the wall looming several feet over his head.

"I'm not climbing that." Keeping his shoulder against the wall, he moved westward until he came to the northern gate.

The museum closed at 6:00pm and a quick check of the cheap watch he picked up at the bazaar to replace the one left behind at Evin told him it was 7:32. He was surprised to find the gate open, the heavy bars ajar just enough for him to squeeze through—twenty years ago. In his present form, he had to force the opening but managed to scrape past.

The shadow stood waiting for him on the steps of the Shah's private mansion, tall, lean, and faceless. The distance between them, about the length of two soccer fields, was covered by freshly mown grass and a large fountain.

Vartan aimed, even though a shot at that distance would not likely hit its mark. The man turned and ran, disappearing into the building.

"You've got to be kidding me." He took the obvious bait with annoyance, running at a jogger's pace into the trap set for him.

His chest heaved by the time he sprinted up the marble steps. Like the gate opened for his convenience, the massive wooden doors were left with a slight gap. He leaned back and pulled the door wide with the side of his foot, his pistol in a two-handed grip moving from left to right.

The smell of ammonia rushed to his nose. Gone were the scents and sounds that once filled this happy place. Auxiliary lighting illuminated the now sparsely furnished space. A large portrait of the king and queen still hung in a place of prominence, though not in the same spot. The myriad chandeliers still hung overhead, giving the room a sparkle even when turned off. Plexiglas partitions had been installed on every side, keeping the visitors on a path that offered a glimpse into the past.

A heavy sadness tugged at Vartan's heart while his blood ran thick with anger, but there was no time for emotions now. He spotted movement on the second-floor balcony. This Rostem was fast.

Vartan made for the staircase, his gun pointed up and ahead. The same Plexiglas protected the banisters all the way to the top, and also offered a reflected glimpse at whatever would be around the next bend. He saw no one, but a sound from above him told him to keep climbing.

At last, he reached the third floor, the former private quarters. The long hallway before him brought a flood of memories. The space seemed to go on and on in both directions though it was no longer lined with the same priceless works of art from around the world. The busts of long-dead poets and philosophers keeping silent watch in intervals were gone, looted and replaced with cheaper statues. The train of hand-woven silk carpeting that ran along the entire length in one magnificent piece had been replaced by a green carpet.

One of the statues exploded next to his head—a missed shot that brought him out of his reveries. *An amateur mistake.* Perhaps this was why Rostem had chosen this place.

Vartan fired back in the direction of the shot, faux marble coming down like rain in the cloud of smoke.

"I thought you might not get the invitation," said Rostem, his voice, it seemed, coming from everywhere.

"It wasn't very subtle." Vartan sprang from behind one statue to the next.

"At last we meet, after all these years. I have hoped for this day for a long time."

"I could have done without it." Vartan rolled, a volley of bullets peppering the wall around him. He spotted another shadow on the opposite side from where he had come.

So that's the trap. More than one player. Vartan listened, trying to hear any clues as to how many shooters he was dealing with.

Coming to his feet, he decided to play on his own terms. More bullets tore chunks from the plaster. He pushed at a panel in the wall where the marble gave way to glittering embossed silver slabs. *It still works!* Vartan dove in through the secret door, crouching in the pitch blackness.

He waited by the tunnel entrance, peering through the little gap he left open. A few seconds later, a man appeared, his face obscured by darkness. He peered with caution to where Vartan had been hiding, his gun at the ready. Seeing no one, he turned to face the other direction. Vartan slipped a hand through the crack and fired two shots. The body lurched forward and dropped face down. Closing the door again, he ran the length of the pitchblack tunnel. The panel on the other end stuck a little but gave way with a shoulder, and he emerged in the queen's private apartments.

With stacks of boxes and crates lining the walls and no sign of Plexiglas, he could tell this section had not been open to the public. Only her drawing room had been made available. The once beautiful space had fallen into disrepair. Wallpaper hung in sheets from the walls. The ceilings, stripped of their chandeliers, left only wires and water-damaged panels. Vartan put the thought out of mind.

He could not be sure which one he had killed, but Rostem or not, even if they discovered the panel, no one would come after him through the narrow pathway. It was a death trap. The only other option was to find the service corridor and take the long way around.

Meanwhile, Vartan looked from room to room, searching for a vantage point. The panel to the escape tunnel that might have enabled him to flank his opponent did not budge. He seemed to have trapped himself. He stepped onto the balcony, using one of the pillars for cover. He saw no movement in the garden. His ribs ached and he needed time to rest.

Vartan slung his arms around one of the marble pillars and then a leg. With a little hop, he slid down the fluted shaft, squeezing to slow his descent. He touched down at the base and, taking another look around, ran for the stone garden. He found a large, ancient relief carving, depicting Darius I. He hid behind it.

How were his wife and son doing? He hoped they fared better than him. He had walked into this trap with the confidence of a twenty-year-old soldier, but he was stuck in an old man's body. Something seemed off. If Rostem wanted him dead, he could have just used a sniper rifle while Vartan sat at the park, or any number of opportunities. Why this drama? There had to be something else to it.

A gunshot went off and the top section of the relief blew up above him.

"Why don't you stand up and fight like a man, Mr. Persian?" Rostem called out.

"Why do you like to hear yourself talk so much?" Vartan called back.

Realizing the next shot might go through him, he leapt to his feet and ran. Moving while ducking, he hurried past the vast number of stone monuments. His muscles ached, his mind was on fire.

Vartan cursed his old legs, his aging tendons, and his broken ribs. He ventured a look from behind a large, square ornament and scanned the area. He spotted a few exit points within distance of a short sprint, but he had no plans to leave here while the other was still alive. Above his head came an explosion of marble, the bullet missing him by millimeters.

Where the hell is he? The shot was way too high to be close. He must have moved off further, but I have to draw him closer. He put on a burst of speed, hoping that his body would hold out just long enough. Rolling, shoulder first, to the ground, he came up behind a six-foot tall red marble obelisk, just in time to avoid another shot that sprayed marble dust on top of him.

Vartan fired back in the direction he thought the shot had originated, but with so many obstacles around him it was impossible to hit anything but stone.

"You can do better than that, Persian. I know you can."

"If you would step a little to the left, I'll show you a trick shot."

Movement caught his eye and he whipped his head around. A maintenance worker had just entered the grounds from the side gate. *Great. Things just got even more complicated.* He had no doubt Rostem would happily kill the man, but he did not want that on his conscience—not at this age.

He fired a few more shots to buy him time then made a beeline for cover a few rows down. There was no return fire this time. *Did I hit him? No. I'm not that lucky. He wants to flank me.* The worker, hearing the shots, darted off out of sight.

Vartan reloaded and moved in the opposite direction, going from stone to stone and keeping low. He took a peek, peering out. He moved again. No shots. He saw the hint of a shadow, the tail of a coat, flicker past his eye. It disappeared in an instant behind the large, brick mausoleum gracing the center of the property.

Got you, you bastard.

Vartan took off after his foe, his gun pointing skyward. He stopped at the end of the structure, his back flat against the blackened stone. Peering around the corner, he saw Rostem kneeling at the other end. He crept up behind this predator turned prey. All the skills, the agility, the adrenaline of his youth returned to him for that one brief moment before the kill. The nozzle of his gun touched the back of Rostem's head. The man stiffened. His finger shifted but then stopped.

"Turn around," Vartan said. He wanted to see the killer's face before he blew it off.

"Please don't kill me. He told me to wear this coat. He had a gun too and..." The man who was not Rostem but the maintenance worker began to shake.

"Oh, shi—"

A shovel came down on his arm, cutting off his words with a thud. He dropped his gun.

The worker ran but a loud shot brought him down. Vartan took the moment of distraction to roll forward into Rostem's legs. He fell on top of Vartan and dropped his gun, but came down with elbows to Vartan's ribs.

Vartan let out a howl. Rostem crawled toward the fallen weapon but was yanked back by one leg. Mustering all his strength through his agony, Vartan drew his ankle blade and drove it into Rostem's neck. A struggle and a gurgle later, the agent known as Rostem was with his many victims.

"Long live the king," said Vartan, rolling off the body.

His blood-soaked chest heaved, and he lay his head back. Just for a moment he needed to close his eyes and rest, but the approaching sirens pulled him back from the brink of unconsciousness. There would be no prison if he was caught here. Only a firing squad. Vartan forced himself up and ran back to the small northern gate, keeping out of the light along the wall. Out of breath and about to collapse, he thrust himself through the still open gate and limped to the edge of the street where he dropped to the curb, unable to move any further.

A dark blue Pontiac pulled up in silence toward him. The passenger door opened, Abbas leaning across the seat with a smile. "There you are. I've been wondering where you ended up. You going to sit there until the police find you, or shall we go?"

Vartan dragged himself into the passenger seat and pulled the door closed. "How the hell did you know where to find me?"

"You were shooting up the royal palace. I heard it on the local radio. I figured only you would be crazy enough, so I circled the place a few times and you popped out."

"Lucky me. And who is following us?" Vartan leaned to his right to get a better look into the side mirror. Several SUVs followed in their wake at an easy pace.

"That, my friend, is our ride home. Now where do we go?"

"Shahyad Tower."

CHAPTER SIXTY-SIX

The sun vanished into the Persian night sky, taking a final bow with flashes of gold and red before relinquishing the stage to the moon and its starry canopy.

Jaleh waited at the steps behind the Shahyad Tower. Her mission now completed, she had no idea if her husband and son had been successful. She had already heard that Dr. Barron was dead, but she had no way of knowing if Armik had gotten away. They were both a half hour late.

She held an open book in her hand, hoping to avoid any unwanted attention by being a woman alone at night. There were still a good handful of tourists and locals strolling about as the tower lit up, so her presence was not completely out of place.

Jaleh's heart fluttered at the sight of an old green Mercedes puttering down the street. With trepidation, she watched it pull over and come to a stop. A man in a long dark coat came out, his face veiled in shadow until he stepped under the streetlamp. It was Armik. When he looked up and saw her, he broke into a run, speeding through the smattering of people and under the giant archway. Jaleh received her son with open arms and held him tightly. After a long embrace, they pulled apart.

"It's done," he said

"I heard. Next to impossible, and yet here you are."

"You have no idea, Mama. How did yours go?"

"Our friend and I had a very harsh exchange over the phone."

"Good, that's excellent. Where's Baba."

She looked up at her son and could see the dread in his eyes already. Jaleh's heart dropped. "He hasn't arrived yet. But don't worry, he'll be here," she said, trying to comfort herself as much as him.

"Yes, of course. Probably just ran into traffic."

"I can see him cursing at the cars in front of him as he's driving behind some large truck, rushing to get here."

"Yeah, you know how he gets."

"How do I get? Speaking ill of the dead already?" Vartan stood behind them with Abbas by his side, quiet as ghosts in their approach.

"Baba!"

"Vartan!"

"All these wet faces, I thought perhaps you heard something I didn't." Vartan laughed but she could see the physical pain in his eyes. The three embraced.

"I take it everything went as planned?" said Jaleh.

"More or less. It all worked out in the end. Thanks to Abbas here, who picked me up just in time."

Jaleh winced on the inside at the words. Something was off. She could tell he shared the same thought but said nothing.

"Are you hurt?" she touched his still swollen cheek.

"Nah, nothing a little rest and alcohol won't cure."

"Well," said Abbas. "This is all great, but we better get you three to the French Ambassador's plane before they figure out all the pieces to this messy puzzle you created and come after us all."

They turned around to face Abbas, who stood there, watching them with a smile.

"We have access to the French Ambassador's plane? How did you manage that? I thought we would have to sneak out through the Turkish border."

"Isn't this better? Diplomatic flight with no checks. We will divert and head to Israel where you will be debriefed by Mossad, then you'll be home for croissants and tea by lunchtime. Her imperial highness is not without connections." Abbas waved and a small fleet of black SUVs pulled up.

"The queen organized this?" Vartan's eyes went wide.

"This wasn't a Mossad operation," Jaleh said. "We just came here to find our son."

"You are both technically still active Mossad operatives, so everything you do is a Mossad operation. Besides, that's the deal we had to make to arrange your safe and easy passage."

"Works for me." Armik shrugged, looking anxious to leave, like someone who had had enough of a vacation.

"Let's get going," Abbas said. "A car is waiting."

They followed Abbas to one of the SUVs. A driver waited at the wheel behind heavily tinted glass. Jaleh noted the diplomatic plates. They would have no problem moving through the city to the airport, as long as the Iranians did not decide that diplomatic immunity was now inconvenient. It did not stop them from taking over an embassy.

Vartan was limping. His part of the mission obviously had not been easy. He was an older man now and had seen better days but was still astonishingly strong. He had better reflexes than most men half his age. She could see much of him in her son. Still, she could not shake the feeling that they had missed something—some piece of the puzzle they were not yet aware of.

"Are you alright, my dear?" Abbas asked with concern as she reached the door of the vehicle, which he opened for her.

"Yes, thank you, Abbas-*jan.* It's been a long, few months. I'm just happy we have Armik back."

"You'll be home soon, and all of this will be behind you."

"Thank you." She embraced her husband's old partner and friend. "For all you've done."

"Please, don't mention it. My part was the easy part, after all."

CHAPTER SIXTY-SEVEN

Vartan did not like it at all. He had a nagging feeling they had left something unfinished, as if they had been…distracted somehow.

He was thankful his old friend had arranged the extraction for him and his family, but he knew better than to ignore his gut feeling. He put his hand in his pocket and gripped the gun still there.

He watched Jaleh hug Abbas and pull away. In her eyes, he could tell she looked uneasy as well. She was an extraordinary woman and a better operative than he had ever been. If her instincts said there was a problem, then there was definitely a problem.

Armik seemed like a tiger ready to pounce. Training had agreed with him, and he would make a fine agent. Not the life he had hoped for his son, but he still felt proud. Now if they could all just get home alive.

"These diplomatic vehicles are quite something, Abbas."

"Yes. Top of the line. The French don't take chances. Triple armor plating underneath, heavy body armor with Kevlar lining inside, and the glass can take an RPG. Several million Euros apiece."

"A bit of overkill for a couple of over-the-hill agents,"

Vartan said.

"Speak for yourself," Jaleh said with a forced smile.

"Not so over-the-hill, my friend, and besides, you've earned a spot on the Republic's top ten list. That's a big payday. A lot of people would love to cash in on those Rials." Abbas laughed.

"I'd probably turn myself in for that kind of cash."

Everybody laughed at that, but it sounded unnatural to Vartan. They all got into the vehicle and the heavily armed entourage made their way through the city.

"We are not flying out of IKA?" said Jaleh to Abbas, who sat in the front passenger seat.

"No, we are flying out of Mehrabad. It's where all government planes take off from since they moved all the international flights to IKA."

"I see. I've been away too long," she said. "I'm not up to speed."

They pulled into a private gate off the highway where they had to cross a checkpoint. Once past, they headed onto the tarmac to the government airstrip where a large, private Airbus A310-304 was being fueled. The solid white plane had the red, blue, and white of the French tricolor emblazoned across the tail.

"Pretty big plane. Are we bringing other passengers back?" Uneasiness in Armik now came through despite his efforts to keep it hidden.

"No, just you three and a handful of staff. But not to worry, it's quite comfortable."

"You're not coming back with us?" Vartan said to his friend.

"Unfortunately, no. I have a debrief at the French Consulate and need to check in with a few old cronies before I head back."

They arrived at the aircraft and stepped out of the vehicle. Men in dark suits, wearing sunglasses at night approached and asked for their weapons.

"What's this?" Vartan raised his eyebrows.

"The French's policy prevents weapons and cell phones from being carried on the plane. They will be returned to you upon your arrival. Relax, Vartan-**jan**. It's just routine."

Reluctantly, Vartan gave up his gun and phone and submitted to a pat down, along with his wife and son, before walking up the stairs to the plane. Vartan caught Jaleh's eye movement and understood that she felt there was a problem. That notion seemed to be confirmed when they walked onto the plane and found more armed men, dressed similar to the ones on the tarmac, waiting for them inside.

He turned to his old buddy. "The guy I killed was a dud. You are the true Rostem."

"I wanted to see if you still had some of that fight left in you after all these years. You were impressive. He was no easy kill. I'm just disappointed it took you this long to put it together."

"All this time you were working for them." Vartan shook his head, cursing himself for not seeing it sooner.

"Of course not, I was working for me. This little cold war has brought me wealth and power beyond measure. I would be nothing but a glorified doorman if I took sides. But playing both against each other—now that was profitable and, dare I say, enjoyable. I'm not blinded by mindless loyalty like you are. This country is dying for a strong leader. Someone who can build a new and improved Iran. Improved for me, anyway. You could have come too, but I knew you would never betray your precious queen."

"So what's the point of all of this? Where are you sending us?"

"To Israel, as I told you, with a small gift. We will leave the plane on the runway just long enough for them to know who sent it."

Jaleh nudged him and he looked out the window near the wing to see an oversized crane loading a massive container into the cargo hold.

"Barron's bomb? You're insane. You'll start an all out war and bring everyone down on your heads. How long will you be able to stand after that?"

"Yes. A nice big war. They will investigate. That will lead them to a French diplomatic plane with two Mossad agents and a half-Jew, Persian, French citizen who happens to be freelancing for Langley. It will cause chaos and confusion. And it won't matter by then, because Israel won't even be on the map anymore. Win-win. All of the Jewish allies will join in the retaliations. The US will topple this inept government like they've done many times, and in the vacuum, a new leader will rise." Abbas smiled, pride oozing in his expression.

"You? You're crazy. What makes you think you can take power?"

"Those that can remove kings can also install them. This has been in the works for a long time. Arrangements have already been made, my old friend. This game is far beyond you now."

"And what is the point in having us on the plane? When it blows, there will be no trace of us."

"Because, Persian, it is a spectacular way for you to die! Your atoms separating from your body and spreading in a radioactive cloud over the country you've killed so many people for. You have a few hours to suffer in the knowledge that your family will die with you, and that you brought them to this. There have been so many attempts to kill you over the years as we played on this chessboard. Shooting you now would be so…anticlimactic. I would never offer you anything less than this beautiful checkmate. I just wanted to see the fear in your eyes before—"

Vartan punched Abbas in the face, his blood coming to a quick boil. He grabbed him in a bear hug, trying to take him for a tumble back down the stairs.

Weapons came up in an instant and a taser was used to get Vartan to relinquish his grip. The energy ripped through his body, causing his jaw to lock up. He fell slack, almost blacking out.

Armik picked up his father and they were shuffled further into the aircraft.

Abbas laughed and spat blood. "Watch them carefully. Don't take your eye off him for a second. He is The Persian, after all. If he tries anything, shoot her first."

Their captors sat them down, keeping them apart with one guard in between. They did not have to wait long for the plane to taxi down the runway and take off. With the barrel of a thug's gun pointed straight at Jaleh, Vartan's options had dwindled to almost none. The other four men had holstered their weapons and now knelt, praying out loud. They were resigned to their mission being a one-way trip.

Yet not all of them intended to land in Israel and blow up with the plane. Vartan spotted two packed chutes in the corner. Armik, sat on the other side of the aisle between two gun-toting men. He looked straight ahead, but his eyes scanned in every direction. His son would be doing the same thing he was—looking for the next move.

Pride mixed with sadness in his chest. His boy had become a man and his skills and talent had proven extraordinary. Yet this was not what he had wanted for Armik, and it would all come to nothing if he could not get them out of this.

He looked at his wife, a cold steel barrel close to her temple. She smiled at him, the perfect picture of calmness and reassurance. But he had learned to see behind the eyes she showed to the world. Her readiness for action stood out to him, from the relaxed pose of her shoulders to the tightness of her jaw. His family sat poised and ready for his move.

The grinding noise of the landing gears retracting vibrated the floor beneath his feet. The overhead lights flickered, and the prayers grew more intense. There would be no turning back.

"If these bastards pray all the way to Tel Aviv, it's going to be a very long trip," he said in French.

"Shut up." The gunman moved his weapon closer to Jaleh.

The craft leveled out after what Vartan guessed to be about twenty thousand feet. The prayers fell silent, much to his relief. They unstrapped themselves and all lit cigarettes. Given the situation, Vartan's cravings that had been non-existent for years made a genuine resurgence.

"Can I get one of those?" he said in a loud voice.

The man who had been distributing the cigarettes reached back into his pocket and pulled the pack out. He placed one between Vartan's lips, and flicked his Zippo lighter with his thumb, sparking a yellow flame to life. Vartan inhaled deeply but could not suppress a cough. He did not enjoy it at all. The taste now repulsed him, and his clean lungs rejected the intrusion.

"Good for you." Jaleh glared from her seat. Anger seethed from her narrowed eyes. "You have to go and smoke again after all these years?"

"What difference does it make? We are all about to die anyway."

"Shut your mouths, you two."

"So you want to die smelling like one of these disgusting pigs?" She pointed to their captors.

"At least let me die quietly. Don't you have anything better to do than complain?" Vartan inhaled more smoke and coughed again.

"Oh, you give me so much to complain about," Jaleh said.

"Really. Please tell me. You might as well get it out now."

"This flight isn't long enough to tell you everything I have to complain about with you."

"I said—" The thug bristled.

"A flight to Mars wouldn't be long enough for your complaints, once you get talking," said Vartan, cutting off their captor's demand. "Can a man just smoke in peace before he dies?"

"Do what you want." Jaleh huffed and folded her arms.

"See what Western culture does to a woman?" Vartan addressed the man beside Jaleh, who had become engrossed in the conversation between husband and wife despite himself.

The thug laughed, ready to give his two cents. Jaleh snatched his pistol in an incredible twisting motion before the words could tumble from his lips. Surprise registered on his face, but the bullet entered his forehead before fear could follow. The back of his skull exploded in a spray of blood, brains, and bone.

Two more shots rang out, the expert marksmanship taking down the two guards on either side of Armik before they had a chance to react.

Vartan sprang on the guard to his left, whose hand had risen to fire. Pinning the weapon with his left hand, he struck the man's throat.

Another shot made Vartan spin around. The last of the guards lay slumped in his seat, half his head missing. Armik stood across from the body, smoke rising from the barrel of the gun he had taken. Vartan returned his attention to the gasping man in front of him. He relieved him of his pistol and fired a shot into his chest point blank.

"The pilot." Jaleh leapt over one of the bodies and moved

to the cockpit door. Vartan followed, Armik right behind him.

"Nice shooting, by the way," he said to his wife. "You too, son."

"Thanks," said Jaleh. "You can spit that disgusting thing out now." She scowled at him as she reached for the door handle.

"Sorry." Vartan had not realized he still had the cigarette in between his lips.

"I'll bet. Damn, it's locked," said Jaleh.

"I'll shoot through it." Armik pointed to the lock mechanism, but Vartan stayed his hand.

"It's three feet thick and will ricochet back at us. Let me show you how Ali Baba did it." Vartan pressed the intercom button instead and brought his face to the speaker.

"What is it?" The voice crackled.

"Konjed Baz." Open Sesame.

"What?"

"Konjed Baz."

"What the hell are you talking about?" The pilot sounded annoyed.

Seconds later, the sound of the mechanism unlocking was followed by the swishing of air from the sealed door opening. A plain-clothed pilot's face appeared from behind the door. Vartan slammed the butt of his gun into the side of the irate man's head, dropping him like a bag of bricks.

"Ali Baba." Armik shook his head and laughed.

"Great, you incapacitated the only pilot," said Jaleh, checking for a pulse.

"Today is your lucky day, madame. I just happen to be a great pilot."

"Oh no. I'm flying." Jaleh nudged him aside.

"Yes, because that turned out so well the last time," said Vartan.

"They fired an RPG at us!"

"Wait a minute. You two were flying a plane together and got shot out of the sky?" Armik's eyes widened, listening to his parent's conversation.

"It was a helicopter," Vartan and Jaleh said in unison.

"We need to have a serious conversation when we get back. I can't believe you two have been keeping all this from me."

"Now you know I'm more exciting than Bobbak's dad—"

Armik gave Vartan a hard shove, sending him toppling into the copilot's seat. A shot rang out. Armik fired back, his bullets hitting the pilot, who had sat up and fired. Sparks and smoke erupted from the console.

Jaleh jumped into the pilot's chair and took it off autopilot. "The controls are okay, but the landing gear is finished. We can't put this bird down."

"Damn. Okay, then we will land it in the ocean." Vartan fiddled with the radio, but only static came out.

"Did you forget we have a nuclear bomb on board? That kind of friction might set it off." Jaleh pulled the stick back enough to level the pitch.

"Not if we get rid of it," said Vartan.

"Get rid of it where?" Armik looked at his father.

"Caspian Sea."

"Oh boy." Jaleh blew her breath out through pursed lips. "Okay, that might work. Then again—"

"Can you turn this tin can around?" Vartan gave his wife a reassuring smile.

"Of course." She smiled back, but with uncertainty behind her eyes.

"Good. Go up and go north. We'll do the rest." He gave Armik a nod and they left the cabin.

On the forward part of the main deck, Vartan searched for the cargo access door. He found two metal handles on the floor and pulled up a small section of carpet, revealing a hatch underneath. He pulled it open and they descended, finding themselves in the electronics bay.

"We need to go aft to get into the forward cargo hold," Vartan said.

Armik followed. There was a heavy fabric wall between the electronics bay and the forward hold. Vartan found the edge of it and pulled but his ribs ached.

"Here I got it." Armik moved in front of his father and tore through the fabric.

Once inside, they both gasped. The crate was so much bigger than it had seemed through the window. Vartan pulled his hidden boot knife out and started cutting the straps holding it down.

"Didn't they search you?" Armik looked amused.

"They hardly ever check the boots."

"We are never going to be able to push this thing out."

"That's your mother's job," said Vartan, cutting the last strap. "Now wrap this around you." He handed Armik one of the straps and went to the com panel. "I'm going to open the forward cargo door. We're going to need a little dip to starboard."

"You're so demanding," said Jaleh through the speakers.

"You ready?" Vartan grabbed hold of the nearest handrail.

"Always." Armik braced himself.

Loud sirens went off the moment Vartan touched the button. The reverberations made him cringe, only to be made worse by the ear-splitting pop of pressure loss. The plane shook as the air caught hold of the doors. The suction pulled at him, and he struggled through the pain to keep his grip.

On cue, the plane tilted to starboard. With a moan and a creak, the gigantic wooden crate with Iran's first nuclear bomb slid across the cargo hold, then dropped out of sight.

The plane shook and straightened itself.

The pressure on Vartan's ribs made them pull apart, pain shooting through him as never before. He felt his grip slipping until he tumbled toward the opening, his atoms to be separated after all. The last words he heard before darkness took him came from his son.

"I got you, Baba."

CHAPTER SIXTY-EIGHT

Los Angeles, California
December 21, 2000

Abbas, the man known as Rostem, got out of his car in front of his hotel and handed the keys to the valet. With the late hour, not too many people were in the lobby. The restaurant was closed, but as he approached, two large security agents let him by without a word.

Most of the lights were out, but there was one man, a cleric, sitting at a large table covered with food. So much food Abbas expected they might be joined by at least six more people, but it was all for the man who sat there.

The cleric did not look up at his approach, so Abbas gave a little cough. After a few seconds, the man ceased from his glutinous feast.

"The man they call Rostem. What an honor to meet you, at last." The young, bearded man with a black turban and brown robes spoke in a nasal, high-pitched voice. He motioned to the empty seat across from him and Abbas sat.

"Can I order something for you? They are running the full kitchen for me at the moment. Better food than they provide for the regular customers, let me tell you. Only the best, my friend. Only the best."

"No, thank you."

"Some tea, then." He snapped his fingers.

The restaurant's classy space was furnished with a grand piano and stunning full bar reminiscent of a James Bond film. A large flat-screen TV hung from the beam above the bar. On it, the evening news was in progress, discussing what everyone had been talking about for months now.

The United Nations is still demanding answers as the Iranian government maintains its silence regarding a reported nuclear blast four months ago. The device is said to have been detonated in the Caspian Sea, just off the coast of the city of Rasht. It is unknown how much damage was caused by the radiation, as investigators have not been allowed in the region. Speculation as to the involvement of the now-deceased Dr. Barron—

A body entered the space between Rostem and the TV.

"Nothing but bad news these days," said the waiter, who placed the fresh teapot on the table. "That government has to go."

"Believe me, I've tried." Rostem muttered the words.

"I'm sorry, what was that?"

"Nothing. I'd like some bread please." Rostem ignored the tea and poured himself a glass of chilled Persian *doogh,* a savory carbonated yogurt drink seasoned with mint, from a pitcher on the table. He downed it and poured another. Nothing seemed to taste as good as it did back home, but it would have to do. His status had been revoked and he was now wanted in every country.

No matter. They would not find him, his hair now dyed blond and left long. He was a master of disguise and had enough money in enough bank accounts to keep him living well for the rest of his life. Or at least until he came up with a new plan. They had not heard the last of Rostem.

He watched the cleric eat without a care in the world and anger boiled within him. He considered killing the man on the spot.

"Why did you want to meet me?"

"Oh, not me. I'm here on behalf of our government."

"Your government. They revoked my status, remember?"

"Yes, that. Well, you were responsible for a nuclear bomb going off, and you were working with the CIA to overthrow them, so I'm sure you can understand why you aren't exactly in their good graces at the moment."

"So what, they sent you to kill me?" Abbas scoffed at the thought.

"Kill you?" The cleric laughed. "No, my friend. I'm here to offer you your job back. With a promotion. How do you feel about being Station Chief in Bahrain?"

A sudden surge of hope grew within him. "You can't be serious?"

"You're right," said the cleric, laughing again, his mouth full of rice. "I'm not. I just wanted to see your face light up."

The man's laughter echoed through the empty restaurant. Abbas's face went hot with rage. His hand went for the knife on the table, but the waiter's body once again came in front of him. This time he set a martini glass down before him, an olive on a stick protruding from the clear liquid.

"Compliments of the lady at the bar."

"What lady?" Abbas turned his head. Seated at the bar was a beauty with long, fine legs and a curvaceous figure hugged by a blue velvet dress.

Vartan's wife smiled and gave him a little wave. He looked at the cleric, who continued to laugh while removing his beard. Vartan's son. When the waiter pressed the cold nozzle of a pistol against his temple, he understood. It would be a good death, after all.

"And this is compliments of The Persian," said Vartan.

The Adventure Continues 2024...

David Alexanian is a Canadian-born author and producer. He is of French/Armenian descent, with roots in Iran. He divides his time between Toronto and Los Angeles. Although he loves the big city life, he will escape to the cottage with his family whenever possible.

David is an avid traveler, a voracious reader, and has an incurable addiction to writing stories. He is the author of the Sword Demon Series, including *Laplace's Demon.*

Base jumping, parachuting, cave diving, and parkour, are all sports David enjoys avoiding. Instead, he can often be found in a cafe or by the beach, writing his next adventure.

David Alexanian can be reached at:
www.DavidAlexanian.com

CPSIA information can be obtained
at www.ICGtesting.com
Printed in the USA
LVHW111039061022
730091LV00002B/213

9 781948 266529